THE DANISH SOLDIER

Wilder Publications, Inc.
PO Box 632
Floyd VA 24091

ISBN 13: 978-1-5154-0323-4

First Edition
10 9 8 7 6 5 4 3 2 1

THE DANISH SOLDIER

by Brian Walters

EAST PRUSSIA
JANUARY 1945

CHAPTER I

Just after midday, snow began to fall. Big wet flakes of snow. An endless mass of thick dark heavy clouds had portended snow all day, but the men had been too busy running for their lives to notice until now. The open farm country of the East Prussian hinterland had made Sergeant Foss and his unit prime targets for the Russian tanks. The newer T-34s and Stalin tanks were so stocked with shells that the Soviet gunners often spent their time aiming at individual German soldiers. One salvo had pulverized a man's chest, splattering his remains in a score of directions and leaving a large red splotch in the snow where a moment before he had stood. While an armada of tanks roamed the countryside almost unopposed, the Soviet infantry either rode atop the steel monsters or followed closely behind, mopping up any Germans stragglers who had escaped the treads, machine guns, and cannon. Foss's small patrol was one of the few that *had* escaped. Despite the freezing temperature and the advancing enemy, the fleeing men of the Reconnaissance Unit had gratefully found sanctuary in a stretch of dense woods. Foss waited until his remaining eight men had dashed past the outermost birch and beech trees before hurrying after them.

They ran for ten more minutes. Foss called a halt when Keller fell face-first into a patch of iced-over snow that had fallen days earlier. Slowly pushing himself to his knees, Keller swayed side to side, panting with exhaustion. Trying to stand on his feet, he fell down again. Foss was also sobbing for air, but he remained on his feet, keeping his ears alert for tank engines. He narrowed his eyes at the prostrate figure on the ground.

"Get up, Keller," Foss said firmly after regaining his breath. His voice was raw and hoarse—he had not had a drop of water to drink for hours; none of them had—so the sternness in his tone surprised him. Nudging Keller's shoulder with a boot, he said again, "Get up, or the Ivans will make you get up. Then you'll wish you had never been born."

All the men knew what awaited them if caught by the Russians. Death certainly, but most likely not a quick one; rather torture and mutilation and the loss of body parts to sharp knives. Keller rose a second time, shaking his head morosely at Foss. Keller's eyes were red beyond description, his nineteen year old face so contorted with tension and fear that anyone outside the unit might have mistaken him for pushing forty.

"I'm done for, Foss," he said, licking his chapped lips. Rising to his knees again, he motioned with his hand toward the woods. "Just go. Go! Leave me here. I've got my rifle with me. I swear, they'll never take me alive."

Foss knew well his meaning. He'd been in situations himself where the last bullet in a gun meant the only reasonable choice left. Crouching down next to Keller, he patted the young Landser on the cheek.

"Pull yourself together, Keller. We're safe for the time being. Now get up and keep walking. Your brain might not want to, but your legs will obey." At that moment one of the other soldiers made his presence known. An unusually tall man who stood slightly stooped, he took in the scene before him.

"What's the matter, Keller?" the tall man asked, stepping to the right of Sergeant Foss. "Not those blisters on your feet again, is it?"

"I'm not sure I even have feet anymore," Keller croaked sadly. "Probably frostbitten."

"Frostbitten! You don't even know what the word means." The tall soldier looked at the kneeling man with disgust. "You want to talk about cold—I was on the outskirts of Moscow in the first winter of the war. Men froze to death taking a crap. Their balls were so iced over that when we tried to bury them they fell off and shattered like glass. Back then we didn't even have proper clothing. Now we have everything from warm felt boots to white helmets."

Foss stood up again. He grinned briefly at Dreyback who nodded back. Dreyback was the veteran of the group. He had served in the Wehrmacht since before the invasion of Poland. Had fought on nearly every front. Been wounded five times, bore an ugly scar running down the left side of his neck; limped, especially when it rained; and was minus half an ear, courtesy of Russian shrapnel. He had also lost his wife and son in an air raid on his home back in Hamburg. Dreybach was a dour man. He had never risen beyond the rank of corporal; twice he had openly disobeyed officers, and nearly been shot for doing so. But the man's tenacity in combat and the Iron Cross on his collar had saved him from the severest penalty.

Foss fingered his own Iron Cross. He had won it at Kursk for extreme bravery. Wiping out several Russian machine gun nests, he'd been shot in the shoulder but still managed to throw a grenade that took out the final one, before dropping unconscious due to loss of blood. Convalescence in

Germany after that, where he had nearly died. But miraculously, he returned four months later to the front. He loathed the war but had missed his comrades. By then the Wehrmacht was in full retreat from the steppes of Russia. And practically all the men he had entered the army with were dead, missing in action, or lying in German hospitals without legs, arms, eyes; many had also lost their minds.

Seeing the two veteran soldiers standing taciturn and seemingly without fear, Keller grew ashamed at his behavior. His conduct was not befitting for a German soldier. With a groan he picked up his rifle. The five other men of the company in the meantime were catching their breath. They waited and watched. Foss gestured to them.

"Five minutes. No more," he said. "Don't eat all your bread. We haven't a clue where the front line is. Ivan might have overrun it. So save your food."

The men had each been issued a small ration of bread before heading out on patrol. They were all experienced soldiers. Going without proper food for a day or more was nothing new to them. They nibbled at the bread—which was half-frozen from being exposed to the sheer cold—but saved the bulk of it for later. A few of the men had found a barrel with near-frozen potatoes in an abandoned cellar the day before. Stuffing as many potatoes as they could in their pockets, they intended to share them over an open fire amongst themselves once they made a proper bivouac.

If they ever did. The rumble of artillery in the distance never ceased. One of the men, Ziemans, lit a cigarette.

"Put that out," Foss commanded.

"Why?"

"I don't need to explain why."

"The light at the end of a cigarette has gotten many a man killed," added Dreybach.

Ziemans, an old hand himself, reluctantly stamped out the cigarette.

"What does it matter at this stage!" Ziemans spit a wad of phlegm at the ground, then cursed. Pushing back a strand of hair that had gotten in his face, he loosened the chin-strap of his helmet, then took off the helmet completely. Despite the cold, his dark hair was matted to his forehead with sweat. "The goddamned war's lost," he said without emotion. "Any fool can see our goose is cooked. What the hell does it matter whether I smoke a cigarette in full view of the enemy . . . "

Ruder, a former Hitler Youth, looked aghast. "You could be shot for saying that."

"Well, then go ahead and shoot me, puppy. Whether your bullet or a Russian's—the result's the same."

Ruder was the least liked member of the unit, yet he stood his ground. "Are you dense in the head? The Fuhrer has promised new wonder-weapons. Once we unleash them—the Bolsheviks won't stand a chance. After we blow Moscow to smithereens, we'll turn west and kick the Brits and Amis back over the channel."

"The Fuhrer has promised us lots of things. He promised the Reich would never be bombed. And that Stalingrad would be conquered in a matter of weeks. Need I go on?"

There was brief chuckling among the men, even though the tone was morbid. Foss didn't join in, but he was glad to see his friends laughing. Over the past year there had been precious little to laugh about. Being a Dane, Hitler and Germany meant nothing to him. He had been forced to fight in this God-awful war, but he had grown to care deeply for the soldiers at his side. Mere individuals like himself—who unfortunately had no say in the matter of being drafted in the military. These average men—only *they* instilled in him a sense of continuing the fight for the simple reason of making sure they all survived, and that none of them fell into the hands of the Russians.

"Alright, the party's over," Foss said, after giving the men a little more time to rest. They groaned and complained, but none of them lingered. The explosions to the east grew louder. The men continued to retreat through the woodland for a long time. On the way four German stragglers from a ravaged regiment joined them, one of them barely able to walk due to a wound in his thigh. Having put a tourniquet on the leg, his comrades took turns giving him support. Foss and the others noted that despite the tourniquet, blood had soaked the man's pants. His face appeared ashen and if no doctor was found soon . . .

All at once they came to a clearing near a frozen stream. Tulm, the lead man, was the first to see a road paralleling the forest nearly a hundred meters away. Visibility was poor, for the snow had begun to swirl and a fierce wind blew into the men's eyes. Calling for a halt, Foss studied the terrain. No sign of Russians, but the road was flooded with thousands of refugees fleeing from the east. Carts and wagons pulled by horses, most of the people afoot, carrying what they could of food and furniture and mementos from their homes. The majority were women with heads wrapped by scarves, holding infants or leading small children by the hand. Some of the children pulled ropes attached to the necks of goats or cows. Foss noted a few ragged army personnel mixed among the throng. Most of them weren't even bearing weapons. Beside them trudged groups of Poles—probably farm workers—and even a smattering of Russian Hiwis, heading west to escape the vengeance of their countrymen.

"Shouldn't we join them?" Tulm's question momentarily startled Foss. Thinking to himself, while studying a small compass he had carried throughout the war, the tall slender Dane knew he had to come to a decision. The woodland made traveling hard with its lack of a straight path and branches and other debris on the ground that caused the men to continually stumble if they weren't careful. The road would be faster, that is, if they didn't get held up by the refugees. But instinct told him to avoid the road. And instinct was what had gotten him through three years on the Eastern Front.

"We'll cut over to the road at dusk," he said with a finality that was not to be questioned.

Tulm was about to say something, but seeing that Foss had already turned his back and left the clearing, simply nodded. Tulm was the only man in the outfit who never ribbed Foss about his heritage. The others were only too eager to let Foss know where he stood in the world. A Dane leading a bunch of Germans! They never let him forget that it had taken Germany less than a day to conquer his lilliputian country. And they cued him frequently over the grammatical mistakes he still on occasion made when speaking Deutsch. Yet they had also grown to accept the fact that Aksel Foss was a superb fighting man. A brave resilient soldier who had risen from the lowest private to the rank of sergeant. Many of his comrades thought he might even become a lieutenant, due to the attrition in the grinding battles of the east. But he was overlooked time and again. To Foss it didn't matter either way—he merely wanted to survive and return to Denmark when the war was over. And this rubbed off on the others. Foss was the one who got them out of rough spots.

And today was a rough spot. Foss kept his face calm, but inside his self-confidence was waning. The front was a mess. All hell had broken loose two days before when the Russians had unleashed their artillery in a massive dawn attack that had wiped out barricades and dugouts as though they were paper houses. The Nazi Party leaders had boasted that the *Festungen*, the Fuhrer Fortresses of the East, would withstand anything the Soviets threw at them. But since Stalingrad, the Soviets had been throwing their whole arsenal and then some at the Wehrmacht, and nothing had stopped them. Now the Red Army had crossed the borders of Germany—something no one could have imagined, even a year ago—its destination: Berlin.

But Foss didn't care about Berlin. He didn't care about Goebbels, or Goering, or any of those gangsters in their immaculate uniforms. They were the bastards who started the war, and finally they were getting a taste of it close up. Keeping his Tommy gun secure in his hands, he motioned his men to return to the sanctuary of the woods.

They walked without letup for nearly an hour when a scream rent the air.

Then a burst of machine gun fire.

Foss didn't need to tell the others to stay down. The snow was falling even heavier, but now crouched behind an uneven row of shrubs, he could see just a stretch of the road through the branches, lying perhaps a few hundred paces to the southwest. The first scream had become an entire multitude of screams; a mad scramble of people and livestock stumbling and running in all directions but east. From that direction more than a dozen T34s were barreling over the snowbanks toward the refugees. And firing.

Several blasts went off simultaneously. Then several more. Carts were snapped like matchsticks, the horses bearing them crushed. Piles of earth flew into the air . . . and piles of people. Those not instantly smashed by the shells staggered in the snow, then were sickeningly ground into red pulp beneath the charging tanks. The machine guns never let up. Dozens of peasants raised their arms to surrender—and died despite the effort. The few who retained a semblance of intelligible reasoning dropped all their belongings and raced for the woods. Mothers left infants and toddlers beside the road. A soldier or two stopped briefly to return fire, but the rifle bullets did no more than ricochet off the unyielding plates of steel. The people who were too frightened or too wounded to flee, stayed where they were. Some of the tanks sped by them. Some stopped. Crew members scrambled out, oblivious to anything but the lust for German women. With machine pistols they shot whatever men they found. As for the women, they shot the old, the frail, the feeble. The young and plump they stripped naked, dumped their clothes in the snow, then forced them moaning and wailing into the tanks, the last of the crew closing the turrets. In a few seconds the tanks turned and raced backed east, though a few remained where they stood.

"My God, did you see what they did!" Keller, losing his earlier weariness, was wide awake and near to hysteria. "Those are German women those beasts are ravishing! We can't let them get away with it."

Keller and a few others turned to Foss. The Dane shrugged. "We only have two Panzerfausts. Even if we can get close enough to use them, the women will die too."

"But they're going to die anyway. The Ivans will shoot them as soon as they've had their fun."

Foss and Dreyback exchanged glances. The Wehrmacht had been in Russia for more than three years. The veterans knew that no one's hands were clean in this war. Entire Soviet villages had been wiped out to the last dog, then burned to ashes that blew away in the wind. The Russians were more than thirsting for revenge—they demanded it. They had given a taste of what was to befall Germany the autumn before in the village of Nemmersdorf. Nearly every person in the town had been murdered horribly, and nearly every woman raped. Some of the victims had been crucified on barn doors. Others were left with the very ropes around their necks that had been used to strangle them. Very few had been left untortured before meeting death. And death at that point must have been a relief. There wasn't a German soldier on the Eastern Front who didn't know this. But civilian deaths were part of the war. Shaking his head, Foss said, "Before Lieutenant Jurtgen died, he ordered us to get back to the army in whatever way we could. And that's what we're doing." He paused. "As much as I'd like to save refugees—it's not possible to rescue them all. We'd only die in the process."

"Would you say the same if those were Danish women out there?" Becoming less hysterical, Keller's face had turned beet-red with a growing hostility born of helplessness. He had seen the face of fate, and it was not kind.

Foss took a moment before speaking. "If they were Danish women . . . I would come to the same conclusion." Just then a rustling of branches forced Foss and the others to raise their guns in alarm. A trickle of refugees, most of them covered with snow, peeked their heads through a clump of birches. Their eyes stricken with fear, they were soon followed by others. Many of the women and children were weeping. Some dripped blood into the white-packed earth. Foss nodded at Steenhagen, the one man of the outfit that had had some medical training.

"See what you can do to bandage the wounded," Foss said to him.

"I wish I could, but we don't have enough for the lot of them . . . let alone ourselves." Steenhagen's voice trailed off.

Foss was about to say more when a tattered old man trudged up to him. "You are German soldiers," the man berated, his entire body trembling. Unable to still his limbs, he tried steeling his eyes at the man he thought to be in charge. "Yet you hid out in the woods. Why didn't you help us! We were promised that the Russians would never be allowed to cross the Reich's borders. My whole family . . . has been killed . . . " The man shook claw-like hands at Foss as though he had been the culprit who had murdered his loved ones. He gritted his teeth. Tears streaked his face. "Why did you not stop them—"

His question was never answered, for just then a barrage of explosions rocked the woods, ripping apart trees and scattering debris in all directions. The sound of more tanks could be heard distinctly, their treads grinding and crunching across fallen branches and logs. Many of the refugees screamed. A madness took hold of them. Terrified, they ran. Foss and his men kept their heads, but the tanks were coming closer. Not panicking, they crouched down and headed for the denser part of the forest.

They soon came to a more open setting with fewer trees—by the look of the area, a frozen swamp that in summertime would have been impossible to traverse. The rumble of the front followed Foss and his eight men, who now were joined by dozens of civilians and other soldiers cut off from their companies and battalions. A goddamned motley bunch, Foss reflected grimly to himself, watching them plod and stumble through the snowdrifts. It was unbelievable that so many of the soldiers had lost their guns. By the look of their ragged uniforms, or lack of any uniform, and their gray wrinkled faces, Foss knew these were the ballyhooed members of the Volksturm: the cradle and the grave. The sixty year old relics from the Great War that the Nazi Party had vouched would stop the Russians in their tracks at the eastern borders of Germany. Men who had not fired a rifle in nearly thirty years, and had no inkling on how to use Panzerfausts and other modern weapons. If there was a prime definition of "cannon fodder," then these miserable old bastards fit that description. At least the Hitlerjugend who were also being sent to the front lines to fight Russian tanks, carried the vigor of youth about them. And the fanaticism that had not been worn away by time and experiencing endless horrors.

Foss's feet ached. He wanted to lie down and sleep. If he were alone with his men he would have ordered them back to the relative sanctity of the forest to rest awhile. But all these newcomers and tag-alongs . . . he cursed to himself silently, knowing he had no choice but to lead them to safety since he saw no officers anywhere in sight.

Yet reaching the German lines was not the only difficulty. The Russians had obviously overrun the line of yesterday in more than one place. Maybe broken it completely. And he had no map of the region. It was also rumored that street and road signs had been removed to confuse the enemy. Of course in Russia, road signs had been a luxury—the villages and outlying farm districts had been devoid of them. Still, the army had made do. Foss only knew that the Baltic Sea lay many kilometers north, and west, along with the larger cities of East Prussia. Koenigsberg, Memel, Kolberg, Danzig. A few others. They were merely names to him. Just like the names of the villages and towns of the entire region. Meeting the eyes of Brohm standing a few paces away from him, Foss asked, "You're on home ground, aren't you?"

Brohm nodded. He was a thickset man, had worked as a field hand on one of the large junkers estates before the war, and was a fine soldier, someone you wanted beside you in a firefight. High intelligence though, was not Josef Brohm's forte. In the beginning the others had teased him frequently because of his lack of brain matter and the slow stuttering way in which he talked, and Brohm often had resorted to fisticuffs in retaliation. Over time he got used to the insults, and learned how to give them back with words instead of bare knuckles. Stepping closer to Foss he said, "I-I-I lived south of here—near Lyck. The landscape's much the same, but I-I-I was never in these parts. Not that I-I remember."

Butting in, Ziemans laughed sardonically. "My dear Josef, I doubt you even remember the hair color of that whore you slept with in the Ukrainian brothel. Was she blonde—or brunette? And I don't mean the hair on her head." He laughed again, louder. A few of the others laughed with him.

Blushing, Brohm said, "At least I-I-I slept with her. That's more than y-y-you did."

Attempting a follow-up, Ziemans began to speak when Foss cut him off. "How far are we from the coast, Brohm?"

Brohm scratched his cheek, then gazed north. "Maybe fifty, sixty kilometers. Don't know for sure. But it c-c-can't be much more than that."

Following the other's gaze, Foss blew out a long breath that looked like a puff of smoke in the freezing air. He scrutinized the civilians slumped on the ground or standing pitifully amid the soldiers. They were waiting for him to make a decision. *A decision that may cost them their lives,* he thought sourly. But lives weren't worth much these days. His only loyalty was to his men—*Good God, is that how I've become!* Callous toward anyone he didn't know? Had the war changed him so much? He had been an ardent socialist back in the homeland and dreamed of a world where no one went hungry, where everyone was equal, where all lived in peace and . . .

He closed his eyes and shook his head as though trying to erase the current circumstances. When he opened them again the people still stared at him. Clearing his voice, he said loud enough so the dozens surrounding him could hear, "My job is to my fellow soldiers. Our goal: to reach the nearest defense line. We don't have a radio, and we've been out of communication with the rest of our battalion since last night. But my guess is that the cities to the north are still in our hands. That's where we aim to go." He stopped to see the effect of his words. When no one interrupted he continued. "Anyone fit to follow can come with us. Otherwise I suggest you head as far west as possible. Perhaps several towns are still free of the Russians. A few trains may even be running. Seek them if you can. If you come with us I don't plan on stopping for any reason unless we're attacked and have to fight. If you can't keep up you're out of luck."

The landscape was totally quiet for a moment. No one contradicted what he said. When he started marching north, the majority went with him. A few went west. Those who were too exhausted or wounded to walk, stayed where they were in the snow. The last thing Foss heard before reentering the woods was their moaning and weeping. Their blunt curses unleashed at him, and at circumstance. But he knew if the situation was reversed, they'd leave him behind without a second thought. In a matter of minutes their wailing was lost to the elements.

Or to the Russians.

Foss wasn't sure which was worse.

CHAPTER 2

They trudged on the rest of the day and early into the night before being halted by a German patrol. Overcome with weariness, Foss counted his eight men as they stepped past him into a bunker about a hundred meters behind the front line. He no longer took any notice of the others who had come with them. Many had fallen in the woods or wandered off on their own. They were no longer his concern. The surviving civilians who had made the trek were ushered out of the battle-zone and hauled in horse-drawn wagons to the rear. Being given a little soup that was barely more than water and gruel, his men lay down immediately and slept on the earthen floor of the bunker. Foss meanwhile waited outside for an officer who was being sent to debrief him. A sentry had given him a cigarette. Leaning against the inner parapet outside, Foss sucked in smoke from the cigarette then blew it out.

Oddly, he had never liked cigarettes before the war. He'd had asthma as a small child. The damned things made him cough. His mother wouldn't tolerate anyone smoking in the house, even his father had to go out into the rain and cold so that little Aksel could try and breathe normally. Now whenever he had cigarettes or cigars he smoked them as though they were an elixir to the soul. But when he considered this fact, he still wasn't certain he liked them. Merely something soldiers did to relieve boredom, relax nerves, dream away time. Part of the motto of—*Live now. Tomorrow you'll be pushing up grass.* Eat gluttonously when you had the food. Drink till you lay in a stupor—if vodka or schnapps were on hand. Anything to forget the killing and dying.

The officer soon appeared with an orderly. He was young, too young, boyish, and especially didn't look like a usual captain. But the war had left a void in the ranks of officers; the Reich had begun to rob its kindergartens to fill the positions. Quickly finishing the cigarette, Foss saluted him.

Raising his eyebrows, the captain seemed nonplussed at the greeting. *No Sieg Heil,* his stare voiced into the winter morning.

But Foss remained silent. In the early days of his recruitment into the Wehrmacht he had Sieg Heiled with the rest of them like a puppet pulled by strings. Since then he had gradually erased the Nazi gesture from his world. Being Danish and an anti-fascist, he would never use it again unless they put a Luger to his head. Even then he might refuse.

But the captain didn't know all that; nevertheless, he let it pass. Quietly reading a report that the orderly handed to him, he kept Foss standing at attention until he had finished. Then he gave the papers back to the orderly.

"So Lieutenant Jurtgen was killed in action?" The captain's cheek had an odd twitch to it when he spoke.

"Yes, sir."

"How?"

"We had completed our reconnaissance of the area and were heading back to our lines. But something must have spooked the Russians. They began using mortars. Heavy batteries. Probably threw everything at us they had. We didn't see their positions but they must have seen us. Or heard us. The lieutenant and two other men were hit by a round."

"Killed instantly?"

"No, sir. The lieutenant survived for a short time. We planned to cut up a birch tree and make a stretcher but he forbade us. Told us to return to our defenses."

"Even though your orders were to scout the enemy's intentions." The captain placed a harsh emphasis on the word "enemy's."

Unable to stifle an angry sigh, Foss said, "We had little choice in the matter, sir. Russian tanks started appearing everywhere. We almost didn't make it ourselves."

A stern look came over the Captain's face, then sighing heavily himself, he told the orderly to file the report with all the others that had recently come in. All the other negative reports. The man left them, and the captain, pulling out a silver cigarette case, opened it, took a cigarette out, put it to his lips, then offered one to the tall slender man before him. The captain then produced a fancy lighter. For a few minutes the officer and the NCO smoked in silence.

"Pardon my inquisitiveness—but you have an accent." Holding his cigarette securely between thumb and forefinger, the captain flicked a few ashes on the ground.

"Indeed I do, sir. Seems no one in the army let's me forget that fact."

Smiling, the captain said, "My guess is that it's somewhere north."

"Yes, Denmark."

"Where . . . in Denmark?"

"Copenhagen."

"My parents took me to Copenhagen as a child. A beautiful city. I remember Tivoli Gardens." The Captain looked wistful.

Foss simply nodded. Thinking about his homeland made him sad. It seemed a century ago since he'd last been there. *Did Denmark even exist anymore . . .*

As though suddenly seeing Sergeant Aksel Foss for the first time, the captain noted the Iron Cross pinned at the neck of his winter-white uniform. Despite the difference in rank, he felt strangely inadequate next to this tall foreigner of few words. He had dreamed many a time of winning an Iron Cross, but having spent most of the war sitting behind a comfortable desk in Berlin, he had not a clue as to the ordinary life of a Landser. Then when Goebbels had demanded for the German Nation: TOTAL WAR; and had decreed that every fit man must be sent to the front, the cushy job became a job no more. So he had been sent to the east a full captain, courtesy of party affiliation. The thought of real action invigorated him immensely, yet after only a few days near the front he had lost his taste for battle, and, embarrassingly—had pissed in his pants twice. Stalin organs ripping up the earth at all hours, Soviet planes strafing field hospitals and even latrines—whoever said that war was glorious must have been a raving lunatic. Then seeing the wounded brought back with their rib cages exposed and minus half their faces had scared him shitless. And here was this Dane who undoubtedly had been fighting a long time by the look of him—fighting a long time and seemingly unperturbed by it all. He had said as much by the manner in which he gave the report of his patrol. This perhaps irked the captain more than the medal the man wore. A German medal for utmost valor given to an outlander.

"Why did you join up?" the captain asked abruptly.

"I was forced to join."

"By the SS?" The captain knew that lately many legions in the SS were composed solely of foreign troops.

Foss shook his head emphatically. "No sir . . . the Wehrmacht." He felt insulted by the question, then he realized that the captain must have heard that many young Danish men had willingly signed up to serve in the Free Corps Denmark, a division in the SS. But Foss had no liking for the SS. Neither did most of his men, native-born Germans all of them. War was brutal, but the SS made brutality a game.

Noting the sudden surliness in the sergeant's expression, and the aloofness in his eyes, the captain refrained from asking any further questions. He left Foss where he was, telling him that he and his men would soon be gathered together with other lost units from mauled divisions. The Russians had to be stopped before they cut off the Reich's armies on the coast.

Knowing that he would shortly be in the thick of it again, Foss returned to the bunker where his men were still all sleeping. His body too ached for restful sleep, but though he lay down on a pile of straw that one of the others had arranged for him, his eyes wouldn't stay shut. Finally giving up, he stared up at the ceiling and beams of well-placed logs and wondered why he was here . . .

Foss knew the captain wanted to dig deeper into his past, but the man must have sensed he'd reached the point of going too far. Yet the questioning unfortunately had pried the lid from an already closed coffin.

Never had there been any intention of joining the German military. Like all Danes, Foss resented the invasion of his country. And also like all Danes—or at least most of them—he had over time come to accept the daily reality of seeing German soldiers and officials stepping through the streets of Copenhagen. There was nothing anyone could do to alter the facts. Denmark had been whipped in a surprise attack, and so as not to further any potential bloodshed between the scant under-equipped Danish soldiers protecting the realm and the mechanized elements of entire Nazi armies, the Danish King Christian X had uttered a proclamation to treat the intruders without visual or vocal animosity. In other words, to show them the attitude of Danish friendliness—even respect.

Being only nineteen at the time, Foss didn't really know what to think of the Germans. The only thing on his mind those days were girls and writing poetry. And he never could decide which one he loved the most. Politically he leaned to the Left, but never so much that he identified with any extremist group. He had been barely more than a toddler when his father, an out of work alcoholic, had stumbled out of a bodega late one foggy night and on trying to cross a street, had been hit and run over by a tram. The Great Depression had caused numerous suicides, and Foss later wondered whether his father had been one of them. But his mother never spoke about the "accident" afterward, and neither Foss nor his older brother ever asked her about it.

His *mother*. A stern, strong woman who raised her two boys alone and refrained from any notion of marrying again. Yet she was pretty. A dark blonde that men turned to look at twice. Foss didn't notice it then, but now being so far away he remembered the many suitors who often ate dinner in their tiny apartment in Vesterbro. One man in particular stood out in his mind: Uncle Henrik he called him. The man was fond of reading and once gave Foss a book about King Arthur and his knights. After reading the book himself, Foss grandly chased his brother around their small apartment, wielding a sword he had made out of wood. Foss smiled thinking about those times.

Then he just as easily frowned. A robust youth he had never been. Though taller than average, and despite being good at football, and having even given boxing a try, he had always been skinny and sickly. More often than not he'd been bedridden with colds and ear-aches and a cough that never seemed to go away. Measles once had nearly done him in. His mother forever worried herself over his health, or lack of it. A doctor had even told her that her youngest son wouldn't make it to twenty. But fate had other ideas—as fate always does. The single good thing he could say about the army—his poor health had disappeared, except for the occasional bout with diarrhea caused by eating the peasant breads and beets of Russia.

He tried sleeping again, but the captain's question remained in his thoughts. A question he'd been asked—*how many times?* Too many to recall. Becoming a member of the German Armed Forces—he was not one of those Danes who'd been swindled into believing the propaganda that a Crusade against Bolshevism was the only means of saving Europe. He could have cared less. Strangely enough, it was his literary leanings that got him into the mess. A Friday summer afternoon at the harbor at Nyhavn with two other writer-friends, a beer or two, another beer or two, and still another beer or two—*who was counting!*—then his friends had to leave, but he didn't want to leave, a waitress had caught his eye, had even smiled at him, but then when he'd gotten up the courage to—*he'd seen no ring on her finger*—ask her name, the world all at once and her beautiful face were lost to him. He found himself lying on a rough bed in what he soon learned was an army barracks. German army barracks. It was the next morning. A hangover like a freight train trying to burst out of his head. *My God*, how had he ended up here? Two men wearing spotless German uniforms approached him as he sat woozy on the edge of the bed. They showed him the sheet of paper he'd signed the night before.

What paper? Screwing up his eyes, he read it slowly. In lieu of the fact that unauthorized Danish citizens were not usually found on the streets during the Blackout, they informed him that he had been kindly offered a place to stay, and thus avoided arrest and questioning by the police. Skipping down, he saw his signature at the bottom of the page. More a scribble of black ink—yet his signature it was. He then went back to the paragraph in the middle that he had neglected to read. The part stating that by signing below, he agreed to join the German Wehrmacht for the duration of the war. Obviously it was all a mistake. He didn't recollect signing any paper. He was sorry he'd caused them any trouble, now was it OK to go home.

NEIN.

He learned quickly enough that the German NO was a lot harsher than the Danish version. And more than a simple command. The threat of fists, whips, dogs, lay behind that brief monosyllable. Sent to a training center in Jutland, twice he tried running away. The first time he'd been caught they bloodied his nose, slapped him around, warned him not to do it again. The second time, the Gestapo became involved. Foss had expected much worse, but they didn't beat him at all. A couple of goons in black leather jackets had glared at him while a smaller man with a calm voice stated that he would be unequivocally shot if there were a third escape. The remains of his body afterward would then be tossed into a sty and fed to pigs.

A third escape . . . No, Mrs. Foss's boy was clever enough to know when a wall could not be climbed. Not that he had given up on the idea, but once he boarded the train down to Germany, and linked with another train that headed east through Poland and didn't stop till he got to Smolensk, then *escape* was not a viable dream . . .

Just then Tulm stirred, opened his eyes, sensed Foss lying awake. Sitting up and yawning, he whispered, "How'd it go with the brass?"

Surprised at the interruption of his thoughts, Foss took a few moments before whispering back, "The usual questions. This one wasn't demanding as most. Young. Looked a few years out of nursery school."

Frowning, Tulm said, "We're scraping the barrel now. Pretty soon there won't be much to scrape."

The two men chatted quietly together for some while about the everyday life they knew. Their constant hunger, the fierce winter weather—possibly the coldest of all the war years—and what each of them planned to do when the war was over. Tulm was one of the quietest men in the outfit, one of the *quietest* men Foss had ever met. A year or so before during a lull at the front, Foss had found inspiration watching a flock of geese heading south in the sky. With what time he had, he had written a short poem commemorating the event. When Tulm learned of this he exclaimed, "I didn't know you wrote poetry! I write poetry too." After that they shared their poems, discussed the merits of modernism versus rhyme and meter. Tulm's works were mostly abstract visions of a futuristic world that Foss had a hard time understanding. But many of his lines were beautiful. Foss always complimented Tulm on this fact.

"I haven't written much lately," Tulm said after Foss inquired about his poetry.

Foss nodded in agreement. "Me neither. Not much I want to write about." And he added to himself that there were no spare hours to write in this hell they currently had to endure.

The other men still slept. Ziemans snored. A gargling, snotty type of wheeze that Foss had first found disgusting in the early days, but now had grown wont to hearing. Tulm shook his head.

"He's forever worried me with that snoring of his." Half-smiling, Tulm continued to shake his head. "Surely the Ivans have heard it by now. He'll bring their batteries on us one day."

Smiling back, Foss studied Tulm. A short dark-faced man with a shyness that never went away, even among his comrades Tulm had been teased about his looks time and again (and often the teasing turned into uglier sentiments) for being a Jew. "Why don't you just admit it?" Ziemans had echoed on countless occasions. "You're a goddamned Jew!" Ruder would pick up where Ziemans left off, and not only accuse Tulm of having Jewish blood, but threaten him with exposure to the military police. And ultimately the SS. Foss had always told them to knock it off, and the bullying would eventually cease. Foss had had a Jewish friend in school, and he never understood the Nazi ideology ingrained in so many Germans. Why Jews were so hated? Whether Tulm was a Jew or not, he'd never asked him about his background. Tulm was a good soldier, and at this point in time, that was all that mattered.

For a few minutes the two men remained silent. Then Tulm said, "What are your plans when the war's . . . over?"

Foss checked momentarily to see whether Ruder was still sleeping. The former Hitler Youth lay sound asleep, his eyelids moving in dream. He looked at the other men. Ziemans' snoring was grosser than ever. "To go home again," Foss stated with resolution, when he knew that none of the others would hear him. "Just to go home."

Fidgeting with his hands as though unsure of what to say next, Tulm kept his eyes averted. "What about your countrymen—will they let you back home?"

The question puzzled Foss. "Why wouldn't they?"

"How long have you been away?"

"Almost . . . three years."

"Have you had a furlough?"

"No furlough."

"I haven't had leave either. I've heard things aren't the same in Dusseldorf, my home town. All the bombings have taken a toll, despite what those in power say to the contrary. People don't have enough to eat. It might be the same in Copenhagen."

Foss scratched at a place on the back of his neck. He and just about every other soldier had had off-and-on problems with one of the greatest scourges of the war: Lice. Continuing to scratch, he said, "Copenhagen hasn't been bombed. At least not extensively."

"How do you know?"

Foss was surprised by Tulm's uncharacteristic probing. He wondered what had set him off. Of course, after the long retreat from Russia, all the men's nerves were on edge. Now that the war had come to Germany, no one knew what lay ahead. Foss said, "I get letters regularly from my mother. And from an old girlfriend of mine. According to them . . . Denmark is still very much intact."

Knowing full well of Foss's correspondence with home, Tulm nonetheless continued to probe.

"But when did you last hear from them?"

What the hell's up with Tulm? Foss thought irritably, then realized that he had not received any mail for many weeks. Months. The system was breaking down. Or perhaps the censors no longer allowed mail to be sent to the front lines for fear of what the letters contained. *Defeatism.*

"I'm sorry, Aksel." Tulm reached over and patted the Dane on the shoulder. "Didn't mean to hammer you like that. Just curious to know about Denmark. I might need a new home after all this is over with."

"New home?"

"I'm afraid Germany's days . . . are numbered," Tulm said, keeping his voice nearly inaudible as he checked to see whether any of the others might have woken. "The writing's been on the wall a long time. Apparently our leaders have been too blind to see it." Closing his eyes all of sudden Tulm appeared as if he was going to break. "The Nazis have destroyed Germany. And now the Soviets are going to destroy what's left."

Biting his lip, Tulm stood up in a hurry. He paced a few moments, stopped, then paced again. Taking several deep breaths, he looked as though he had something on his mind—something important to say. Foss waited. He had never seen Tulm when he wasn't composed, even when accused of being a Jew. *Is he trying to tell me that he's indeed Jewish? Is that why he wants to go to Denmark?* The obvious pain etched on Tulm's face left Foss speechless. He wanted to reach out and embrace the other man. Then a boom louder than thunder slammed the bunker and Foss found himself pelted with flying dirt and debris.

But it was not just a single boom. A series of tremendous blasts followed, and to Foss, they felt like the end of the world. From so many similar experiences, Foss surmised that the Russians would pound the German lines with massive artillery till they were reduced to rubble, then launch an attack. Crouching with his Tommy gun in a corner of the bunker, Foss shut his eyes to keep out dust and splinters. The rest of the men had woken instantly, almost as though they had never slept. Each of them stayed low to the ground like Foss, some holding their ears, some gazing anxiously at the wooden support beams that shook precariously with every round of the tumult raining down on them.

"Those Red scum!" someone shouted, though Foss didn't open his eyes to see who it was. There were times such as this one when even the most battle-toughened veteran could lose his mind. Men would weep or scream till something burst in their brains, then they'd run amok, even go outside and nearly foaming with fear, dash over the parapet and trenches and end up being killed. Occasionally a man had to be put down by his own side, so that his terror did not become contagious and send everyone over the edge. Foss forced his eyes open momentarily to gaze over his men. They all hugged the dirt like he did.

The explosions went on for nearly an hour.

Somehow the bunker held. But other bunkers nearby were blown to bits. Foss surmised this from the hideous shrieks and calls for help that periodically eclipsed the shells in sound. When the last explosion faded, Foss waited two minutes, then leaped up with his gun and sprinted outside. Not needing a signal, the others followed him in the same manner.

Sure enough the Russians were on the move. Foss crawled into a crater made by one of the recent shells. He peered cautiously over the top. Dozens of tanks were racing toward him, just a few hundred meters away. Russian infantry ran behind them. Foss glanced from right to left. The German lines had been bombed into disarray, in a number of spots totally obliterated. Other men, many shaking and covered with so much dirt and dust that they resembled ghouls, had crawled out and were gazing wide-eyed at the enemy approaching them. This section of the front had once been secured with a long stretch of barbed-wired fence. Foss was not surprised to see that the fence had nearly disappeared.

For the Volksturm units, the Russian advance was alarming. To Foss and his men—they'd witnessed the same scene a hundred times or more. A machine gun began to bark from the German side, and Foss told the newcomers to stay low in the trenches . . . what remained of them. He was shocked to see that many of the Volksturm bore rifles used in the First World War. One of the youngsters, probably no more than fifteen, openly wept. Foss took the boy under his wing.

"Stay close to me, son." Saying the words made him feel strange. He was a young man himself, but to the boy he must seem like a grandfather. The tanks began firing; great holes were made in the German lines. Half a leg flew into the trench where Foss kept a hold on the boy. The sight of the bloody remnants of a human limb sent the boy into a spasm of terror. Breaking free from Foss, he screamed hideously and flung himself over the trench—straight toward the Russians.

Foss peered over the parapet to see the boy sprinting. Hands held high, he sought to surrender to the Ivans when another blast tore up the ground in front of him. Foss ducked down as shrapnel and shell splinters whipped through the air over him. When he peered over the trench again, he saw the boy sprawled on the snow and dirt not twenty paces away. His helmet had been torn from his head, and half his face with it. The boy had bright red hair. Foss had not noticed it earlier.

Checking his Tommy gun to see if it was fully loaded, Foss waited till the Ivans were in range, pointed at a group of infantryman beside a tank, then let out a burst.

The Russians dove to the ground. Early in the war they had mounted mass attacks at German positions and had absorbed casualties in the tens of thousands. Now they were warier, and let their artillery and tanks chew up the German fortifications before attacking.

Panic engulfed Foss as he waited for the German artillery to open fire. *Why the hell aren't they shooting?* He knew the German Army lacked supplies these days, lacked everything. The Russian tanks were closing in. He was ready to give up hope when he was nearly concussed by the sound of a battery from the rear. An .88 millimeter gun had somehow survived the earlier barrage; one of the few guns that could knock out Russian tanks, it fired off another round as Foss once more peeked over the trench.

Miraculously, two tanks sat immobile, ablaze; from one of them a Russian tank-man was trying to squirm his way out of the turret. But the fire caught him first. He writhed and screamed like a banshee as the fire quickly engulfed his entire body. The sight was sickening, even to an old hand like Foss. Forcing himself to take a deep breath, the Dane turned his gaze and instantly forgot the horror as thousands of Russians shouting their famous battle-cry, "Urrah!" sprinted toward the trenches. Most of the Russians wore white clothing that blended well with the snow, though many in the front of the pack bore darker uniforms. Foss knew these men to be recent recruits, or members of penal battalions punished for some infraction. Another German machine gun spat out a long burst of bullets. Many of the Ivans crumpled in the snow.

Waiting for the enemy to get closer, Foss finally aimed his Tommy gun and let fly a brief burst. He turned to see several of his comrades doing the same with rifles. A couple of grenades were tossed. Russians were dying by the scores. The T-34s kept firing. Endless thunder rocked the earth, and part of a body landed in Foss's trench. Sensing the precariousness of his position, the Dane slid on the cold soil toward another fox hole. He noted Dreyback and Ruder firing their guns. Dreybach stopped firing when he noticed his sergeant kneeling beside him.

"Can we hold?" Dreybach's face was a mask of grime and sweat, his words scarcely audible above the uproar.

Foss started to answer when several Tiger tanks drove up from the rear. They had somehow survived the earlier barrage intact and now began to pummel the Russians with their own salvos. Seeing this, the Landsers took heart and began to fight furiously. But the Tigers soon left. With fuel and ammunition dangerously low all across the Reich, the tanks would be needed in the rear areas in case of a Russian breakthrough. Many of the inexperienced Volksturm ran after them, believing the battle lost.

The Russians kept throwing more men and tanks at the front line. It was always the same—at least since Kursk. Though giving all they had, the German soldiers were simply overwhelmed by men and materiel. Time and again. The Ivans had too much, the Landsers too little. Soon they'd have nothing.

This thought ran across Foss's mind as he blasted away at the enemy. Something tugging his shoulder nearly caused him to whirl and fire at whatever did it.

Tulm. The man was shouting at him and he barely made out the words. "Laursen's been . . . hit. Not bad. He'll . . . make it. The rest are wondering . . . what to do . . . "

Foss ground his teeth at the man as though he were a dimwit. "You know what to do—if he's injured, find a medic."

Tulm shook his head. "I mean—do you intend to stay here or what? Everyone else is taking to their heels. Most already have." He pointed at the German lines to left and right that now held scarcely a company to man several hundred meters of pockmarked entrenchments. Even the majority of these remaining men began to trickle out of their foxholes in retreat.

Whether a retreat had been ordered or not, Foss waved his hand toward the rear. Tulm needed no other words. The two men crawled out of the trench, made for the others who were waiting behind the concrete wall of a ruined bunker, then all of them hurried west as fast as they could run.

We won't be able to run forever. Foss kept repeating this silently to himself the closer they drew to Greater Germany. An hour had elapsed. He and his men had found new lodgings in a half-finished bunker overlooking a broad flat landscape that reminded him of the country in Northern Zealand where one of his uncles owned a pig farm. He smelled the sea in the wind, and knew they were not far from water. From the look of the new positions, it was obvious the High Command was trying to consolidate as many forces as possible in one area to stop the Russian onslaught. Tanks and gun emplacements lay hidden beneath camouflage amid small groves of trees; machine guns were carefully concealed by mounds of sandbags and heavily packed soil. The Wehrmacht had been doing the same since the final hours of Kursk . . . but what had any of it accomplished? Certainly they had slain Ivans by the tens of thousands, crippled whole army groups, yet there was no stoppage to the amount of troops the Russians threw at them. They just kept coming. A bottomless pit of men and machines, while the Germans had almost no reserves left. Foss rolled this over in his mind with sickening reality. He had no desire to end up in Siberia, a slave-laborer, worked and starved to death. Or trussed up and tortured. With the cold barrel of a Nagan shoved up against the back of his neck and—

"You look worried, Aksel." Laursen, an ethnic Dane from Flensburg in Schleswig-Holstein, looked worried himself as he broke the sergeant's thoughts. A white bandage covered Laursen's forehead; it was red in spots.

Caught off guard, Foss nodded. "You must have read my thoughts. But sorry to say, nothing new with the situation. Same dilemmas. Same shitty lack of solutions. How's your wound, Laursen?" Since the two men were not too near the others, they spoke quietly in Danish.

"Got nicked by a piece of shrapnel." Laursen gently probed his fingers along the front of the dressing. Wincing, he pulled it back when he felt a wet spot. "It would have pierced my brain from any other angle. Then I'd really be out of the war."

Foss nearly said that the war would be over soon enough, but he checked himself before uttering anything. In these times, words too often were heard by the wrong ears. Veteran soldiers, even those who had earned an array of medals, had been strung up on trees and telephone poles for the mere hint that Germany might lose the war. Placards proclaiming their "traitorous defeatism" were usually attached to the bodies by the Gestapo or the SS to frighten others from holding similar sentiments.

Lighting a cigarette, Foss handed it to Laursen, then lit another for himself.

"Might not be a bad idea to have a real doctor look at your wound." Blowing out a ring of smoke, Foss narrowed his eyes as he scanned Laursen's bandage.

"Why the hell should I do that?" Laursen asked sarcastically, his face grimacing from a sudden stab of pain in his head. "They're emptying the hospitals right and left. Unless you've had your head blown off, the army's going to stick you in the front line. I'd probably get thrown in prison for malingering."

For a while Foss didn't respond. Then he said carefully, "I would have it checked anyway, if I were you. You never know, you might get sent to the rear. Infection can spread in such wounds."

Looking puzzled, Laursen said, "You trying to get rid of me?"

A hint of a smile curved Foss's lips. "Yes. For your own good. The time for heroes is fast fading."

"But what about you?" Laursen puffed on his cigarette, then blew out a ring of smoke, followed by another ring. "You're the one who should leave . . . hell, you're not even a German."

"Oh, I plan on leaving this war at some point." There was a faraway glint in Foss's eyes that Laursen noted. The Dane was silent a moment. He turned to the direction where he sensed the sea. Continuing to stare north, he said, "It's strange now to consider that I actually sympathized with some of the communist ideas before the war. Marxist, rather. I thought democracy was on the way out, what with the Depression and people never having enough food. There simply had to be a better way of going about life. Of helping the poor and malnourished. But the whole scheme is nothing but a nightmare. I wish my Marxist-sympathizing friends back home could see the way the Soviets brutalize and murder their own people. Their system is a fucking travesty. I've seen all I ever want to see of communism—Russia can have it! And I have no desire to linger in Germany either. The Nazis are rotten to the core. Choosing between Nazism and Communism is like choosing between plague and cholera. No one-party systems for me. Give me quaint little Denmark and I'll be content the rest of my days."

Foss's words made Laursen think of his own hometown, Flensburg. Once a part of Denmark, before the Prussians conquered the entire province of Schleswig-Holstein nearly a hundred years earlier. Laursen sighed, thinking of his mother's homemade pumpernickel bread. And the smoked slab bacon his family would get from his grandparents, who owned a farm in the country. His mouth watered at the thought of all the times as a child when he'd dipped slices of the bread into a pan of bacon grease. My God, he'd give the rest of his army pay to eat some now.

Laursen was about to say something else when a drone in the sky caused him to glance upwards. Foss too craned his neck toward the eastern horizon. It took a few seconds for the men to register what the noise was. Stormoviks. One of the Russians' most common planes, they often attacked during large-scale offensives, using rockets to destroy German tanks and armored vehicles. But more often than not they were inaccurate with their weaponry, and could be shot down with precise anti-aircraft fire or by Messerschmidts. Though lately German fighter-planes, or any German planes, were scarcely seen in the sky over the Eastern Front. They were mostly used nowadays to try and protect German cities from American and English bombers.

Taking Laursen by the arm, Foss moved him toward a grove of trees. The Russian planes flew directly overhead, then veered south without attacking. A few minutes later they were no longer heard. Ziemans and Keller presently appeared among the trees.

"Some other poor bastards are going to buy it," Keller said without emotion, while rubbing at a red spot on his cheek. Foss noticed that the spot was inflamed, and the rubbing only made it redder.

"Better them than us." Coughing suddenly, Ziemans cleared his throat by spitting out a thick wad of phlegm into the snow. "I've had enough of hightailing it every single day. We haven't had a proper rest in weeks."

"And we won't have a proper rest till we kick those Russian scum back to the holes they crawled out of." It was Ruder. The others turned in surprise to see him stepping over a fallen tree trunk, and slipping and nearly falling in the process. He cursed, glancing angrily in the direction the Stormoviks had flown. "We'll blast them out of the sky once the Fuhrer unleashes his new weapons."

"Just shut up with that shit!" With the heel of his hand, Ziemans thrust it at Ruder's chest, shoving the former Hitler Youth leader roughly to the ground. Scrambling to his feet, Ruder pointed his rifle at Ziemans.

"You'll regret that, you ass." Ruder seemed on the verge of firing when Foss grabbed the barrel of the gun and pushed it aside.

"And you'll regret it more for shooting a fellow German soldier. If the Feldgendarmerie don't hang you, then I will." Foss's eyes were like cold daggers, and peering into them, Ruder knew the Dane meant every word he said. Spinning away with a scowl of hatred, Ruder stalked off. Ziemans whistled after him with contempt.

"It's brown nosers like him that got us into this lousy war in the first place." Snorting, Ziemans spit out another wad of mucus. "If he wants to kill Russkies, let him go right ahead."

"Keep your thoughts to yourself, Ziemans." Foss had had enough of the asinine bickering. He also didn't want Ziemans to get the unit in trouble. "Men are being executed every day for saying a lot less than what you just said. If you want to throw your own life away . . . fine. Just don't expect us to sing at your funeral."

"I wouldn't want you to sing at my funeral anyway, Foss. You'd probably botch it up with your Viking accent." Slinging his rifle over his shoulder, Ziemans trudged off in the opposite direction of Ruder.

"No one's in a good mood today," Laursen emphasized after Ziemans was gone. Keller nodded in agreement. Foss merely shrugged, and the three men stood there a while in silence, before heading to a long ditch dug hastily by a Volksturm unit several days earlier. Most of the other men were there, though there was no sign of Ruder. Food was brought up from the rear by the cooking staff, a watery lukewarm soup that contained a few pieces of stringy meat.

"They're killing the horses again," a voice echoed down the line.

"I heard in Stalingrad—*people* were being eaten," another voice clipped in.

"Keep your mouth shut, you idiot." Dreybach rose from his spot to glare at an older man whom he thought had spoken. The man shook his head emphatically to say that it was someone else. Dreybach cursed silently, sat down again, began to eat. Foss found a spot beside him.

The Dane gazed for a long while at the sky, which was dark and overcast. It reminded him of the sky at home, similarly dark most of the year. One of his brother's friends, tired of poverty and the lack of work in Denmark, had gone to Spain to fight in that country's Civil War. When he returned, he spoke high praise of Spain's warmer climate, the frequent sunshine. Though when asked about the war, he turned to other subjects. "You had to be there to know what it was like," he said.

Foss knew now what he meant. In his letters home, to his mother, and brother, and to his former girlfriend Ingrid, he rarely wrote anything more than descriptions of the landscape and weather, and the friendships he had made. He never mentioned the Russian villages he had passed through, torched and burning, with the bodies of the villagers often sprawled haphazardly beside the blackened ruins of their hovels, or the captured partisans he had witnessed being strung up on gibbets, or the Russian prisoners who had been shot out of hand. He had shot some himself. They did the same to German prisoners, and worse. One didn't surrender on the Eastern Front. Not if you wanted to keep your balls.

Dreybach slowly sipped his soup. He noticed Foss staring off at the sky. "Still worried about the Stormoviks?" he asked gruffly.

"No, just reminiscing about home. The weather in Denmark is much the same as here. I don't know how I got used to all that gray. All that rain."

The veteran didn't respond, and Foss knew that the mention of "home" must have brought painful memories to Dreybach. His friend's apartment in Hamburg had been obliterated in the infamous fire-bombing several years earlier, and with it all his family had perished. Foss wasn't sure how Dreybach had kept going all this time, continuing to fight in Russia with distinction, and rarely if ever letting down his guard to reveal the wretchedness of his loss. The man's taciturnity was admirable, though Foss guessed the sorrow was hidden away somewhere. The suffocating agony and bitterness. The Dane said, "Why don't you come up and visit me in Copenhagen after the war. I'll treat you to some Danish beer—real beer!" He laughed. "Beer and smoked herring. Or sausage if you prefer. Though you Germans have the trademark on that."

Dreybach briefly grinned. "I'll consider it, Foss. Never traveled outside Germany until the war started. Seems odd now. I've seen more countries than I knew existed. In the last six years I've hardly been home." His words trailed off. There was silence, except for the conversations of others in the trench. Foss turned his head at an abrupt rumbling in the distance. Barely a few minutes respite from the war. Never enough time to relax and shove it out of the mind. He turned back at the sound of Dreybach's voice. "How about you?" the German asked with earnestness. "What will you do when this mess is over?"

"I haven't thought that far ahead. I suppose I'll get some type of education. Though Denmark is limited as far as jobs. I don't fancy working in a factory. After being out in the open so long, I'd get claustrophobic staying cooped up inside for ten or so hours a day. I don't know . . . maybe I'll travel. Maybe you and I can travel. I guess we could always be mercenaries. The world never lacks for wars."

Dreybach didn't answer right away. Then he said, "Don't you think we've had enough war? Fifty years ago men still made cavalry charges. Then some idiots invented machine guns, gas, tanks. Dive bombers. Stalin organs. So what are they going to invent for the next one? I'd rather not consider it. And I hope I'm a million kilometers away, hidden in some silent bunker with an arsenal of schnapps to keep me listless. I'll never be a soldier of fortune—for there's no fortune in war."

Nodding slowly in agreement, Foss glanced again in the direction where the shelling had become noticeably louder. Snow flurries swirled in the air. The temperature was dropping as night drew closer. A prelude to another blizzard, he thought somberly. He'd experienced three years of blizzard-like weather. Three years of a bitter, frozen hell. Yet—what remained for him in Denmark? He longed to return home, see his mother, his brother, and hopefully Ingrid was waiting for him. If not with open arms, then at least with . . . but what if she wasn't waiting. And what if his family had other concerns to occupy their time. Suddenly Denmark felt like a place he'd never known. *But it's only been three years!* A mere thousand or so days. Could a man change so utterly in such little time? A foolish question; in war he'd seen countless men change in a matter of minutes.

A matter of seconds.

One moment sitting and playing cards with a buddy, and a moment later seeing your buddy's body, minus a head decapitated from a sudden howitzer blast, sitting in the same position as though ready to deal. Foss shut his eyes as though trying to rid himself of this memory. But it didn't go away, not completely. Nor the others of equal horror. The day he and his outfit had come across two Germans who'd been captured by the Russians and crucified on makeshift crosses. Castrated, and mutilated beyond recognition, the men had had excrement smeared across their naked corpses. For the next month Foss and his unit vowed to take no prisoners. And they kept the vow. Russian soldiers, partisans, commissars, civilians, had all been mowed done ruthlessly. One of them, a beautiful girl no older than twenty, had pleaded for her life, claiming innocence, despite the fact that she had concealed a pistol and several grenades under her skirt.

Ziemans wanted to rape her first, but Dreybach shot her through the heart before the other Landser could satisfy his lust. "We don't have time for that," Dreybach had groused, and when Ziemans got angry, Dreybach pointed his rifle at him. It took a lot of urging from Foss to get the older man to lower his gun. A letter had just come informing Dreybach of the loss of his family in the bombing raid. He would have shot anyone at that point, friend or foe. Foss realized then that all of them needed to get away from the killing. Needed to stop shooting every Russian they saw.

But there was no getting away from the killing. It only got worse.

Verheizen, the word that every Landser knew as the only reality of the war. Cannon fodder to be sent into the fields of fire and slaughtered. The Eastern front was nothing but an enormous maw of shark-like teeth tearing to shreds the souls of millions. Foss had no idea what the western front was like, but somehow he doubted it was as bad. Nothing could be this bad. No longer was there any innocence left in the world. But maybe innocence was only a fairytale. His father's suicide, the impoverishment of the Depression—who in the world had not known despair. He looked at his hands. Would he be able to wash the blood from these hands once he was back home? Could he ever adjust to life in Denmark again knowing what he knew . . .

An explosion rocked the earth behind him. A man screamed. Then another explosion somewhere to the left, showering debris over the spot where Foss and Dreybach lay hugging the ground. Putting his fear aside, the Dane grabbed his Tommy-gun and stared out over the trench.

The Russians had appeared from out of nowhere and were attacking in a mass formation of tanks and infantry. Foss heard Dreybach curse. Other men cursed. Then a cannon boomed. As though a giant sword had cleaved through it, the turret of the lead Russian tank was knocked clean off. Seconds later the turret landed among a group of Russian soldiers, smashing them to pieces. Rifle fire erupted up and down the line. A machine gun started, sputtered, then started again.

"I didn't even get to finish my goddamned soup," Dreybach shouted above the din, firing off several rounds from his Soviet machine pistol. More durable than the German-made sub-machine guns, and capable of firing up to a thousand rounds per minute, the Russian brand was coveted by many Landsers. Dreybach had taken his from a Russian partisan he had killed a year before.

"You're not the only one," Foss hurled back, as he let out a burst from his own gun.

"Where the hell did they come from? We should have been warned."

"Patrols were sent out an hour ago. Must have been snuffed on the way." His weapon suddenly empty, Foss pulled a cartridge from his pocket and reloaded it. Snow continued to fall. He wiped a flake off his eyelid. A soldier next to him had dropped to the bottom of the trench, his face a mangled mess. The man's blood ran over Foss's boots. The battle lasted only a few more minutes. The Russians must have been as surprised at the enemy defenses as the Germans were at the surprise attack. They retreated back to where they first started. Soon they were all but hidden in a distant woods. A few desultory shots were fired by both sides, then silence. Except for the screaming of the wounded. Foss and Dreybach took awhile before lowering their guns.

"It's not like the Russkies to quit that fast." A major appeared and was looking through binoculars at the retreating enemy. Gazing from side to side and back again, he continued to observe the horizon for some time. Then putting the binoculars away, he turned and smiled at Foss. "Sergeant, that medal at your neck—I'd lay any bets you won that in our eastern campaign."

"Yes, sir, I did. Kursk."

"Well done!"

"Thank you, sir." Taken aback by the officer's casual tone, Foss made note of the Knight's cross with oak leaves pinned to the major's tunic, just visible through the top of his thick winter coat. Only extreme gallantry could win such a medal.

"They'll be back," the major said grimly. "And with a lot more than what they just brought." He swerved around to scan the German lines, manned mostly by Volksturm units, then shook his head with disgust. "I wonder if Stalin knows he's now facing mostly untrained farmers and schoolboys. I just spoke with one of our soldiers a while ago. The man could barely walk. Lame. A cripple! When I asked him his age . . . do you know what he told me?"

"No, sir."

"Seventy years old! He's seen seventy turnings of the earth. And there are many others like him. Do you think—such men can stop the Red Army, sergeant?"

It was a loaded question. One Foss knew instinctively not to answer. Instead, he said, "Sir, with your permission, may I take this pause in the fighting to find my men. One was wounded in an earlier firefight. The others are scattered among the breastworks. Hopefully they are all still alive."

"I hope they are too," the major said in a low tone. "Godspeed to you and your men." He immediately began scouting the terrain with the binoculars again. Foss and Dreyback saluted him as they went to search for their comrades.

When they were out of hearing, Dreybach asked, "What did he mean by that: *Godspeed?* Didn't exactly sound positive."

Foss shrugged, unsure himself. "Any sod with even a smidgen of brain matter knows we are constantly moving these days. Though—always backwards."

It took nearly an hour to gather their group in one place. But thankfully they found everyone alive. Even Laursen had returned to the fray, holding his rifle across his lap as he sat smoking a cigarette. His head was still bandaged beneath his helmet. The snow was falling in heavier flakes. A murky brooding twilight westered behind them. Up and down the fortifications sentries took turns staring into the darkness. Because of the cold, they were relieved every twenty minutes. Past experience had taught the army that men too long exposed to sub-freezing temperatures often fell asleep and never woke again. Or had their throats slit by partisans. For Foss's group Ruder was given first duty. As Ruder sullenly gazed over the parapet, Ziemans quipped, "Let him guard all night. With luck, he might freeze his nuts off. Then we won't have any more little Ruders running around the world. And what will the Party say to that! For lack of diligence in the fight against Bolshevism—I'm sure the headhunters will find a nice telephone poll to strap his ugly carcass to. I can just see it now, the placard on his chest: **A traitor to the Fatherland. He surrendered his weapons and his balls to the enemy without a struggle.**"

Ruder scowled. "More likely you'll be the one the military police apprehend, you filthy swine. When it's your turn, I'm keeping my eye on you the whole time. If your eyelids droop for even a second, I'll be right there to remind you of your duty."

"Go right ahead, chum." Fingering the knife at his belt, Ziemans grinned evilly. "We can have a nice friendly midnight chat."

Continuing to scowl, Ruder went off to an outpost some distance away. Ziemans then settled down and fell asleep almost instantaneously. Foss, watching it all with a sigh, said to Dreybach who sat next to him, "We'll take turns, each of us. And if you don't mind, keep an eye on those two."

"I'll keep more than an eye on them," Dreybach responded, adding a fresh cartridge to his Russian weapon.

The snow continued to fall. So did the temperature. A wind, first barely noticeable, began to whip across the open landscape with fury. Men huddled low to the ground in the half-sheltered trenches. But they shivered regardless. Occasional coughs were heard. One man mumbled in his sleep until he got a kick in the shin. Foss slept for an hour, then took his turn at the sentry post. He and a private from another unit gazed into the cold darkness that was eerily silent. Keeping his hands on his gun, Foss felt a foreboding. He noticed the private—who unbelievably looked no more than twelve in age—trying hard not to doze. But the boy's head kept tipping toward his chest before he would raise it swiftly in wide-eyed alarm. He glanced at Foss in fear that the sergeant had seen him sleeping. Falling asleep on sentry duty at the front was punishable by death. Though that didn't grab Foss's attention as much as the fact that this obvious newcomer had no sense of danger. Had not built up years of keen intuition, instinct. Could not perceive when an attack was imminent. Or when a plane might appear out of nowhere to strafe an entrenchment. Or when a shell might slam into a—

Foss tackled the boy. They both tumbled deeper in the trench as explosives lit up the entire front line like a grand display of fireworks. The boy shrieked. Foss clapped a hand over his mouth.

"Artillery!" Foss yelled above the din. Though the word was redundant. The crash of shells tore up the ground around them. Snow and earth that a moment before lay still, now were heaved up in the air in great mountains of debris. Then the Stalin Organs came, the shrill of their high-pitched launch frightening even the hardest soldiers. The nightmare of every German infantryman.

How long they huddled at the bottom of the hole, Foss couldn't tell. The boy was bawling. The Dane continued to clamp his mouth shut. My God, when is this going to end, Foss thought, biting his chapped lips till they cracked and bled. The taste of the salt from the blood caused him to focus on something other than the terror of the shells. That was the only thing

to do. You were either killed, wounded, or survived. That was all there was
to war. Afterwards, life went on for the survivors.

He knew once the shelling stopped, the Ivans would mount an attack.
The shelling stopped. He waited as usual a short time, then grabbed his
sub-machine gun and peered over the parapet. Gesturing to the boy to do
the same, Foss left the post and ran to his friends. He turned back to
glance over his shoulder once. The boy had not followed him. Still half-
submerged in the trench, he stared at Foss with a look of terror. But there
was nothing to be done. He would either find his way back to his own unit,
or he wouldn't.

Explosives continued to pummel the earth. Foss had dealt with countless
artillery barrages, but this was one of the worst. He barely jumped into a
foxhole before the whole world seemed to belch out fire and thunder. For
a moment Foss lost his bearings. His head swam. His chest ached as if he'd
been mauled by a giant hammer. Palming his hands over his eyes, he tried
breathing deeply. Men often got concussed from such explosions, but Foss
soon felt his sense of time and place returning. Grabbing his gun again, he
left the hole and zigzagged at a crouch to the spot where he thought his
men might be. He'd been taught to zigzag early in the war; bombs and
bullets had a way of specifically targeting men moving in straight lines.
Foss dropped whenever he perceived a shell coming close. The explosions
temporarily turned night into day. One landed off to the left and for a split
second Foss thought he saw Steenhagen tending to a wounded man above
the parapet. Then another shell slammed into the snow and Foss lost his
footing.

He leaped up just as quickly as he had fallen. *Keep going, keep going.* He
wasn't sure whether he spoke aloud or yelled in his mind. It was dangerous
to brave the cannon fire without cover—but he didn't want to be parted
from his men. *But where the hell are they?* Piercing screams erupted from
seemingly everywhere. Soldiers were dying. He prayed they weren't his
friends.

Finally he heard someone call his name. It was a pinprick of a needle
amid the bombardment. Then it called again: "Aksel, over here!"
Immediately the Dane whirled to what appeared to be a huge dark crater
cut out of the snow. Panting with exhaustion, Foss jumped in, banging his
shoulder against something hard.

"Aksel, are you alright?" It was Tulm, who was fully shouting because of the din.

"I think so," Foss said, rubbing his shoulder where he had hurt it—the same shoulder where he'd taken a bullet several summers before. He saw that he had hit it on a helmet. He tried moving the helmet but it was too heavy. Then he noticed a face beneath it. A man he'd never seen before. A man now dead.

"Did you know him?" Foss asked.

"Just some guy I shared a foxhole with," Tulm winced, as another bomb went off close by. "He got taken out early. Probably a shell splinter. I didn't even say two words to him."

No longer interested in the dead man, Foss scanned the rest of the crater. "Where are the others?"

"Steenhagen was here—before the Russians started their fireworks. He and another man. Then a bomb went off right in front of us. Nearly blew our trench to pieces. I must have been knocked out, briefly. When I came to—the two of them were gone. I yelled out his name several times, but he didn't respond."

A flash of worry crossed Foss's face. "I almost collided with Steenhagen out in No Man's Land. Bandaging one of the wounded."

"That sounds like good old Steenhagen. He patched me up once right in the middle of a firefight. I told him to get lost, but he never makes himself scarce. He wanted to be a doctor once."

"I know. That's what worries me. He feels a need to wrap even the tiniest scratch. If Stalin were lying in No Man's Land, he'd be out there treating him."

For a few seconds both men peeked toward the open field. It was too dark to see except when falling bombs jettisoned their deadly flames. But flying shrapnel was not conducive to one's well-being. They finally stopped searching. There was no sight of anyone. Then the shells ceased to fall. Checking to see that his gun was loaded, Foss once again peeped over the top.

Now that the barrage had ended, moans and screams became audible. One raspy voice cursed God; another cried for his mother. Most just shrieked in agony. Dugouts along the entire line had been hit hard. Small fires crackled and the sickening smell of burnt flesh burgeoned in the wind.

Medics raced to and fro, but they were overwhelmed. Then drowning out the noises of them all were tank engines.

"Shit! You'd think . . . those bastards would run out of tanks by now." Tulm, choking on his words with fear, kicked at the earth in frustration. It was at that moment Steenhagen reappeared, bearing a wounded soldier on his back. The man was unconscious. Steenhagen didn't stop. He kept moving steadily toward the rear.

"He won't make it," Steenhagen labored to say, "unless I get him to a proper doctor." Foss and Tulm saw that the man was missing a leg at the hip. Steenhagen had strapped a tourniquet around it as best he could to halt the bleeding. Covered in blood, Steenhagen might have been taken for being wounded himself. Foss showed a gesture of concern, while Tulm stood up, seeking to assist him.

"I'm fine. Don't fret about me." Knowing the intended question, Steenhagen calmed Foss's worry. "And I need no help, Tulm. I'll be back as soon as I find a surgeon."

Steenhagen staggered off with his load, and Foss and Tulm soon forgot about him. The Russians would be on them in a matter of moments. Hearing footsteps, Foss raised his gun.

"Don't shoot! Don't shoot!"

It was Keller, followed by the others. All except Brohm. Foss waited a minute, but there was no sign of him.

"Where's Brohm?"

The men kept their faces averted. None of them spoke.

"Well? Where is he?"

Still no one said anything.

"What the hell is this—a conspiracy of silence?" Foss stared at each man in turn. Finally, when Foss was about to lose his patience, Ruder spoke up.

"The idiot ran off."

"Ran off?" Foss was shocked. "You mean deserted?"

"Not . . . exactly."

"Then what *exactly* did he do! He didn't surrender to Ivan I hope?"

"Brohm would never do that," Dreybach broke in. "He'd put a gun to his own head before throwing himself to the mercy of the Mongolians. He simply ran back home. To Lyck. I wasn't there when he made his decision. Ruder tried to stop him but he wouldn't listen."

Foss paused, trying to collect his thoughts. Lyck was one of the towns that had already been overrun by the Russians. The news was not official, for the Nazis shoved under the rug anything resembling defeatism, even if it was an utter fact. Unless it suited their own purposes, such as whenever the Russians committed atrocities. But what purpose did Brohm have in going home? His family would no doubt have been evacuated by now—and even if they hadn't left, Foss shuddered to think what the Reds might have done to them. God damn the man! Returning to Lyck was a death certificate. Yet . . . he couldn't blame him entirely. No one could question Brohm's loyalty to his fellow soldiers, and his bravery in battle. But love of kin came before country. As it should.

"We'll speak no more about it," Foss said, his tone gruff. "Brohm went missing in action. That is what the record will state."

The men knew what he meant. If Brohm were listed as a deserter, not only would he receive a sentence of execution, but his family would suffer as well. Imprisonment, torture, even a firing squad. The men looked at their sergeant and kept mum. Even Ruder stayed silent.

The rumbling at the front grew louder. Bursts from several machine guns erupted periodically. The Russians had long made a habit of attacking at night—and they were good at it. A German artillery piece unleashed a salvo. Foss put his hands over his ears. But there were no further shots. The artillery was so low on ammo that each gun was given a quota it could not exceed. Orders were shouted into the driving snow and wind. Men yelled out in confusion. There were few anti-tank weapons available at this stage of the war; instead, Panzerfausts and the rocket-launching Panzerschreck, similar to the American Bazooka, could be operated by a single individual. And since the range of these weapons was limited—up to 180 meters for a Panzerschreck, and much less for a Panzerfaust—it took a stout soldier to hide and await a Russian tank at close quarters. Several of Foss's group carried them—Ruder and Brohm. But now Brohm was gone. Before leaving he had given his Panzerfaust to Keller. Turning to Keller, Foss saw that the man was uneasy with his new toy. Ruder, on the other hand, appeared overeager to match up with a T-34.

They didn't have long to wait. Driving out of the dark horizon, dozens of Soviet tanks flattened the earth beneath their treads. In the first trenches the treads flattened any men unable to hide themselves. Their thin screams barely rose above the roar of the tank engines. Looking like an eagle intent on a kill, Ruder fired his weapon at an oncoming tank. The resulting explosion reverberated across the landscape. Keller fired immediately afterward. His shot missed. The tank he had aimed at began to spray the area with machine gun fire.

"Duck down!" Foss yelled. Though everyone had instantly taken cover. More tanks went up in flames as other Panzerfausts hit their targets. Russian infantry following the armor were mowed down by rapid German fire. Many however escaped the withering hail of bullets to fire their own guns. Jumping into the destroyed remnants of the German fortifications, they engaged in hand to hand fighting with the defenders. There was the sound of gun-stocks smacking on helmets, spades cleaving through flesh. Men growled, cursed, shrieked, slew. And slew again. The Russians kept coming.

The world was a blur. Foss tripped over a body in the trench. He rose in a second. A Russian appeared in front of him. His eyes met the slanted eyes of an Asian. Foss fired his machine pistol point blank at the man's face. Blood splattered back at him. A bullet ricocheted off the barrel of his gun. A grenade exploded in a trench nearby, bringing screams. He fired at another Russian who was trying to bayonet Keller. "Pull back!" someone commanded in German. Men began fleeing. As he scrambled to follow the others, Foss's boot lodged against something soft. Human flesh. He stooped down to look closer. *Laursen.* His helmet was gone. The white bandage on his head torn and hanging about his face in disarray. Foss bent down to help him.

Too late.

The left side of Laursen's head had a hole big enough to put a fist in. Inadvertently Foss yelped. For a few seconds Foss clutched at the dead man's jacket and shook it fiercely. As though shaking the corpse would will it back to life. Then the clamor of Russian voices brought him back to the moment. The blast from grenades and the continued *tattattat* of machine guns just as quickly drowned out the voices. Men still fought like maddened animals in the dirt and snow. Hearing a groan, Foss spun around as a Russian toppled down on Laursen's corpse. The Russian, too, was dead. Foss hurriedly searched the ground around him for his comrades. No one. Only the remains of Laursen. Reaching around Laursen's neck, Foss broke off the dog-tag to verify his death. The ethnic Dane from Schleswig-Holstein would never have a proper burial. He and thousands of others. Taking one last look at his friend, Foss wiped tears from his eyes. Not wasting any more time, he heaved himself over the parapet and took off toward the only route left to him.

CHAPTER 3

The counterattack went badly. Having faced German tactics time and again, the Russians were waiting for it. The rattle of machine guns started even before the first German soldier got within several hundred paces of the new Russian lines. Mortars, then cannons, tore up the ground the Landsers tried to traverse. But orders were orders. The men were commanded to retake their previous positions. A direct order from Berlin.

"The hell with Berlin," said Ziemans reproachfully. Crouching behind the wall of a blown up house, Ziemans smoked a cigar in the predawn grayness. He had found a case full of cigars lying beside a dead colonel he'd come across in the earlier retreat. Now he and the rest of the men were smoking away. Even Ruder had been given one.

Occasionally eyeing the horizon to the east, Foss gently massaged the shoulder he'd smacked on the helmet the night before. He was bone weary. All of them were. Still, he and the others had managed to make a semblance of an attack in the wee hours of the morning. But there was no use continuing. The Russians had them pinned down. A fly wouldn't escape unscathed with the arsenal being unleashed at them.

"With the way things are going, you'd think the generals might unleash some of Adolf's wonder-weapons now." Ziemans glanced scornfully at Ruder, while flicking cigar ash on the ground. "Or maybe the Fuhrer's waiting for Ivan to take all of Germany before he shows the world how big his balls are."

Ruder's face reddened, but he said nothing.

Changing the subject, Tulm said, "I wonder if Brohm made it back."

Steenhagen raised his eyebrows. "Back here or back home?"

"Back home."

"Not much of a choice," Ziemans said with a cackle. "He's a goner either way."

Finishing his cigar, Dreybach threw the stub into a wooden bucket sitting against a broken wheelbarrow. "Have you ever had a single uplifting thought in your life, Ziemans?"

For a moment Ziemans assumed a pensive air. "To be or not to be, that is the question. And out here . . . none of us are going to be for long."

Just then a missile struck a stand of trees not fifty meters from the remains of the house. All of the men crouched lower.

"I guess the Russkis didn't like your answer." Dreybach gave a rare smile, surprising Foss. Perhaps the man was finally coming out of his long depression.

"We better get going." Foss waved them up with his hands.

When Ziemans cursed, Foss said, "No need to fret, boys. We're holding off on the blitzkrieg. At least today."

"That's the first good advice I've heard in a long time," Ziemans said, visibly relieved.

They moved out, heading back on a path that wound around other once-tidy homes smashed by artillery. The rotting carcass of a cow lay sprawled under the tiles of a fallen roof. Ziemans stopped to investigate but Foss grabbed his arm and pulled him away.

"Leave it. I know what you're thinking: Food. But it might have lain there for days. There's better ways to die than eating foul meat."

The sight of the cow suddenly made Foss regret his words to Ziemans. They brought back his last memory of Laursen. As though sensing Foss's grief, Tulm stepped along side of him.

"Sorry about Laursen," Tulm sympathized. "I just hope he went quickly."

Foss nodded, sad. "He did. He went quickly."

The men rarely spoke the rest of the way back to the German positions. Instead, they spent the retreat dodging explosives, throwing themselves down in the snow, or hiding behind large trees. Over time they were joined by other units, some bearing severely wounded soldiers on stretchers. A man who had had his hip smashed by a shell, died en route. Once back with the troops that had remained behind, they awaited the inevitable Russian onslaught. Fortunately though, the Russians were patching up their own wounds, consolidating their lines, reestablishing contact with divisions spread out in disarray across the German countryside. Foss and his men slept in the meantime. It wasn't until nightfall that the Russians launched a new barrage.

Jutta Scherbenske was a twenty six year old blonde who had spent her whole life in East Prussia. Tall, and buxom, she had lived with her father for most of her years, helping him tend to a farm that had been in the family for three generations. She didn't remember her mother. The woman whom she resembled physically (the few photographs attested to that) had died when Jutta was two, trying to give birth to a stillborn son. Her father never got over her loss, and he treated his only child like a precious ruby. He rarely even let her go beyond sight of their farmland which lay on fertile soil just south of the confluence of the Alle and Guber Rivers. Especially after she began showing signs of becoming a young woman. Jutta's good looks prompted many a suitor to ask her father permission to court his daughter. But the old man (he was nearly fifty when Jutta had been born) always managed to turn them away time and again. He told her straight up that he was loathe to let her go to another man. For some reason Jutta didn't mind—she loved her father, despite his jealousy and overprotectedness. He doted on her, and she never felt deprived. It was good she stayed with him, for just after her sixteenth birthday he became sick with a rare cancer. For four hard years he fought against withering illness and fatigue, striving to keep the farm going. But there was no getting around the truth that he was dying. Frail and bedridden at the end, he finally relented to the wishes of a young man eager to marry his daughter. Rolf, a local boy from a minor aristocratic family, promised to run the farm with the same diligence as Herr Scherbenske had. Promising to take care of Jutta forever, he moved into the household.

But then the war started. Poland was attacked and conquered in a month. France and England declared war on the Reich. While the old man still clung to a thread of life, his son-in-law Rolf was drafted into the military. Joining the Wehrmacht, Rolf was sent to the western front, where he took part in the invasion of France. A week before the French surrendered, he was killed in an attack on a British rear guard unit on the outskirts of Dunkirk.

The news not only affected Jutta. Her father expired a day after they received the official letter of Rolf's death. Rarely one to show emotion, he gazed at her with tears in his eyes, then sighing, closed them—and never opened them again. Jutta had witnessed pigs and cows die suddenly, and wild birds, but never a person. Then in a matter of days to lose the only two people in the world that meant anything to her . . . seemed worse than cruel.

Whether due to desperation or painful loneliness, Jutta threw herself at the first man she met. Another soldier, Werner had seen action in both Poland and in the attack on Norway. After a brief courtship, they married. But Werner was only allowed a few weeks furlough before heading back to the army. Jutta never saw him again. Werner was in the spear-thrust of

Operation Barbarossa. Just two months into the invasion of the Soviet
Union he was killed in the Battle of Smolensk. *For Fuhrer and Fatherland.*
Two letters in little more than a year proclaiming the same stark finality.
This time Jutta kept her tears inside. She had barely known Werner. Then
again, she had hardly known Rolf. She decided there would be no more
men in her life. She wore black from that day on. Even when she toiled in
the fields planting potatoes and turnips. On the rare occasions she visited
the small village nearby to sell eggs and vegetables she avoided gossip and
smalltalk with the locals. She knew they called her a recluse and other
things behind her back. Her only human contacts were a middle-aged
Polish husband and wife "loaned" to her by the authorities to assist in the
farm work. But even contact with them was limited, except
communicating through hand gestures and the small vocabulary of German
words they understood. She gave them a portion of the barn to sleep in,
and once a week paid them what they were owed. After each work day she
took her meals alone, eating whatever the Polish woman had prepared for
supper.

Now they too were gone from her life. Once word reached the district of
the impending Soviet invasion of the Reich, most of the Poles fled. A good
many of them to the west. They feared the Russians more than they feared
the Germans. Jutta had remained on her farm alone, even when the
sensational rumors trickled in concerning the fate of Nemmerdorf. When
the rumors became official news, local people began to pack their
belongings on wagons and carts. Regional Nazi bigwigs tried dissuading the
population first with false promises of safety, and later with serious threats
of imprisonment, execution. But people still left. Refugees from the
farthermost eastern borders of Germany passed by her property almost
daily. Some occasionally stopped to spend a night or two at Jutta's home.
They were a pathetic lot, often half-starved, poorly clothed for the
upcoming winter, and delirious with fear and lack of proper sleep. They in
turn looked at Jutta as though she had lost her wits.

"How can you stay here when the Russians may come any day now?" An
older woman had railed at her incredulously one eve. "Do you have any
idea what those devils are doing?"

When Jutta shook her head to say no, the woman pointed to a small
adolescent girl asleep on the floor of Jutta's kitchen. "Poor Gerda
there . . . more than a dozen Russians raped her. Her mother who tried to

stop them—they stabbed with a bayonet. And her father . . . they shot him point blank in the face. Then tossed his body on a dung-heap. If our forces hadn't retaken the area, who knows what might have happened to us."

Jutta found herself sympathizing with the plight of these victims of war, yet she also found their stories hard to believe. *Were the Russians that close? Were they really perpetrating such horrors on the German population?* Things couldn't be that bad. Or were they . . .

Then a day came during a heavy snowfall when she awoke in the night to what sounded like a constant thunder. She sat up listening to it, expecting the noise to stop at any moment. But the noise didn't stop. It became louder. Nearer. Until Jutta arose and stood by the bedroom window. A faint fiery glow lit up the eastern sky. She shivered. And not from the winter cold. A different winter approached, and she recalled the fearful looks of the refugees whenever they heard footsteps or a door opening. Jutta tried putting the thought out of her mind. But each day the rumbling became more distinct. The glow more visible. As a precaution, she began to pack several chests with clothes and provisions and carried them to her only cart. And she saddled the one horse remaining from the three her father had once owned. The beast was old, and partly lame. Jutta wondered how far he could carry her if she needed to flee.

Most of her neighbors on outlying farms had already skedaddled. The few who chose to stay, couldn't bear the thought of leaving their cherished homes. They would take their chances with the Russians. Jutta eventually came to feel the same way. It didn't seem possible that men were as barbaric as what the newsreels stated. No, it was nothing but a scare tactic. To paint the enemy as evil. To make the German nation revile them even more.

Yet the uneasiness inside never went away. Then circumstances decided for her. Soviet planes one evening riddled her house with bullets, forcing her to hide under the bed. Not an hour later shells from artillery fire smashed the barn, setting it ablaze, and slaying her last hog. Her heart pounding, her eyes flooding with tears, Jutta without hesitation placed more belongings in the cart till it was full. *Yes, it is time to leave.* Tying the horse to a halter, she rigged the animal to the cart. There was just one more item to bring. A photograph of Rolf in uniform before he went off to war. It was not a necessity. She remembered him clearly in her head. But it lay in the dresser in the living room. Only another minute. Then she'd be on her way—

Jutta's scream rose from her throat involuntarily. The hands that grabbed her hair from behind yanking her to the floor were not hands, but paws, and there were more than one pair. Three men in white parkas growled at her in a foreign tongue, their breath stinking like vodka. For a moment Jutta was too astonished to do anything but stare at them in bewilderment. She screamed again as they began to rip off her clothing. She fought, scratching one of them on the cheek. Cursing vilely, the man backhanded her across the face, drawing blood. He punched her again in the stomach as the others pulled off her coat, blouse, then using a knife, sliced off her bra. The men whooped and hollered as Jutta's large breasts jiggled before their eyes. They began to squeeze and pinch them. She writhed and squirmed, trying to break free of their hold. They punched her repeatedly in the face and neck. After a while she lay stunned, bleeding, hardly feeling her dress being slid from her body, her panties being cut apart by the same knife that had destroyed her brassiere.

Only the sudden gunshots woke her again. Then two more shots. A groan. A gurgling noise, like someone choking. Bodies hitting the floor. Then a thudding sound. Once. Twice. Three times. Four. Flexing her chin to her chest, Jutta watched in a daze as a German soldier kicked and stomped on the heads and faces of her attackers. His hard boots sprayed their blood everywhere. Though it was easy to see that the men he kicked were dead. She gasped at the nightmare before her.

Foss continued to dig his heels into the eyes and noses of the Russians he had just gunned down. "This is for Laursen, you bastards!" His mind didn't register the snarl of his voice. "This is for the girl!" He booted one corpse in the groin, and was about to do the same to another when he felt hands gripping the back of his coat.

"Aksel, stop! They're dead! We've got to get the hell out of here or we'll be as dead as they are."

Through a fog, Foss recognized the voice of Steenhagen. He whirled around and met the other man's gaze. For a moment he shook with the fury of one who has gone berserk. Livid with anyone who sought to curtail his need for revenge, he lifted the butt of his gun and was three inches from smashing it down on Steenhagen's skull. Then the fury aborted. As rapidly as it had risen. Taking in huge lungfuls of air, Foss was aware he had only twice before in his time at the front lost his reasoning completely. This was the third time. He recalled the horrors of the last few days. Laursen. The German lines dissolving again under ceaseless pressure from Ivan. He and the other Landsers running pell-mell to wherever they could find safety. Men caught under the treads of tanks and squashed into pulp. The screams of the wounded that had to be left behind. His unit scattered. Only Steenhagen remaining with him. Dodging shellfire. The endless crackle of small arms. A barn burning. A farmhouse. Entering the house. Three Russians assaulting a naked woman. Three Russians ravishing . . .

No need—to remember the rest. Telling himself aloud to calm down, Foss muttered an apology to Steenhagen. Glancing at the floor, he saw the blood. Then the girl, who was still naked, and staring at him with utter shock.

"She's alive!" Foss exclaimed.

"I know." Steenhagen, unable to keep his eyes off the beautiful female, was at a loss for words. The woman, finally coming to her senses, reached for her torn clothes.

Foss too felt shy. "Do you have other clothing?" he asked while trying to look away.

"I do," the woman answered meekly, still stunned by the carnage that had suddenly become her world. "They're hanging in the closet in the bedroom."

Turning his back toward her, Foss gestured to Steenhagen to do the same. "Go dress yourself. We won't look."

The woman quickly left the living room. She returned five minutes later, fully clothed and with a thick woolen sweater. Though showing bruises on her face and neck, she had cleaned off all the blood She was about to speak when another round of artillery crashed close to the house.

Foss glanced at the door. "We must leave, Frau—"

"Scherbenske. I was about to leave myself. Before those beasts tackled me." Her voice breaking, Jutta began to sob, cupping her face in her hands.

Foss nearly put a hand on her arm, then thought it wise not to touch the woman. Not after what she had been through. He said, "The Russians have broken through. Unfortunately, we can't hold them back from here. We have to regroup. It's safer if you come with us."

Regaining some composure, Jutta nodded. "My horse and cart are ready to go. But—the three of us may be too much to pull. The cart contains most of my life's goods."

"Let's have a look," Foss said.

"We'll manage somehow," Steenhagen chimed in, trying to sound more positive than he felt.

They hurriedly walked outside. Shells were bursting in the distance. As Foss and Steenhagen surveyed the horse and cart, Jutta thought the facts ought to be put aright.

"I want you to know—they didn't rape me. You saved my life. Thank you." She gazed first at Foss, then at Steenhagen, giving each of them a brief smile.

At that moment a shell burst overhead. On impulse Foss dove beneath the cart, pulling the woman with him. They lay there cowering as two more explosions reverberated across the landscape. When the noise died down, they slowly crept out.

It was then Foss noticed Steenhagen lying on his back beside the cart. He wasn't moving. Foss bent down to him.

"Gerd! Are you hit?" But there was no response to Foss's question. Steenhagen's eyes were still open; his face held a gaze of astonishment. Foss removed his friend's helmet. A slight trickle of blood seeped down from the forehead. Shrapnel. Aksel checked the wrist. No pulse. A splinter from a shell had gone into Steenhagen's brain. A tiny speck of steel had taken the life of a man in less than a second.

"Oh my God! Is he—"

"He's dead." Foss answered the woman's question with a voice that was bleak as a graveyard. The abrupt staccato of machine guns sounded close by. The war. The goddamn war. The Russian vanguard had broken through. The first elements must have been the very men who had tried to rape the blonde woman standing here by the cart. *But why am I thinking about that now?* He gently touched Steenhagen's cheek. "I won't be able to bury you, Gerd," Foss said sorrowfully, snapping off the part of the dog-tag that contained his personal information. *I said the same thing to Laursen.* "But you understand that. There's no time with the Russians coming." Tragically, he had said the same to many fallen friends. With his own life at stake, he had to carry on.

Leaving Steenhagen where he lay, Foss motioned to the woman to get on the cart. Without looking back, he hopped up on the seat, took the reins, and they bounded off down the road to the west.

For a long time, Jutta held a hand over her mouth. Foss glanced at her occasionally from the corner of his eye but kept silent. He knew the trauma of the past hour or so must have overwhelmed her. Often people felt a need to vomit when first experiencing the horrors of war. He could tell she was trying to hold it in.

It occurred to him that he didn't even know her Christian name.

The minutes rolled by—but the horse was slow. Old. Explosions and gunshots continued to rake the areas behind them. Gradually, the horse slowed even more. Then stopped moving altogether.

"Something must be wrong. It is unusual for Sturm to stop like this." Jutta's face was etched with concern. She jumped off the cart. Running a hand soothingly over the horse's back, a look of bafflement fell over her. Her hand was covered with blood.

Joining her beside the now listless animal, Foss was not surprised to see a number of wounds along its back and flanks. Shrapnel from the same shell that had taken the life of Steenhagen had penetrated the horse's body. The animal began to wobble. Foss unrigged it from the cart, removed the halter, led it to the side of the road. Several seconds passed, then the legs of the horse buckled. Falling awkwardly to the ground, it twice neighed in agony, twisting its head side to side. With one heave the wounded horse pushed its body up briefly, though the legs would not allow it to rise. Sitting there, its breaths came in ragged gasps.

"I'm afraid your horse is done for," Foss explained in a mild tone, trying to lighten the harsh truth to the already stricken woman. He had witnessed the wounding and demise of countless horses during the war. Their deaths always saddened him. Their innocence derailed by the corrupt ambitions of men.

Jutta bit her lips. Tears welled in her eyes. "What will we do now?"

Foss took a few seconds before responding. "We'll have to journey on foot."

"And Sturm?"

Without answering, Foss lifted his gun and calmly shot the horse above the ear.

"My God! Why did you do that?" Jutta was beside herself with shock and sudden rage.

"Whether me or the Russians, it is all the same. And they might start carving meat first before shooting him. What I did was humane."

Foss's tone brooked no argument. His years of leading troops in battle had given him an air of authority that was evident from his demeanor. Jutta gaped at him, but no words formed from her lips.

The horse would have made good eating, Foss thought sensibly, but he realized that might push the woman over the edge. Besides, the Russians were not far away. No time. Turning back to the cart, Foss began to rummage through one of the chests.

"What are you doing with my things?" Jutta stood close to him.

"Searching for food. We'll need every morsel we can get. I doubt there'll be any inns open along the way."

"Let me find it." Jutta reached in and brought out four small sacks containing flour, bread, potatoes, turnips, peas, smoked ham. She gave the two heaviest sacks to Foss to carry. "What about the rest?" she asked in a choking voice.

"Take what you need. Just remember: this isn't a holiday trip." With that Foss jerked his head in the direction where guns still rumbled like thunder.

Crying silently, Jutta grabbed the clothes that were most practical to her and stuffed them into one of the sacks. That they would take on the odor of the food made no difference now. Taking a last mournful look inside one of the chests, she pulled out a small framed photograph of her father. This she placed carefully among the clothes.

"I'm ready," Jutta said stiffly, not bothering to wipe the tears that left trails on her face.

She walked a few paces behind Foss, unable to mimic his soldier's pace. For a moment Foss wondered whether he should let the woman fend for herself. He wanted to find his friends. And get off the road. The road made him nervous. Russian tanks might be on the road. And if they weren't now, they would be soon.

Then he sighed with relief. Luck was with them. A stretch of woods several hundred meters ahead.

"Best we avoid towns," Foss said almost to himself. Having temporarily forgotten the woman's presence, he turned around to make certain she still followed. "The Ivans—Russians, usually sack towns first. Plunder. That's all most of them think about. Liquor, and—"

"You don't need to say any more." Jutta had ceased crying; her face resembled hard stone. "I got an earful from earlier refugees about Russian behavior. It was hard to fathom anyone could be so barbaric. Unfortunately . . . they were right."

As they neared the woods, Foss kept a finger on the trigger of his gun. The previous snowfall had dropped more than a foot of snow here. He found no footprints. Or the long marks left by skis. Which meant no Russians. At least he hoped not. "You need help?" he asked, concerned. The woman had stumbled on a snowbank and for a moment had trouble regaining her balance.

"No, I can manage well enough." The woman's tone was curt. "I've handled a farm on my own for the duration of the war. And I did just fine."

Foss brushed snow off his sleeve that had dropped from a branch. He glanced pensively at the woman. She appeared hardy enough. And . . . *attractive*. He suddenly wanted to learn more about her—her past. Her reason for living alone. How long had it been since he'd thought of a woman in such a way? The army brothels he'd frequented in the Soviet Union offered little in the way of curiosity. Only momentary pleasure. A fleeting taste of female flesh. A Ukrainian or Pole he'd never see again.

"You didn't mention your first name," Foss said. They had left the road behind them. A narrow path meandered through the woods. Foss halted for a second to let the woman catch up with him.

"Neither did you. Nor your last." Jutta kept her eyes steady when she spoke.

Foss smiled. "Aksel Foss."

"Jutta."

"Jutta . . . a beautiful name. Not one I hear often."

"The same can be said for yours."

"Well . . . maybe not in Germany."

"Are you not German?" Jutta was surprised.

"Danish. Can't you hear my accent? I've been ribbed by your countrymen for three years now because of my inability to speak standard German."

"Your accent is not strong. I would say North German. Of course, to Bavarians, anyone from East Prussia sounds foreign. They sound foreign to us."

They walked through the woodland until coming to an open field. This led to another woodland. Foss scoured all directions carefully before waving to Jutta to follow him. Finding a half-frozen stream, Foss dipped a cup into the frigid waters and gave it to Jutta. They took turns sipping the water. Not far away lay the remains of a half-eaten cow.

"Looks like wolves got it. Or human wolves." Foss pinched his nose at the putrid smell.

"No Prussian farmer would leave a carcass like that lying around." Shaking her head in dismay, Jutta again appeared on the verge of tears. "Why is this happening? What have we done to deserve this? I have lost two husbands, was nearly raped by a horde of cutthroats, and now have been forced from my house and farm that my family has owned for generations. I own nothing at the moment but what you see. I have nowhere to go . . . "

Foss put a hand on Jutta's shoulder to comfort her but the woman roughly pushed it off. "I had nothing do she with starting this war," she said vehemently. "It is always men who start wars. And the women have to pick up the pieces. I just wanted to be left alone."

"You're not the only one who wanted to be left alone." The sarcasm was thick in Foss's words. "My country wanted to be left in peace altogether. I can't think of any Danish men that desired to conquer Poland . . . and the rest of Europe with it. If there were, I didn't know them." Swearing coarsely in his native tongue, Foss gripped his gun till his hands hurt. "If it hadn't been for a case of bad luck, I wouldn't be fighting your damned war right now. And I wouldn't have ended up in your farmhouse shooting three strangers who'd have had their way with you otherwise."

Foss's last sentence hit hard. The anger fled Jutta as quickly as it had flamed. Exasperated with an inability to control the upheaval of emotions that threatened to drain her energy, she broke out in a long sob.

"Forgive me," she breathed huskily after a minute had passed. "I should not have spoken to you like I did. I am at a loss to deal with all that has happened. I fear the future. Where am I to go? I have no roots elsewhere. Please! Don't be mad at me."

"I'm not mad at you."

"I . . . always prided myself on being strong—but now I feel frightened of everything." Her chest convulsing, Jutta began to cry uncontrollably.

This time when Foss slid an arm around her shoulder, Jutta drew close to him. She buried herself in his embrace.

"All of us are uncertain, Jutta," Foss said gently. "Everyone is scared. Our instincts have reverted back to the Stone Age. The future . . . getting enough to eat every day, and a place to sleep at night. And hopefully wake up the next morning." With his tongue, Foss licked his lips that were chapped and blue with cold. "None of us know how much longer this hellish war can continue. This displacement from our lives. The Russians seem unstoppable. And—they won't be stopped!"

Jutta lifted her head from his chest to gaze at him. "What do you mean—they won't be stopped?"

"Nothing to deter them from enacting revenge."

"Why?"

"You heard about what they did in Nemmersdorf and other places."

"Yes, but I thought it was an exaggeration. A way for the government to rile up the people."

"Maybe it *was* partly propaganda. But the atrocities were true. Too true."

"And they intend to do the same to all the German people?"

Foss shrugged, turning away to stare to the east. "We weren't too kind in Russia either. We did horrible things."

"You mean like what those monsters tried to do to me!"

"I never did that. But there were Landsers that did. You reap what you sow. I used to think that was a corny expression. Fit only for smug priests, gossipy crones. Out of date and overused. But it makes a hell of a lot of sense when you've experienced what I have . . . "

Jutta began to weep again. Removing a glove, Foss wiped the tears from her face. "We better get moving," he said simply. "Save your tears for later. That might sound harsh, but in this weather tears soon become icicles. You don't want your cheeks to freeze." Releasing her, Foss picked up his sacks and entered the woods. Clenching her teeth to refrain from crying, Jutta picked up the remaining baggage and followed him without a word.

Worried about the Russians overtaking them, they trudged through snow and brush until it was almost too dark to see. The sounds of the war faded behind them. A lull in the fighting, Foss told Jutta. Thinking they would have to spend the night in the open, Foss began to cut a lean-to, when Jutta grabbed his sleeve.

"Over there, Aksel. Look." Jutta pointed with her head toward what appeared to be a small cottage. "A hunter's lodge."

Picking up his sub-machine gun where he had stood it beside a tree, Foss crept up to the dwelling. His boots sounded noisy in the snow; the silence of the surrounding forest unnerving. Before him a small wooden structure. The single door broken on its hinges as though someone had tried a forced entry. Finger on trigger, he peeked inside.

No one.

Going in further he stepped on something that crackled beneath his feet. He was about to shoot when he noticed it was only a newspaper scattered on the floor. Lighting a match, Foss peered around the place. Barely spacious enough for more than a few people, the lodge appeared as though it hadn't held human occupants for some months. Maybe years. Curiously, he scanned the newspaper. The date: August 1943. Almost a year and a half ago.

Foss spun around when he heard a twig snap.

"Don't fire, Aksel, it's me." Jutta stood trembling at the door. Her eyes wide and staring.

Whether she trembled because of fear or the cold, Foss didn't know. "I don't make a habit of shooting beautiful women," he said with a smile, trying to mollify her. He spread out his arm in a half circle to indicate the surroundings. "I've found better places to shelter from the elements, but this will suffice. We need rest. I intend to leave before dawn."

Foss tried to shut the door as much as it would allow. The only two chairs in the hovel he placed in front of the door. Anybody seeking entry would bump into them, giving themselves away. He found a woolen blanket in a corner, partially wet from exposure. Jutta in the meantime sat down and propped herself up against a wall. She appeared exhausted. Foss spread the blanket over her legs.

"This should keep you warm tonight," he said affably. "If you don't mind a few wet spots."

"What about you? There's no other blanket."

Foss laughed. "I haven't really had a proper blanket since I was forced to leave home. These days I'm used to sleeping without one. Whatever the weather."

They decided to eat a little before sleeping. They were famished, but Foss said it was best not to over-stuff oneself. Especially when you might have to sprint for your life at a moment's notice. Jutta brought out a loaf of rye bread from one of her sacks. With a knife she sliced two thick pieces for each of them. Then spread on top of each slice a generous amount of blackcurrent jam.

"Delicious," Foss commented between bites.

"I made it myself." Jutta closed the jar of jam and returned it to the sack. "I preserve lots of food. My cellar is filled to the brim with delicacies." She paused, and Aksel thought she might weep again. Sniffing, she said, "The Russians are going to find a whole banquet in my cellar."

Foss was about to answer that the Wehrmacht would one day soon push the Russians back over the border, but he knew the words would sound banal. He no longer himself believed in a German victory. Instead he said, "Forgive me if I intrude, but you mentioned you had had two husbands."

Chewing her last piece of bread with jam, Jutta was taken aback by Foss's lack of subtlety. But she had experienced the same directness from other soldiers she'd met. Perhaps war destroyed civilized etiquette. Just like it destroyed people and places. Letting out a long sigh, she said, "I did. They were both lost in the war."

"I'm sorry." Foss's tone was sincere. Germany had become a land of widows. It took a resilient person to deal with the untimely death of a spouse, but Jutta had dealt with it twice. He admired her. "Do you have any other family?" he asked. "What about your parents?"

"My parents are both dead. There's an aunt I haven't seen in years. My father's sister. Last I heard she was living in Danzig."

"Have you been to Danzig?"

"Several times as a child. Back then it was a city unaffiliated with any nation. The Free City of Danzig. Even though most of the inhabitants were German. I think one of the objectives Hitler had was to claim Danzig for the Reich." Jutta appeared wistful, as though touched by a memory. "My father never liked cities. He was born and bred in the country. As was I. I suppose that's why we didn't go back once I reached adulthood."

"It might be in your best interest to go there now," Foss suggested. "Having some family is better than having none."

"Aunt Elke is an old spinster. She seemed old even when I was a child. Never married. Apparently liked living alone. She probably doesn't want company. Not at this stage of her life."

"Well, you know the old saying: There's only one way to find out." Foss wondered how he would be treated if he suddenly barged in on relatives he hadn't seen in years. Danes could be very reserved when it came to social etiquette. "I can try and help you get to Danzig, Jutta. Once we reach the German lines. There are trains carrying refugees to all points west."

Jutta was silent for a while. "What if I don't want to go?"

"No one can force you," Foss said, shrugging. "Unless the regional Gauleiter makes it mandatory. But you know what awaits you if you remain here."

She knew only too well. "What about you? Are you heading for Danzig?"

"I have to find my unit first. What remains of it. I'll go wherever the army sends me—Danzig, or, excuse my language—the gates of hell."

Jutta was quick to acknowledge the sarcasm in Foss's tone. She cast a long glance at the Dane. *A handsome man.* Even in the darkness. And a strong man. She remembered how he had killed the Russians single-handed. Brutally. Now he spoke in such a civilized manner. Is that what war did to people? Turn normal human beings into killers? She wondered how many others Aksel had killed. Not sure why she was switching the subject, Jutta said shyly, "You haven't told me much about your life. Are you . . . married?"

Foss grinned. The question brought back memories of his many girlfriends. And the one girl whom he still thought of with fondness. "No, I'm not married," he returned. "Though I would like to marry one day. But—only when there's peace. Too much heartbreak otherwise. I've seen a lot of soldiers go mad worrying about wives and children back home. Losing sleep because a letter arrived two weeks late. Or no letters for a month. One man I serve with lost his entire family to a bombing raid. He was a boisterous laughing type before he got the news. Now the life's gone out of him. All he has left is the war."

Jutta took all this in with a nod of her head. *Suffering for everyone.* She closed her eyes, trying to fight back tears. "After my second husband was lost at the front—I decided not to get close to anyone. Besides, all the young men were gone from the district. An old farmer up the road from me showed interest in establishing a relationship—but he was old enough to be my father. There was also a friend from school: Hans. He'd lost a leg in North Africa. Told me he'd commit suicide if I didn't marry him." Sighing, Jutta raised up her arms in exasperation. "I don't know why I'm telling you all this. You must think I'm crazy."

"Well . . . if you're crazy, we're all crazy. We've all been affected by loss."

Jutta sighed again. "I haven't had anyone to talk to in so long. Thank you for listening to me."

"That's what ears are for," Foss grinned. "If you don't mind my asking: your name: Jutta. Is it not Jewish?"

Jutta was cautious a moment before answering. Then she remembered his honest feelings about the war. "You're very perceptive. My father gave me the name. He had been in love with a Jewess when he was a young man. I don't think he ever got over her. He named me after her . . . "

Foss thought it improper to probe deeper. But the woman was staring at him intently. Breaking the sudden silence of the room, he said, "In Denmark there was never an anti-Jewish crusade. I knew Jews and liked them. All the energy the Nazis have used downgrading Jews has been a sick waste of time." Foss looked around him as though expecting the walls to have ears. "This is the first time I have ever stated such an opinion to a German. Men have been thrown into concentration camps for a lot less."

"I value your opinion, Aksel. It's refreshing to hear someone speak without thinking they have an ax hanging over them. My father hated the Nazis. And I loathe them too. I'll say it again: *I loathe them.* Without those fanatics making a muck of things, we would all have gone happily about our lives."

Foss nodded in agreement. He suddenly recollected a poem he'd once written about the sun shining down on the earth despite man's despairs; the continuance of light not bothered by an individual's or even a nation's darkness. Life went on. The world went on.

"What are you thinking, Aksel?" A note of concern crept into Jutta's voice.

"About something I wrote?"

"Wrote? A letter?"

"No. A poem."

"You write poetry?"

"Try to—when I have the time."

"My father loved poetry. He used to read it to me when I was a little girl. I liked listening to it. Though I was never a writer myself."

"It's funny—no one in my family ever wrote. I don't know where it came from."

Jutta tapped a finger over her heart. "My father told me some things come from the head and some from the heart. Poetry comes from the heart."

"I fully agree. Perhaps you might be a poet in the making."

Jutta smiled. "I'm just a farm girl. Always have been. I love animals and plants. From an early age I learned the names of all the trees and flowers in this part of the country."

"That's commendable. Not many can say that these days. Not people in cities."

"Not many people read poetry either." Jutta gave Foss a quizzical look. "But why poetry? It certainly doesn't seem a soldier's art. I don't mean that badly—but I always thought of soldiers as gruff and ignorant of the finer arts. My two husbands hardly even read the newspaper."

Foss thought a long time before answering. He recalled writing some doggerel in school, rhymes to deal with the boredom of listening to teachers whose lectures otherwise would have put him to sleep. Then one day he penned a poem to a girl with bright red hair—though he had been too reticent to give it to her. That love poem led to other poems, other subjects, the Depression, the sky, the sea, the changing seasons, drunkenness, anything and everything. *What couldn't one write about!* A fierce gust of wind blew outside the lodge. Foss thought again of Jutta's question.

"Poetry's not only for sickly men dying from tuberculosis," Foss said with emphasis. "The Great War spurred a lot of poets to put words to paper. Some of the greatest Viking warriors were poets. They'd even compose poems in the midst of swinging a sword at an opponent's throat."

"Is that right?"

"That's right."

"Do you compose poems in the midst of battle?"

Foss was surprised by the question. "I haven't yet. Maybe battles with spears and swords were more heroic, more poetic. I don't find much heroic about the current war."

"You were more than a hero today . . . "

Foss shrugged. He did not take compliments well. Partly it was his upbringing. Jante's law. The unwritten set of rules Danes seemed to govern their lives by: not to consider yourself greater than your neighbor, or anyone else. Rather stupid, when he thought about it. What was wrong with feeling good about yourself when you had a talent. He'd witnessed in the war how some men were simply finer soldiers than other men. Some people were smarter. Some better looking. Some crueler. And some were nothing but assholes. Humans never had been born with equal talents, and despite what Marx or Lenin or anyone else said, they never would be equal.

"Where is your mind drifting to now?" Jutta's query broke Foss's reverie. He turned to look at her.

"It depends on how you define the word *hero*," he said impassively. "I'm no more a hero than any other man. War just forces us to make decisions swifter than we would normally. You might find it hard to believe, but I'd never even handled a gun before I was drafted into the Wehrmacht—now I can't imagine living without one. Comes in handy. Like back there at your house." He paused, running a hand over his gun. He noted how the woman near him was ardently listening to his every word. "Without it I wouldn't have met you. We wouldn't be talking like this. We wouldn't even be here. I'm not sure what I'm trying to say, Jutta." The girl's attractiveness suddenly became more noticeable. "I just know I like talking to you. Which makes me wonder if things have a purpose. Maybe the events of today were meant to happen. Seems a perverse way for two people to get to know one another, yet we can't undo the past. The good and the bad are all one stream."

Are they? Jutta found herself wondering how rape and death had anything to do with good. The image of the three Russians swarming over her earlier in the day made her shudder. If it had been peacetime, Aksel's actions would be the ultimate in heroism. Then she thought—such actions must be a common occurrence in wartime. Practically the whole world was at war; men and women were dying in droves every minute of every day. Closing her eyes, Jutta tried blotting out the image. But it wouldn't go away. She barked out a swear-word she rarely used.

The word was not lost on Foss. "Are you alright?"

"I'm not sure. I can't get those three awful men out of my head. I've never gone through anything like this before. But . . . you seem to have put it out of your mind."

"You have to," Foss said with conviction. "That's the only way you survive."

"You can forget your friends? The man who was with you today."

The blood running from Steenhagen's wound flashed before Foss's eyes. He took a deep breath. "No. You never forget them. But you remember the joyful times you spent. Remembering the horrors only makes things worse."

"But what if there is only horror? My introduction to the war was not exactly a tiding of joy."

Despite the unaccustomed stirring he felt in his groin, Foss was growing weary of the woman's melodramatics. He wanted to sleep soon. He missed his fellow Landsers. He missed Steenhagen. Laursen. Frohm. When a fellow soldier died you discussed the fact briefly with friends, then let the matter drop. How could he impart this to Jutta? She had not experienced three years on the Eastern Front where millions had bled out their lives and were lost forever. Who remembered them? Statistics. A battalion, a regiment, a division, a Corps, entire armies, erased from the military lists like stray pencil marks. Women perhaps, needed to wring out their nightmares. Foss considered this. He had not shared a long conversation with a female in years. He had forgotten what the fairer sex was like.

"We all have to come to terms with our inner shadows," Foss declared evenly. "I am sorry you had to go through what you did. I don't mean to sound harsh when I say this—but you simply have to get over it. One thing the war has taught me: Tomorrow may bring worse."

The advice did not completely satisfy Jutta. "I don't see how anyone can get over it. What about you? Do you ever think about the men you've killed?"

The question jolted Foss's memory. The first man he had shot at close range had been a Russian officer. The man had been trying to rally a retreating band of infantrymen to turn and face a German attack. Foss's bullet had entered the man's body just below the heart. The officer, dropping a pistol he'd been holding, stumbled with buckling knees, as though drunk, until finally falling face-down on a pile of thatch blown off the roof of a bombed peasant's hut. Other shots rang out. The thatch caught fire. And with it the officer too went up in flames. Foss had watched in numbness as first the dead man's hat and clothes rippled and blackened in the orange heat. Then the dark hair. Then the flesh. Burning no differently than a chicken's or a pig's. The awful stench made Foss gag.

Whoever said burning corpses smelled sweet must have been mad. The rest of the Russians were driven further from the scene. The war moved elsewhere, and Foss, encountering other deaths, forgot his first kill.

Until now.

"There are some things best left to a person's own memory." Foss placed his gun a few feet away on the floor. Far enough away that he wouldn't roll over it in his sleep, but close enough to grab if need arose. Stifling a yawn, he then cracked his knuckles, cleared his throat. "Like I said, we leave before dawn. Sleep well, Jutta." And he lay where he was with his back toward her and tried to sleep.

But sleep did not come to Aksel Foss. He sensed Jutta did not sleep either. He heard her breath distinctly in the darkness of the otherwise still room. Then her voice: "Aksel!?"

Foss lifted his head. "What is it?"

"I . . . want you to hold me."

Without hesitating Foss moved near her. He slid under the blanket. He took her in his arms. For a long time, they lay entwined, feeling awkward. Not speaking. Until the stirring of other emotions brought their lips together. Their movements were at first clumsy. Some minutes passed before the last of their clothing was tossed on the floor. Then they forgot all awkwardness. They forgot the war.

CHAPTER 4

They left the hunter's lodge at dawn as Foss had said. The world outside was silent. The Russians had not renewed the attack. Eventually meeting up with other battered groups of soldiers and civilians, Foss and Jutta trudged along the snow-filled countryside toward the coast. A drifting mass of human flotsam, the whole of East Prussia seemed to be on the verge of fleeing the province forever. Would the people ever return? Foss wondered about this. He had never seen an entire civilian population pack up its wares and run without looking back. Centuries of heritage gone in the blink of an eye. The Russians would not be kind. Just like the Germans had not been kind in Russia. Tit for tat. Revenge moved nations to decisive action more than practically anything else. A sad way to progress. If you could indeed call it progression.

Foss kept Jutta close to him, not wanting her to lag behind. The woman's blue eyes lit up each time he turned to gaze at her. He wanted to embrace her, kiss her, even in the middle of the march, for he didn't know if there would ever be a moment to do so again. But in the midst of all the misery of others, he thought such caressing would be frowned upon. Deemed improper.

An aircraft flew overhead. Someone shrieked. People ran, threw themselves in the snow. Squinting upwards, Foss shook his head. "A German plane," he told Jutta confidently.

"Why only one?" Jutta held a hand over her eyes as she arched her neck to scan the eastward path of the aircraft.

"It's scouting the Russians. Recording their movements, positions."

Just then a woman ahead of them lurched forward, dropping a bundle of rags in the process. Foss helped her to her feet. He picked up the bundle. It contained a dead baby. The infant was frozen blue.

"Give me back my child," the woman rasped, her own face nearly as gray as the clouds that ranged overhead.

Foss gave her the bundle. He didn't speak. The woman grabbed the bundle and held it tightly to her chest.

"We have family in Berlin," she said, her eyes glaring in no particular direction. "Little Willy and I are going all the way to Berlin." The woman muttered something else unintelligible. Then limped off on her own.

Shaken, Jutta took hold of Foss's arm. They walked this way for some time in silence. No one paid them any attention. All the others wrapped up in their own misery. Two Panther tanks rumbled by at one point, forcing everyone off the road. They headed east. Part of a rearguard to try and stem the Soviet advance. Foss had been part of countless rearguard actions. He didn't tell this to Jutta—for he feared he might be yanked from the retreat at any moment and thrust back into the fray. The glow from last night's lovemaking had not left him; unlike any other woman he had met at the front, Jutta seemed special. *Is special.* He gave her a sidelong glance. Her cheeks were red and he wondered whether it was from the cold or if she too blushed from joy. Joy—a nearly extinct word in the last three years of his life. Foss suddenly felt the urge to throw his gun down and take this woman with him to Denmark. Flee the army. *Escape.* They could find a town to hide in until the Russians swept by on their way to the interior of the Reich. Then emerge, find a boat. Sail the Baltic. Reach one of the many beaches of Denmark. Then go underground . . .

A dream. They'd neither outrun the gamut of the Russians or the Geheime Feldpolizei, the secret German military police. Besides, he'd never sailed a boat in his life. Foss cursed quietly, but Jutta must have heard him. She pivoted towards him, alarmed.

"What is it, Aksel? You look angry."

"I am angry. Angry at the war. We're all of us so helpless." He wanted to explain how he felt about her, though he didn't want to scare the woman off. It might be too early to speak of deeper feelings. But when was too early nowadays? He'd lost two friends in the past forty-eight hours—he might lose Jutta at any moment.

The blast from a heavy battery pounded in the distance. Followed by a second blast. Apprehensive, the soldiers and refugees on the road looked over their shoulders momentarily toward the rear. Foss found it to be a sign. Halting where he was, he pulled Jutta into his arms. He kissed her.

Embarrassed at first at Foss's open display of emotion, Jutta gradually returned the fervor of his embrace.

"One thing the war has gifted to me," Foss said expansively, "is the fact that I now rely on intuition above anything else." He kissed her again, his tongue meeting hers in a playful dance. "We don't have much time left together, Jutta. I can feel it in my heart."

"Why do you say that?" Jutta gaped at him, appalled that the sadness of his words were in stark opposition to the vigor of his kisses. "I don't want you to go!"

"Neither do I." He hugged her fiercely. "But when has the army ever cared about what a lone man and a lone woman thought? Wasn't it Hitler who stated that the individual is unimportant? Only the State matters. Only the State . . . "

Doing her utmost to refrain from pouting, Jutta winced at the sound of an explosion that boomed much closer than the last. She reached up to Foss's cheeks with her hands, caressing them softly. His stubble felt almost like sandpaper.

"I think I'm falling in love with you, Aksel Foss." She couldn't believe the sentence came out so easily. She'd only known him a day! But if hate could arise so quickly—like it had with the Russians who'd entered her home—why not love? Swallowing, she said it again, this time louder, "Yes! I'm falling in love with you. The world is my witness to that. So you can't leave me!"

Stunned, Foss hesitated, but not for long. "I'm falling in love with you too, Jutta. No. It's more than that—I do love you." Like the woman clinging to him, Foss found it odd to utter such a binding endearment. He hardly knew her. Then again, he hardly knew himself anymore. It seemed only yesterday he was writing poetry to girls he knew in school. Or kicking a soccer ball with friends. Had that person really existed? And who was he now? Suddenly unsure of the intentions behind their vows Foss fumbled at words. "Jutta . . . I wonder—would . . . you have even given me a second's notice in peacetime?"

Jutta was caught off guard. Temporarily. Then her lips curled upward with a smile. "Would you have looked me over twice?"

The tables turned, Foss could only smile back. "I would never have stopped looking the first time. You're a beautiful woman. More than beautiful."

Her heart fluttering, Jutta was about to respond when she heard someone snickering.

"Here Stalin's breathing down on our beloved Berlin—and Aksel saddles up with a wench."

Foss whirled around to find Ziemans standing with a toothy grin. Beside him stood Tulm, Keller (the scab on his face redder than ever), Ruder, and

Dreybach. For once, Foss didn't know how to react. Keeping hold of Jutta, he cleared his voice and nodded at his men.

"I thought I lost you," Foss said to them a little unevenly. Half-embarrassed, he introduced Jutta to his brothers in arms.

Noting the unusual gleam in Foss's eyes, the men surmised quickly that the woman beside him was more than a physical need for gratification. She and Foss appeared almost as if they were long lost lovers—reunited by circumstance. Ziemans made another snide remark, but the others ignored him, until he stepped a few paces away and lit a cigarette. Ruder and Keller turned away too; being so young, neither of them had much experience with women. Dreybach patted Foss on the shoulder. Tulm shook Foss's hand. His handshake said all the things he wanted to say with words.

Sensing that the men were half-starved, Foss doled out food to them from the sacks. Jutta didn't mind. It was a way to become more accepted by them. Then, taking on the role of a sergeant again, Foss led them west. They blended with the rest of the traffic. Some people went north. Wagons pulled by horses, army trucks, occasional tanks and half-tracks, but mostly a motley mix of individual military personnel and civilians, foreign laborers, even French and British prisoners, and a hodgepodge of farm animals, all in some way mental or physical casualties of the war, all seeking safety from the rampaging Russians.

Little was said along the way. What was there to say? Everyone was hungry, footsore. Jutta no longer clung so closely to Foss, not wanting to cramp his style in front of his friends. But whenever Foss threw her a smiling glance, her entire face brightened with joy. It made her believe that she was not just another momentary whim, another brief pleasure for him in between combat.

The men were quieter than usual. Much quieter. No banter, no perverse jokes. The presence of the woman had stolen their tongues. Even Ziemans was like a stone, an ever-present cigarette locked between his lips. Foss knew that Jutta could not remain with them forever. At the next defense line soldiers would be separated from the refugees, and most likely cast back out to fight the Russians. Where the civilians would go from there—who could guess? Rumors flew all around the Reich these days. Some party officials told the civilians in their districts to stay put. The Soviets would be thrown back. Only a matter of time. Other leaders secretly or openly made it plain that those who stayed, would imperil their lives. Forget your homes, forget your family mementos; save your skin! Foss had heard stories of mayors and even Gauleiters proclaiming on one hand that they would never flee from the barbarian menace from the east, while at the same time packing all their earthly goods into cars or even planes, and hightailing it to areas well out of the combat area. One high official purportedly had flown as far as the Alps.

Were such men cowards? Foss believed they were. Leaving their people in the lurch was beyond shameful. Though he wondered whether he would do the same if the circumstances were reversed. It was human nature to want to live, to survive, to stay out of the grave for as long as possible.

After another hour of walking through slush and snow they were forced to halt. A cordon of military police had blockaded the road. Big, mean-looking men who had no qualms about proclaiming a rigid authority. They checked the papers, the credentials of everyone passing through. Soldiers, they sent back east—or arrested. Poles, and anyone else considered as riffraff were herded into makeshift pens. German civilians were after questioning, waved on to the west or north. To follow the roads to Danzig Koenigsberg, or Berlin.

"We've reached the end of the trail, Jutta." Foss tried to reassure the suddenly sad-faced woman by squeezing her hand gently. He would not risk a kiss with the bulls watching his every move. She was shaking. And it was not from cold.

Bending down, Jutta went through the sacks. She gave a number of food items to Foss and his men. Foss protested, but she wouldn't relent.

"I know what you're going to say," Jutta interposed, "but they'll be food somewhere. It would appear bad if the authorities let civilians starve. You soldiers need it more. Since you have to stop the Russians." She attempted a smile with her last words, but was unable to hold it. She didn't want to cry at this point. Willing herself to be strong, she found a pencil and a small notepad in one of the sacks. She wrote down her name and the address of her aunt in Danzig. Tore out the paper and gave it to Foss. Then handed him the notepad and pencil.

"Here, write down your address in Denmark."

He wrote it down. They hugged, not wanting to let go. Noting several policemen scrutinizing him, Foss whispered gently to her, "I never say goodbye—goodbye is too final. Let's make a pact, Jutta: Until we meet again."

A tear ran down her cheek. "Until we meet again, Aksel." Her hands lingered in his for a moment. Then she pulled away and was gone. Hesitant at first, Jutta willed her feet to move toward the growing line of refugees heading westward toward Greater Germany. She looked back once, waving. Then Foss lost view of her.

Foss expected to wake from a dream at any moment. Laursen and Steenhagen were still alive and Jutta a figment of his imagination. But when he observed his men waiting for him by the roadside—Laursen and Steenhagen were not there. And the warmth from Jutta's embrace—still present. No dream.

Not wishing to converse, Foss nodded at the others to follow him. They went back the way they had come. New orders had been issued. The Russians were to be beaten back to the borders of their own land. Further retreat was out of the question. The Fuhrer demanded every able-bodied man in Germany to fight to the end. To death, if need be.

Which made Foss hate the war even more. Germany's not my country. Why the hell should I give my life for it? He cursed under his breath in Danish. The road was dotted with military policemen who kept an alert eye open for stragglers and potential deserters. In a field a short distance away a group of police had surrounded a single soldier without a gun and were lambasting him, their harsh language spoken loud so that all could hear them: "You cowardly swine! Running from the enemy is penalty enough—but to throw your gun away! That is property that didn't belong to you. Traitors like you are nothing but dung!" The man's protests to his innocence were lost in a flurry of fists and boots pummeling him. The last Foss saw of him, he was being hauled away further into the field.

"Those bastards won't get that far with me." Ziemans spit out a large wad of phlegm in the direction of the doomed soldier. He patted his Tommy gun as though it was a beloved pet. "They'll get a taste of this old girl if they try and manhandle my bones."

"Ziemans, you're nothing but a lying imbecile. You'll crap yourself when they get their hands on your worthless carcass." Looking daggers at his nemesis, Ruder kicked at an empty wine flask that had been left on the road. The flask came close to hitting Ziemans in the ankle.

Ignoring the bottle, Ziemans spit in the direction of Ruder, causing the other man to do a swift dodge. Ziemans grinned and spat at Ruder again.

"Hey puppy, you make it sound like I'm already marked down for arrest. Seeing me dangle in the wind—is that your life's goal, you little shit!"

The two continued to tangle verbally but Foss didn't care this time whether they argued or killed one another. Landsers were being gathered into groups—assault groups—and Foss and his small unit soon found themselves attached to the remains of a regiment that had been mauled in the recent fighting. The recollection of last night made him sad—sad that the time had been so brief. He hoped to God that Jutta made it to Danzig safely. Foss was no praying man, but inside he said a prayer his mother used to whisper over him whenever he went through one of his nightly asthma fits as a child. Taking the address of Jutta's aunt from his pocket, Foss read it over and over till the number of the apartment and street became as known to him as his home in Copenhagen. During a battle he might lose the slip of paper at any time. He willed himself to focus on the picture of Jutta he held in his mind. The blonde hair curled at her shoulders. The blue eyes. The ruddy face of a farmer-woman. As long as he drew breath, he'd remember that face.

Though how long would that be. A truck pulled up. An officer was yelling down from the back of it at the infantrymen standing in scattered lines by the road. Foss felt himself being nudged, then taking a deep breath, he hauled himself up into the truck. When he made sure his friends were all there, and when the vehicle was packed, a signal was shouted by the officer to the driver. Slowly, the truck revved into propulsion, stalled a bit, then lumbered forward.

"Well, here's to the party, gents! In hopes that Adolf uses his wonder weapons before we all grow too old." Pulling from his coat a bottle of kirschwasser he'd pilfered from an empty house during the last retreat, Ziemans took a long swig, then handed it to Dreybach who followed suit. Dreybach in turn shared the bottle with Foss.

Tipping the flask to his lips, Foss drank the cherry brandy slowly. He wanted to savor the taste. He wanted to savor the memory of Jutta. Then rubbing his mouth with the back of his hand, he passed the bottle to Tulm. Looking at his gun, Foss checked his pockets to make certain he still carried enough cartridges.

He would need them. They were heading back to the front.

CHAPTER 5

The German tank was burning. No screams came from within. The tank had been hit by numerous shells that had not penetrated its thick armor. Finally, one shell turned the tank into an inferno. The detonating impact must have killed the entire crew instantaneously. Nearly a dozen Russian tanks were similarly burning and immobile in the field ahead, knocked out by this one German tank that had been hidden behind a stand of trees. Most of the trees had been cut in half or smashed into splinters by the continual Russian shellfire. A sudden haunting stillness swept over the battlefield, interrupted only by the crackle of the flames in the wind.

"What do we do now?"

Hidden behind the wreck of a German staff car half-toppled over in a ditch, Aksel Foss roved his eyes from one Russian tank to another. He was certain more were out there, certain some had not been destroyed. The man who had asked the question was named Mehler. He held a Panzerschreck. He started to aim it. Foss motioned to him to wait.

"God knows we can't afford to waste a shot." Foss took off his helmet and ran a hand nervously through his hair. He put the helmet put back on. "With the Tiger gone, we're like hogs in a slaughter pen."

Mehler noticed Foss's nervousness. It made him nervous. He was an older man who had been called up to serve months before, back in the autumn. "Why don't we just mosey on out of here? The brass is probably long gone by now."

Foss shook his head. "We were ordered to hold this position until nightfall." Foss looked at the sky. "That's an hour away."

"Who would know the difference?" There was a note of pouting in Mehler's high-pitched voice. "I bet the rest of the army has already reached the coast."

"If Sergeant Foss says we stay here until dusk—then we stay here until dusk!" Dreybach, who had been filling his canteen with water from a small stream nearby, approached the others in a crouch. He gave Mehler a look of contempt. Many of the Volksturm had proven themselves useless in battle. Offering the canteen to Foss, Dreybach took a seat beside the ruined car.

Foss drank. The cold water relieved his parched mouth. He offered the canteen in turn to Mehler, but the man refused. Foss took another swill.

Though outwardly he kept control of himself, his mind felt numb. The battle had been a nightmare. More than usual. The rush of Soviet tanks upon the German positions had unnerved Foss. The officer sent to command the sector had been slain at the very outset. Then in the midst of a bombardment, Foss had lost contact with the rest of his men. At that moment he had screamed out in fear. All soldiers reach a breaking point; he knew that. But this felt different. He wondered if it was because of Jutta. Before, he only thought of his men, getting them back to safety. Surviving. Now it seemed he had something else to live for—a woman. He silently cursed himself for a fool. The chance of ever seeing Jutta again was slim. Maybe she'd end up in Danzig—maybe she wouldn't. War was that way. His thinking about her had caused a sudden indecision at the sight of the tanks. And indecision in battle got men killed.

He swore. One of the Russian tanks started to move again. In a straight line towards them.

"Should I shoot?" Mehler's voice was a frightened squeak. With shaking hands he tried aiming the Panzerschreck.

"Hand it over, you bastard." Dreybach grabbed the weapon from Mehler, who made no effort to retain it. Taking careful aim after bracing it on the side of the car, Dreybach let the seconds go by as the tank rumbled closer.

"What are you waiting for?" Near to hysterics, Mehler's face was as white as marble.

"Just a little more. I want to make sure this shot sends that whore-monger to hell."

"Shoot for God's sake!"

"Shut up, Mehler!" Foss was beside himself with rage at the sniffling oldster. He knew much of the rage was directed against himself. He too quaked at the tank's approach.

A mere thirty meters away, the tank stopped. The turret swiveled. The attached cannon slowly moved toward the car in the ditch. A half-second before it lined up with the car Dreybach launched the rocket.

The resulting explosion was like a howling windstorm. The three men were tumbled to the ground. Luckily for Foss and Dreybach, they somersaulted backwards into the snow. Mehler fell awkwardly beneath the car which rolled over on him. Lying stunned where he was, Foss heard the other man's frantic screaming.

Picking themselves up, Foss and Dreybach, ran to the car. There was nothing they could do. The car had rolled over Mehler, crushing him. Only his head and neck were visible. His screams became whimpers. Dreyback tried pushing the car off—but it was no use. Mehler soon lost consciousness. Foss checked his pulse.

"He's gone . . . "

Dreybach nodded once at Foss's words. He gazed at the tank. The T-34 was ablaze. One of the crew had managed to crawl out of the burning monster, but the man did not last long. His body burned alongside the tank.

"Let's look for the others." Shaking the cobwebs from his head, Foss found his gun and gingerly stepped across a field away from the destroyed tanks, away from death. Dreybach followed. The two men moved in silence. Only once did they glance back—at the sound of gunshots. But they saw no one.

A short while later they came across Ruder and Tulm. The two were holding a thin line at the top of a small slope along with several dozen other weary-looking soldiers. Foss was astonished to see a number of the men wearing the uniform of the Luftwaffe. One of the airmen noticed this. He said, "We're part of a ground crew. Our airfield got overrun. Last night. I'm a mechanic myself. But since there's no planes to fix, they gave me a rifle and sent me here." The man shrugged as though there was nothing to do but accept his predicament.

"Where's Keller and Ziemans?" Foss turned his attention to Tulm.

"Keller got a slug in the shoulder. Really bad. He was put on a stretcher. Ziemans helped carry him back to the aid station."

"He lost a lot of blood," Ruder added, his usually terse tone softer, sad. "God, it looked like he got torched by an incendiary."

Foss absorbed the news with a grunt. Dreybach said nothing. They were both as tired as they had ever been in the entire war. Another night was approaching, the gray of the westering skyline becoming darker by the minute. It struck Foss that he hadn't thought of Jutta for some time. Savage combat could make you forget your own name. He wondered where she was at the moment. He hoped on a train traveling further west. If not to Danzig then to a place Ivan was nowhere near. He wanted to see her again. Wanted to see her badly. Wanted her—to feel the same about him.

Half-frozen, the Landsers waited anxiously on the hill. A few aircraft flew overhead but no one knew which side. At one point they saw a Russian tank approach to the south, but it turned around soon afterward. Then a German officer appeared. He commanded them to "strategically retreat" five kilometers to the north. Another defense line. Another festung. Falling back daily drained even the most tenacious soldiers. But not a single one of them protested the new order.

Word spread that they were being pulled all the way back toward the outer defenses around Koenigsberg. Except for several bombing raids by the Soviets early in the war that had caused minimal damage, the beautiful city beside the Baltic had largely gone through the war unscathed. But the previous August the RAF had mounted two enormous raids within several days of each other. These attacks had ended up destroying nearly half the city. The older part, and many of the churches and cathedrals were completely gutted. Foss secretly hoped that Jutta had been sent to Koenigsberg. It was possible. The large port was being used by the German Krigsmarine to shuttle out civilians and wounded military personnel to more western cities in the Reich. If he could gain access to the inner part of Koenigsberg he would search for her. But the Russians had other plans.

Before he and hundreds of other Landsers had even been employed in the latest dug entrenchments, the hell of war fell upon them.

A rain of shells from Russian batteries hammered their positions. Men dove under whatever cover they could find. When the artillery ceased, tanks and infantry raced forward to mop up the survivors. The Wehrmacht as always fought tenaciously. But they simply couldn't match the enemy numbers. As dozens of T-34s tore the defense lines into disarray, Foss and his group found themselves cut off from the last road leading to Koenigsberg. Instead of backpedaling north to the safety of the city, they had to run for their lives first south, skirting Russian advance units, then make west when there was opportunity. Other groups of cut-off Germans followed the same direction.

Ruder was bleeding from a neck wound where a bullet had grazed him. Dreyback staunched it with a cloth while Ruder gritted his teeth in agony.

"Another inch or so, puppy, and you'd being doing more than gritting your teeth." With a smirk on his face, Ziemans, who had returned in time to fall back with the retreat, looked as though he wished the bullet had done more damage. He was about to say more when Dreybach gave him an icy stare. Not wanting to confront the older veteran, Ziemans shrugged and walked toward a grove of trees. Undoing his trousers, he took a piss.

"How is he?" Removing his helmet to wipe the sweat from his forehead, Foss watched Dreybach carefully putting a new cloth against Ruder's neck.

"He'll live," Dreyback said calmly. "Won't you, Ruder?"

A tear down trickled down Ruder's right cheek. He was trembling. "I want to see my parents again. I'm . . . their only child."

It was clear Ruder's earlier bravado had evaporated. Yet all of them had nearly reached the end of their tether. Foss wiped his forehead again. His hair felt like a mop. Inside *he* was trembling. Closing his eyes, Foss wished he was back in Denmark walking along the wharf. He loved listening to the sound-waters lapping against boats at anchor. Inhaling deeply, he tried pulling himself together. Foss thought of Dreybach. The man was like an immoveable boulder. The type of man that was needed to keep everyone else sane. Inhaling again, Foss opened his eyes, put on his helmet again

The sun had come out, briefly. Now the sky had returned to its dismal gray. Winter and war. Shells continued to fall to the north. Koenigsberg was under siege. Foss felt perversely glad that someone else was taking the brunt of Ivan's attack. Then he mused that Jutta might be in the city. No, she would have gone to Danzig, he was sure of that. At least he hoped so.

Ziemans let out a fart that caused some of the men to laugh. The cigarette dangling from his lips smelled of mahorka, the cheap Russia tobacco so common in the east. Foss asked him if it was.

"Yes. I grabbed a bunch of this evil-smelling shit off a dead Russki." Ziemans took the cigarette out of his mouth, gazing at it with disdain. "But you have to take what you get in this war."

"How'd it go with Keller?" Foss's face was twisted with concern.

"Not good. The doc that looked him over didn't say too much. He gave Keller a shot of morphine, but the kid was already unconscious by then. I expect he might lose his arm. What remained of it was hanging by a few sinews."

This morbid news affected Foss. His men were dying one by one. Steeling his mind against the sorrow that was overtaking him, he said, "At least he's out of the fire."

Ziemans glowered. "You think so? He's lying under a thin canvassed tent in Koenigsberg, next to scores of other bastards with pus leaking from all parts of their bodies. If the surgeons don't kill him, then the Russians or the weather will."

"He'll be evacuated." Foss didn't care for Ziemans' pessimism. "The Kriegsmarine are bearing the wounded toward western Germany. At all hours of the day and night."

"So I've heard." Ziemans continued to glower. "Maybe all of us should get wounded at the same time—then we can throw a party on the way back."

"Or maybe you can just keep quiet." Making his presence known, Dreybach walked over to stand beside Foss. He raised a fist a few inches from Ziemans' face. "All of us are tired of the shit that's coming out of your mouth. It's bad enough simply trying to survive this God-awful war, without having to listen to your morbid crap. Zip your lips—or I'll do it for you."

Every man in the unit knew that Dreybach was not one to make an idle boast. Clearing his throat, Ziemans spit a big wad into the snow that had turned to slush in the earlier sunlight. "Whatever you say, grandpa," he said acidly. Raising his hand in the air, he clicked his dirty boots together. "Heil Hitler! May we all meet happily in hell."

The bombardment of Koenigsberg had grown louder in the distance. Foss at first thought it might be best to sneak through the Russian lines back toward the city. But what good would that do—hemmed in and surrounded with dwindling supplies. Gazing from left to right at his men and the many others that were also cut off from their former positions, he speculated that the only way left was to flee the area entirely. He had gathered enough information from reports and rumors to realize that most of the East Prussian hinterland had already been conquered by the Russians. A counterattack might take back a few miles, but beyond that it was hopeless. Such an endeavor would only get good men killed. He had seen enough killing. The face of Jutta appeared in his mind; the blue eyes that were as bright as a summer sea. He desperately wanted to see her again. Danzig, he told himself. She must have gone to Danzig. Anywhere away from the front. He looked at his men.

"There's nothing left for us here, comrades. We can't turn back the tide." Foss spoke not only to his own men, but to the large numbers of grimy-faced Volkssturm, the old men with white hair, the young boys with girlish voices. Silent to a man, they listened with marked attentiveness to his every word. To them, the Iron Cross on his chest spoke louder than words. His voice was quiet, but resolute. "Everyone is on their own from here on out. If you want try and make it to Koenigsberg—Good Luck! If you want to come with us—well, I can't promise we'll be any luckier. I aim to reach Danzig, or some other port on the Baltic. That's the only chance I find viable." He paused, to see how his speech had affected those listening. No one spoke up against him. No one showed any signs of defiance. He let out a long weary sigh. How many times had they been cut of behind the lines? How many of these speeches had he given before—*too many*. The road ahead would not be a row boat ride on a calm lake. Many of these men and boys—if not most of them—would die. "The Russians are everywhere now," Foss said stoically. "Avoid them if you can. Fight them if you must. I don't think I need to reiterate what will happen if you're captured. We all know that score."

He had wanted to add what all of them knew—*that the war was finished*. But some of the young faces in the crowd of scared soldiers reminded him of Ruder. In these days of darkness, one denouncement was enough to permanently stretch a man's neck. Aksel Foss would easily give his life to save his friends; he'd not give a hair off his head to save the Third Reich.

Studying a decrepit map he'd come across in the retreat, Foss jerked his head in the direction he was going, then began to walk. His friends shouldered their guns and walked with him. Frankly, he didn't care whether the rest followed or not. But turning around once briefly, he saw them following. Even officers, who had had no experience in war. Their anxious faces betrayed the fact that they were glad someone else had had the guts to make a decision.

And *some* decision is better than *no* decision.

Wondering where and when they might replenish their scant rations, Foss calculated the distance to Danzig was roughly one hundred fifty kilometers. And that was without taking into account the detours they'd have to make to get around any advancing Russians. Scrutinizing the map again, he realized there were other towns and cities much closer than Danzig. Balga, Rosenberg, Heiligenbeil. The names meant nothing to him. He realized too it was wrong of him to lead his men on a longer march when they might reach one of the other places in half the time. Besides, Jutta might not have ended up in Danzig. She could have been sent to Berlin for all he knew.

Foss suddenly wished Brohm was still with them. Having a local man as a guide would have taken the brunt of the journey off his shoulders. It was unfortunate he had not known of Brohm's desire to return home; he might have dissuaded him. Then again, was he not doing the same by heading toward Danzig? Hoping to find a woman he had spent one night with? Who could explain a man's motives, especially in a time of disaster. Foss didn't fault Brohm for placing the love of family above that of his comrades. But no organization ran efficiently without discipline, an army most of all. If every soldier decided to allow his personal fears and whims to influence his actions, then . . .

There was no need to finish the thought. Tulm, who as usual, had gone to scout the terrain ahead, was sprinting back without stop.

"Tanks in front of us!" he blurted out.

"Are they ours?" One of the older Volkssturm queried hopefully as Tulm raced up to Foss.

"Ivan, you idiot." Ziemans spit in disgust at the man's stupidity. "You think that Jew-boy would be running like a jackrabbit otherwise."

Tulm gave Ziemans a look of loathing, before speaking to Foss. "They're all over the place. I pray to heaven I'm wrong, but it sounded like they had overtaken a group of civilians. Refugees on the road. I heard them screaming. Terrible. I still hear their pitiful cries in my head."

Foss stiffened with alarm. Jutta might be among that group. Then he remembered the decision he'd made days ago concerning the women who'd been hauled naked into the Russian tanks. Keller had pleaded with him to attack the tanks—but Foss had remained impervious to anything but getting his men out of danger's way. Losing their own lives to save a few unfortunate women had not seemed practical at the time. *Is it any more practical now?* The berserk mania that had enveloped him when he shot the three Russians returned. He wanted to lash out at something; kill. If they hurt Jutta—*I'll kill them all . . .*

"There's a large stream not far from here." Tulm's statement brought Foss back to reality. "Partly melted. We'll have to cross it if we want to continue to the coast."

"Where else do you propose to go?" Ziemans had stepped into the circle of speech.

"South." Tulm sidled up to Foss as though seeking support for his idea.

"No." Foss shook his head. "We'll run smack dab into the whole of the Red Army. They're aiming for Berlin. Not a chance in hell we'd escape going south."

Tulm didn't argue. Ziemans shrugged. Dreyback, who had come to stand beside them, said nothing. Ruder remained a few paces away, not wanting to cross paths with Ziemans.

Retracing his steps, Tulm led them to the stream. The temperature had risen enough in the last day to thaw portions of ice that had earlier covered the water completely with several inches of thickness. They spent half an hour searching for a ford—Foss would allot no more time than that—but though they didn't find one, they found a spot where the ice was thicker.

"We'll have to cross here," Foss ordered, testing the ice near the banks with his boot. It appeared sturdy enough. Luckily the stream was only twenty meters across. "I doubt the water's very deep anyway. This is a puddle compared to the rivers we've waded through in Russia."

Following Foss's lead, they guardedly stepped over the ice one man at a time, in case someone fell through and needed help. Cracks were visible in the middle part of the stream. Foss slipped once but regained his balance before grabbing the branches of a beech tree on the other side. He hauled himself up. One by one the others did the same. Then gunshots were heard in the rear. And what sounded like grenades. Men were shouting. Suddenly like a herd of frightened livestock, the rest of the soldiers rushed over the stream, slipping and sliding and accidentally tripping each other in a frantic urge to reach the farther shore. Ice in places began to crack. One men screamed out as his legs broke through a thin layer and he fell in the stream up to his waist. Foss could sense the man's agony as he yelled out against the frigid stabs of the freezing water. Several others toppled in after the first one as the ice started to break away completely. Then more gunshots erupted in the background, closer than before. A cry went up: "Russians behind us! Tanks!"

Men scrambled toward the far side of the stream in a mad-dog frenzy. Many threw their rifles away, dove into the water, tried to swim. Others fell in and floundered, grabbing at anything to keep them afloat. Some never came up again. Foss called to them to hold on to their weapons. Then he heard more gunfire. The stream began to run red.

Not bothering to witness further the outcome of those still thrashing in the stream, Foss waved urgently to those around him to keep going. A series of explosions shook the air. Foss was tossed like a rag doll face first to the ground. For a few moments he couldn't breathe. Slowly pushing himself up, he felt wetness on his neck. Fearing a terrible wound, his hands shaking, he probed the area with his fingers. His glove came away matted with gore and flesh. But . . . not his. A group of men had been running behind him. He spun his head around to look for them. They were gone. They had not even had time to scream.

More explosions. This time Foss heard screaming. A man was shouting for his mother. Another wailed like an infant. Foss's knees buckled on him. He could barely stand, let alone run. Then rough hands grabbed his arms and began to drag him.

Foss thought he'd been captured by the Russians. Until he noticed Dreyback trying to utter something to him. The man's mouth moved—but no words came. The continuous bombardment obliterated all vocalization. Tulm was there too. Both of them were pulling him to safety. Foss felt a strange surge of new strength course through his limbs. He gritted his teeth and forced himself to his feet.

"I can manage on my own," he said loudly, though not loud enough to be heard through the tumult. He was still weak, but he didn't want anyone held up because of him. Dreybach and Tulm stood beside him like a couple of mother hens. They eyed with concern the bloody mess dripping down his neck. Foss pointed back toward the stream, then at his neck. "Not mine," he repeated several times. Whether they understood, it didn't matter. Hurrying their pace, they climbed over a stone fence that appeared out of nowhere. Then sprinted like all of hell was chasing them.

They didn't let up until reaching the wreck of an old oak smashed by a shell. Ziemans, Ruder, and several others crouched warily behind the trunk of the fallen giant.

Panting, Foss, Dreybach, and Tulm took several minutes to catch their breath.

"Where's everyone else?" Ruder asked, his eyes widening as he noticed the gore staining Foss's upper jacket.

Eyes downcast, Foss shook his head. No one questioned any further. Scooping up a handful of snow, the Dane tried his best to wash the muck off his neck. The others sighed with relief when they saw he wasn't seriously hurt. With a bare hand, Foss put some fresh snow in his mouth, letting his tongue melt it. The cold drops of water running down his dry throat made him shiver. Despite his thirst, he drank only a little. Veterans knew from experience that drinking snow water stole heat from the body. Stamping his feet to stay warm, he glanced back once at the stone wall. Beyond that his vision was blocked by stands of trees spread out across a flat landscape blending in with the occasional slope or hill. Ivan was somewhere out there. Somewhere not too far away. Sporadic gunfire pierced the stillness of the otherwise quiet day.

"Let's get the hell out of here," Foss exclaimed, his voice gruff, strained. The men needed no further prompting. They were tired, thirsty, hungry, but their legs moved with renewed strength born from inner terror—death stalked them, and death was not kind on the Eastern Front. Foss had observed countless men die in his young life, and their end was no romantic floating away toward a happy heaven. Men wept, shrieked, cursed, bit their lips till they bled, convulsed hideously, hemorrhaged, choked on their own vomit and blood. If they were wounded and trapped in no man's land, they'd swallow their own fist to keep from screaming—rather that than fall into the hands of the Russians who'd slice off their penises then stick them down their throats. Or else the wounded would put the barrel of a gun into their mouths and pull the trigger. An old Landser once told Foss before a battle: "The only thing harsher than death—is living out the last hours of your life wishing for death. Don't ever let the Russkis capture you." Foss had always kept that in the back of his mind; and being Danish instead of German made no difference. Made it worse. The Russians held an especial loathing for satellite nations that helped the Nazis. If the Soviets had their way, those countries would reap the same fate that awaited Germany. Some already had. Bulgaria. Rumania. Hungary. Finland had been forced to accept the harsh terms of a Soviet peace treaty, or else face another invasion. Foss couldn't imagine the Russians getting as far as Denmark.

Or could they . . .

Foss made them quicken their pace until well past nightfall. No one complained. At least not openly. Even Ziemans stayed taciturn. A few men lost their way and stumbled off on their own. But no one was spared to search for them. There was no time for anything but to find refuge. Safety.

The night was long and cold; they took turns sleeping only a few hours at a time. Foss didn't want anyone freezing to death during sleep. One of the older Volkssturm at one point lost his head. Babbling incoherently, he began to strangle another soldier before Dreybach clouted him on the jaw, knocking him senseless. When Foss had all of them ready to march before dawn, the unconscious man still lay where he had fallen. No one had bothered to check on him during the night. A boot nudged against his ribs revealed that he was frozen stiff.

"Ah, look what we have here! Another brave German soldier—fallen for Fuhrer and Fatherland." Ziemans' sarcastic cackle seemed inappropriate to Foss, but he let it pass. The frozen corpse would be a warning to the rest of the Volkssturm.

Foss told them not to eat all of their rations. "Save it for later. Eat a little here and there. Just enough to keep your blood flowing."

"Damn it, Sergeant—I was just getting ready to sit down to a meal of schnapps and roast pork." Ziemans' false joviality made some of the other men grin. Foss himself cracked a smile. Though it was the last smile he'd show in a while.

Trying to keep to wooded areas to avoid Russian patrols, Foss pushed the men relentlessly with barely a halt. All complaints by the Volkssturm of his slave-driving ways fell on deaf ears. Those not able to maintain the fast pace were left behind. His comrades from the Reconnaissance unit, knowing the rapidness of their march was the key to survival, stayed silent. Around noon, after plodding for kilometers through snow and mud, Foss suddenly gestured to the men to stop at the bottom of a hillock. He smelled smoke. Pointing to Tulm and Ruder, he had them crawl cautiously to the top to find out what lay beyond.

Ten minutes later they returned. Ruder looked shaken. Tulm kept his eyes averted.

"What is it? What did you see?" Foss placed a hand on Ruder's forearm.

Ruder swallowed several times before speaking. "A train."

Foss was puzzled. "Surely we'd hear the engine from here. Unless it's not running."

"It's not running, Aksel." Tulm's voice rose barely above a whisper. "It's never going to run again."

Foss turned to Dreybach, who raised his eyebrows, equally nonplussed. Motioning with his eyes for the veteran to follow him, Foss lumbered up the slippery hill. At the crest the two men lay prone and scoured the landscape. Ruder and Tulm had told the truth. There was a train—at the bottom of the other side of the hill. Or what had once been a train. And there was not only the train. Watching for movement of any kind, Foss waited a long while before deciding there was no longer any danger lurking. Standing up wearily, he waved to the others below to follow.

The train's engine had derailed. But more than that, it had been nearly obliterated. What remained lay scattered in a slew of fragments on the ground, the metal twisted, scorched. Foss quickly surmised that Russian tanks had been in the vicinity, their numerous tread-marks visible in the snow and earth. The passenger cars were damaged and burned in places. But what they carried, fared worse.

"Dear God! A nightmare." A stab of pain crossed Dreybach's face. "I thought I'd seen everything in this damn war. I thought I'd seen everything . . . "

Foss found himself retching, though nothing came out. A number of the Volkssturm were less fortunate. They vomited up the small amounts of food they'd eaten earlier. Most of the men had turned completely pale from shock. A few of the younger ones cried.

"The Russians must have broken through here," Dreybach said in a voice without tone. "That much is obvious. But what's also obvious is they took their revenge out on civilians."

Surveying the scene in all directions, Foss lost count of all the corpses of naked women covering the ground beside the ruined train. Nearly all of them had been shot or stabbed or beaten to death, most with dried streaks of blood staining their genitals. His heart pounded. Not wishing to seem perverse, he roved his eyes over each female body briefly, hoping silently that Jutta was not among them. She was not. Though some of the women were so mutilated he could not be positive. Foss kept looking. Dead children lay also among the slain. Not even infants had been spared the massacre. And the bodies of the few men lying in and outside the carriages, had been horridly brutalized. A number had been run over by tanks—probably intentionally—and flattened till they resembled little more than strips of flesh mashed into the melting snow.

"A goddamn shame we can't bury them." Tulm appeared next to Foss. His hands shook as he gripped his rifle tightly. "That's the least they deserve."

But there was no time to bury anyone, and all the men knew it. The Russians could be in front of them, behind them, or waiting close by to spring an ambush. Foss put two fingers in his mouth and whistled shrilly.

Getting the men's attention, he began to walk away from the train in the direction they had originally taken. He went no more than 10 paces and stopped, holding his hand up in the air. Other soldiers crowded around him, their faces tense, fearful. "Tanks!" someone yelled.

"Yes!" Foss added, his voice taut from strain. The unmistakable sound of tank engines. He swerved around, trying to pinpoint the exact location.

"It's coming from the road," another voice burst out. The road lay a short ways from the railroad tracks. Foss held a hand over his eyebrows to get a better view. The sun had broken through the earlier cloud cover sending spears of light across the countryside. He still could not see the tanks, but the grating of their treads grew nearer.

"Scatter!" Waving his arms wildly, Foss shouted the word again. "Take cover inside the train. Those with Panzerfausts—be ready to use them! Now move, you bastards."

With a speed that belied their fatigue and forlornness, the men hurled themselves aboard the empty cars. Windows not already shattered by the Russians were smashed outwards to give better aim for their guns. No one spoke. Ziemans had come across a Panzerfaust—or more likely had snatched it from one of the young recruits, Foss thought—and now propped it on the remains of a window frame. Several other men did the same.

They waited. Foss looked at his watch. He counted the minutes: 1, 2, 3 . . . before the first tank rolled into the clear, fifty meters away. Ziemans was about to let the rocket fly when Foss gripped his forearm.

"Hold your fire!"

Ziemans stared at Foss as if he were insane. "But I have a clear shot!"

"Look at the cross! They're ours." Foss felt a relief he had not felt in a long time. His body sagged. Tears welled in his eyes.

"By God, they are." Lowering the gun, Ziemans rubbed his arm where Foss had clamped down hard on it.

Jumping out of the train unarmed, Foss realized he was throwing caution to the wind. Yet he didn't care. With hands overhead, he stumbled toward the first tank shouting, "Deutsche Soldaten! Deutsche Soldaten!" It only occurred to him later that the tank crew might have distrusted his Danish accent and machine-gunned him as a potential Russian infiltrator. Instead, the hatch opened slowly, an officer stood up—in his hand he bore a Luger. He pointed it at Foss's chest.

"Deutsche Soldaten!" Foss continued to yell, halting a few paces in front of the winter-camouflaged Panzer IV, the most common German battle tank in the war.

The officer lowered his gun. Ordered to move at lightning-speed to face a Russian tank thrust reported to be ransacking the region, he was perplexed not only to see a single German soldier approach his tank, but dozens of others following behind him. The men were caked with mud and grime and looked like they had just fled the pits of Hell.

"I am Major Horst Steckel, of the 3rd Panzer Army," he said in an officious manner. "And whom may I be addressing?"

Foss felt oddly faint. The world was spinning. His legs buckled on him. Going to one knee, he tried saluting the officer. His lips moved slowly. "Sergeant Aksel Foss, sir. With me . . . the remnants of . . . various units that once manned the Festung outside—"

But Foss never finished the sentence. His sight dimming to blackness, he fell face first into a patch of bloody snow.

CHAPTER 6

Foss wondered how long he had slept. Groggy, head throbbing as if he'd been clobbered by a hammer, he was sure he had a hangover. A bad one. His eyelids felt like lead. A minute passed. Another minute. With no stars overhead, no clouds, no sun, in fact no sky at all—Foss slowly became aware that he was lying on a cot under a large tent. Raising his head, he studied the surroundings. A dressing station. An infirmary. He could tell by the pervasive smell of pus, and by all the doctors and orderlies moving constantly to and fro, tending to patients. He blinked his eyes several times, believing that he was in the throes of a bad dream. Then he heard a horrible rasping screech. He swiveled to the right to see a man lying on a cot next to him with a completely bandaged face and no legs. Bile rose in Foss's throat, but he calmed himself by closing his eyes and turning away. The man's muffled scream was heard again: "Doctor, help me! Someone help me! I can't see! I can't see!"

Foss decided that he had no hangover. Thrusting off the blanket that covered him, Foss propped himself up on his elbows. He wanted to leave this place. He hated hospitals. Had visited too many mangled comrades in makeshift medical tents over the past three years; hospitals were where wounded men went to die. Having been badly wounded himself once, he knew firsthand the septic nauseating odors that emanated from hospitals. Impatiently he tried sitting on the side of the cot—but his head swam, and he nearly fell off. Then behind him an abrasive voice grated in his ears.

"What do you think you're doing, you damned fool!" A grim-faced orderly appeared. "Get back in that bed," he said without preamble.

It was then Foss wondered if he too were wounded. In a rising panic, he gazed at his hands—the fingers moved freely, he could clench his fists. He ran his hands down his legs—*still there!* He wiggled his toes. He could see his arms: no bandages; and his torso and chest were intact. He felt his neck. Touched his face: chin, lips, nose, eyes, eyebrows, ears, forehead. He still had his hair. So what was wrong . . .

"If you don't lie back down on your own, I'm going to strap you down." The orderly, now standing in front of Foss with arms akimbo, glared. His burly figure was so close that Foss noticed stains of gore on his dirty tunic. Feeling less dizzy, Foss nodded compliantly to the face above him, then taking a deep breath, and without hesitation, rammed a fist into the man's gut.

The orderly doubled over as if he'd been shot, blowing out a gust of sausage breath that made Foss's nose twitch. "Bastard," the man wheezed, holding his stomach and in obvious pain from the punch. Foss stood up on wobbly legs, his fists raised. He anticipated that he might have to hit the man again. From his previous stay in a field hospital, he had learned quickly that many orderlies were untrustworthy. Many were outright thieves. Foss had woken one morning to find his watch stolen.

"You bastard," the orderly blew out again, trying to right himself. His own fists were drawn, but before he could use them, a man wearing a bloody white gown intervened.

"What is the meaning of this?" the man asked authoritatively.

"Sir, this bast . . . this soldier slugged my in the stomach as I was trying to help him."

The man in the gown turned to Foss. "Is this correct?"

Foss shrugged. He surmised the man that questioned him was a surgeon. "Depends on how you define the word 'help.' Seems like he was more bent on tackling me."

Fuming, the orderly began to deny Foss's accusation, but the other man cut him off.

"Attend to the patient in bed number four," the man in white directed to the orderly. "I'll see to this one."

Foss, still standing with clenched fists, watched the orderly sullenly stalk off. Making eye contact with the man in the gown, he said, "I take it you're a doctor."

"I am, indeed."

Knowing full well he could be severely punished for punching a medical worker, Foss bowed his head. He didn't want to be thrown in prison this late in the war. "I apologize for my misdeed, sir. I lost myself temporarily. I reacted like a soldier does when he feels threatened."

The doctor made Foss wait a long moment before answering. He was tempted to enforce discipline, but the wounded man's honesty made him overlook the infraction. Grinning warmly, he said, "Apology accepted." Looking around to make sure the orderly was out of hearing, the doctor added with an amused expression, "I'm surprised it hasn't happened earlier.

That man's a brute. I've long wanted to send him to the front lines just to scare the piss out of him."

Nodding gratefully, Foss said, "Sir, with your permission, I would like to gather my belongings and return to my unit."

Raising his eyebrows, the doctor stayed quiet a moment. "Did the orderly bother you that much?"

"No offense to your profession, sir, but I want to get back to my men in the field. I have no visible wounds."

The doctor sighed. He cracked a weary smile. "You're a rare case these days. Most men are doing whatever they can *not* to return to the front." A terrible screaming rang out from another part of the tent, shifting the doctor's attention momentarily. When he turned back to Foss his smile was gone. "Though no one wants to lose an arm or leg, it's often the invisible injuries that are the worst. Do you remember collapsing?"

"Collapsing?"

"That's why you were brought here."

Foss was confused. He racked his brain. "No, sir. I only remember . . . running from the wreck of a train. German tanks had appeared. They saved us from the Russians."

"Yes, they saved you alright—you rode back to the nearest garrison ten kilometers away and never woke up once. A long way to go on a tank with nothing but fellow soldiers to keep you from tumbling off."

Now Foss was doubly confused. "Is that true? I had no idea."

"Very true. One of your friends related the story to me personally when they brought you in. Don't recollect his name; he had a scar on his face—"

"Dreybach?"

"That might have been his name. But I've treated so many soldiers in this war that I easily lose track of names. Nevertheless, he told me you were the finest soldier he'd ever served with. Pleaded with me to make certain that you'd become well again."

"And will I become well again?"

"Only God knows the future—though I'm inclined not even to believe that any more." The doctor threw a sorrowful glance at the heavily bandaged man in the bunk next to Foss. The man was softly moaning. "No doubt, sergeant, your luck has allowed you to go through this conflict without losing a limb, or an eye—but at some point in time you incurred a concussion—probably more than one. Add to that months, if not years of service in the field without letup, then you are a prime example of a soldier who has bitten off more than he can chew. The medical diagnosis is extreme combat fatigue. And the only real solution: rest, recuperation, and a prolonged vacation far away from all battlefield experiences. Perhaps a permanent vacation. Somewhere peaceful, with no noise. A nice little mountain hamlet would do."

Foss tried to register what was being said to him. He wondered if the doctor was being sarcastic. His legs beginning to shake again, he sat on the edge of the bed. "I didn't think anyone was allowed to rest at this stage of the war. Doctor, there are complete cripples being sent to the front. Men old enough to be my grandfather. You really think the army would let me shirk?" The image of soldiers strung up with nooses around their necks on bridges and telegraph poles by the SS was branded vividly in Foss's mind. Running a hand through his shock of white hair, the doctor said genially, "If I write an order proclaiming you unfit for duty, then that order will be obeyed. The army has not broken down so much that a doctor's word will go unheeded. Tomorrow I might be wrong about that—but not today."

"And you would write such an order?" Foss shook his head with disbelief.

"I would . . . and I will." Rubbing his chin, the doctor gazed at Foss speculatively. "I detect an accent in your speech. You're not German, are you?"

Foss was not surprised at the question; he'd been asked the same a score of times. "Danish, sir."

"Ah, Denmark . . . a nice little country you have. Beautiful women, if you don't mind me saying so."

"I don't mind."

"And a sincere compliment it is. Though you might think less of me when I tell you that I served with the invasion forces that crossed the borders of your nation. Hard to believe that was nearly five years ago." The doctor appeared almost pained, his forehead wrinkled in thought. "Of course, I never shot any of your countrymen; I've never shot anyone. Only tried to patch them up. Which seems to be a lot harder than shooting them."

When Foss didn't say anything, the doctor continued. "What I'm about to tell you might sound like drivel to your ears, but a day of reckoning is coming. Your friend . . . Dreybach . . . was that his name? He mentioned that you served your entire time in the east. I've served my share of time there too. We both know"—his words became deeper, slower, almost a whisper—"the appalling things that happened in Russia. I can't speak for the other fronts, but my guess is this war has caused the deaths of untold millions. The world will not look kindly on Germany once it's over. No, there will definitely be some payback. That is why we Germans need to make amends for what we have done. The least we can do. I fear the allies will not be gentle in their punishments. Not this time. They forced us to pay reparations after the first war. This time . . . they might wipe the state of Germany off the map." The doctor paused to cough several times. When he regained his composure, he said, "I myself can't make amends to the whole world, but I can do so on an individual basis. I can help a man whose country was wronged by Germany. I don't know what your political convictions are, but you did you time for us, sergeant. No need to drag a Dane down the cesspools where we are likely headed. Go home, sergeant, and make a good life for yourself. You are to be invalided out. I'm writing an order for you due to your wounds, to head for the coast to one of the port cities. Koenigsberg, and even Pillau, are probably out of the question, now that the Russians have cut them off. But there are other cities to the west, Stutthof, or Zoppot. Once there, your medical order will suffice as an official pass for you to board a vessel sailing away from the battlefront. Somewhere west at least. My advice: find a ship sailing to Denmark. Then you'll be out of this mess forever."

His heart thudding wildly, Foss was astonished to the point of speechlessness. Unlike most doctors, who were touchy and impatient, worn out from overwork, this man seemed genuine. But why would he go out of his way to help one soldier? A non-officer; a non-German? He had stated his reasons. Yet Foss found them so out of character for the moment at hand. Through three years of the worst nightmares one could imagine, the Dane had grown wary of trusting those in authority. Too many mistakes had been made by those on top. Mistakes that had caused the misery and deaths of too many common soldiers. And were still causing them.

The doctor sensed Foss's deliberation. Placing a hand on the younger man's shoulder, he said, "I'm not giving you counterfeit money. This pass is a guarantee home."

The doctor's grave tone struck a chord in Foss's mind. *I can go home! Damnation, I can go home.* The unbelievable was coming true. He might even find Jutta and sail with her. Then guilt bore down on him. What of his men? He couldn't leave so readily. Could the doctor not give them similar passes?

"Your kindness exceeds anything I have ever experienced from a doctor," Foss uttered with gratitude. "Exceeds almost every experience I have had in this war, for that matter. But I don't feel like I'm ready to be an invalid. And what of my comrades? I cannot betray their trust in me at this hour." Foss paused, trying to formulate the right words so as not to sound greedy. Nervously, he said, "Herr doctor, it would not be right for me to leave unless my fellow soldiers come with me."

"I feared you might ask that—though it shows that you are a man of character. Your Dreybach related that much to me as well. But I am not a Gauleiter or Reich minister to shower favors on everybody wishing to make themselves scarce of the Red Army. The pass is only for you. Your comrades are not wounded, at least not enough to send them to the west." The doctor stopped speaking and whirled about as the impact of a shell-burst nearby brought the war back into their midst. Gradually the booming of artillery could be heard rising in the east.

Foss was torn. He thought again of Jutta. "I accept your medical pass," Foss said after coming to a decision. "And I thank you for it. You are a man of honor, sir. Rare, these days. But I won't forsake my men. I'll use the pass if there is no other option. I'll keep it secret. But my duty now is to my comrades. My friends."

"The choice is yours. Give me a few minutes, and I will return with the paperwork." When he returned, he said, "Just remember, you are not fully well. I have seen battlefield fatigue in soldiers the entire war. It is not a like a rash that goes away—the symptoms of sudden frailty and loss of mental coherence can return at any moment. Be aware of that. Good luck." He stuck out his hand.

The doctor's grip was strong. Then the man was gone.

Perhaps I am too weak to go back to the front, Foss thought with trepidation after retaining his equipment. Gripping a tent pole to steady himself, he stepped out into the cold of a rainy afternoon. The doctor's words were true. His entire body ached. The pain in the head lingered. Yet remaining here might prove worse in the end. Foss had once seen a dressing station in the Ukraine the Russians had overrun. The wounded had all been bayoneted, the unarmed medical staff murdered. To die was a part of reality for everyone at the front—but at least a man could die with some semblance of dignity. Foss took several deep breaths and steeled himself to put one leg in front of the other. He'd rather take his chances in the open with a Tommy gun. Especially now.

He had a get-out-of-jail-free card.

*

If there were food and drink to be had, Ziemans knew where to find them. His latest scavengings included bacon, potatoes, a whole loaf of rye bread, and three bottles of French wine. Though confrontational by nature, Ziemans was never stingy. Yanking the cork from one of the bottles, he took a long swill, a trail of red liquid tracing from his mouth down to his white winter coat. Licking his lips, he handed the bottle to Ruder.

"Drink up, you little Nazi. I can't say much for the landscape here. But the Prussian aristocrat this belonged to, made a damned good purchase."

Aristocrat? Ruder wondered whether Ziemans had pilfered the wine from one of the many estates that had stood empty during their recent "tactical withdrawal." East Prussia was one of the richest regions in Germany. The land mostly owned by the old nobility. Ruder decided not to ask Ziemans where he had gotten it. He drank. The wine was incredibly smooth. For once, he agreed wholeheartedly with his tormentor.

"Too bad Aksel's not here," Tulm said in between bites of a roasted potato. The potato was hot. It burned his tongue. "Ouch! I just hope he gets released from the infirmary soon."

"Why? So he can come back to this shithole." Ziemans gazed at Tulm as if he had gone nuts.

"Knowing Foss, he'd much rather be sitting here with friends than with a bunch of amputees."

The men had attempted to play cards earlier, but Dreybach had lost interest. In Ziemans' mind, the man wasn't much interested in anything. The scar on Dreybach's face only added to his already sullen demeanor. After eating a piece of bacon, Ziemans lit a cigarette. For a while he watched Ruder and Tulm pass the bottle of wine back and forth between them. Then he laughed.

"I bet old Grofaz would have a heart attack if he saw a dedicated Nazi supping happily with a Jew." Ziemans laughed even louder.

Early in the war, the German press had labeled Hitler as the Greatest Field Commander of all time.

But when losses began to mount, ordinary soldiers shortened the phrase to *Grofaz*. Now they only used it as a term of belittlement.

Tulm reddened, but stayed quiet. Ruder kept his eyes averted. Ziemans persisted with his digs until a rough hand clamped hard on his shoulder.

"Shut your ass, Ziemans." Dreybach's gruff voice cut through the stale air of the bunker with finality. But Ziemans had had enough of the veteran's sour attitude. He shoved the hand away and stood up.

"Why don't you rot in hell, you bloodless worm. I am tired of your shit. Who do you think you are lording over the rest of us?"

Ziemans barely got the last word out when Dreybach's fist crashed into his jaw, knocking him into a wooden support beam. It took a few moments, but with a grunt and a heave, Ziemans' picked himself up and again faced Dreybach. There was blood on his lips.

Ziemans wiped a hand across his mouth. He stared at the blood as though he had never seen blood before. In a strangely subdued tone unlike him, Ziemans said, "You haven't been the same since your family was killed. No one can negate the agony you must have gone through. But we've all lost people in this war. My brother was killed fighting in Sicily. My best friend went to the bottom of the Atlantic in a U-boat. And there is not a man here among us who has not mourned the death of a comrade. Except maybe them." He pointed at a group of young recruits sitting taciturn and shocked at the animosity displayed between the two veteran soldiers. "But they've probably lost someone too. Dreybach, if you want to go through the rest of this goddamn war being bitter and angry, I won't stop you. But at least let other men be the way they wish to be. Yes, I know I'm a pain in the ass much of the time. I know I make wisecracks when I shouldn't." He looked at Tulm, then Ruder. "You two no doubt hate my guts. But if you were wounded and lying in no man's land, I'd be the first one to crawl out to try and bring you back in."

"And I'm sure deep down they realize that."

Caught off guard by a voice in the background, everyone turned to see who had spoken. At the entrance to the bunker stood Aksel Foss. He was grinning.

"Foss, I . . . we . . . thought . . . we'd never see you again." Stuttering, Dreybach came near to breaking out with elation as he ever would. He went over to Foss and patted him on the back. "Are you really back?"

"It's not my ghost standing here."

The others crowded around him. Foss told them everything about his hospital stay except for the reason of his recent collapse and the medical discharge he'd been given. Sharing the food and wine, he was glad to be back among friends. Later, when he spurned off their attempts to keep him from doing sentry duty, he strode outside into a night of snow flurries. Dreybach went with him.

"Ivan's quiet tonight," Dreybach said laconically, trying to adjust his sight to the utter darkness surrounding them. "At least in our sector."

Rubbing his hands together to keep them warm, Foss nodded agreement. To the northeast a distant continuous drone meant that someone somewhere was getting shelled. Most likely the unfortunate inhabitants of Koenigsburg, who were now trapped in a siege.

"The Russians in front of us are most likely regrouping." The words had barely left Foss's lips when an errant shell whistled over them, bursting far back in the rear. "Guess I opened my trap too soon."

Crouching in a trench, he and Dreybach waited for an onslaught of Soviet artillery, but none was forthcoming. They resumed their lookout.

"You surprised us in there," Dreybach declared, referring to Foss's appearance in the bunker.

"You surprised me. Throwing a hay-maker at Ziemans—he must have really gotten under your skin."

Embarrassed, Dreybach avoided Foss's gaze. "I was angry. I'd had enough of his bullshit. He taunts people like it's a natural way of talking. I know I shouldn't have done it—but I did."

"Forget it. If any man deserved a good hiding, it's Ziemans. I did the same thing to an orderly not an hour ago."

For a long while they kept their thoughts to themselves. Then Dreybach said, "How'd you inveigle your way out of the infirmary?"

Not wanting to alarm the men about his diagnosis of shell-shock, Foss had neglected to tell the truth about the reasons behind his recent collapse. *Extreme exhaustion*, he had explained with a shrug, knowing full well that all soldiers in the field related to the lack of sleep and over-activity so common among them. Foss had told the men he'd merely been ordered to rest by doctors due to chronic insomnia. But Dreybach was too wily a veteran not to see through his friend's explanation. Foss was honest with him, even though it hurt inside to admit that he was as vulnerable to the rigors of battle as the rawest recruit. Dreybach listened without interrupting, then he said consolingly, "Nerves, exhaustion, take a toll on everyone in the field. Remember Captain Herling?"

"I remember him well." Herling had been the company commander more than a year earlier. A strict but fair officer, the man had been the most competent and fearless soldier Foss had ever come across. Going into battles with nothing but a pistol, he always led from the forefront, seemingly oblivious of all gunfire and grenades the enemy directed at him. Then one night after a particularly vicious skirmish when over half the company had either been wounded or slain, Herling broke down. The men later found him curled up in a fetal position in the ruins of a Russian barn, wailing like a baby. He was immediately relieved of his position and sent home. The company lost all contact with him.

"I'd never count myself as brave as Herling," Foss commented with a shake of his head. "Few leaders are of that caliber."

"Don't berate yourself, Aksel. None of us would have made it this far without your leadership."

Foss wanted to respond that not all of them had made it—Brohm, Laursen, Steenhagen, and Keller could attest to that. But he realized Dreybach was not a man to give compliments lightly. It was a rare event for him to open up the drawbridge of his closed castle.

"Your . . . sentiments mean a lot to me," Foss said appreciatively.

"We're just glad to have your back," Dreybach mumbled swiftly. Feeling all of a sudden awkward, he turned away to keep his expression hidden.

Worrying about frostbite, Foss stamped his feet and walked the perimeter of the trench. The drone he had heard earlier was no more than a distant drumbeat. It was moments like these when sharing guard duty with a comrade gave him the sensation of butterflies in his chest. Feeling suddenly poetic, Foss searched the sky—but there wasn't a star to be seen.

"We ended up burying them after all." Dreybach's words cut through Foss's thoughts. "The people from the train."

It took a few moments for Foss to understand what his friend meant. Then he remembered the smashed train; the scattered clothing, ripped up luggage and other debris littering the ground, the scores of civilian corpses lying haphazardly everywhere, both inside and outside the carriages.

When Foss stayed mute, Dreybach said, "I just thought I'd tell you. To give you peace of mind."

"It does—to a degree." The horrid scene was one among many, now stashed away in his memory. Seeing soldiers die in battle was hard enough; seeing innocents suffer seemed far worse. Foss wondered whether the massacre of the train passengers caused Dreybach to consider the brutal way his own wife and children had perished in Hamburg. He had never asked Dreybach about them previously, but though he was curious, he thought it inappropriate to begin querying now.

Relieved an hour later by two other men, Foss and Dreybach sought shelter in the bunker. Despite their winter attire, they were cold to the bone. Dreybach fell asleep immediately in a spot next to Tulm. Foss stayed awake a while longer to make certain the rest of the men slept soundly. The visit to the field hospital had not altered the familiar leadership skills that were thoroughly ingrained in him. Sensing all was well, he lay down, shut his eyes, and slept.

But all was not well. Shortly before dawn the Russians unleashed a barrage that rocked the bunker as if it were a small boat foundering on a stormy sea. Everybody awoke simultaneously, scrambling about in the darkness to find their weapons. Some of the Volkssturm recruits yelled out in near-panic. Already screams were heard from outside. Shells rained down all around them. The bunker shook, but held. Barely. The wooden roof beams creaked and one of the poles supporting them showed a crack running down the side. When the artillery ceased half an hour later, Foss led the way to the trenches.

Or what was left of them. An impenetrable fog limited vision to a few meters. Great chunks of earth had been torn out of the ground. Men tripped and fell into holes that earlier had not existed. Lieutenant Vogel, the new officer in command, rallied the men around him, some of whom were as white-faced as the clumps of snow left untouched by the shells. "Stay alert," he called out to the men, racing up and down what remained of the strong-point to make certain each of them had a gun and was ready to use it.

Foss and the other veterans needed no such prodding. Already they had assumed firing positions. All of them knew it was only a matter of minutes before the Russians thrust themselves at the German lines.

A tank materialized out of the fog, momentarily frightening the men situated in its path. Foss got a brief glimpse of it before someone let loose with a rocket from a Panzerfaust. The tank burst apart like a teapot smashed to pieces by a sledgehammer. From the shape of what remained, Foss guessed the tank to be a Sherman. One of the many lend-lease vehicles given to the Russians by the Americans. Poorly armored, the Sherman could usually with ease be destroyed by one solid hit from any decent anti-tank gun.

The burning tank offered the men a visibility that was lacking only a moment ago. In seconds they spotted Russian infantry sprinting toward them. The Russians were not shouting their usual battle-cries, but instead, hurled themselves at the trenches in grim silence, determined to obliterate everything in their path. The Germans were equally determined to stop them. Grenade blasts sent hot slivers of metal into bodies. A machine-gun barked to life. Bullets ripped through flesh. A hideous shriek almost burst Foss's ear drum. He fired at anything that moved in front of him. He lost track of time. Men were screaming in defiance; others screamed in agony. As though a tide receding, the Russians all at once fled. The Germans cheered. Those that had survived.

A wounded Russian was captured and taken back to headquarters for questioning. Other wounded Russians were shot where they lay writhing and whimpering on the broken ground.

Foss checked up on his men. Thankfully, all had come out unscathed. There was also tragic news. Lieutenant Vogel apparently had been killed instantly. Shot through the heart. Yet another officer lost in the blink of an eye. Foss had not even said two words to the man.

But there was to be no lull in the fighting. Just as soon as the Germans began to relax and receive their breakfast rations, the Russians launched a fresh attack. By then the fog had lifted, and Soviet planes flew unhindered overhead to spray the German lines with withering rocket and rapid machine-gun fire. Men died by the dozens. Then the tanks came. Hordes of them, followed by massed infantry. This time Foss and the others were unable to hold. Forced back, they maintained a semblance of order by retreating while firing. Officers on the scene gathered men for counterattacks. Foss took part in one of these when he saw Ruder halt suddenly beside him. The man teetered a moment before falling to his knees. A second later he fell to his stomach.

"Ruder!" Kneeling on the ground, Foss checked to see whether Ruder had spinal injuries. Not finding any, he rapidly pulled Ruder on to his back. Foss's stomach churned. From the blood on the front of his jacket,

Ruder had taken a bullet in the chest. Half conscious, Ruder wheezed spittle and blood with each moaning breath. Dreading the worst, Foss surmised he had a lung shot.

The counterattack had no chance of success. Almost as if they had been tipped off with the German plans, the Russians had set up a series of machine-guns and were pummeling the terrain with mortars. Men found shelter where they could, behind trees, in craters made by shells, beside the wrecks of wagons and sleighs abandoned by refugees who had fled the area days before. In a frenzy of fear, most of the men dashed back to where they had started. They ran without listening to Foss's pleas for help. Finally a medic stopped to probe Ruder's wound.

"He won't make it," the medic stated bluntly. The man looked with anxiety back toward where the Russians were still firing.

"He will!" Foss answered the medic with equal bluntness. "Help me carry him."

When the medic made as if to leave, Foss pointed his Tommy gun at him. "Either you help me, or I'll shoot you in the leg and leave you here for the Russians."

The medic thought he was bluffing until Foss took aim at a spot right above the man's left knee.

"You'll be court-marshaled for this," the medic said, unsure whether the crazed Lander would really pull the trigger. He tried to inch his way back to the German lines.

"Take another step and your leg is history."

"I'll report you!"

"And I'll report you too. Leaving behind a wounded man to the whims of the enemy. A more despicable thing is not found in this army."

The medic thought a moment. Cursing under his breath, he picked up Ruder by the legs while Foss lifted from beneath the shoulders. Unconscious now, Ruder was borne back through mortar rounds for close to a kilometer. By the time they reached a dressing station, Foss ached from head to toe. The medic briefed an attending doctor of Ruder's condition. Glancing at Foss, he said nothing of the incident in the field.

On the heels of the retreating Germans the Russians continued to press. Foss barely had time to relay his fears about Ruder's wound to the doctor when he was forced again into combat. Reshuffling decimated regiments into a makeshift battle order, the high command threw every man available into the contested area. Foss found himself next to men blind in one eye or missing part of their face. Others hobbled out on crutches to meet the new attack. Cooks, mechanics, orderlies, radiomen and other soldiers that had never lifted a gun the entire war, were thrown into the inferno. Despite their overwhelming superiority in manpower and heavy weapons, the Russians, after several hours of some of the most vicious fighting witnessed on the Eastern Front, were forced back. When it was over, Foss, drenched in sweat and hardly able to hold himself erect, ran his eyes wearily over the battlefield. He had an unobstructed view of death. Russians by the score lay in mass heaps, some so meshed together that it looked like a giant orgy of arms and legs. German corpses were also plentiful. And somehow a group of unfortunate refugees had wandered (or been chased) in the wrong direction and ended up being butchered like helpless animals. Overturned wagons, crushed sleds, horses with their entrails splattered over snow and dirt, the wreckage of smoldering tanks and trucks, small arms strewn in disarray everywhere, and the sickening sight of bodies—staring at the mayhem Foss felt himself trembling. He wanted to run away.

He closed his eyes for a long time. They stayed that way until someone gently placed a hand on his shoulder.

"Aksel . . . it's over. For now. We survived again."

"Dreybach . . . " Foss wanted to say more to his friend, but the words were stuck in his throat.

Ziemans appeared, as did Tulm, who looked as though he'd been through hell and only half of him had come back. They'd heard about Ruder.

Later, when the four of them went to the dressing station to inquire about their comrade, they were told Ruder had died on the operating table. They stood silent for a long time afterward. To assuage the men's sadness, the attending surgeon gave them a pack of cigarettes. They smoked most of them by midday.

Then the barrage started again. This time the lines didn't hold. Even the rear area was overrun. A few ambulances and transport vehicles hurried off with what wounded could be taken aboard, but most were left to the mercy of the Russians. Foss felt an odd sense of relief that Ruder would not experience such a fate.

The day dragged into night; explosions rent the air without cease. Reinforcements were rushed up to stem the Russian advance. But never enough to do more than give a brief respite.

"You'd think they'd run out of men by now," a soldier declared aloud, worriedly turning back to note every blast that came nearer. Limping from a wound to his knee, the man was falling behind the others in the long retreat. Ziemans, who was closest to him, stopped to give the man a hand.

"We've been saying the same damn thing the last three and a half years," Ziemans responded acidly. "But old Adolf never got the message."

The man, an aged member of the Volkssturm, surveyed Ziemans with shock. He was not used to hearing anyone curse the Fuhrer.

Ziemans groused, "I know what you're thinking, grandpa, but at this point I'm more concerned about Ivan than our beloved Fuhrer."

They trudged on like this for awhile until Ziemans felt his own strength begin to wane. "I can't bear you anymore," he said, releasing the man's arm from around his shoulder.

"But I won't make it," the man trembled, tears forming in his eyes. "Please, I beg you, help me."

Ziemans turned away. He stepped a few paces when he spied Foss standing a short distance ahead.

"We wondered where you were." A sense of relief spread across Foss's face as he saw that Ziemans was not injured. He didn't particularly care for Ziemans as a person, but the man was still part of his unit—and that counted for everything.

"That old-timer held me up." Ziemans jerked his head toward the soldier who was frantically trying to keep pace. "Otherwise I would have been drinking a beer in Berlin by now. And finding a loose whore."

Foss suppressed a smile. Ziemans would never change; his sardonic attitude gave Foss a feeling of continuity in a world where all else seemingly had broken apart and vanished. He patted Ziemans on the back. "Let's help the old one."

Despite protesting, Ziemans helped Foss bring the limping soldier to safety.

But hardly had they reached the newest vantage point when rumors flew about that the Russians had effected a pincer movement to the west. The truth was confirmed when refugees fleeing toward the interior of the Reich, streamed back in panic to the coastal towns and cities of the Baltic. A

number of German armies, decimated divisions from other armies lost
further to the east, and hundreds of thousands of civilians, were now
trapped between the Soviets and the sea. Foss took the news
grimly—though in the back of his mind, he was calmed by the fact that he
could leave for Denmark once he reached a harbor city.

Yet . . . he couldn't leave—not while the others trusted him with their
lives. Running his fingers through the whiskers that were now becoming
a beard, Foss realized he hadn't shaved in nearly a week. Dreybach, Tulm,
and Ziemans also appeared like ruffians. Dusk was approaching. In the sky
overhead the noise of aircraft loomed menacingly. Since there was a ninety
percent chance they were enemy planes, Foss didn't even bother to look
up.

"How's the Austrian corporal going to get us out of this pickle?" Ziemans
was his old self as he smoked the last cigar from the batch he'd found days
before. This time he didn't share it.

A strange silence ensued when all of them realized that Ruder was no
longer there to boast of Hitler's wonder weapons. Tulm was about to utter
something, then chose not to.

"We're doomed," Ziemans said matter-of-factly, chomping on the cigar
like it was the last one he'd ever smoke.

"There's still hope," another soldier opined. "It's only a matter of time
before the Amis and Russians come to loggerheads. Then the Amis will
need us on their side."

"Where you'd hear that crap? Probably something Goebbels cooked up."
Ziemans rolled his eyes in dismay.

"You can't expect capitalists and commis to be friends forever."

"They don't need to be friends forever. Just long enough to carve us into
pieces."

Ziemans' words made Foss recall the American tank that had been blown
up before his eyes. He'd seen a lot of them used by the Russians. And
American jeeps. And all types of food rations, including canned fruit, and
meat. As far as he knew, the allies had not yet quarreled.

An explosion halted the conversation. More explosions forced everyone
to seek cover. The men had been sitting in hastily dug trenches that
afforded little protection against bombs from the air.

"Stormoviks!" someone yelled, but Foss was well aware what confronted
them. The planes were zeroing in on the German entrenchments.

Throwing caution to the wind, he motioned to his friends to sprint toward a small stand of pines about a hundred meters to the right of them. Stumbling several times, Foss dived under the first tall tree he encountered and rolled underneath its wide branches. The others followed suit. All of them were panting as if they'd used up every last breath in their lungs.

The explosions only lasted a few minutes before the planes flew back to the east. It was only then that Foss realized they were not alone. Hearing a twig snap, Foss whirled around gun in hand to meet the terrified eyes of an SS man kneeling on one knee. The man too was bearing a gun. Not far from him a half dozen other SS were crouching in equal terror. At their feet lay what appeared to be women dressed in filthy rags that barely covered their skin. The women—Foss guessed there must have been twenty to thirty, more skeletons than human females—had all been shoved face down in a mixture of slush and pine needles. Foss was astonished that none of the women wore winter coats. And more astonished that the few SS were pointing their guns at them.

"Those damned planes gave us a start," the first SS man confided uncertainly, straining his eyes through the tree tops to see whether the Stormoviks had indeed left. Foss noticed that the man's hands shook uncontrollably.

"This your first time in the field?" Foss's question was more a statement. His voice, caustic.

Reddening with embarrassment, the SS man saw that Foss and the other Landsers who now stood along side him, were staring at the women. Clearing his throat, he said, "The front line exists everywhere these days, if you know what I mean. Each of us has a part to play."

"A part to play? I wonder what part you've played to make you shudder so."

Crimsoning in his face even more, the SS man crossed his arms to hide his hands. He looked condescendingly at Foss, as though he were dealing with a simpleton. "War is about duty. All of us have our duties. All of us are fighting the enemies of Germany. We each deal in our own—"

"Spare me your shit!' Foss interrupted; then he spit on the ground a few inches from the other man's boots. "Are those women enemies?" A sudden boiling anger was overflowing inside him and it began to dawn on him why. He'd seen equally appalling scenes in Russia, but something was churning inside, ready to seethe into flames. He remembered the doctor's words about his condition—but this was more than a case of shell-shock. The whole damned idiotic reason he was standing here under these trees had finally come full circle in his head. He was enraged at the Germans for impressing him into their demented vision of world conquest, resentful that he had been forced to take arms against people from nations he had no quarrel with. *Fucking Nazis!* he thought savagely. The fear, the expenditure of energy from fighting battles and trying to survive the last number of days, weeks, months, years, had run him ragged. A part of him didn't care now whether he lived or died. He was tired of fighting, tired of running, tired of fulfilling a *duty* that should never have been his to do. This SS creep was the epitome of everything he hated. Duty, discipline, destruction, death. Foss stepped closer to the man. "Are those women enemies?" he asked again. Then raised his Tommy gun until the barrel was level with the other man's stomach.

Unnerved at the vehemence in Foss's tone, the SS man slowly backed away, keeping his eyes glued to the weapon aimed at him. Another SS stepped to the forefront. A heavy, thickset man with small pig eyes, his lips curled in open disdain at the common soldier. "Whether they're enemies of the Reich or not," he said brusquely, "is of no importance to you."

"What if I beg to differ?"

"Then you'll find yourself in hot water. Very hot."

Foss shrugged. "With Ivan breathing down our necks, I find myself in hot water every day."

"You're wasting our time. Go back to your Festung, soldier-boy."

"You never answered my question . . . "

Growing impatient with the relentless probing, the SS threw a brief glance at the women on the ground before turning back to Foss. "Alright . . . I'll tell you. They're Jews. Vermin. And . . . no concern of yours. I'll say no more on the matter."

The man pivoted around and started to walk away. Foss had no doubts now that the women had been interned in a concentration camp. Probably from one of the many camps in the east that recently had undergone a hurried dismantling before being overtaken by the Russians. Foss knew little of such camps. What little he had garnered from his three years of service in the Wehrmacht was that they were brutal places, surrounded by electric wire fences and sadistic guards. Tulm had mentioned that one of his mother's uncles had been sent to a camp for sedition against the Nazi government. He had died there. Later, his cremated remains were delivered to his family in a shoebox with a death certificate stating that he had perished from typhus. Though keeping their thoughts to themselves, Tulm and the rest of the family believed otherwise. They had no doubts that the uncle had been tortured and murdered.

"At least give them proper clothing," Foss blurted out as the SS men began to harshly prod the women with the front of their hob-nailed boots, forcing the prisoners to stand. The man who had just spoken to him whirled around, his face a mask of rage.

"One more peep out of you and I'll file a report of your misconduct."

"File it, you evil bastard."

One of the women turned her head to stare directly at Foss and got a kick in the shin from one of the guards.

Retrieving a small notebook and a pencil from his pocket, the SS man began to write. Keeping his eyes on the paper, he asked, "Your name, soldier?"

"Kiss my ass, you SS pig!'

The SS man's jaw dropped.

"Leave it, Aksel." Dreybach, realizing that his friend was nearing a danger zone, tried pulling him aside.

"No, I won't leave it."

"Then you will be arrested." Drawing a pistol from a holster on his belt, the man with pig eyes began lifting it when Foss went berserk.

Shouting at the top of his lungs like a man gone mad, Foss unloaded his Tommy gun, spinning side to side and spraying everything in his path. The SS man fell back with a roar of pain; the other half dozen guards too were gunned down where they stood. Most of the women still lay hugging the ground, but three who had already risen were hit by bullets from Foss's gun. Their emaciated bodies crumpled like empty sacks to the earth—their red blood mixing with the red blood of the dead SS.

Foss would have continued shooting if Dreybach had not tackled him. The two men wrestled like lions on the ground, Dreybach trying to subdue the bellowing Dane while Foss punched and poked at his attacker. When Ziemans and Tulm eventually came to Dreybach's aid, Foss ceased struggling. His eyes glazed; he babbled incoherently. Spittle, snot, coated his cheeks. *Who were these strange men holding him down?* He didn't recognize them until Dreybach slapped him hard on the face, twice.

"What the hell was that for?" Foss blinked. Coming to, he saw the bodies on the ground, and the women, now huddled in a group, gazing at him with shock and fear. "What happened here?" he asked, swiveling his head around to get a better look at the men beside him.

Dreyback, his demeanor stark with resignation, could only whisper. "You killed them, Aksel."

Memory flooding his brain, Foss felt aghast. "I did kill them . . . didn't I?" His sense of duty to his men overwhelmed him. *What have I done? I've jeopardized their lives.* His own life was now forfeit. Beyond a doubt. Murder of fellow soldiers—and especially the SS—was a crime punishable by execution. *But I acted alone!* His friends had had nothing to do with it. He would make that clear to any tribunal. He glanced around, expecting to be arrested at any moment.

But there were only his men and the surviving women. Hidden by the pine woods, the event had not been witnessed by anyone back in the trenches. Though a voice was heard, several voices. Other Landsers curious to know the reason for the gunfire. Hoping to stall for time and create a diversion, Ziemans cupped his hands around his mouth and shouted.

"Russians! On our flanks! Head to the northeast—or we'll be cut off!"

A flurry of activity ensued. Men began to assume defensive positions. Crouched behind the trunk of a tree, Ziemans made certain no one was near before intimating with the nod of his head that no other persons had followed them into the woods.

Rising from the ground as they let go of him, Foss knew he was now under the close scrutiny of his friends. "You have no choice but to turn me in," he said, dropping his chin to his chest to avert their their gaze. He offered his gun to Dreybach. The veteran refused to take it.

"There's not a man among us that likes the SS." Dreybach kept his voice low, so that the women could not overhear. Tulm nodded assent. Still viewing the trench-works, Ziemans said with his back turned, "I tangled with one of the bastards in a bar some years ago. Gave him a knot on the head, then got the hell out of there. So I'm on their shit-list too." Spinning around, he cracked a wry smile. "Guess that makes us brothers, Foss."

Foss felt at a loss for words; felt drained, as though he had run for hours without stop. His eyes alighted on the women. For a moment he had forgotten them. Pulling a half loaf of bread from his pocket, he held it out to them. It was the only food he had. "Here, take it." Unsure what nationality they were, he enunciated each German word slowly. "This . . . is . . . bread. Nourishment." When none of them moved, he wondered if they had been so maltreated that they trusted no one. Not wanting to dither any longer in the dark grove, Foss placed the bread on a mat of pine needles. He then pointed a finger southward. "Go that way. You will find the Russians. You will be safe. SS kaput." Though he doubted his own words. The women wouldn't last long slogging through bitterly cold countryside in the midst of a war. And who could guess how the Russians would act. Everyone was a refugee now. It was a time of no mercy.

Ziemans meanwhile had begun rifling the corpses of the SS. He found four packs of cigarettes, a flask containing a strong-smelling schnapps, and six cans of salted herring, one from each of the dead. "A taste of Denmark," he said, showing the fish to Foss.

But Foss wasn't listening. He had already begun to walk away, heading for another stretch of woods just visible to the east. If he didn't meet up with any Russians, he'd hole up there until nightfall. Then skirt around the German lines and make for the Baltic. It was risky, but it was riskier staying here with the probability that the military police might want to question him. Under the present circumstances, he wasn't sure his unstable temperament could hold up to an interrogation.

The women watched him pass. They still had not taken the bread. Foss moved beyond them when a series of shots caused him to spin around.

Ziemans was shooting at the women. As a dagger pierced Foss's heart, he suddenly realized that Ziemans was not shooting at them—but in the air directly above their heads. Panicking, the wraith-like females, some of them little more than slow moving sticks, poured out of the woods in the direction Foss had earlier pointed them towards. One of them snatched the bread before fleeing. A few minutes passed and they were soon gone from sight. Foss stared at Ziemans, bewildered by his action.

"Someone might have questioned them about the slain SS," Ziemans explained while reloading his gun. "We don't want any witnesses—especially since we won't be sticking around either. Now let's hurry if you want to live."

"Looked like you were making for that woods over there," Dreybach added, his eyes meeting those of Foss.

Foss realized his men had been with him so long that they thought the
same way he did. One mind. A soldier's mind. It made him happy—and it
made him sad. For the first time in a million years he wanted to cry. *Am
I fit enough to lead such men?* A tear rolled down his face. He wiped it away.

"Might be better if *you* pull the strings from now on," Foss advised.

Dreybach was about to answer when Tulm rushed up to them. With
Ziemans concentrating on pilfering the death, Tulm had kept an eye on
the German entrenchments. Having attended to the dead and wounded
from the attack by the Stormoviks, those remaining now turned their
attention to the earlier firing from the woods.

"A patrol's on the way," Tulm pointed out, his face twitching with
nervousness.

"No doubt coming to investigate," said Foss apathetically. "Maybe I
should just give myself up."

Ziemans spit out a huge wad of green phlegm, hitting the chest of one of
the dead SS. "Don't be a moron, Aksel. If you jump ship now, we're all
going to drown."

Foss gradually realized he was right. Once the military police became
involved, they would most likely blame more than one man for such a
killing spree. Ziemans, Dreybach and Tulm too would pay for his rabid
outburst. Taking a cue from Ziemans, Foss lifted his gun and fired up in the
air. "That should give them pause. Alright, let's go. Quick time."

They ran. Foss looked back once to see if anyone followed. He saw no
one. After entering the woods, he and the others hid themselves behind
a large tree that had been knocked over by shellfire. Then they waited for
nightfall.

Recently returned to duty after nearly a year convalescing in a hospital in
Dresden, Colonel Friederich von Wert had been given a command in the
same theater of the war where he had almost died. A professor of
philosophy at Heidelburg University and a man from an esteemed family
that had helped serve in Germany's rise to power since the time of
Bismarck, von Wert wanted to do his share for the war effort. Having
connections enough to procure a colonelcy in the Wehrmacht, he had
been slated to join the 6th Army at Stalingrad when the Russians suddenly
cut it off from the rest of the world. Though he counted himself fortunate
not to have been plunged into that debacle, the loss of hundreds of

thousands of irreplaceable soldiers had struck a depressing chord in von Wert's brain. From then on as the war become one losing battle after another, he began to brood daily and to question the meaninglessness of life on the Eastern Front. During his spare moments he turned to his favorite philosopher, Nietzsche, who bore out repeatedly in his works: Adversity makes a man stronger.

But what if the adversity is constant? And with no happy ending in sight? Did a man become more durable, more complete, just because he had come close to his own mortality? Von Wert considered these questions as he recalled the previous spring. While observing from a forward position the enemy's preparations—a fragment from a Russian mortar had ripped through his left thigh. He had almost bled to death, and at one point, the field doctors attending him contemplated amputating his leg. Conscious and in unbearable agony, von Wert had pleaded with them not to, and so they had removed the jagged metal from his body in a touch-and-go operation, patched him up, sent him home, and told him the rest was in the hands of the Almighty.

Whether due to the wishes of God, fate, or simply from having a robust constitution, the former professor had regained his health. Yet, despite this recovery—remarkable many said, for a man of fifty-eight—von Wert, once back at the front, had lapsed again into periods of morbidity. Periods such as now. Sitting at a table in an abandoned house merely a kilometer or so behind the main lines with a glass of whiskey in front of him, von Wert wished he was back in the hospital in Dresden. The war was worsening by the hour—in fact, he had become part of the large group of German soldiers that days before had been penned in along the coast by a huge Russian drive toward the center of the Reich. Rubbing his leg that strangely had begun to hurt again after months without any pain, von Wert reflected grimly on the event that had brought him to where he was. Having had his leg restored to him had not vanquished his doubts about the war and his place in it.

But now other matters took precedence. A junior officer stood patiently at attention in front of the desk. The man, whose eyes were bloodshot, and who was attired in a dirt-stained combat uniform, had just relayed to him the harsh facts of a potential crime. A report told first by a non-com about a dying SS man. A report of murder committed by a band of German soldiers against their own.

"Are you certain you heard correctly?" von Wert queried his subordinate.

"Yes, sir, I am quite certain. One of the non-coms found him alive. There were five others—all dead. And the bodies of three women—I believe they were inmates from a camp. The dying man didn't last for very long, though. But long enough to say that they had all been gunned down by four members of the Wehrmacht."

"That's a serious charge." Von Wert's usual even temperament was ruffled. It was dire enough being encircled by entire Soviet armies, but to add to that murder perpetrated by his own men against fellow soldiers— even though they were SS, which von Wert considered in most cases no better than thugs—meant a total breakdown in military discipline. Such a criminal act would have to be reported to the higher ups—perhaps even to the Gestapo. Von Wert wished he had time to be alone; maybe reading Nietzsche might produce some insight on what to do. Then again, it might confuse things further. Nodding to his subordinate, he said, "Have an official report written up on the time, the date, and everything you observed at the scene. I will take care of the rest. And oh, by the way, make sure you get it down in full detail."

"I will, sir."

Putting the matter out of his mind for the moment, von Wert decided to read Nietzsche after all when the subordinate suddenly spoke up.

"Sir, there was one more thing the dying man said."

"What was that?"

"He said the main instigator had an accent. Was a foreigner."

"A foreigner?"

"That he wasn't German. But Dutch, or Scandinavian. Tall, fair-haired. And . . . he even recalled his rank: a sergeant. Decorated with an Iron Cross. Then the man expired before we could question him further."

Von Wert mused on this. "Interesting. We could possibly check the background of the men in our units with such a description."

"I thought of that too, sir. But lately we have become a hodgepodge of units thrown together from all branches of the military. It might be hard, sir, to single out one man. Especially with the Russians bearing down hard on us."

Realizing the truth in this, von Wert sighed. "I suppose we'll have to turn it over to a higher authority. As much as I think the military should handle its own dilemmas, the state police are often more adept at gathering needed information. Since it was SS men that were slain, the SS must be notified of the circumstances surrounding their demise." With that von Wert wrote out an order to be delivered promptly to the nearest SS office. He figured Danzig was the best bet for finding the right men to conduct an official investigation. When the subordinate had left with the order, Wert pulled out his book of Nietzsche and began to peruse his favorite aphorisms. He always found comfort in the wise words. An aerial bombardment was going on some kilometers to the west. Wincing occasionally at the disturbing noise, von Wert wondered about the murders of the SS. What had caused German soldiers to attack their own side? And who was the foreigner involved? Maybe they had all been foreigners—God forbid, they may even have been Russian infiltrators dressed in uniforms of the Wehrmacht. Or maybe there was another reason. Maybe several men had been arguing and one had simply gone haywire. Drunk and beyond control. Or fighting over a woman. He'd heard stories that Landsers, even from well-respected regiments, had been found looting and desecrating homes and villages left deserted by refugees. The German aptness for obedience and order was breaking down. With bombs still dropping in the distance, von Wert speculated wearily on the chaos that was spreading. But what could one officer do to prevent such turmoil? Whatever had happened in the case of the slain SS, it was no longer in his hands.

An orderly arrived presently bearing a tray filled with slices of ham and boiled cabbage. Von Wert put the book down and began to eat. After he had finished, he decided he'd read later. Instead, he picked up the glass of whiskey and speedily drained it. Then poured himself another.

CHAPTER 7

Far from sober, Ilya Grigolyuk had a brief return to sobriety as he gazed at fourteen German-made watches strapped to his left forearm. Watches that he had personally taken from the enemy. A peasant's son from a small village midway between the Ural Mountains and the city of Orsk, Grigolyuk, with little more than a week of training—he had hardly learned to fire a gun—had been hurriedly shipped to the front in the late winter of 1943 with hundreds of other raw recruits in unheated cattle wagons aboard trains that bounced and heaved repeatedly at each rough stretch of track. It was nightmarish enough dealing with the rickety transportation system, but if he thought getting off the train would be a relief, he suddenly found himself assembled in a division that was quickly thrown into the hellfire that became known as the Battle of Kharkov. Escaping from that costly defeat with his life, his rifle, and little else, Grigolyuk had endured the gradual push west toward Germany with a foreboding that he wouldn't last out the war. So many of his comrades had died, or been sent back home minus body parts, that he was certain it was a matter of time before he too became fertilizer for the earth.

But entering Germany had changed his negative presentiments. He and nearly every soldier around him (and only a retarded person would not have become wide-eyed at the wealth they now were encountering almost daily) were astonished beyond words at the land they had invaded. Farms with numberless cattle and pigs roaming freely; neatly spaced towns and villages with tidy homes adorned with baths and flushing toilets (something no one in his village had ever seen), chairs, tables, clocks, clothes, toys, and food and drink unimaginable in the Soviet Union—the so-called "Worker's Paradise." Why had the Germans attacked a country as poor as the USSR when they already had everything and more? He and his friends asked themselves this constantly. And why would those same Germans go to such lengths to destroy every city, town, and village their troops marched through? Grigolyuk had seen up close the devastation the Germans had wrought all across Russia. Towns buried under rubble. Whole villages erased from the map. Partisans, but mostly innocents, strung up on gibbets, their dangling corpses left to be picked to the bone by rooks and crows. He had not been to Stalingrad, but he'd heard from veterans of that campaign that the entire city was a gigantic ruin. A moonscape. The same was said of much of Leningrad. Not to mention the starvation of tens of thousands of her residents due to the years of German encirclement. He and the other men didn't need propaganda leaflets to stir them to a frenzy of revenge once they crossed Nazi soil, though there were plenty of government-sponsored rabble-rousers to add a greater pitch toward the effort of making the enemy bleed until there was no blood left. *Kill the German men! Rape their women! Kill! Kill! Kill!* Such broadcasts were becoming an hourly part of the Soviet soldier's education.

But the men as a whole were no longer preoccupied with merely slaying German soldiers and civilians. Ravishing the women had of course not lost its appeal (Grigolyuk smiled to himself thinking of the petite blonde he and twenty-two other soldiers had taken one right after another just the night before), but it was also the wealth of goods, the extravagance that was so alluring. He had already sent back a package containing silverware and candlesticks to his parents; now he prepared another filled with shirts, skirts, trousers, shoes. He only wished he could show his family in person what he had stumbled across.

Feeling the effects of a hangover, Grigolyuk smashed off the top of a wine bottle with his bayonet and chugged down the red liquid till it was nearly gone. An old hand had told him the best way to overcome a hangover was to drink more spirits. The wine revived him. He preferred vodka, as did most Russians, but the wine and schnapps he'd found in the German cottages and estates along the way were not to be turned down. One of his comrades, Bogdan, lay sprawled at the bottom of the foxhole they shared. Passed out from overindulging in alcohol of all kinds, the man's snoring sounded like the grunting of a wild boar. It was Bogdan's turn to keep watch over no man's land. Grigolyuk was about to rouse him, but decided to let his friend sleep. The entire company was in the same predicament. Becoming suddenly lethargic from the wine going to his head, Grigolyuk felt like snoozing himself. At this stage of the war—what the hell did it matter anyway? The big hats were often drunker than the enlisted men, and there were whisperings that some Red Army units had become so soused from all the excess alcohol they'd consumed in East Prussia, that they had begun gunning down their own officers and even commissars when ordered back into battle. At one sector a group of tanks led by drunken drivers had accidentally run over scores of fellow soldiers without even knowing what they were doing. Listless artillerymen had unknowingly let loose salvos on their own positions. Grigolyuk mused on all this without surprise or anger, gazing again at the watches that he had stolen off the corpses of dead Germans. Anything and everything could happen in war, and it did.

A little rain started to fall. A cold rain. Three hours after dusk. Grigolyuk, not caring about the cold or the darkening night, shut his eyes and drank more wine. It was only when he had tipped back the bottle that he vaguely heard the sound of someone stepping behind him. Opening his eyes and turning slowly, he barely had time to register a hand being clamped across his mouth, and even less time to register the knife blade being thrust into his neck, severing his jugular. Losing all sensation in his body, his last sight on earth was another knife being plunged into the neck of Bogdan. The stupid man was still snoring, then this too vanished from Grigolyuk's world.

"The bastard never even woke up." Wiping the blood off the knife that he had used to kill the sleeping man, Ziemans was astonished as the rest of them how easily they had pulled it off. Dreybach had done in the first sentry, and was now rifling the dead man's pockets. Foss grabbed the man's Tommy gun and tossed it to Tulm.

"Once you use that you'll never touch a rifle again," Foss said with conviction, rummaging through an ammunition pouch he had found in the trench. Foss had wanted to be in on one of the kills to prove he was mentally stable again, but Dreybach had dissuaded him. "Give yourself time, Aksel," he had told him, convincing the Dane with a gentle punch in the arm. Foss wasn't sure they trusted him any more. It had been Dreybach who came up with a plan to take out the Russian sentries. Running into strong Soviet positions after leaving their forest hideout, the four men had soon found themselves completely cut off from the German lines. Foss no longer had his compass—probably lost during his stay in the hospital tent—and the sounds of distant firefights seemed to carry from all directions. From his experiences in Russia, he knew very well how easily front lines became a mishmash of friendly and enemy units crossing one another's paths amid the turmoil of constant attack and retreat. Not knowing where they were in relation to any major town or city, Foss had ordered the men to return the way they had come, back to the forest. Dreybach, for once, had overruled him.

"Ivan's forward units might be kilometers ahead of us by now," Dreybach said with an authority he rarely used with Foss. "We can't afford to fall too far back." Tulm and Ziemans said nothing; they merely looked at Foss awaiting his response. When Foss nodded in agreement, they decided to find a weak point in the Russian lines and make a break toward the north.

"You were right, Dreybach." Foss gave his friend a bottle of wine that he had found beside the ammunition pouch. "Let's drink up when we get out of here."

Taking the bottle and stuffing it in a coat pocket, Dreybach squinted up at the rain that was continuing to fall from the sky. "Still have a long way to go, I'm afraid."

"Then let's move." Trying to regain a sense of command, Foss slipped out of the trench and ran at a crouch away from the Russian line. Caught off guard, the others had no choice but to follow.

"Hell, I wasn't finished!" Ziemans objected, cradling in one hand the two packs of cigarettes he had stolen from the corpse. He was sure there was plenty more booty to be found.

The rain hid the sound of their boots from all ears. It wasn't until they had sprinted past the last entrenchments that a Russian sentry, momentarily waking from a drunken stupor, saw the white uniforms fleeing into the darkness. "Stoi!" he screamed. "Nemetskiye soldaty! German soldiers!" Then picking up his sub-machine gun, fired erratically at the vanishing forms.

Grunting loudly, Dreybach slipped and lost his balance on a muddy spot. Foss turned back to help him up. "Go on . . . I'm fine." Dreybach's whisper sounded like a gasp.

Instinct told Foss that something was wrong. "Erwin . . . are you hit?"

"Go on, I said. I'll make it."

Swallowed up by the darkness and rain, Tulm and Ziemans halted beside a lone tree and waited for the other two men to appear. Seconds crawled by, and Tulm, panting from the sprint, became apprehensive. "If they don't show up soon, I'm going back to look for them."

Chewing his lower lip, Ziemans felt himself sweating despite the chilly rain. Putting a hand on Tulm's arm, he said, "You wouldn't find your mother's tit in this weather. Give them a few more minutes."

"They might not have a few minutes! If they are shot and bleeding—."

"Then there's not a damn thing we can do. The Russkis will shoot us too."

"You cynical bastard!" Uncharacteristically angry, Tulm shoved away Ziemans' hand and began to carefully retrace the way back.

He had only gone several paces when Foss staggered into view, pulling Dreybach along with him.

"What happened?" Tulm's voice sounded close to breaking.

Tulm must be near the edge like the rest of us, Foss thought to himself. He had draped Dreybach's arm over his shoulder and was practically dragging the man's whole weight. Glancing first at Tulm, then to Ziemans, Foss said, "Help me, for God's sake. He's been shot in the back."

A bullet had clipped Dreybach's right shoulder blade, leaving a mess of splintered bone and exposed tissue. Dreybach was gritting his teeth, trying not to cry out. The three other men half-carried him until they were well out of range of the Russian lines.

"To go through the whole goddamned war—and then this!" His arm hanging limply, Dreybach grimaced as the pain spread.

The rain fell harder. Fighting through his own anguish, Foss tried to steel his nerves. With Dreybach gravely wounded, and all of them lost on a dark night in the middle of a freezing downpour, not knowing where the German front line was, or even if the front line existed anymore, he simply had to control his wayward emotions and be the leader he had been in the past. The minutes trudged on, slowly to became hours. They halted for brief periods whenever Dreybach groaned in agony, though none of them slept. Foss wished he could have given Dreybach a shot of morphine, but mostly the veteran bore the pain without uttering a sound. Sometime before dawn the rain turned to mist, then ceased altogether. As a gray tinge spread across the eastern horizon, Foss and the others found themselves suddenly facing a machine-gun. Ziemans raised his own gun to fire when Foss knocked it aside. "They're Germans!" Foss yelled out.

The men tending the machine-gun were also about to fire. Then they saw the familiar coal scuttle helmets, and hesitated. The loader nervously called out, "Password?"

"We don't know the password." Keeping his gun lowered, Foss looked at the two men beseechingly. "We don't even know where the hell we are. The Russians shot our friend." Foss jerked his thumb toward Dreybach who was barely being held up by Tulm.

The machine gunners glanced at each other, uncertain. They were both older men, part of the Volkssturm. Natives of the East Prussian city of Elbing, they had been pressed into military service shortly after Christmas. Elbing itself was under attack by the Red Army, and the men were frightened at the predicament of their families. They had had no contact with home for over a month. Thrust into the forefront of the latest Russian incursions, they held no illusion about their own outcome.

"You either have to shoot us or let us through," Foss said impatiently, sensing the older men's indecision. "Our comrade needs prompt medical attention, else he'll bleed to death." Foss had tried staunching the blood flow with a strip of his coat sleeve that he had sliced off, but he knew it was merely a temporary bandage. Dreybach's wound would become infected soon, if it wasn't already.

The two Volkssturm continued to wrestle with uncertainty when a massively built sergeant appeared from behind their gun pit. His eyes becoming slits, the sergeant stared at the four wet and bedraggled Landsers with suspicion.

Sensing a deteriorating situation, Foss quickly pulled out his paybook and tossed it at the other sergeant's feet. "My soldbuch has all my information," he said steadily. "But don't ask for the password, because we haven't a clue. We've been seeking our lines the whole night. If you don't trust me, then place me under arrest. But please . . . find a medic for my friend."

The near despair in Foss's voice did not go unnoticed. The man who now paged through his identity booklet took no more than a minute before returning it.

"You were in Russia for quite a while," the big sergeant said.

Foss nodded, but didn't answer.

Holding up his left hand, which was missing the thumb and forefinger, the sergeant sighed sadly. "Lost these outside Leningrad. Spent two years besieging that accursed place. What the hell were we even doing in Russia?" Not wasting any more time, the sergeant sent one of the Volkssturm back to seek medical aid for Dreybach. Two orderlies with a stretcher arrived in minutes. They carried the now unconscious man to a dressing station. Foss, Tulm, and Ziemans wanted to go with him, but protocol wouldn't allow it. Instead, they slumped down beside the machine-gun. The sergeant gave each of them a cigarette.

"Sorry about your mate," he said, as he offered them matches.

Foss took awhile before speaking. "We've been through a lot together. Erwin Dreybach is a first-class soldier."

"I'm with you there." The sergeant glanced disdainfully at the Volkssturm men manning the machine-gun. "Hard finding good recruits these days. We're left with nothing but the scrap heap."

Scanning the area, Foss noticed that the gum emplacement lay near a side-road. He commented on this fact to the sergeant.

"That's because the main roads are so clogged with civilian carts and milk-cows that military traffic can't go more than a few meters without coming to a complete halt. Nothing but a goddamned mess. Then when Ivan shows up it becomes pandemonium. The civilians scatter like crazed mice and our soldiers can't fire for fear of hitting our own people. Though usually the poor sods get run over by Russian tanks or gunned down in droves. I've seen horrific sights. Things I'll never forget."

"We've all seen such sights," Foss agreed, with Tulm and Ziemans nodding grimly in confirmation.

"So that's why we're guarding the side-roads," the sergeant went on, "to allow our vehicles and men safe access. Or as safe as can be, considering we have almost no ammunition."

A picture of Jutta ran through Foss's mind. "Where are the civilians headed?"

"Everyone's trying to get to Pillau. To the port. Where the Kriegsmarine can hopefully carry them safely away from Ivan."

"Pillau? I thought we were closer to Danzig."

"Then you really are lost."

"Isn't Pillau near Koenigsberg?" asked Tulm.

"It is."

"But we got cut off from Koenigsberg."

"Tulm's right," Foss added. "That was days ago. So where is the front line?"

The sergeant cracked a strange smile. "There's no longer any coherence in the front lines. Turn right—you'll meet a German. Turn left—and Ivan's pointing a rifle at you. Some days we clear enough of a path through the foremost Russians to allow the civilians to go west. Even a train or two has gotten out. Then Ivan counterattacks and we lose everything we gained. But each time we renew the battle, we have fewer men, fewer tanks, fewer rounds of ammo. And the Luftwaffe hasn't helped us in a thousand years. Often we have to blow up our own tanks because there's no more petrol." The sergeant shook his head and swore. "I've heard stories that the top brass confiscated the last barrels of petrol to keep their damn cars running while they fled to the western ports. And they leave orders for us to fight to the last man. Those swine! What do they expect us to do—fight with tooth and nail!"

"No—we're just waiting for Adolf's wonder-bombs." Ziemans, not holding back the sarcasm, finished his cigarette, then pulled out a pack he had stolen from the dead Russians. Lighting another cigarette, he began to smoke again.

Foss realized the other sergeant needed to let off steam. Apparently in charge of untested Volkssturm units, he probably hadn't spoken with veteran soldiers in a long time. The man continued talking, but Foss shut his eyes after awhile. Drained from the previous night, he fell into a dreamless slumber.

How long he slept he never knew. A thunderous explosion woke him instantly. Clods of dirt smacked him in the chest. A piece of metal flew by an inch from his face. He rolled, his instinct refined from years of dodging shells. Another explosion lifted the earth around him, lifting him as well. He landed on his back with a thud, knocking the air from his lungs. It felt like he was trapped under a huge boulder. Trying not to panic, he willed himself to turn slowly on to his stomach, then crawled for the nearest depression in the ground. The Russians were now shelling without stop. Foss hugged the ground like a baby would its mother. He dug with his hands through the rain-wet soil until his whole body was covered with mud. A long drawn-out scream sounded from close by. Foss didn't raise his head to see who it was. For a brief moment the shelling ceased. Without hesitation, Foss leaped up and sprinted away as fast as he could. Another man ran beside him. It was Tulm.

The two men made it to a trench where other Landsers crouched low to the earth, barely even looking up to note the newcomers. Foss was breathing heavily. "Where is Ziemans?" he asked, as he gulped in air.

Equally fatigued, Tulm shrugged. "No idea. One of the first shells took out the sergeant and one of the machine-gunners. The other hightailed it out of there. I didn't see Ziemans anywhere."

Foss deliberated whether to go back and look for him. He got up to go when the Russian guns started thundering again. The shells fell for another hour. Men died, horribly. When quiet finally reigned, the inevitable Russian attack ensued. Tanks, assault guns, infantry in the thousands. What remained of the battered German line was overrun. Foss and Tulm, anxious at the whereabouts of Ziemans, waited until the last moment before escaping with a few dozen other Landsers who had remained behind as a rearguard. They ran to the next defense line, but the Russians overcame it after a short, fierce battle in which the dead from both sides piled up on the wet earth. Finally the Russians were thrust back with the appearance of a group of four Jagdpanzers. These formidable tank destroyers, which the soldiers nicknamed "Hetzers," knocked out eight T-34s in a matter of minutes. The Russians called off their attack.

His greatcoat torn and muddy, Foss found a nearby corpse and removed the jacket from it. Some of the inexperienced soldiers gaped at him, but he didn't care. Taking off his old coat, and making certain he left nothing in the pockets, he draped it over the corpse, then put on the new one. Despite a few blood stains, it was mostly dry, and significantly warmer. Gesticulating to Tulm to follow him, they moved to a spot out of hearing of the others.

Foss yearned to look for Ziemans, but going back now would be suicide. He surmised the Russians had taken up positions in the old trench line. He wouldn't get five meters before being shot. "If there's anybody who will make it back, it will be Ziemans," he said, trying to display more confidence than he felt. The shoulder he had banged on the helmet days back had begun to hurt again. His whole body in fact, ached from fatigue. He thought of the sergeant at the machine gun nest—now dead. Snuffed out in the blink of an eye. Foss sensed that he was again losing control of himself. He wished he could talk to Dreybach. *Dreybach.* The most indestructible soldier he'd known the entire war, but even he had succumbed to the frailty of being human.

"I wonder if I'll ever be able to write a poem again?" Foss asked aloud, though more to himself than to Tulm.

"It won't always be like this, Aksel." Tulm rubbed his hands together to keep the circulation flowing. "We had a life before the war. We'll have one after, too."

"Maybe. Maybe not."

"Of course we will. I don't plan to spend the rest of my days contemplating my time in the war."

Foss looked at Tulm. The man was shivering. His face, pale. "Are you sick, Tulm?"

"No! Just cold."

Foss was surprised at the surliness of Tulm's tone. It was unusual. "Here, take this coat. I'll find another one."

"No, I'll find one myself." And with that, Tulm stood up. He walked back to the area where Foss had found his. There were other corpses in the vicinity. "I'll get us some chow, too," he called back over his shoulder.

"Be careful," Foss admonished, but Tulm was already lost to view. Foss suddenly felt alone. Dreybach and Ziemans were gone, and Tulm appeared ill. Then he remembered the medical pass. Reaching into the front pocket of his tunic where he had stashed it, Foss's heart began to thump.

The pocket was empty!

He frantically checked the rest of his clothing but there was no paper. Not even Jutta's address. He nearly rose to return to the body on the ground, but he had already gone through the pockets of his old coat thoroughly before discarding it. What could have happened? He must have lost it during the retreat. Or perhaps the shock from one of the many explosions had blown it clear away. Regardless of what had happened, he no longer had an official pass back to Denmark. He swore, but there was nothing to be done about it. There was no leaving the war. He'd end up lying on the cold earth like the coat-less corpse. His family in Denmark never to know what had befallen him.

Lighting a cigarette, Foss inhaled the smoke deeply into his lungs. Maybe he could induce the asthma to return. That might get him out. Or give himself a self-inflicted wound. A bullet through a hand or a foot would suffice. But Foss was too aware of what happened to such cases. He'd end up getting another bullet. And that one from a firing squad.

Continuing to smoke, he huddled in his new coat in the muddy trench. The wind had picked up, and was blowing fiercely from the east. Foss closed his eyes and thought of nothing. Hunger stirred inside him.

So he waited for Tulm.

FEBRUARY 1945

CHAPTER 8

Dozens of scattered and decimated German units found themselves cut off and forced back toward the coast by the Red Army's unending pressure. They soon learned that they were enveloped in a pocket between the towns of Braunsberg and Heiligenbeil. Those from divisions that had been almost annihilated, were attached to other combat groups. Some who had gotten lost—whether by accident or on purpose—wandered the sandy dunes along the Frisches Haf, the freshwater lagoon that separated the mainland from the Frische Nehrung. The Frische Nehrung was a thin peninsula bordering Danzig Bay, and connecting with the port of Pillau in the north with that of Stutthof, nearly a hundred kilometers to the south. With Koenigsberg already besieged, word carried that the Russians were thrusting hard to capture Danzig, but no one was certain of anything. With their backs to the sea, and the Russians in front of them, Foss and Tulm and a few others decided to head north toward Pillau. The lagoon had frozen over and thousands of refugees were making their way on foot or were borne hurriedly by horse and carriage. People and animals slipped on the ice, and in some places large cracks juddered, causing widespread fear that the ice was beginning to thaw. When Tulm looked apprehensive about venturing out too far, Foss squeezed his shoulder.

"Don't worry about it melting," Foss said with more reassurance than he felt inside. But they couldn't stay where they were. "The weather's too cold, Tulm. We'll make it to Pillau."

"I think you're right," one of the other Landsers said. Snow was falling, and a forceful gale blew inland from the Baltic. Foss stepped first on the ice. The rest gradually followed suit.

The going was slow. The traffic of refugees impeded their progress. Carts had broken down, horses went lame, and people who had been fleeing the Russians for weeks, suddenly began weeping, or screamed with the fever of hunger, fear, madness. Some wandered off alone to die. Mothers, too weak to feed their new-borns, left their babies to freeze on the ice while they continued toward the safety of the ports.

Like those that continued the trek, Foss focused only on the task of reaching Pillau. The plight of the refugees was beyond his control to alter. His feet felt like blocks of granite, but still he plodded through the ice and snow drifts. Occasionally he glimpsed behind him to make certain Tulm was keeping up. He was. Though some of the other soldiers who had started with them, were nowhere to be seen.

Then the unmistakable drone of aircraft. Approaching from the northeast.

"Goddamn it!" someone exclaimed.

"Planes aren't supposed to fly in weather like this," came another voice, drained of hope.

But despite the weather, a squadron of enemy planes flying low to the ground, bore down on the hapless hordes of humanity seeking to cross the Frisches Haf. Machine guns raked the long lines of people and carriages. Some of the rounds fired were tracers, making a beautiful pyrotechnics display against the gray winter landscape, except for the fact that the bullets were meant to tear apart human flesh. German military trucks and other vehicles, making headway across the densely packed ice, were set afire, and exploded when their gas tanks were ignited. Hideous screams rent the bitterly cold air, and for a moment, Foss stood transfixed at the horrors occurring around him. There was nowhere to dive for cover. Expecting to be pulverized at any moment by a round, he suddenly espied a discarded sled a short distance away. Tossing himself to the ice, Foss slid beneath the sled, lying on his stomach and holding his head in his hands. A burst of fire ripped close to the sled, sending splinters of ice against Foss's helmet. Then as he held his breath, the planes flew off as quickly as they had come. Once the roar of their engines became a faint buzz, Foss crawled out and immediately looked for Tulm.

There was no sight of him. "Tulm!" he yelled. *Don't let me lose my last friend.* He searched frantically wherever he found a body on the ice. And there were plenty of bodies. He saw one corpse lying atop another. He pulled it off. Tulm was sprawled underneath it. Foss bent down to him.

"Don't die, Max," Foss pleaded, caressing Tulm's cheek with a shaking hand. Then the eyes slowly opened.

"I'm still here, Aksel." Tulm attempted a weak smile, but there were tears in his eyes. Foss too, cried. A few minutes passed before they were able to croak out any words.

"I don't know what happened," Tulm said vaguely. I heard gunfire and I ran. Then this man"—he gazed down at the corpse that was spattered with blood—screamed out and bumped into me. The next thing I knew, the whole weight of his body had pinned me down."

Foss had heard such stories before. A soldier saved by lying beneath the dead body of his comrade. The corpse would take the brunt of the bullets and shell fragments. Wiping his tears away, Foss glanced in the direction where the planes had flown. He was certain there would be more.

Tulm read his mind, and the two men returned to the business of marching toward sanctuary. The sights they saw were little different from what they witnessed in Russia. A fire raged where a truck transporting wounded soldiers had been blown up. All the men died instantly, or were too weak too call out for help. Horses riddled with bullets littered the ice. Starving refugees, no longer abashed at crude and uncivilized behavior, took out knives and saws and greedily cut off great slabs of meat from the dead beasts, then wrapped them in scarves and blankets to be cooked at a later time. Surviving family members grieved over fallen loved ones, but that was all they could do. There was nowhere to bury them. When the lagoon eventually melted, their bodies would sink below the waters. Foss looked straight ahead. There was no looking back. If he had learned anything from the damned war it was that trying to resurrect anything was not only pointless—but a mark of insanity. The stricken and wailing refugees on the Frisches Haf merely reiterated that fact.

So he walked on, Tulm keeping stride with him. Nothing else in the world mattered at the moment. Except getting to Pillau. *And once we reach Pillau . . .*

They reached it just before nightfall, having paused only once to quench their thirst with water and to share a few morsels of frozen bread. The last food they had between them. Exhausted to the point of collapse, they along with other soldiers in similar condition were afforded a day and a half to sleep and rest. A luxury among luxuries at this stage of the war. So as to reestablish army discipline away from the massed exodus of refugees now crowding the port, the high command moved most of the soldiers who had come over on the ice to a spot close to the coast a short distance north of Pillau. Here the men recuperated. There was even talk of a new army being assembled by Hitler that would be sent east to throw back the Russians. But most just scoffed at this. They were mainly concerned about their own reassignment. Not a few hoped they'd be transferred by ship to Danzig, or Stettin. Some of the more optimistic men spoke of being moved to the Rhine region to face the British and Americans (where more than a few planned to willfully give themselves up just to get out of the war).

But the majority of the Landsers who were veterans of the Eastern Front considered this a hope beyond hope. Reality had become too bleak to believe in anything so fanciful.

More imminent worries were even closer at hand. On the outskirts of Pillau as the men limped in from the Frisches Haf, they were greeted by a young soldier—probably no more than sixteen by the look of him—hung from a lamp post. His face, a mixture of purple and gray, bore signs of terror, as though his last moments alive were beyond bearing. On his chest was hung a placard: "I deserted my post. I declined to defend German women and children." But if the Nazis intended the effect of his execution to scare other soldiers into remaining more vigilant, they mostly failed. Men instead became angry, or apathetic. They had little chance of surviving anyway. They didn't need to see this.

Foss and Tulm sat with a score of other men beside a burned out building next to a deserted quay just west of the town of Fischhausen. Further west stood a forest that extended a little inland from the coast and stretched almost to Pillau, some ten kilometers away. They had been given a mug full of lukewarm soup, devoid of anything nutritious except for the taste of turnips and a few pieces of stringy meat. No one dared to guess what type of animal it was. The repetitious booming of artillery thundered somewhere to the northeast. Most of the men had finished eating when gunshots erupted from a bomb-ruined warehouse across the street. Everyone grabbed his gun. Foss and Tulm and a handful of others decided to investigate. Orders had been issued earlier to hold the road to Pillau at all costs. Precious time was needed to allow the Kriegsmarine to evacuate the tens of thousands of German refugees and wounded who waited along the pier anxiously staring seaward. Foss entered the warehouse first, pushing stealthily through a poorly boarded-up entrance. The sight that met his eyes glued his feet to the floor.

"Oh, my God!" exclaimed Tulm, coming to a standstill beside his sergeant. The rest of the soldiers crowded beside them.

Below, on the floor, blood poured from four bodies lying on their backs beside one another in a pile of sawdust. Civilians. All had been shot in the right temple. Two small girls, an adult woman, an adult man. A pistol was clenched in the man's right hand.

"Didn't want to get captured by the Russians," a man standing next to Tulm said, while crossing himself.

Noticing a ring bearing a swastika on one of the dead man's fingers, Foss said darkly, "That . . . or they didn't fancy living in a world not run by the Nazis." *Though were his daughters even given a choice.*

Foss led the way out again. None of them thought about burying the corpses. Or even covering them. Death was present everywhere—the suicide of a petty Nazi official and his family members made small news these days. A freezing wind blew off the sea. The sky was dark, and already snowflakes were tumbling to the earth. Sitting down again, Foss whirled abruptly when he heard Tulm shouting his name with excitement.

"Jesus, Aksel—the man must have nine lives!"

"Who?"

Another voice behind him. "Who do you think, you stupid Viking."

Turning again, for a long moment Aksel was beyond speech. Then he said, "The devil must have thought you were too much to handle. Or else he sent you back to plague the rest of us."

Cracking a grin, Ziemans smoothed a hand gingerly across a scabbed cut that ran down his forehead and across the top of his left eyebrow. Dirty, disheveled, his coat and pants torn in various places, Ziemans indeed appeared as if he had just come back from Satan's lair. Despite past differences, he hugged Foss and Tulm with affection. Then opening up his coat, he removed a bottle of schnapps.

"Where in the world did you find that?" Tulm was beside himself with envious surprise.

"My father told me once that the army is filled with drunks. And where there's drunks, there's bound to be booze." Ziemans broke off the top of the bottle, took a swig, then passed it to his comrades. So they drank, and Ziemans related his story. Sheltering as best he could when the Russian bombs fell in the same attack that had thrown Foss into the air, he barely had a second to leap aside as a T-34 rolled over his position, crushing two other Landsers hiding with him. Running for his life, he luckily found a woodsy area to lie low while enemy infantry swept the German lines.

Pausing to drain the last drops of the schnapps, Ziemans surveyed the ruins of the small seaside village where he and the others were now quartered. The entire coastal area around Pillau had for some time come under Russian bombing raids, and now resembled a place that had been razed to rubble by a horde of vandals. The usual tidiness of German towns was lost. Emptying too much of the drink down his throat at once, Ziemans began to cough. Foss patted him on the back.

Taking a moment to regain his composure, Ziemans glared at the now empty bottle, then swore vilely. "I think I'd rather be crushed under the treads of a tank than go in the way that nearly finished me. Some Russian bastard tried to torch me with a flamethrower when I lay in the woods. But I shot him in the balls before he could fry me. He was crying for his mama when I got the hell out of there." Throwing the empty bottle down, then closing his eyes, Ziemans sighed several times before resuming his tale. "I didn't think I was going to make it. You two were nowhere to be found. I'd thought you'd both bought it. At one point I had no choice but to play dead. Russkies swarming over the ground like fleas on a dog's ass. One of them booted me in the head to see if I was really a goner. Gave me this nice little scratch"—he pointed to the cut—"but then we counterattacked. Ivan was thrown back, and I managed to get a lift on a truck before it ran out of gas. I remember someone shouting that we could reach Pillau by crossing the frozen water. And so that's how I made it all the way to the wonderful seaside resort of Pillau. I take it you journeyed here in the same fashion."

Nodding with a smile, Foss never would have thought he was glad to see Ziemans again—but he was. Tulm, he knew, felt the same.

"Any word on our grumpy friend from Hamburg?" An unusual tenderness tinged Ziemans' voice.

"I inquired about him once we reached the port area," Foss said, slowly. "We didn't expect good news, but . . . would you believe it, Dreybach is in Pillau. He and some other badly wounded were taken out by boat. A channel had been cut through the ice. He probably made it here before we did." Foss became emotional but he no longer cared about maintaining his composure. The days of being stoic all the time were over. Wiping away several tears that had rolled down his cheek, he said, "Dreybach was shot up rather badly. I don't think any of us realized it at the time. But at least he's being looked after. He's bedded down in a make-shift hospital near the wharf. Waiting with the other wounded for a reliable ship to sail them the hell out of here."

"Any chance we might be able to go with him?"

"No chance of that, Ziemans. Every able-bodied man is needed to halt the Russians."

Tulm gave Foss a sharp look, almost a glare. He was about to utter something, then averted his eyes when Foss noticed him staring.

"I've never been in a big boat before." His face wistful, Ziemans lit a cigarette. "Always fancied sailing aboard one of those huge cruise liners. A pal of mine once told me that it's nothing but drinking and fucking—a garden of Eden on the sea. I'd trade that anytime for this hellhole."

Foss shuddered visibly. "I suppose you haven't heard?"

"Heard what?"

"About the *Wilhelm Gustloff?*" Tulm broke in.

"No, I haven't," Ziemans said. "Sounds like one of Adolf's buddies."

Foss shuddered again. He ached to know at this moment where Jutta was. *Had she been on the Gustloff!* Inhaling deeply, he looked at Ziemans and said, "We only just heard the news ourselves. It was a ship that took off from the port of Gotenhafen. About a week ago. Sailing for the west. But it never got there. Sunk by a Russian submarine. No one knows the exact number of people on board—refugees, mainly. Five thousand. Maybe even as many as ten thousand. No one was able to count them all when they boarded. But whatever the amount, the survivors supposedly numbered only in the hundreds."

Ziemans whistled. "If that's true, that makes the *Titanic* look like a side show."

"God, I hope Jutta wasn't on board . . ."

"I hope not either," Ziemans said, after a few moments elapsed. "A pretty girl. You seemed to like her." His words were sincere.

"I did . . . I do." Foss wondered suddenly if by uttering the past tense, that Jutta might indeed by dead. He tried to throw it off as superstition—but the feeling of dread did not go away.

They spent the rest of the day digging anti-tank ditches alongside hundreds of other soldiers. An order had been given that a new line of fortifications was to be erected. Mounds of earth, sandbags, wrecked vehicles, and bricks and pieces of wood gathered up from the ruins of houses and buildings were knitted together as barricades to help delay the eventual Russian attacks. None of the soldiers from the general staff down to the lowest enlisted man felt any confidence that the Soviets would be delayed for even the briefest of periods. Only a smattering of tanks remained to guard the entrances to Pillau, and these were nearly without fuel, and needed repair work to be fully functional. A small number of anti-tank guns remained, but shells were scarcer than turtle eggs as one man put it, and could only be used sparingly. Once the Red Army got close, the Landsers would have to rely on Panzerfausts, which, despite their limitations, were plentifully stocked. Machine guns and grenades would then be used to knock out the infantry. Yet all of them knew they would be overwhelmed by sheer numbers in the end. Only the most die-hard Nazis believed in final victory at this point. The writing was on the wall. The prospects of getting out of Pillau were dimming by the day.

And for that very reason, military motorboats and ferries, as well as merchant vessels and the occasional cruise ship, continued to reach the pier to take people away. Large sorties of Russian planes several times flew over to strafe and bomb the cues of people lined up along the quay. But the proximity of formidable German naval vessels in the bay kept them from flying over the town too often. The threat of being hit by flak from persistent anti-aircraft fire, and the ever-present harsh winter weather, kept most of the Soviet pilots grounded, or scouring other areas for easier targets. The heavy guns from the German ships also forced Russian tank formations to become wary of venturing too close to the coastal defenses. Precise coordinates estimating the Russian positions had been wired from the Wehrmacht to their naval brethren. Soon Russian tanks trying to rush Koenigsburg were smashed to pieces by accurate cannon fire delivered by the Kriegsmarine. The Russian high command decided to wait and let the Germans starve awhile before they'd attempt another major attack. In the meantime they would shell the German city with savage regularity.

The next morning Foss obtained permission for he and Tulm and Ziemans to visit Dreybach in Pillau. Normally under such dire circumstances no soldier was allowed to leave his post. But the officer in charge was an older man, a former civilian who had been forced to put on a uniform. He did no more than raise an eyebrow at the request.

"I don't need to tell you the penalty for desertion," the officer said without trying to sound condescending. "It's one thing to give the excuse of being cut off by a Russian attack, but if the Feldgendarmerie catch you milling about for any extended length of time around the lines of civilians near the pier, then you haven't a prayer. And don't expect me to try and save you. Be back by suppertime, or else I'll alert the military police myself."

Foss saluted the officer with graciousness. Nine times out of ten, for such a request, he'd have been turned down with a harsh word. And maybe even be disciplined for misconduct.

They hitched a ride on a half-track and found Dreybach in a makeshift infirmary of torn and weather-worn tents. Such poor shelters were barely a deterrent to the icy breezes whipping in from the strait that led to the sea.

"They must have been using these since Operation Barbarossa," Ziemans remarked mockingly. Barbarossa had been the initial invasion of the Soviet Union, more than three and a half years earlier.

Dreybach was in a tent with four other soldiers, all of them in seemingly critical condition. Half sitting atop a matting of straw spread loosely on the ground, and covered by a dark woolen blanket, Dreybach appeared to be in a deep sleep. His breaths were loud, labored.

"Should we even wake him? He might need to rest." Tulm kept his voice to just above a whisper.

Foss dithered. Disturbing a wounded man could set him back. Yet they probably wouldn't get a second chance to visit him. Not wanting to disturb his friend, Foss decided it best to leave. He could send a note or letter later to let Dreybach know that they had come to see him. Foss gently placed a hand on Dreybach's forearm. Lifting it just as gently, he then beckoned Tulm and Ziemans to follow him out of the tent.

Just then one of the other wounded men cried out in pain, causing Dreybach to stir. He opened one eye, then the other. Seeing his comrades shocked him into full awareness.

"Aksel . . . "

"Yes, Erwin, I'm here. So is Max. And Johann."

"When . . . did you come?" Dreybach's voice sounded stertorous, his face racked with extreme effort as his mouth formed each word.

"Just now," Foss answered, putting his hand back on Dreybach's arm. "We're stationed some kilometers north of Pillau. Things in this sector are rather peaceful at the moment . . . considering what all of us have recently been through."

"Yes, we even have dancing girls," Ziemans added, "and ten flasks of liquor for each man."

Dreybach reacted to this with a brief smile. Then the smile vanished. "I've been told," he croaked, that I'll be sent home soon. But I don't believe the doctors. They're lying."

"Why would they lie about something like that?" Foss tried sounding more positive about Dreybach's chances than he felt. The man had a gray demeanor, and anyone with even the most rudimentary knowledge of wounds, could tell that his condition was grave. Foss glanced a moment at the other wounded men in the tent, one of whom was missing both legs, then he said, "People are embarking on boats here day and night, Erwin. Your turn will come—"

"I'm not sailing on any goddamned boat! If I'm to die—I'll make certain to die on land."

Dreybach's brazen interruption caused one of the other wounded to wake with a start. A teenage boy by the look of his smooth face, his eyes darted back and forth with unchecked terror. He then began to call out for his mother.

"Tell that little bastard to shut up," Dreybach said gruffly, raising one arm from beneath the blanket to weakly shake a fist at the boy. He tried to sit up from the floor but the effort taxed him and he lay back down, his breaths coming out in ragged gasps.

"Erwin," Foss said, "if you wish to live, you have no choice but to be evacuated by ship."

"Who says I want to live! What the hell do I have left to live for?"

A grim quiet overtook the tent; even the boy stopped muttering. Dreybach, his voice turning monotone, said, "There's nothing left for me in Hamburg. It's not home anymore because there's no one there waiting for me. No one there to greet me when I return . . . "

Foss and the others didn't know how to answer. The fire had gone out of Dreybach, had gone out long ago, but at least the war had kept his mind occupied, focused. Now with his wounding, there was indeed nothing left. But Foss couldn't stomach the notion of his friend dying so meekly. Men had suffered with loss for centuries, yet they had had the will to continue to survive. Kneeling down beside Dreybach, he said, "Erwin, you are still young. There are plenty of widows all over Germany. Plenty of women. They may not mean anything compared to your wife, but you could fall in love with at least one of them. You could even have more children, one day."

Dreybach didn't respond for awhile. Outside the tent it was snowing. The boy who had earlier cried out for his mother, had again fallen asleep. A steady rumbling could be heard far away. Koenigsburg was being shelled. Or bombed. Or both. The war had gone on for a long time. A generation of young men had known little else but war. And not only young men. But the entire German population. Dreybach reflected on this. Then he said, "I don't want to be alone. Like I said, there's no one left waiting for me. You"—he looked at Foss, Tulm, and lastly Ziemans—"are the only family I have. And now . . . I no longer even have you. They want to put me aboard a fucking ship with thousands of strange faces—I'll be all alone. And when we get torpedoed, I'll drown in the sea—all alone."

Foss knew his friend referred to the sinking of the *Wilhelm Gustloff*. After such a tragedy, even the most doughty of souls would be afraid of sailing under the current conditions. Foss had been told that refugees at Pillau, on learning of the sunk ship, had taken to the road again, following the long sand spit known as the Frische Nehrung that separated the Frisches Haf from Danzig Bay. The spit ran some sixty kilometers from Pillau in the northeast to the small town of Stutthof in the south, where the refugees decided they would rather take their chances trying to find a path through Soviet armies than to brave the submarine-infested waters of the Baltic. Foss empathized with Dreybach—but what else could be done. To stay here in a primitive hospital in an overpopulated port that would, in good weather, increasingly become a target for Russian bombers, was tantamount to kissing the world goodbye. And even if he survived the bombing, there would be eventual starvation rations to consider, and the fact that a Russian army would one day soon force a breakthrough and conquer the entire region of the Peyse and Pillau peninsulas. Any wounded Landers left behind would be shot en masse.

"You must go," Foss said with rising conviction. "If not for yourself, then do it for us—your comrades. Return to Germany and live. When this damn war's over, we'll all get together and drink a beer. I promise."

Dreybach grimaced. "I won't go alone. I told you that. And if they try to force me, I'll shoot myself first."

"What if one of us went with you?" Tulm's question was unexpected. Foss was as shocked by it as Dreybach.

"You mean sneak aboard?" Ziemans laughed harshly. "We'd be hung from the ship's rail as a warning to all other would-be stowaways."

"Not if a legitimate pass was produced." Tulm's face was earnest. He gave Foss a long glance before looking away.

"And where the hell would we get that?" Ziemans, his tone even more derisive, lit a cigarette, then gave it to Dreybach. He then lit one for himself. "Your heart's in a good place, Tulm, but I can't say the same for your brain. Every goddamned German soldier in East Prussia would trade ten years of his life for a sick-card stamped by a proper Nazi doctor. Even a kike like you would accept one gleefully."

"Don't be an idiot, Ziemans," Foss reprimanded.

"Aw, I'm just kidding. I couldn't have spent half the war with Tulm if I didn't like the bastard." Turning to Tulm, he smiled. "And I mean that! From one bastard to another."

Tulm didn't return the smile, but he nodded, accepting Ziemans' peace offering. Returning to the subject at hand, he said, "So Erwin, if one of us went with you, would you get on a ship?"

Puffing away at the cigarette, Dreybach shrugged. "I might."

One of the other wounded man, his left arm amputated at the elbow, stirred, then woke. Seeing Dreybach smoking, he said, "The doctor told you not to smoke. Because of your condition."

"I don't care what the doctor said." Dreybach continued to smoke.

"You should give it to me. You're just wasting it."

"Rot in hell, you scum."

The one-armed man turned to Ziemans. "Could you spare me one?"

"Sorry mate, but these are the last I had," Ziemans lied. He had three packs in his coat pocket. But good cigarettes were scarce these days. He had no intention of handing them out to every stranger who asked for a freebie.

Just then a doctor entered the tent. He frowned when he saw Dreybach smoking. Noting the three fit soldiers, he said quietly but sternly, "You men will have to leave now."

Not wanting to tangle with authority, Foss led the others from the tent. But before leaving for Fischhausen, he told Dreybach that they'd be back to visit again. Soon.

That evening while Ziemans performed sentry duty, Foss found Tulm sitting by the quay. Thinking he might be getting inspiration for a poem, Foss tiptoed away when Tulm turned and called out to him, "What is it, Aksel?"

"I couldn't sleep. Then I saw you weren't in your bunk."

"I'm not sleepy either."

"Were you composing a poem?"

"No. Just sitting here."

"Do you wish to be alone?"

"No, not especially." Tulm glanced slowly side to side, as though worried someone might be listening. "I actually wanted to talk to you without Ziemans hearing what I had to say."

Foss hesitated a moment. He thought back to the conversation they'd had weeks earlier before the Russian breakthrough. The discussion about Germany's downfall and the possibility of moving to Denmark. "Is something wrong?"

"Yes, there is something wrong. Dreybach. He looked pitiful. A shell of what he was. He's dying. And there's not a chance in hell he'll improve unless he receives better medical treatment than they offer here."

"I realize that as much as you do." Pensive with worry, Foss heard the lapping of wavelets against the wooden poles holding up the pier. The soothing sound reminded him of the fishing boats tied to the dock at Nyhavn in Copenhagen. The smell of salt in the air. Suddenly he felt homesick. Tulm's words brought him back to the moment at hand.

"So since we realize it, Aksel, what do you propose we do?"

Foss noted a harsher-than-usual tone to Tulm's voice. But then Tulm had been acting strange as of late. His mannerisms had turned gruff, and he became distant whenever Foss approached him with small talk.

"I'm devoid of answers," Foss said straightly. "Ask me to blow up a T-34, and I'm your man. But with this situation I'm clueless."

"Do you mind if I offer a suggestion?"

"You know I don't mind—why even say that!"

Tulm knitted his eyebrows, as if he was clearing his brain before finding the words he wanted to use. Then he said, "We all have our secrets, Aksel. And I suppose it's naive to expect a sergeant to share everything with his men. Though I once thought otherwise of you."

Momentarily speechless, Foss was taken aback by Tulm's continued coldness. "Something's obviously eating at you, Max. Alright, I've rubbed you wrong. So tell me what the hell it is."

"This." Pulling an envelope from his pocket, Tulm handed it to Foss.

It took Foss a few seconds before he realized what he held. *The medical pass.* "Dear God," Foss said faintly, "I thought I lost it."

"You did lose it. I found it next to you when you were sleeping. Soon after Dreybach had been hauled off to the rear. I was going to give it back to you, but then the battle occurred."

"So . . . you opened it?"

"Not then. Not until later. I saw it was a medical form of some kind, and I guess curiosity got to me in the end."

Foss was a little annoyed at Tulm's intrusion into something that did not concern him. He would never have peeked into another man's personal belongings, regardless of the demands of the occasion. But maybe I'm being too hard on him. He may have opened it out of worry, thinking I had a fatal disease. Putting his irritation aside, Foss stared at the envelope with disbelief. He'd been given a reprieve—a second time.

"Now Dreybach can sail without feeling alone."

His face tightening with emotion, Foss looked at Tulm, then looked away. Like so many other things he'd lost in the war: friends, mementos, his very youth, he no longer concerned himself with the supposed fate of the letter. It was in the past. But this time—the past was still present. The unexpected had become a miracle. Maybe there was a God after all. Maybe something was looking after his welfare.

"I guess you had your reasons for not telling anyone," Tulm said coolly.

"I would have told you in time. But I wasn't sure I would even use it. Didn't want to leave you and the others." Foss sensed that Tulm didn't believe him. "That's the truth, Max. The doctor practically had to force me to accept it. He said I was unfit for duty because of extreme combat fatigue. But even now—I'm uncertain whether to use it . . . "

Tulm didn't speak for several minutes, but instead wandered a few feet along the quay. Russian mortar fire could he heard on the outskirts of Fischhausen. When Tulm wandered back he said, "I know it's petty of me to be angry with you. Probably I'm just jealous. But you've been a good soldier, and more than that—you've been a good man. A good friend. You'll be more than a fool, Aksel, if you don't leave this killing ground and return to Denmark."

It was Foss's turn to stay silent. He placed the letter carefully in his pocket, then tapped on the spot twice just to make sure it was where it was. Releasing a tired sigh, he said, "You don't need to put me on a pedestal. I did what I had to do to survive—and for all of us to survive. Though whatever I did, or didn't do, wasn't good enough for those who are never coming back. It seems unfair that I receive a ticket out of here, while you and Ziemans are left to hold the line."

"Stop being so Danish. You told me on many an occasion how you couldn't stand your national attitude of loathing men of talent, men with a gift. What do you call it . . . "

"Jante's Law: Never think you're better than your neighbor."

"But you are better," Tulm said pointedly. "You got us back to Germany from the inferno of the Soviet Union."

Foss felt embarrassed by Tulm's praise—again, it was his Danishness coming to the forefront. Not wanting to seem ungrateful, he smiled, and shook his head. "It wasn't just my doing. None of us would have made it if we hadn't acted with one head on one body. You're the best lead man I've ever served with—and there have been many. You saved us from many an ambush, many minefields."

"Yes, we all played our parts. Even Ziemans. He supplied us with fine wines."

The two men laughed. Then Tulm said stolidly, "You have to go. Those are doctor's orders. More importantly—it may save Dreybach's life."

Tulm was right. There was no getting around the fact that Dreybach would benefit from the presence of a friend. Foss held no doubts that Dreybach might follow up on his plan to commit suicide if forced to do something against his will.

"Alright, I'll go," Foss agreed."

"What do we say to Ziemans?"

"I'll tell him shortly before the time. He might react badly if we tell him now. First, I'll need to make sure I can book a passage. There's a long cue of refugees at the port."

"Soldiers always get preference. Especially wounded ones."

Sighing again wearily, Foss wasn't so certain. "All these hapless civilians running in desperation for their lives have made the Nazis appear inept. You and I both know they've handled this crisis in East Prussia badly."

"Like rank amateurs. The whole lot of them are rotten." Utter disdain was in Tulm's voice. "I'll go relieve Ziemans now."

As Tulm turned to leave, Foss stopped him. Hesitantly, he said, "Awhile back you seemed on the verge of telling me something. About your past. Your family. Your heritage . . . "

Tulm waited, his face unreadable.

"You know I've always meant well concerning Jews, and I've loathed the imbeciles who bullied you at times. You don't have to tell me a damned thing—but if you ever need to unload, well, I'm not sure what I'm trying to say. Just that—you can trust me."

Tulm made a gesture with his eyes, and once more turned to go. Then just as quickly spun around again to face Foss. "I've never told anyone in the army this," Tulm began slowly. "My . . . father was Jewish. He was wounded severely during the Great War. Was sent back to Dusseldorf. My mother worked in a hospital where he was being treated. They fell in love. Even planned to get married once he recovered. She never told her parents. They would have disapproved." Pausing to swallow, Tulm took a few moments to compose himself. Taking a deep breath, he said, "I was conceived a few months after the war ended, though sadly—my father never got to see me. My father was mostly healed by then. But because of the times, and because of the shame of being unwed, my parents chose not to live together until they could come to a practical arrangement. But then . . . my father became involved in one of the Bolshevik groups that were assembling all over Germany at that time. The local government, anticipating riots and potential street battles, hired ex-soldiers to guard the streets and buildings. During a march that was meant to be peaceful, a shot rang out, or someone threw a brick at the mercenaries, and then all hell broke loose. Dozens of marchers were gunned down. My father unfortunately . . . was one of them. When my mother learned this she was beyond grief. Still living with her parents, she knew eventually she would have to tell them the truth about her pregnancy. So she made up a story that she had had too much to drink one night and afterwards had been seduced by a soldier on furlough. And that he had later returned to the front and been killed. Whether they bought it or not, I'll never know. My mother kept it a secret. I first learned the truth of the matter when I turned eighteen. She wanted me to know who my real father was. And to be proud of him."

"And you should be proud," Foss affirmed. "Your father sounded like he was a brave man." In saying this, Foss thought of his own father. A drunk who couldn't keep a job. *But might he have had another side to him?* Foss would most likely never find out. His mother was steadfast in her refusal to discuss anything about her former husband.

A lone aircraft could be heard faraway in the sky, the distant drone of its motor like a soft hum. Despite that and the still-occasional mortar rounds, an expression of relief swept over Tulm. A burdensome secret had been shared. "You are the only person besides my mother who knows my real past."

Feeling honored by Tulm's trust in him, Foss said, "Be assured—I'll keep it solely to myself."

Tulm smiled. "That's why I told you. I doubt I would ever have told a fellow German. As a boy I was occasionally teased about having a Jewish profile, but I never took it seriously. I assumed all along that I was Aryan. Then when the facts were unleashed—my world was jolted. I became paranoid. Always looking over my shoulder. When I was drafted in the military the hazing about my looks caused me more than once to consider running away. Even to the point of fleeing Germany. I thought of climbing the Alps and crossing over to Switzerland."

"It must have been bad."

"It was. But the consequences would have been worse. I may very well have succeeded, but my family would have suffered. I couldn't bear the thought of my mother being arrested by the Gestapo and forced to dredge up the past under torture. With the possibility of ending up in a concentration camp. So I knuckled under and dealt with the taunts by remaining silent. Assholes will usually leave you alone if you constantly ignore them."

Foss thought of Ziemans, then Ruder. He remembered others as well who had poked fun at Tulm's supposed Jewishness. Recalling the conversation in the bunker, Foss said, "So is that why you asked me about journeying to Denmark after the war?"

"Yes. A new start. A new place. With people unstained by Nazi propaganda."

"We have plenty of bastards too, just like anywhere else."

Tulm snorted. "Not like Germany. Here, I already have two strikes against me. My father was a Jew, *and* a communist. The two worst sins in the eyes of the Nazis. For once, I want to live in a nation where no one judges you on your bloodlines, or political convictions."

"I'm with you on that," Foss seconded. "Believe it or not, I dabbled with communism to a degree years ago. But after what I've seen in Russia—it's just another form of Nazism. Red fascism. Not for me. No thanks."

"I'd rather not have any government lording over me," Tulm opined. "Or as little as possible. Maybe one day we'll be luckier to have such a world where each man can govern himself."

"Anarchism . . . "

"I guess that's the best definition."

Foss decided not to comment further. Dreaming about changing the world was best left to idlers sitting in cafes sipping coffee and throwing out their opinions to other sedentary philosophers. The war had killed any ambitions he'd once held about creating a better world. Tulm must have sensed his change of mood, for he checked his gun and began to saunter off toward where Ziemans was patrolling the town.

"I feel we've talked enough for one night," Tulm said over his shoulder. "I hope I didn't wear your ears off."

"Not at all. I'm glad you opened up. I respect you even more now—though I've always respected you."

"Let us talk again . . . before you go."

"We will. I promise," Foss said. He had noted the growing sadness in Tulm's voice. Foss heard his boot steps gradually fade into the dark night, before he was lost from view. Feeling suddenly alone, Foss bit his lower lip to keep a hold of himself. The doctor had been right. He wasn't whole any longer. An image of Captain Herling wailing like a baby passed before him. Foss wondered what had become of the man. *I don't want to ever be like that,* he thought. But it was simple mathematics. The longer time he spent in the field, the greater the chance he'd once more turn berserk. Maybe even shoot one of his own men by accident. Like he had shot the SS. A matter of time. Foss removed the letter from his pocket. Took it out. Held it. The letter was real. He would go home. The decision was made.

He would be leaving the war . . .

CHAPTER 9

SS Major Otto Meyer had a bad headache. He had put in a ten hour day and still was sitting at his desk. He was the only one left in the office. Even the cleaning lady had gone home for the night. Taking a couple of aspirin and washing it down with a barely warm cup of coffee, he lit a cigarette and leaned back in his chair. If only he could go home and sleep.

But sleep was a luxury, and even more than that—an impossibility. A colleague had told him the only ones that got a proper rest these days were the dead. Reflecting on this, Meyer, a man who long ago had given up the delusions of religion and an afterlife, wondered if indeed, death was a more peaceful state.

Not that he wanted to find out anytime soon—he had just turned thirty two, and despite not having found a suitable woman to marry, he was certain he had many years ahead of him. His father's family was well known for its longevity, and Meyer reckoned he had at least another fifty years or so on earth. That would take him close to the end of the twentieth century. He found the thought both appealing, and a little frightening. What would the world be like in 1995 . . .

But first, he had to survive 1945. And so far, 1945 had been an utter disaster. The Russians were on the move everywhere; Allied armies in the west were waiting to cross the Rhine. There was no longer a safe haven anywhere in the Reich. Especially not here in Danzig, now surrounded by a number of Soviet armies bent on obliterating every German.

His head throbbing unmercifully, Meyer wondered whether two aspirin were enough. He really should go home, but the paperwork piled on top of the desk looked like a small mountain. Mostly bureaucratic crap that needed his signature, and the run down on the typical hum-drum an SS Criminal Inspector had to deal with on a daily basis: letters of complaint, people asking favors, an accusation of a lower officer sleeping with a higher officer's wife, scandals in the making including bribery, theft, blackmail, and the occasional corpse that needed someone to find its murderer. With the Russians storming all across Prussia east and west, Meyer was nonplussed how he was supposed to solve crimes that now seemed less than petty. And solve them with a *much* reduced work force.

Meyer had only been at the job a year. But in that time, the staff had been cut in almost half. His immediate superior had all of a sudden become

"ill" around Christmastime—some unusual stomach ailment the man's
doctor had stated—and soon after was whisked off back to his home in
Austria, while of course taking his entire family with him. Stomach
ailment—better known as the *Russian illness*. Meyer reflected with derision
on the fact that many top members of the party, and—God forbid, even the
SS—were becoming unwell these days. Many healthy men who hadn't had
a touch of the flu or even a cold in years, were checking themselves into
hospitals in growing numbers, with the result that most of them were being
relocated back to safer areas well behind the front lines in order to be
treated at sanitariums by recognized specialists. Meyer was fully aware that
more than a few doctors in Dazing had become a good deal wealthier in the
past six months.

Deciding to read one more memo before calling it an evening, Meyer
picked up the top paper from the stack. At first he perused it lazily, then
noting the seriousness of the crime described, he scrutinized each line
carefully a second time, just to make sure he wasn't hallucinating. *SS
guards escorting a small contingent of foreign women laborers to the west, gunned
down by four soldiers of the Wehrmacht. Their group leader, a sergeant, was
described as tall, blond, and spoke with a noticeable accent. Possibly Norwegian
or Danish, or Dutch. They were last noted to be traveling away from the
German lines, and may have run into the Russians. No more information has
been gathered at this—*

The boom of faraway artillery caused Meyer to stop reading. His head did
not feel any better, but now he had another headache to worry about. The
murder of SS troops could not go unpunished, even with the world falling
apart. He knew it was too late to begin scanning files for any leads into the
case. Better yet, he would get his secretary to do so in the morning. But he
was intrigued by the mystery behind the murders. Apparently the women
laborers had escaped to the east, but they were of no consequence. The
Russians would probably ravish them then leave them for dead. The
German troops involved, on the other hand, had to be brought to justice.
Such killings would destroy morale, even though morale overall was
quickly vanishing in the rising turmoil that was currently evident
everywhere in the Reich. Meyer had recently ordered the execution of
more than a dozen Poles accused of breaking into a bakery and stealing
bread. The old saying was true: Chaos only led to more chaos. A fire had
to be stamped out before it raged into an inferno.

Meyer stood up and yawned. He looked out the second story window. Darkness had enveloped Danzig, and because of the threat of Russian bombers, a complete black-out had been enforced. Meyer heard an army truck rumble through the street followed by two more. Troops going off to the front.

Pondering on the foreign accent of the culprit behind the murders, Meyer was certain a German would not have mistaken a Northern European accent for that of a Slavic one, or a Lithuanian, or Estonian. The Wehrmacht (and unbelievably the SS!) in the last few years had enlisted lots of different riffraff from other nations. Scandinavians, Balts, Dutch, Frenchmen, Hungarians, Croats, Albanians, Muslims, and even a division of Spaniards sent by Franco to thank Hitler for his help in that country's civil war. Not to mention the scores of Russians that fought for the Germans against their own countrymen. The field was too wide and the time too waning to search every foreigner that wore the gray-green uniform of the Wehrmacht. So Meyer decided he would only search for those whose origin was Aryan. A man from the northern nations. Holland, Norway, Denmark, perhaps even Sweden—Swedes too in small numbers had joined up in the great fight against Bolshevism.

But being prone to perfectionism, should he not also check the possibility that the perpetrator spoke a German dialect. Swiss, Tyrolean, or an ethnic German from one of the many outlying territories spread throughout Europe. Maybe even a German pretending to speak as a foreigner, thereby giving himself a disguise. All potentialities had to be investigated, yet, how much time would he have to find a needle in a burning haystack! A year before would have been much easier, but now? A mishmash of humanity was streaming toward Germany and the West, a smorgasbord of people from dozens of nationalities, all trying to escape the clutches of the Soviets. Just a week before, Meyer had been told a peculiar story that a group of British POWs had even offered to fight with the Germans against the Russians, instead of waiting for liberation. They feared being sent to a concentration camp in Siberia.

Another truck hurried by outside, followed by what sounded like several tanks. Meyer shuddered at the fact that the front was drawing nearer. A noose was being placed around Pomerania, around West Prussia, and what was the likelihood that Danzig would remain free for any great length of time? Another month? Two? Or maybe just a matter of weeks. Meyer looked again at the piece of paper, and for a moment, his mind churned with the idea of tearing it into shreds. Then burning the shreds in his fireplace at home. He regretted the loss of his fellow SS, but what was the point in seeking the arrest of a handful of criminals, while Rome was engulfed in flames. He cursed, silently. He knew even before he thought of doing away with the paper, that he would never destroy such official evidence of a crime. It would be like destroying himself. A duty had been given him to perform, and besides that, honor to its very core, was at stake. He was proud to be a member of the SS, and pride meant carrying the flag through to the end. He would begin his search tomorrow. But first, he had to get over this damned headache. He had to get home and sleep.

Foss never realized that so much scrutiny would be paid to a single document. He had first shown his medical pass to his superior office, who in turn had passed it on to an officer just above him. This officer then passed it further down the line to a head doctor in the unit, who looking it over, and finding nothing out of sorts, had it sent to the headquarters of the military police. There it was carefully probed for any illegality, but not finding a single thing wrong, they stamped an approval on it, then handed it back to Foss. A pockmarked giant of a man returned it to him with a scowl. "You're damned lucky to be getting out of here," was all he said.

Foss wasn't so certain. Many of the wounded were frightened now of boarding a boat after the disaster of the *Wilhlem Gustloff*. Similar to Dreybach, they preferred to die on land than to drown in a frigid sea. Feeling the same jitters, Foss began to have second thoughts about the whole venture.

"If it weren't for Dreybach, I wouldn't be going anywhere," he said to Tulm while they cleaned their guns as part of a general order sent through the ranks. "From a medical standpoint, I'm fine. A touch of shell-shock. Nothing that other soldiers haven't had. Now it's over with."

"So . . . have you become a doctor all of sudden?" Tulm, unusually sarcastic, shook his head and frowned. "That's not a diagnosis that disappears after a few days rest, and you damn well know it."

Foss was set to argue the point, but inside he knew his friend was correct. "I still don't fancy the notion of leaving you and Ziemans behind to face Ivan. Seems like I'm welshing on my duty."

"It never was your duty. You were forced into this bloody army."

Foss thought back to the morning he found himself impounded into the Wehrmacht. The memory, even after all this time, still left him feeling sour, his right for individual choice abused by a foreign power. "You have a point. But I can't go back and change what happened."

"No, none of us can." Tulm's mood was bleak. Polishing the barrel of his rifle, he said gloomily, "What about Ziemans?"

"What about him?"

"Did you tell him?"

Foss had first considered telling Ziemans that he was being transferred to a division in the west. Then decided that lying would only make him feel more guilty about leaving for home while the others had to keep fighting. *Honor.* He had never given that word a thought while growing up. Somehow it wasn't a part of the lifestyle in Denmark. Danes were content with their beer and bakeries. But in Germany it was at the root of all things German. Which meant strength—but also weakness. Honor entailed throwing yourself on a grenade so that your comrades would not die. Honor, as well, meant obediently bowing to a psychopath like Hitler—without once standing up to kick him in the balls.

"I plan to let him know tonight," Foss said, with a hint of worry that Ziemans might not take it well. "He probably won't like the idea, but it is what it is."

But surprisingly when the time came to give Ziemans the news, the Berliner took it without rancor.

"I suppose someone has to keep that dour bastard company," was Ziemans' comment. "In a way, I'd rather take my chances with the Russkis than to deal with Dreybach on an ocean voyage." Though Foss knew such words were no more than bravado. There wasn't a Landser in the whole area known as Samland that didn't wish to be far away from the Red Army once it resumed its push toward the sea.

Foss and his last two men from the reconnaissance unit sat up long into the night drinking the last bottle that Ziemans had pilfered along the rapid retreat through East Prussia. A wonderful bottle of Hungarian apricot brandy. Other men in the bunker tried to sleep, while still others played cards or sat by themselves looking forlorn, empty. It was bitterly cold outside, and though Foss would have liked to take the conversation out of doors, he also didn't want to freeze. Arrangements had been made for Dreybach to sail in two to three days, with Foss to accompany him. Foss had learned from a sailor in the port that the journey would probably take at least several days to reach a city in the west, depending on weather and sea conditions, and how many people were aboard the boat. If Russian airplanes and submarines were in the vicinity, the voyage would take longer.

Or be aborted before it even began . . .

Inhaling deeply, Foss closed his eyes and tried to put the last thought out of his head.

"Get yourself drunk, Aksel!" Ziemans handed Foss the bottle. "This might be the last decent drink you'll have in awhile."

Maybe the last drink ever. The morbid thoughts would not go away. His hand shaking, Foss drank. Despite the fact that he was he sailing home, a huge part of him wanted to stay. To abandon these men at this stage, seemed a crime. Tulm had noticed Foss's tension. It made him tense. Trying to lighten the mood, he said, "You should write a poem about the sea voyage once you return to Copenhagen. Didn't Vikings write about their sea-jaunts?"

Foss smiled. "I just might take you up on that. And yes, they wrote a lot about the sea."

Ziemans gave Foss a long stare. "You write poetry! What's the world coming to . . . "

Foss returned the bottle to Ziemans after taking another swill. He wished they had another bottle or two. The idea of getting drunk appealed to him now. "I wish I had time to write more often," he said ruefully."

"I never wrote anything more than a letter. And hardly that. I always thought that stuff was for sissies."

"You never gave a love-note to a girl?"

Ziemans snorted, then pointed at his crotch. "This is the only love-note I give them. And believe me, it's enough!"

One of the men playing cards cackled at Ziemans' response. Another voice then rang out, shouting for everyone to shut up and let him sleep.

"You shut up, you moron," Ziemans returned. "The lot of us—are going to be sleeping forever soon."

Ziemans' words struck a somber tone, and for awhile, no one in the bunker spoke. Even the men playing cards paused, their faces turning melancholy. Then swearing, Ziemans stood up and walked out into the cold night.

Foss ran after him. He found Ziemans standing alone beside an anti-aircraft gun. Such guns recently had been used more against Russian tanks. "Are you alright, Johann?" Foss asked, concerned.

Keeping his back to Foss, Ziemans shrugged. "I don't know how to answer that."

Foss let several moments pass before he said, "I can understand if you're mad that I'm getting out of here and you're not. But the doctor that wrote the sick order practically forced it on me. It was either that or he was planning to have me removed as group leader. I only accepted it then." Foss knew that he was embellishing the story, but there was truth in what he said. Unfit leaders were more often than not, relieved of command.

Ziemans knew it too. He turned around to face Foss. "Look, I realize I'm a shithead much of the time—but I'd never accuse you of being a shirker. It's just . . . that everything's breaking up. The old crew is all gone."

There was a gleam in Ziemans' eyes. A gleam of sadness. Foss was touched by it. "We'll have a reunion once the war is over," Foss declared, trying to sound more positive than he felt. "The drinks then will be on me."

Ziemans smirked. His old self returning. "Perchance we'll celebrate the liberation of Denmark. I wouldn't mind a few Viking women to keep me company."

They both turned as they heard a noise. It was Tulm. His face appeared red, angry.

"What's the matter, Max, you lose all your back-pay playing skat?" Skat was one of Ziemans' favorite card games, and was popular throughout the German Army. He patted Tulm on the back. "I'll win it back for you."

"I wish it *were* only a card game. One of the sons of bitches said I looked like a Jew."

Now it was Ziemans' turn to become angry. "I'm the only one that can call you a Jew. Let's go pound those scum."

Foss blocked his path. "Forget it. I don't want to get thrown in the guardhouse right before I'm to sail. I'll go back and retrieve the brandy."

"No need to." Tulm removed the bottle from his coat. The three of them drank the rest of it in the damp cold that was so prevalent in winters along the Baltic. They uttered few words. Even Ziemans was at a loss for language. They sensed the finality of the occasion. Their time spent together had reached an end; now only apprehension remained, the specter

of the unknown, but not a happy unknown. Even after finishing the
brandy, they lingered. Used to being out in the elements in the frozen
steppes of Russia, they only returned to the bunker when they believed the
others had finally gone to sleep. Foss, as always, made certain his men slept
before he did. It seemed like any other night among the countless nights
he had witnessed during the war. But he only told himself that because this
night was different. The same rumble in the distance meant the enemy was
nearby. Koenigsberg . . . under bombardment. Foss glanced at Tulm and
Ziemans and something whispered that he would never see them again. At
least not alive. Orders had come in earlier that all the men in the vicinity
of the Peyse peninsula were to be redeployed. Even at this stage in the war,
those in command still used the official wordage. Though they could just
as easily have said, "You're being sent to the Front." Sent to the charnel
house.

For some minutes Foss chewed his fingernails, a nervous habit he'd had
since he was a toddler—according to his mother. And one that he had
picked up from his mother. He was tired, but he didn't want to sleep. Then
the weariness in his limbs caused him to lie down. His eyes became moist
as he closed them. The continuous shelling of Koenigsberg acted like a
mantra. He had grown so accustomed to such noise, that not hearing it
would be strange. As he eventually drifted off, he wondered whether he
could get used to not hearing it.

CHAPTER 10

Having blocked all land routes to the west, the Soviets intensified air raids on Pillau. Stalin didn't have enough air or naval-strength to stop every vessel from moving in and out of the Gulf of Danzig, but he and his generals planned to hit and sink as many as possible. Whenever the weather was clear enough for flying, Stormoviks and heavy bombers swarmed over the port strafing the dense crowds of exposed refugees and blowing up what remained of a town mostly destroyed from previous attacks. Pillau now resembled so many other towns and cities across Europe. Destruction everywhere. The stink of refuse and unburied corpses left where they had perished in the wreckage of fallen buildings. Several weeks earlier, whether by aircraft or human error on the ground, an ammunition dump at a military installation had exploded, killing hundreds of people. Jammed like kippers in the army hospitals, thousands of badly wounded soldiers lay waiting for rescue or the end. Adding to the horror, uncountable hordes of refugees, many sick and fatigued to excess from having spent weeks constantly fleeing for their lives, huddled miserably on the rubble-strewn streets.

Foss, taking stock of the surroundings, was shocked by the degradation. Not that he hadn't seen Pillau already—or Russian towns with worse damage—but the misery was unbelievable. Ever since the moment he had first entered Germany on his way to the war being waged in the Soviet Union, he had considered the Germans a capable people, a nation built on efficiency and organized to the hilt. But here, their capability had gone awry. Their resources sapped. Refugees wandered about dazed and weeping, their clothes and shoes often in tatters. Soldiers held the blank stares of men who had ended up in an insane asylum, and were never coming out again. Because of a lack of proper dressings for wounds, the doctors and nurses had had to resort to using paper bandages, and even these were running low. Suicides were common among both civilians and soldiers. Others drooled and shouted out with an unmistakable madness. At the same time, there were those that worked tirelessly to mandate a semblance of order amidst the mass chaos. Officials and officers of both the army and navy, who toiled without sleep to keep civilization from reverting to complete barbarism. Almost immediately after the beginning of the Russian offensive in mid-January, Grand Admiral Karl Doenitz, the head of the Kriegsmarine, had set in motion the sea-borne evacuation of the inhabitants of potentially all of Prussia, both East and West. Operation Hannibal—was the last lifeline for those trapped between the enemy and the sea. But despite continuing successes in bringing numerous non-combatants, and soldiers with war-ending wounds out of the eastern theater of war, the overall task was almost beyond daunting. Dunkirk in comparison was a brief historical event. Dealing with Russian submarines, planes, and underwater explosives proved to be a daily dilemma, and now the western allies were also adding their dreaded weight of arms. British aircraft had begun dropping air-borne mines into the Baltic, forcing ships to rearrange their normal routes, and sometimes wrecking or even sinking them. Yet . . . what other choice was there except to escape by sea? The brief corridors of non-enemy held land opened up by infrequent German counteroffensives against Russian entrenchments, were no more than minor victories in a war not winnable. Twenty-four hours, sometimes forty-eight, a few days at most, before the Russians re-closed the gaps. And each new try meant a reduced number of tanks and armored vehicles to start with, less fuel, and . . . fewer men. The barrels were being scraped, like Tulm had once voiced. No untapped barrels remained.

Something tugged at the back of Foss's coat as he continued to stare at the astounding scenes around him. Turning, he was surprised to meet the gaze of a young girl whose dark hair was partly covered by a gray scarf. Her chapped cheeks showed lines where tears had streamed down them. The girl wore a dirt-spattered sweater. One of her shoes had a hole it at the toes. She carried a small suitcase in one hand. In the other hand a photo, which she showed to Foss.

"Can you help me?" the girl asked in a pleading voice. "I've lost my parents. This is what they look like. Have you . . . by any chance . . . seen them?" Tears formed in the girl's eyes.

Not wanting to be the harbinger of bad news, Foss didn't know what to say. Then taking a few moments to look at the photo, he said, "No, I'm sorry. I have not seen your parents. But perhaps I can lead you to someone who might assist you in finding—"

The girl began crying before he even finished the sentence. Taking a piece of bread out of his pocket, Foss offered it to the girl, but she shook her head.

"I can't eat not knowing where my mother and father are."

"Like I said, I'll take you to one of the assembling areas beside the dock. The town officials working there might be able to help."

The girl was silent a moment. "I've already been there."

"And they didn't know?"

"No, they didn't know anything."

"Maybe your parents are looking for you."

"They would have already found me. They told me to wait beside the lighthouse if we ever got separated. I waited three days . . . " The girl began to cry louder. Foss took one of her her hands and gently stroked it.

"But how did you get separated in the first place?" he asked.

Between bouts of weeping, the girl said, "Enemy planes . . . flew over. I ran. Hid myself under a cart filled with . . . baskets. I stayed there . . . until . . . the planes were . . . gone. But by then . . . it was nighttime. I called out to them. Then a man yelled at me. Said he would hit me if I didn't stay quiet."

Foss wondered if they had become casualties from the plane bursts. He said quietly, "Have you checked the hospitals? Maybe your parents thought you were injured and went to a hospital to search for you."

The girl's eyes widened. "I asked at two hospitals that treat only refugees, but they weren't there either."

Not knowing what else to add, Foss watched as a small trawler slowly steamed toward the port. The winter had been so harsh that the waters around the embarkation area had frozen solid. Icebreakers were required constantly to create a path for all vessels. Noticing the throng of civilians clamoring and pushing to be first in line for the incoming trawler, Foss wondered whether the little girl's parents had boarded a boat and already sailed away. It seemed inconceivable, unless they thought their daughter had been slain in the plane attack. More likely *they* had been killed. Perhaps they had fallen in the icy water and drowned. The girl had for the moment ceased weeping. Foss thought it best not to overload her with the potentiality that her mother and father were not coming back. Unwrapping a scarf from around his neck, Foss used it to wipe the tears from the girl's face. Then he smiled at her.

"What's your name?" he asked.

"Traudl."

"And how old are you, Traudl?"

"I'm . . . seven," the girl sniffled.

So young. "Do you have any other family nearby?"

"My grandparents. But they chose to remain behind. Said they were too old to run. They're still in Lyck. I wish I could just go home." A new fall of tears.

Lyck was Brohm's home town. The girl suddenly shrieked as she stared at the sky. An airplane. But Foss quickly noted it was German. Strange. The Luftwaffe was rarely seen anywhere these days. Most German aircraft were grounded for lack of fuel. The plane made one pass over Pillau, then flew off to the west.

"Don't worry, it's a German plane." Foss comforted the girl by briefly caressing her back. Then he said, "I was on my way to a soup kitchen. In one of the harbor sheds. Would you like to go?"

The girl glanced at Foss skeptically, then wiping her nose, nodded. Makeshift shelters, and kitchens doling out soup and porridge had been set up in areas all along the pier. Yet so many thousands crowded the waterfront that there wasn't enough space for everyone. Once at the soup kitchen, Foss made sure Traudl received a bowl of hot porridge. He took none for himself.

"Why aren't you eating?" Traudl looked at him quizzically.

"The food is for civilians. I'll eat at the army mess."

"Then why did you want to come here?"

How to explain? "I'm going to try to get you aboard one of the ships."

"Aboard one of the ships? What do you mean?"

"There's no need to panic, Traudl. But I think"—and he hoped she believed him—"your parents probably feared when you couldn't find them, that you had already been put on one of the boats sailing to other parts of Germany. And so they in turn embarked. Now, if you want to find your parents, it is best you leave Pillau as soon as possible. You never know when there might be another air raid."

Craning her neck, Truadl peered fearfully at the sky. "Will you be coming too?"

"Not on this trip. I have to travel in a few days with a friend of mine who is wounded."

"I . . . have to go alone?"

Foss was surprised the girl had become so attached to him. A random soldier she met in the street. He wondered whom he would trust if he were in the girl's shoes. He didn't answer her directly, but instead asked about her home life. Her friends, her school. When she finished the food he led her to a small recently constructed office near the quay. Inside, sat a naval official surrounded by a mob of refugees, all trying to get his attention at once.

"I've told all of you over and over," the official spoke up loudly, clearly irritated. "Each of you in time will receive a boarding pass to sail. Those with children come first."

A heavyset young woman wearing a black mink coat was about to say something, then shaking her head, stormed out. Foss grabbed her arm as she reached the door. "May I have a word with you, Fraulein?"

"Frau—for your information. And take your hand off of me."

But Foss didn't let go. "If your intent is to board a ship—I may be able to find you a berth."

The woman was distrustful. "How?"

He released his hold. "Do you have children?"

She was quiet a second. "Obviously not. Otherwise I wouldn't be walking out of this office now."

"What if I gave you a child?"

The woman looked at Foss as though he were mad. Then she noticed Traudl. "You mean her!"

Turning to Traudl, Foss patted her on the head. "Just remain here for a moment. I promise I'll be right back. I need to talk to the lady—outside." Then gesticulating to the woman in fur to follow him, he stepped out of the office.

The wind had increased, and wafted chillingly over the harbor. Foss was reminded of the frigid gusts of air that had blown regularly across the endless landscape of Russia. He was about to speak, but the woman spoke first, haughtily.

"What do you want from me?"

"To take the girl with you to the west. It will be your ticket out of here."

"Who is she? Your daughter?"

Foss told her the story. The woman's previous demeanor softened a little. "I suppose I could. We've all lost somebody in this awful war."

It was then that Foss noted the woman was dressed entirely in black. He said, "Are you a widow?"

The woman grinned sadly. "Yes, how can you tell."

"My condolences." And thinking of his lost friends, he meant it. He said, "Is your home elsewhere?"

She shook her head. "No. I'm from these parts. East Prussian to the core. Born and raised in Braunsberg." She paused, then sighing heavily, stared Foss straight in the eyes. My husband was as well. I know it might not interest you, but he was a Captain. Last fall—he was killed fighting in Italy." Suddenly looking deflated, she dropped her gaze. "I still haven't gotten over it."

Foss thought she was about to cry, and tried to console her, but she waved him off. "I've shed enough tears to fill an ocean bed. Now it's only bitterness. Hate and anger toward those who have led us astray."

Time was running short. Foss thought of Traudl standing by herself in the office. He recalled the tales he'd heard of refugees without children going so far as to kidnap babies and toddlers to improve their chances of being first to board the outgoing ships. Some people once aboard, had even thrown infants down toward relatives waiting on the quay, so that they too could lie their way to safety. But often the falling infants would miss their outstretched hands and instead drop into the iced sea, where they quickly drowned or died of exposure. Foss looked at the woman. "So will you take the girl?"

Shrugging, the woman said, "Nothing to lose by doing so. But what if her real parents all of a sudden show up? Or if the authorities quiz me about her past? I can't exactly say I'm her mother."

"Her parents would surely have found her by now if they were alive." A thought ran through Foss's mind that they may have been arrested. All the more reason to get the girl out of Pillau safely. "Don't worry about the rest," Foss continued. "At this point our esteemed leaders just want to get people out of here before the Russians arrive. I'll tell Traudl to act as though you're her aunt. Her mother's sister. Once both of you are ship-bound, no one will care. But I trust you to look after her until you reach land again. Then the authorities can take over. She's got a life ahead of her—with or without her parents."

The last sentence he uttered made Foss feel like an idiot. He knew nothing about Traudl. She might as easily wither away and die with no family, as to survive and go on living. He thought of his own past, most of his years spent growing up with no father. Indeed, he himself had survived—but at least he had a mother. Unless a miracle happened, the little girl would have to fend for herself. Alone.

It took some time, but in the end Foss persuaded Traudl to accept the woman in the fur coat.

"But what's her name?" Traudl looked suspiciously at the woman, who made an attempt to smile back at her.

"You can call me Aunt Margot."

Traudl knitted her eyebrows. "Is that your real name?"

"That's my real name."

Seeing that the little girl now had someone to look after her, Foss felt a sense of relief he had not enjoyed in many months. Quietly, he said, "I have to go. A friend is waiting for me." He nodded at Margot, who nodded back, then took Traudl's hand and held it a moment. "Good luck to both of you! Maybe one day we'll all meet again—when the circumstances aren't so hectic."

He turned, then felt a hand on his sleeve. It was Traudl. "You never told me your name."

"No, Traudl, I certainly didn't. How silly of me." He gave his full name. Not knowing why it was necessary, he also told he was from Denmark.

"Denmark . . . I learned about Denmark in school. Mr. Foss, doesn't your country have a king?"

"Yes, we have a king. And you can call me, Aksel." He softly patted the little girl's cheek. "But I must be on my way. Now stay close to Aunt Margot." Foss waved goodbye. He didn't turn around until he was well out of the area of the wharf. But there were too many people milling around, waiting for incoming ships. Traudl and Margot were nowhere to be seen.

He hoped Margot kept her word. Wearing a fur coat and having been married to an officer, she was probably not used to doing favors to people she deemed beneath her in status. Foss had not found her attractive, and for Traudl's sake, that was possibly a good thing. Margot wouldn't be a major distraction for the men on the ship.

Dreybach was propped up in the same place where Foss had seen him days earlier. He appeared more haggard than before, sallow. His mood had not changed either. Had worsened.

"So when are we supposed to leave?" Dreybach's words were slurred, as though he had been drugged.

"Tomorrow night. From what I've been told." Foss noticed that two of the wounded men who had previously been in the same tent with Dreybach were no longer there. He decided not to ask why, but Dreybach must have read his thoughts.

"They died," Dreybach said without remorse. "One of the bastards screamed the whole night, before finally croaking. Good riddance, I say! At least I can sleep a little now—though I never rest much without pain."

"Aren't you getting morphine?"

"Occasionally. But the damn stuff wears off. And there's not enough for every wounded man who's been *shot*."

The emphasis on the word "shot" drew Foss's attention. He wondered whether Dreybach was comparing their injuries. To Dreybach, I must seem whole, standing here without bandages or crutches. Foss tried to steer the conversation in another direction. "Tulm and Ziemans wish you well. They're being sent off to fight again."

For awhile Dreybach didn't answer. Then he said, "I envy them."

Foss shook his head at Dreybach's callous statement. "You don't really mean that, Erwin."

"I most certainly do." Dreybach clenched his teeth.

"Everyone these days going to the front is earmarked for death. And you damn well know it."

"And so what! At least they're on their feet, moving. I've gotten so weak, I can't even stand any longer without some mug-faced orderly holding me up."

Looking concerned, Foss said, "Sorry. I did not know that."

Dreybach closed his eyes a moment. "Just forget it. I'm not even sure what I'm saying half the time. Lying around here with all these other sickos is turning me into a basket case. I still don't like the idea of boarding a goddamned boat."

"I'm not wild about the idea either, but Ivan hasn't given us any other path to take."

Foss turned as shouts were heard outside the tent; then scuffling, vile curses. A wounded man was being accused of shooting himself in the hand. The military police were involved. They were in the process of arresting him. Then the man was dragged off, whimpering.

"We can count ourselves lucky we're not in his boots," Foss said, a sudden fear rising in his mind that he too might be a wanted man. With the need to survive overtaking all other considerations the past week, he had forgotten his last temperamental outburst. The blurred memory of the shooting in the forest. The SS men. The emaciated prisoners. Foss remembered Ziemans' words about never being taken alive by the Feldgendarmerie. He had seen enough death in the war not to overworry about losing his life. But torture . . . no man wanted to face that. Checking his Tommy gun to see that it was fully loaded, Foss gripped the weapon hard as though it were a talisman.

Aware of Foss's nervousness, Dreybach said, "My bet is they line the poor sod up against a wall and shoot him immediately. They don't have the resources or time to detain people any longer for questioning. At least not here in Pillau."

"What makes you so sure?"

"Things I've heard since lying here. Rumors are rampant. One deserter they caught dressed up like a woman. The sonofabitch even had lipstick on—and that's what no doubt gave him away. There aren't too many fashionable females roaming the quayside."

Foss thought of the heavy woman in fur. He didn't recall her wearing any make-up. "What did they do to the guy?" Foss said, still turned toward the tent's entrance.

Dreybach looked at Foss wryly. "Come on, Aksel, do I need to answer that?"

Sensing that the police were gone, Foss lowered his gun. "I felt spooked for a moment. So much has happened the past month."

A light clicked on in Dreybach's mind. Gradually, he began to fathom Foss's fear. "If you're antsy about the SS . . . then just hop the next ship. You've got your pass. I won't mind."

"You mean go without you?"

"Yes. Get your ass back to Denmark in one piece."

"Erwin . . . you misjudge me." Foss sounded hurt, and irked. "I won't leave you to fend for yourself. Not in your condition."

Dreybach gave a brief laugh, before wincing as he felt a twinge in his back. Recovering, he said, "You speak like a sergeant again. I suppose you want me to follow orders."

"You're still a soldier, Erwin. And so am I. Until we hear otherwise."

Their conversation halted abruptly as the noise of planes overhead became apparent. Stepping outside, Foss peered up toward a partly clear sky. When he returned, he said in a barely audible tone, "Russian bombers!" Dreybach merely sighed, but some of the other wounded in the tent became frightened and began to moan. One of the greatest nightmares of a wounded man was to be trapped in a burning building. Sudden bursts of flak from anti-aircraft guns drowned out the moans in the tent. Then the bombs fell. But luckily, for the soldiers, they were aimed at the boats anchored dockside. Faint screams from refugees could be heard in between the explosions. The bombing seemed endless, though lasted no more than a few minutes. The hospital escaped without damage or loss of life.

After it was over Dreybach appeared more haggard than ever. Worried, Foss went over and put a hand to his forehead.

"Erwin, you're burning up. Does your doctor know you have a fever?"

"Screw the doctor," Dreybach said abrasively. "They hardly have any medicine as it is. Besides, all the men in here have fevers."

"All the more reason to get you out of Pillau."

For the first time, Dreybach did not appear adverse to the idea. Nodding slowly, he said, "So the boat's scheduled for tomorrow evening?"

"That's the time I was told."

"Big boat or little boat?"

"Big boat. An ex-liner. "

"Oh no—not another *Wilhelm Gustloff* . . . "

Not wanting Dreybach to revert to his previous despair, Foss told him there would be less chance of getting seasick on a larger vessel, compared to sailing on a torpedo boat or a dredger. And besides that—Foss was guessing—there would be a sufficient convoy to discourage any further submarine attacks.

Hearing this, one of the other wounded spoke up. "I don't care if I have to float on a fucking raft. I just want to get far away from here before Ivan comes."

The rest of the wounded that could still speak, backed him up with a chorus of yeas. Dreybach looked sharply at Foss. "Dammit, I hope you're right. Does the ship have a name?"

"The *Steuben*," Foss answered. "Named after a Prussian general."

"The *Steuben* . . . " Dreybach's words drifted off as his eyelids lowered. Foss wondered whether he had fallen asleep. But he eventually lifted them again. "I certainly hope you're right."

Foss heard the sound of planes again. He hoped he was right too.

CHAPTER 11

Foss had lost track of time during the constant retreat over the past month. But he knew today was the ninth of February—one of the seamen had told him—and that he would be sailing aboard the *Steuben*. He had learned from asking around, that the ship had once been christened the *München*, and for a decade or so had been a trans-Atlantic passenger liner sailing from Germany to the United States. Later changed to the *General von Steuben*, then finally *Steuben*—for the duration of the war up till now she had been kept in port and used mainly by members of the Kriegsmarine as a place of lodging. But with the onslaught of the Russians in the East, there had been pressure on the navy to use every craft available to salvage human lives. Besides that, she bore no other cargo.

Watching through the cold morning hours as thousands of the wounded were lifted up to the ship and taken below, while a similar number of waiting refugees pushed and shoved in a frenzy to be aboard, Foss was heartened by the fact that the *Steuben* was to sail to the German city of Swinemünde. Though he would have preferred to sail directly to Denmark, at least the distance home was shortening. The same seaman he'd chatted with earlier had relayed the news that if accommodations could not be offered in Swinemünde, then a ship from there would carry most of the passengers further west to Kiel. Located in Northern Germany, Kiel with its huge naval base, was situated within the province of Schleswig-Holstein, just south of the Danish peninsula of Jutland. Foss felt a stirring in his chest at the thought that he had survived the war, and would soon be out of it forever.

Well . . . not yet. He crossed his fingers. Dreybach's woebegone attitude had rubbed off on him. An hour before noon he made his way up onto the ship. Taking nearly ten minutes before locating Dreybach on the Promenade Deck strapped to a stretcher head to toe with other severely wounded soldiers secured in the same way, Foss sensed a great tension in the air. The same tension he'd get before heading into battle when the odds lay with the enemy. He still carried his gun. Many of the wounded bore a weapon of some sort. Foss found a spot beside his friend and waited till the last refugees were hauled aboard to seek what little space was left on the main deck and the gangway. There was little food. And no shelter from the elements. Time passed. Foss tried to snooze while final preparations were made to begin the journey westward. Several tugboats drew up to the *Steuben* to start the arduous task of pulling her away from the quayside further into the gulf. Foss noticed that the sea was gentle; the ship hardly rocked at all. But a thick steady snow fell from a dismal-looking sky. Foss gazed at Dreybach, who was lying with his eyes half-closed. Foss was about to ask him whether he was cold when a biting voice snapped at him.

"The main deck is only for wounded who are immobile." The voice juddered like a stiletto through the frigid air. A thin naval officer with gray eyes and a weather-beaten face. He glared at Foss. "All other wounded must report to the cabins and rooms in the lower decks."

For a second Foss was stunned into inaction. He thought of making up a lie about an internal injury, then decided to be honest. "I'm taking care of my friend. And I have a pass."

The officer shook his head. "A nurse or doctor will attend to him if he needs care. Proceed to the next deck—and that's an order!"

Foss felt a sudden foreboding. A voice inside urgently telling him to stay with Dreybach, don't let Dreybach out of your sight. Don't go to the lower decks. *Am I being foolish?* How many times had he experienced more dire circumstances in the past, and not come to harm. But the trepidation did not leave. "I'm staying with my friend, officer," he said slowly, his voice filled with a determination not to be deterred "We've spent three years together at the front. I'm not abandoning him. Especially not now."

His forehead wrinkling with displeasure at being challenged by a mere enlisted man, the officer was about to threaten Foss with arrest, when a sailor approached, gesturing about a problem on another part of the ship. Swearing irksomely under his breath, the officer gave Foss a dirty look, swore again, then followed the sailor to check on the disturbance. Foss expected him to come back. But the minutes passed, and there was no sign of him. Only the wounded all around, bound tightly to stretchers so that they would not fall out when the ship weaved in the waves.

Foss checked on Dreybach. He had not reacted to the appearance of the naval officer, and was unresponsive when Foss tapped his leg. His face looked wan, and Foss was about to call out for a doctor when several Russian fighter-bombers swooped over the bay.

Stunningly, they did not fire at the *Steuben*. Instead they attacked the lead ship of the convoy that had sailed out from the Hela Spit, a torpedo boat, which returned fire. Their bombs having exploded harmlessly in the water, the planes hurried off as quickly as they had appeared. The people on board for a long time studied the sky, believing they would come back in greater numbers. But only snow fell. Beginning to zigzag as a protection against torpedoes from submarines, the ships continued on course.

But the planes had alerted Foss and others to the vulnerability of the expedition. With alarm, Foss noted that only two vessels acted as part of the convoy. The torpedo boat, and one smaller craft. *These were the ships that were supposed to stop a sub!* He didn't say anything about it to Dreybach, who still lay half-comatose. Foss touched his friend's forehead. It was hotter than the day before.

Worried about Dreybach's condition amid the falling temperature, Foss got up to search for a doctor, but he saw the officer again, standing at a distance. The man looked through binoculars at the horizon to the north. The trip would not take more than a day or so—but Foss wondered whether his friend would even make it through the long night, when the ship did most of its sailing? No planes would attack in the darkness, but darkness was no hindrance to what lurked beneath the sea. A sudden shiver ran down Foss's spine, and he found himself regretting that he had been so pushy toward Dreybach about boarding the vessel.

The tugs released their hold, and sped back to Pillau. It was mid-afternoon, the snow continued to fall, and the *Steuben* was heading for the Baltic.

If those aboard the three German vessels thought that they had escaped unscathed from the Russian planes, then they were mistaken. For after flying back to the airbase, the lead plane radioed the information that a large vessel was leaving Pillau. Guarded by only a small convoy. And the only direction it was traveling: west.

Whether this direct report was immediately relayed to Commander Alexander Marinesko, or whether he concluded himself that the enemy had a large ship on the water that night, in the end did not matter. For the commander of the S-13, one of only about a dozen modern Soviet submarines, had been on the prowl for German shipping since the previous autumn. As a Soviet naval officer, duty demanded revenge for all the devastation and murder the Fascists had inflicted on the USSR. Marinesko had sunk the *Wilhelm Gustloff* less than a fortnight earlier. Though even now he still was uncertain what exactly his prize had been. The Soviet

Naval Command, either due to jealousy or outright dislike for a man many considered a drunk, were highly skeptical he had sunk such a large ship, or for that matter, any ship at all. Which not only irked Marinesko, but drove him to take unnecessary risks in his search for the enemy. Already the S-13 had nearly collided with a German submarine in a dense fog; there were also depth charges from torpedo boats that had to be avoided at all costs. Not to mention the countless mines scattered across the entire Baltic. Seething inside at the recent lack of action, Marinesko had taken the S-13 to the surface. Having been underwater for days hiding near a natural seawall known as the Stolpe Bank, the S-13 had nearly run its batteries to exhaustion. Now from the conning tower, Marinesko scoured the endless blackness of the seascape when one of the crewman touched his arm.

"Commander, look! Straight ahead!"

Turning toward the direction the man was pointing, Marinesko saw nothing at first. Only what he gauged to be puffs of smoke barely visible against the dark background. Then suddenly tiny sparks of light, almost like miniature shooting stars, blinked briefly amid the drifting smoke. They stopped, then started again. And . . . they were growing closer.

What could they be?

"Perhaps the ship burns coal, Commander," the crewman said.

"Yes . . . of course," Marinesko nodded. "An older boat. And the crew are feeding it to keep up speed." Aware that the unknown ship—or ships?—was cutting a path straight towards them, Marinesko ordered the S-13 to crash-dive. And quickly.

They remained submerged deep under water for thirty minutes, hoping the Germans—and who else could it be—had not detected them. Sweating with anxiety even in the cold of the Baltic, Marinesko and his crew waited for the inevitable depth charge.

None came.

Unbeknown to Marinesko, the flashes of light he had seen earlier belonged not to the *Steuben*, but to one of her escorts, the TF 10, a torpedo recovery ship. An older vessel pressed into service due to the constant need for ships to assist with Operation Hannibal, she burned coal for fuel as Marinesko's sailor had surmised. Also unbeknown to the Russian commander was that a huge liner such as the *Steuben* was even this close. Using his periscope, Marinesko with precision swept the area where the ship would have passed over them. To his amazement he caught sight of something that momentarily took his breath away.

"What is it, Commander?" Nervous, the navigator nearly bumped Marinesko in his eagerness to learn more.

Marinesko continued to rove his eye over the winter sea. "Silhouettes in the sky," he said, his lips curving into a wide smile. "The silhouettes of at least three vessels. I'm"—he moved the periscope slowly side to side, then back to center again—"searching for others, but, no, that's it. Three."

His closest officers all looked at him at once. Then the navigator cleared his throat. "What type of vessels?"

"I'm not sure about the smaller ones. The Fascists are using everything these days from barges to rowboats. But the big one is an Emden." Marinesko uttered the last sentence with relish. "Fifteen thousand tons, I'd say."

The officers clapped one another on the backs, but kept their voices constrained. Noises carried far in the sea, and radar had been the bane of many a sub. But if the commander's words were true, then they had in their sights a cruiser. And to sink a cruiser would mark the greatest victory in the short history of the Soviet Navy.

"These Nazis are arrogant." Putting the periscope away, Marinesko scratched his cheek. Like all the other men aboard the S-13, he had begun to grow a beard, and it itched. "To depend on such a mini-convoy is a slap in the face to us. But the bastards have been arrogant all along. Attacking our nation and expecting us to become their slaves. Slaughtering our people like hogs. I have nothing but contempt for all Hitlerites. All Germans." His words tapered off, but the loathing in his demeanor was evident to everyone in the S-13. Marinesko beckoned to Kurochkin, the torpedo gunner's mate. "It's time we send these fascist thugs to the bottom of the sea. Make ready to fire torpedoes at the cruiser."

No one needed further instructions. For most of the war, the men of the Soviet Baltflot, the Baltic Red Banner Fleet, had been holed up in Kronstadt, one of only two ports in the western part of Russia that had not been conquered by the Germans. The Germans and Finns from 1941 on had laid a string of mines in various places in the Gulf of Finland, immobilizing the entire fleet from submarines to heavy cruisers. Vast numbers of sailors and cadets had then been forced to fight and die in the land battles around Leningrad. Those that remained with their vessels, ached for the day when they could break out and resume the warfare at sea.

And here was their chance to make history. With the torpedoes now loaded and ready to be fired, Marinesko noted the time. A little before 0100 hours, the tenth day of February. He looked at Kurochkin. Then drawing an imaginary knife across his throat, he ordered the gunner's mate to launch two torpedoes toward the enemy ship.

Watching through the periscope, Marinesko felt as giddy as a child at Christmas as the torpedoes struck the starboard side. He estimated a direct hit just below the Bridge and the aft funnel—*but should I shoot more?* He was debating what to do when one of the men spoke urgently. Marinesko turned away from the periscope. It was Vinogradov. The expert at reading German codes.

"Commander, I advise that we get out while we can."

Marinesko stared hard at the man for a second. "Is that advice from your gut? Or from your head?"

"My head. The enemy torpedo boat is bearing down on us. She won't catch us if we go now."

Being blown to pieces by a depth charge would be hell enough. But if they didn't return to base, no one would ever know it was the S-13 that had sunk another large German ship. Marinesko took one more quick look through the periscope, then put it aside. He said evenly, "Back the sub out of range. Comrades, we're going home. Once ashore, the vodka's on me."

He was tempted to reverse the order and try and sink the two other vessels, but it was now a cat and mouse game. And he had become the mouse. *Safety before stupidity.* A submarine commander lying at the bottom of the Baltic was of no help to the Soviet Union.

The S-13 moved north, then east. Marinesko knew he had hit something big. He could only hope that it would sink fast with all hands lost. The more fascists killed now, the fewer they'd have to kill later. And he wanted to kill as many as possible. The bastards deserved worse for all that they had done. They deserved worse!

The worst thing about the voyage was the elements, Foss thought, as he tried to bundle up against the cold, against the snow. From time to time he checked on Dreybach. But without light to see, he could only guess how his friend was holding up. As a precaution, the Captain of the *Steuben* had extinguished all electrical lighting, leaving the passengers in pitch dark. Thankfully, the sea had remained relatively smooth, without jarring waves. If not for the war, the many wounded, the exhaustion and lack of food, Foss might have regarded the trip as adventurous. Even poetic, in a way. Perhaps he would write about it in the future, once they were on land and safe. Yawning, Foss stretched his arms overhead when a shock reverberated across the ship. Losing his balance and rolling over a wounded man who cried out in pain, Foss thought he heard a muffled explosion, then screams drowned out the noise. Standing up, he was nearly knocked over again when a second shock rocked the *Steuben*. This time a distinct explosion.

"What the hell was that?" One of the wounded next to Dreybach had woken. Secured to a stretcher, he could do no more than lift his head. "Are we being attacked?"

His gut tied in knots, Foss searched the lightless horizon from side to side, then behind him, but saw nothing. No sound of planes in the sky either. The ship had lost speed, but had not stopped completely. Or am I mistaken? Foss thought, uncertain. He wondered whether one of the engines had blown up. Then the *Steuben* began to tilt. A continuous piercing howl was now heard all over the ship—and it didn't cease. A madness overtook those on the outer deck. Refugees scrambled over the wounded who cursed them vilely. Those that had been issued with life-jackets tried to put them on, though most had no idea how to secure them properly. The crew had not had enough time to give instructions before leaving Pillau. A woman tripped and fell against Foss. She screamed so loudly he cupped a hand over her mouth.

"Calm yourself," he said, keeping his palm firmly over her lips. But she fought him like a wild beast. Finally he released her.

"We've been torpedoed! Everyone to the lifeboats!" A sailor had appeared. He was waving frantically for people to follow him. It was then Dreybach awoke from his stupor.

"Aksel . . . where are you? What's happening?"

What words to use? "I'm still here. The ship's been hit."

"Hit?"

"A torpedo. More than one, I think."

Dreybach opened his mouth to speak, but abruptly shut it again. A large beam of light temporarily blinded those on the main deck. A searchlight from the torpedo boat—roamed back and forth, trying to make sense of the chaos. The ship was listing to starboard. And sinking. The bows had already slid under and people were leaping into the water. The crescendo of screams ascending from the lower decks was deafening. Thousands trapped who could not get out. Gunshots also erupted from below. Then one went off nearby, causing Foss to take hold of his own gun.

A wounded man had pulled out a pistol and shot himself in the head. Then more shots. Those without guns began to plead for one. Seeing Foss's weapon, a legless man reached up to try to steal it. Foss stepped away before he could do so.

"Just shoot me," the man begged. "Don't let me drown." Other men began to clamor for the same.

Foss couldn't think anymore. The ship was sinking further. Dreybach was trying to free himself from the stretcher, but too weak to loosen the straps, gave up. His feverish face looked up at Foss.

"I never wanted to get on this blasted boat," he said, his voice toneless. "Aksel—you must do it. You must shoot. Now!"

The screams had not abated. Had gotten louder. Mixed in with weeping and guns still going off. His throat constricting, Foss tried speaking but the words would not form. He shook his head.

"Erwin, I won't shoot you. Or any other wounded."

"Then give me the damn gun!"

Fearing suddenly for his own life, Foss glanced out at the sea swarming now with people. He had not been issued a life-jacket. And though he was a fine swimmer, the water was too cold for anyone to last long. A matter of time.

"Give me the gun, Aksel."

Foss bit his lip. The ship began to list to the point that if he didn't get away in minutes, then he'd be pulled down with it in the resulting undertow. For a moment he considered shooting himself. Then he thought of Jutta. And . . . decided he wanted to live.

And he wanted his friend to live too. He believed with a little effort he could get Dreybach's stretcher in the water safely. *We'll both survive!* "Hold on, Erwin!" Foss bent down to pull the stretcher off the deck when several other wounded men grabbed at him, grasping for his gun. Just then the ship lurched. The men strapped to the stretchers began to slide seawards, their horrid shouts for help echoing momentarily, before stopping altogether. The rising waves buried them. Yelling out in desperation while holding on to a thin rope attached to the rail, Foss looked for Dreybach—but he was gone. Foss continued to yell like a madman. When he saw a small girl fall into the water holding to a doll, he jumped in after her.

As he went under fully, the sea stabbed his entire body with thousands of icy needles. He rose, spitting out a mouthful of salty water, the air nearly knocked out of him by the endless chill. Gasping, he tread the waves, searching in all directions. The child had vanished. Foss swam. Despite the terrible cold, despite the tragedy of losing Dreybach, he knew he must get far from the ship. Then something hit him, scratching his forehead.

"I can't swim!" A man floundering in the water grabbed Foss's hair, pushing him under. Unable to breathe, Foss lashed out like a man possessed. He punched the man in the groin. He punched again. A second later he was free. He swam away. A few meters ahead, he saw what appeared to be a boat. Reaching it, he put a hand on the wooden rail and tried to yank himself up. Then his hand was on fire and he fell back.

"Go find your own boat, you bastard. This one's full!" Foss couldn't see who had spoken, but surmised he would have to fight to board the boat. His energy ebbing, he chose to look elsewhere. Scouring the sea for anything to cling to, he knew he could not last much longer. A life-jacket. A piece of wood. He was so cold now he felt numb. Then without realizing it at first, he bumped into an object. Hard. It was wood. Another lifeboat! Bracing himself for another attack, he grabbed hold of the rail as subtly as he could. Then not meeting any resistance, with one strenuous heave, crawled over the top and fell in.

Some seconds passed, before Foss regained his senses. He was breathing heavily. Trying to wipe the stinging salt from his eyes, he gazed around the interior of the boat. Empty! How could this be? A whole lifeboat without anyone in it. But just as quickly as he thought this, another person climbed up out of the sea. Then another. Two more people after this were pulled in by the others. One, a woman. She was crying. Over the next few minutes those with sufficient strength, pulled up six more human beings out of the swirling water. Shaking with fear and freezing temperatures, the eleven individuals sat dazed in the boat, not sure what to expect next.

Slapping and rubbing his body to regain warmth, Foss looked over the boat's rim and was shocked to see in the distance the *Steuben* falling out of the world. Incredibly, there were people clinging to the railing at the stern, no doubt hoping that the ship would not sink completely to the bottom in the shallow Baltic waters. But as Foss watched entranced, the *Steuben* twisted on its side, with those still on the stern having no choice but to leap. Horribly, dozens fell directly on to the whipping blades of the still-running propellers, screaming as they were cut to pieces. A woman beside him retched, then vomited over the rail. She then tried to rouse a man lying beside her. But he didn't wake. He was either unconscious, or dead.

Those who remained in the water were running out of time. But no one else swam towards the lifeboat. Shivering and unable to stop, Foss looked at the other people in the boat. A thought ran across his mind that these would be the people he shared death with. Then he remembered Dreybach. Nothing to do now. It was over. But thinking about Dreybach made him think about the long cold nights in Russia. Men would often huddle together to share warmth. And this had kept them alive. The same could be done here.

His voice hoarse, Foss said, "All of us must bunch up together to pool heat. An old soldier's trick. Otherwise we'll freeze to death." He moved closer to the woman. Several more people gathered around him. Eventually everyone but a lone man, who stayed by himself near the bow.

Foss was about to let him be when a sudden anger boiled over. "You there! Yes, you! Either help us keep warm—or I'll throw you back in the water." Foss wasn't sure he would have backed up his words, but what he said worked. The man grumbled, but slid over to huddle with the rest of them.

The people in the boat were a mixture of wounded soldiers and non-combatants. But at the moment it didn't matter what they were. They all had survived a torpedoed ship. They all hoped to be rescued. The woman who had earlier vomited, did so twice more over the rail. Like most of them, she had swallowed sea-water and was at the end of her tether. The man she had sought to rouse still lay sprawled in the boat, unmoving. Foss noticed that the man was completely bald, and looked old. The tremendous skirl of human voices that had gone on non-stop when the *Steuben* was sinking, had dwindled to nothing. Almost as though such frightful terror had never occurred. And neither were their voices anywhere in the water. The sea was quiet. Like a tomb. The body of the woman slouched against Foss, and he held her. He thought of the little girl with the doll—*could it have been Traudl?* He didn't want to think anymore. The boat drifted, and he was drifting in and out of consciousness. Someone began to moan. Someone prayed; recited the Lord's Prayer twice. Someone else cursed the Russians and the war and Hitler and even God and then the voice trailed away. With a start Foss raised his chin from his chest and knew that he had been dozing. *How long?* Despite the close proximity of the other people, he continued to shiver. The boat seemingly had not moved. It was too dark to see whether they were nearing a coastline. They might drift all the way to Sweden before it was over. Then a light flashed in various spots on the water.

"A rescue ship!" The man who had spoken aloud stood up waving his hands, lost his balance, and nearly toppled into the water if Foss had not caught him in time.

Those in the boat who were still coherent began to scream and call out for help. Foss opened his mouth to join in, but a morbid thought stopped him. What if it was a Soviet ship? Squinting against the darting beams, he tried to make out the vessel's logo. He decided he'd rather drown then be captured by the Russians. Then he heard a voice. A German voice. A loudspeaker blaring through the frigid air.

"This is the Captain of the T-196. Stay where you are. We are taking you aboard."

Foss realized it was the same torpedo boat that had been part of the convoy. But it had not done enough to protect the *Steuben*. He wondered if the submarine was still lurking in the vicinity. Near collapse and wanting to rest, Foss caught sight of the bald man still lying at the bottom of the boat. It renewed his desire to live. Gritting his teeth, he took hold of one of the ropes that had been thrown from the rescue ship. With trembling fingers he tied it around his waist. Three sailors then yanked him up. Being smaller, the torpedo boat was even more packed with people then the unfortunate liner had been. Foss found himself in the middle of a scene of distraught, weeping people. Wet and chilled to the bone, he felt someone wrapping a coarse blanket over his back. Wanting to thank whoever it was, Foss turned around to make out in the darkness the face of young sailor. The man nodded at Foss's appreciation, then moved on to assist another of the rescued.

Foss pulled the blanket tightly across his chest. He looked out at the black sea that had nearly claimed his life; the same sea that had claimed the life of his friend. An indifferent sea. Foss continued to look until his eyes filled with tears. They ran down his face, and he sobbed. But no one heard him. There were too many others with similar tears.

CHAPTER 12

The survivors were taken to Kolberg. A sandy seaport in Pomerania. Like so many other German cities in the path of the Red Army, Kolberg was mostly cut off from the rest of the Reich. In weeks, if not days, the Russians would encircle it entirely. No good news anywhere. Though it was forbidden to speak openly about the disasters of the *Wilhelm Gustloff* and the *Steuben*, word passed around that many thousands of passengers had gone down with both ships. The exact amount of survivors from the *Steuben* was officially unknown, but only a tiny percentage of all that had embarked from Pillau were brought ashore again. And those that *had* survived were burdened with the lingering effects of being too long exposed to wet and cold and severe mental anguish. *Why me, and not my son and daughter? Why did I make it and not my friend?* Such questions did not leave the minds of the living so easily.

The living. What was the rational definition of a living being? What did such words mean? To Aksel Foss, Danish citizen, and a decorated sergeant in the German Wehrmacht, he wondered if anything in the world held meaning anymore. Two weeks after the sinking, he sat alone in a refugee tent close to the waterfront. He was told after the fact that he had become delirious on the torpedo boat, and once the survivors had reached Kolberg, he had been carried on a stretcher straight to a hospital. The doctors had diagnosed him with overexposure to the elements, which in turn had caused him to develop pneumonia. Days went by when he lapsed in and out of consciousness and couldn't even say his name when asked. Then the symptoms subsided, gradually, and Foss became aware of his surroundings. Another few days, when he had eaten his fill of warm food, and no longer felt chilled, he stepped out of the bed, and told the doctors he was fit enough to leave. Countermanding their insistence that he was not fully healthy again, Foss refused to stay in the hospital any longer than required. Then, having been outfitted with a used army uniform—*had it belonged to a dead man?*—Foss was given orders to remain in one of the shelters close to the pier. He was to be called back to duty, if needed—*and what man wasn't needed these days*—otherwise he would be sent further west on one of the first available boats.

Foss smoked a cigarette. He glanced off and on at snow swirling outside the tent. He thought about Tulm and Ziemans. Wished he were with them. Even considered putting in a request to be taken back to Pillau. Then realized the pointlessness of such an action. Those in command would think he had lost his wits; besides, his remaining friends might be fighting on a different sector of the front. Or . . . they might be dead.

Like Dreybach.

Foss closed his eyes. Then opened them almost immediately when he heard footsteps crunching on old snow. A woman with blonde hair . . . a nurse was walking by the tent. She was in a hurry. Foss felt his heart leap. He nearly called out to the woman, but thought, *No, it can't be her.* But what if it was? Throwing his cigarette down, he ran after her.

"Jutta?"

The woman walked a few more paces, then stopped.

"Jutta—it's Aksel!"

Turning around slowly, the woman looked puzzled. Then meeting Foss's eyes, she gaped.

"Oh my God! Aksel! I thought I was imagining things. It is you . . . "

For a few moments they stood silently staring at each other. Then Jutta ran to Foss and fell into his embrace.

"I never believed I would see you again," Jutta said, her voice happy as she stroked Foss's cheeks with both hands. "Aksel, you are so thin. Has the army not been feeding you?"

"Yes. With the meager rations they offer. But I haven't had much appetite lately."

Surprised to see that Foss was all by himself, Jutta asked, "Where are your friends?"

Shrugging his shoulders limply, Foss didn't respond.

"Aksel, they're not . . . ?"

"Some of them are," he answered, his eyes downcast. "A few may still be fighting in the lines south of Koenigsberg. One of them—went down with the *Steuben.*"

"Oh no . . . "

"I was supposed to take care of him."

"You were with him?"

Foss made the slightest of nods.

Showing sincere sympathy, Jutta gently squeezed Foss's hand. "Oh Aksel, I don't know what to say."

"There's nothing, to say."

For some minutes they continued to hug and caress one another while snowflakes fell on them and on the ground. Then slipping from the embrace, Jutta pointed down the street. "I'm staying in an abandoned building with two other nurses. I have a place all to myself. It's only a short walk from here."

When Foss began to ask her how she had ended up in Kolberg. Jutta put a finger over his lips. Then she kissed him on the cheek. "We can speak of that later. If your unit seeks your whereabouts, I'll say I was ordered to give you medicine."

"I don't have a unit anymore," Foss muttered.

"Then we won't have to worry." She led him by the hand down a deserted street. Foss observed several burned out automobiles and trucks, and the skeletal carcass of what had once been a horse. He thought of Jutta's injured horse that he had shot in the snow on the road to Koenigsberg. Jutta seemed to take no notice of the carcass. In a few minutes they came to a five-story apartment building made of red brick. Shards of glass from broken windows filled the street near the entrance. A building one block down had been flattened like a pancake. A heap of rubble. Foss discerned it must have taken a direct hit from a Russian bomb, while the residences nearby were mostly spared of any damage.

Turning to him and smiling, Jutta waved her hand to follow her as she leaned on the front door and turned the nob. It didn't budge at first. Foss put his weight to it. Finally the door opened with a creak and they stepped inside. Jutta closed the door behind them.

"It's on the second floor," she said. "Are you hungry, Aksel? Let me cook you something."

"I'm not hungry," he said resignedly, as they entered her apartment. "Maybe in a few hours."

"I was planning to make potato soup. Working with the medical unit—we are privy to a little better fare."

"How did you become—" Foss halted in mid-sentence as he began to cough violently. It took him nearly a minute before regaining his composure. In the meantime Jutta led him to a chair. Appearing concerned, she was about to ask him a question when he put up a hand.

"I had a bout of pneumonia," he said. "That's all. After the *Steuben*."

"Well, then you should be back in the hospital," she scolded. "A bout! Pneumonia can be deadly."

"Just about everything in this war is deadly."

She looked at him as a mother would a child. Foss knew that he must seem almost like another man to her. His body frail, his voice without tone or authority. She said, "I'm cooking the soup whether you like it or not. You need food inside you."

"Alright. I'll eat your soup. I meant to ask how you became a nurse. I thought you'd be on the other side of Germany by now."

They didn't talk in depth until after the meal. With no butter or spices, they ate the soup plain. There was enough for two portions for each of them, along with a small loaf of rye bread that Jutta had also obtained. Foss was surprised when she pulled from a sack a bottle of beer for each of them. Then Jutta gently pressed Foss to speak of his trials. Without excessive details, he told her about the trek to Pillau, but when he tried to relay the terrors of the brief sea voyage, he found himself quaking, and near tears.

"Dreybach never wanted to get on that boat," Foss said between pauses. "I kept drilling it into him that he needed to go. That I would be there to help him. Instead, I caused his death. I . . . " Faltering, he turned aside from Jutta's gaze.

Stroking his forearm, she said, "Don't blame yourself, Aksel. The culprits of this war are in Berlin. *They* killed your friend. You tried to save him."

Foss agreed with her, but what one opined as right or wrong didn't alter harsh facts. Never in the past and not now. Trying to recompose himself, he said, "His wounds were so bad he would have died if he remained back at Pillau. Medical supplies there were almost non-existent. But regardless of the truth of the matter—it doesn't ease my mind that he died in an undertaking I encouraged."

Sitting beside him on an old brown sofa that had seen its share of use, Jutta moved closer to him. She ran a hand through his hair. "You were the person who made me realize that one can't go back."

There was no judgment in her words. "What happened to me back in my farmhouse still haunts me daily. Still plagues me with nightmares. Maybe I'll always be haunted. But what can be done about it . . . ?"

Nothing. Foss didn't need to say the word aloud. Viewing the apartment as if for the first time, Foss noticed a wind-up gramophone on a table. "I haven't heard a record in ages," he said nostalgically.

Jutta shook her head. "Doesn't work, unfortunately. Maybe that's why the family that lived here didn't take it with them. Besides, there are no records anywhere in the apartment. I surmise they took their records with them, wherever they went. They didn't leave much in the way of valuables, that's for sure."

Foss began to see how bare the place was. Almost as though it had been ransacked. A few torn curtains, a pair of leather shoes without shoestrings, an umbrella hung from a hatstand. "Where'd they go?" he asked.

"The same place you wanted me to go—West. Ships have been carrying residents out of Kolberg for many weeks. But now the city's been flooded with refugees from everywhere. Estimates are up to a hundred thousand." She paused, her face grim. "It's been rumored the Russians could attack in force any day now."

"Then for God's sake, why haven't you left?"

Jutta smiled at the question. "I was waiting for *you*."

At first Aksel thought he had not heard her right. "What made you think I was coming to Kolberg?"

"A whim. When I left you on the road, my intuition told me that I would see you again."

Foss recalled vividly the sad parting that had been forced upon them, and the thought then, that they would never again cross paths. He had been wrong. *The strangeness of life.* The small wonders amidst the greater turmoil. A far-off rumble sundered his reminiscing. He frowned, wishing it would go away. It did not. Jutta too, acknowledged the sound.

"I never thought I'd get used to hearing the guns," she said with a shrug. "Odd, but they don't frighten me much anymore. Treating the wounded everyday—I know those poor soldiers have gone through a lot worse."

"You haven't yet told me how you became a nurse? Was it here, or earlier?"

"Here. In Kolberg. After you went back to the front, I was taken with other refugees by truck to Koenigsberg. There, I got out on a ship that was meant to travel to Kiel—but either engine trouble or the threat of aircraft forced us to set anchor at Kolberg. I never did find out the facts as to why we didn't sail further. Perhaps the captain was scared. Or they needed the ship elsewhere."

"But certainly you could have sought a berth on another vessel. I thought originally you were headed for Danzig—to search for your aunt."

"Yes, that was the plan," she said, yawning. "But she might have been evacuated herself. And I was never given the opportunity to decide where

I wanted to go. You might have heard—the situation in Danzig is just as precarious as Kolberg. There's no safe havens anymore."

Foss glanced around the apartment again. It was getting almost too dark to see. The little light left from dusk had dwindled to a thin dull light in the snow-filled sky. Jutta had earlier lit several candles. She proceeded to blow these out.

"We have to maintain the black-out," she said without reproach. "Don't give the Russian planes a bombing target."

For several minutes they sat silent in the darkness. Then Foss said, "You never answered my question."

"What? You mean about the nursing?"

"Yes."

"Didn't you believe me when I said I was waiting for you?"

Foss wasn't sure whether she was serious, or merely pretending to be hurt. He put an arm around her shoulder and she snuggled closer to him. He felt a sensation in his groin, but for some reason he felt hesitant, nervous. Then her eyes met his, and on impulse he kissed Jutta on the lips.

"So you still like me?" Jutta questioned a little teasingly.

Foss smiled. The first smile in many weeks. "Always and forever," he said as he kissed her again, this time longer.

The rumbling to the south grew heavier. They continued to kiss and hold each other. Then Jutta said, "Maybe it sounds old-fashioned and very German—but I became a nurse because felt I needed to do something for the war effort. Something to help. Do my Aryan duty!"

Even in the darkness Foss saw her sarcastic smirk. He said, "No insult intended—but you had no prior skills—or maybe you did."

"I did. If you can remember me telling you—I nursed my father for years when he was sick. At the hospital they gave me and a few other volunteers several days of rudimentary training. Then threw us into the fire." She emphasized the last word with a weary sigh.

A particularly loud blast sounded close by. Instinctively Foss stood up and looked around for his gun. Then remembering where he was, he sat down again.

"I feel naked without my gun," he said abruptly.

Jutta didn't respond, and Foss said, "You mentioned two fellow nurses living here. Friends of yours?"

"Two other women I met on the same boat. They too have lost their husbands in the war. They volunteered like I did."

"Why aren't they here with you?"

"Oh, they found separate apartments. The same building, but it's best this way."

"Wouldn't it be safer if you lived together?"

"Perhaps," Jutta laughed. "But I doubt I'd get much sleep."

"What do you mean?"

"It wouldn't matter with the one girl—she always works the night shift. The other though"—Jutta paused, searching for the right words—"is performing another night shift. She's having an affair with one of the surgeons. And he's married."

A sense of sudden unease swept across Foss's mind. He knew it was petty of him, but he asked the question anyway. "So, do you fancy one of the doctors?"

Jutta was shocked at Foss's obvious jealousy. "Of course not! Would I be sitting here kissing you if it were otherwise?" Then a wave of jealousy overtook her. "What about you? Maybe you've been spreading your wings a bit . . . "

Foss felt all of a sudden stupid. He took Jutta's hand and kissed it. "Sorry. I'm being an idiot. No. No others for me. You're the only female I've been thinking about. You're the only want I want."

A silent awkward moment. Then soothed, Jutta said, "The former occupants did leave one important thing behind."

"What?"

"A bed . . . " Jutta uttered the words in a tantalizing manner. "Of course . . . only for sleeping in," she quickly added.

Foss noted the amusement in her voice, then without thinking, began to tickle her just above the hips. Caught off guard, Jutta giggled uncontrollably. When Foss stopped after a few seconds, she said, "How did you know I was so ticklish?"

"I have a good memory."

Several moments passed before Jutta understood. "Yes. Now I remember. In the hunter's cabin."

"Fortunately, I clamped a hand over your mouth. Else you might have had the entire Red Army on top of us."

Foss regretted his choice of words almost as soon as he spoke them. But though Jutta remained quiet a moment, she didn't bring up the bitter topic. Instead, she circled Foss's knuckles gently with her fingers. "I'm going to bed, Aksel," she said in a voice that brokered no argument. Then taking off her shoes, rose, and walked to the bedroom.

Foss was experienced enough to know not to lag behind. But the surprise that awaited him nearly stopped his heart. In the short time Jutta was gone from the living room, she had unpeeled her clothes. They now lay in a pile beside her naked feet. On a dresser beside the bed she had lit a single small candle which danced off her nudity and emphasized the golden tinge of her hair. Her large breasts fit perfectly with a body that was well-muscled from years of manual labor, yet still shapely enough to be feminine. How long Foss stood there staring, open-mouthed, he would never know. Her eyes cat-like, she beckoned him to the bed, then blew out the candle. If a man needed more than that to get in the mood, then he was missing something in his brain. Foss removed his own clothing in a hurry. The night was bitterly cold, but Jutta gathered three blankets over them. After awhile, they only needed one.

In time, they fell asleep. Periodically, one of them would wake, rouse the other, then they'd begin again. Or begin where they had left off. Finally Jutta dozed off in Foss's arms, and though every part of his body was fatigued beyond recall, Foss's mind wouldn't—couldn't—completely shut out the world.

What did it all mean? Was it a dream? Foss felt Jutta's breath on his chest, her hair spilling on to his skin. No dream. But why such beauty after all the ugliness, all the killing? Do I deserve this—after what happened to Dreybach? A soldier shouldn't think too much, he told himself. If you can't resolve something, let it be. Live live live, and live some more. In a week's time you may not be around.

Yet the poet in him continued to search for meaning. Search for truth. He ran a hand slowly down Jutta's spine and she stirred, mumbled something, but didn't wake. Neither of them had the energy for any further play—at least he didn't!—but Foss suddenly wanted to talk. Share. Despite her physical presence, he felt alone.

Alone. The bed hurt his back. It was lumpy. The springs had little bounce to them. He wondered who else had made love in this bed—and where were they now? Did they shed tears the last night they slept here?

Or lie awake all night unable to sleep? The future remorselessly upon them, rushing them off to a better life . . . or a barren unknown.

The thoughts drifted by, and the bombs still pummeled the hinterland miles away. The regularity of their sound made Foss think of the ticking of a clock. Time moving. Time unaware of itself. Unaware of the war. He remembered summer days sitting by the Øresund, the strait that separated Denmark from Sweden. The coast of Sweden was often visible when no fog or heavy cloud cover lingered. But Foss loved fog, loved clouds. Poetic. Mysterious. Silently going wherever the wind blew them. White and gray clouds moving harmlessly. Large and small clouds shifting east and west freely without borders, without ideologies. It was this that led him to relax. He coughed briefly, sighed, and his mind went blank.

CHAPTER 13

He wanted to believe that it was not running away, but rather, saving himself to fight on another field. Armies had done this since the beginning of warfare. The Russians had merely more men and more equipment at the moment. But he had learned that new divisions were being formed in the west. With these troops, the Reich would once again assert its dominance as the supreme military power in Europe.

Otto Meyer, though, was a practical man. Despite his loyalty to Adolf Hitler, to the SS, to Germany, he was skeptical about the reports of newly-formed German armies with an unprecedented number of Tiger tanks. Even more skeptical about the heralded weapons of wonder that would turn the tide. The V1 and V2 rockets had certainly damaged London, but they had not forced the allies out of the war. Not even close.

Awaiting impatiently a transport ship to whisk him away from the dock of Danzig, Meyer lighted a cigarette. Then for the umpteenth time checked carefully through his two bags. The only luggage he carried. Yes, everything was in order. He had not forgotten anything, not left a single important thing behind. He even brought along a photo of the Polish whore who had kept him company the past six months. The bitch had wept and pleaded to take her with him to the west. Even threatened to commit suicide if he reneged on the German passport he had once promised her. But it had only been a ploy to keep her content. *Go ahead—kill yourself,* he had told her. Poles weren't allowed to travel with officers of the SS, and that was that. Not totally uncaring, Meyer had given her several gold rings he had once taken off inmates that had been gassed at a concentration camp. He of course had not told her the truth about the former owners. Whether the gold bought her much, he would never know. She was terrified of the fate that awaited her once the Russians captured Danzig. And they would capture it. That was why he and other top Nazi personnel were being evacuated before the guillotine was let loose. Danzig was already under heavy daily bombardment. Meyer's own office had been hit. Luckily, he had been late to work that morning. Usually punctual to perfection, he had cut himself shaving, and because of it, his life had been spared. The rest of his staff had all been killed or seriously injured. Four dead outright, one losing an arm, another rendered comatose, and near death.

Meyer's attention was diverted when he heard shouts and curses nearby. A scuffle had broken out between a group of women refugees fighting over a small sack of potatoes. Meyer was about to go over and break it up, when one of the women grabbed the sack and ran off with it. Shrieking with anger, the rest of them chased after her.

The mob mentality. Meyer had never liked large crowds of people, and looking at the women, he felt a sense of irritation at the way civilians were behaving themselves at time when calmness and reservation were what was needed for society to remain whole. Cynical that such people would ever contribute toward helping Germany in this hour of plight, he shook his head with disdain. The core was rotten. And it reminded him of the case he had not yet cracked. His slain compatriots had been murdered by a foreign criminal impersonating a regular soldier. Meyer had scoured all the Wehrmacht files he could lay his hands on, probed the lists of the Army Groups and divisions spread throughout East Prussia, but it was a nightmare trying to locate one single suspect out of hundreds of thousands of troops, many of whom were now dead, missing in action, or trapped behind the Russian lines. He had come across a wounded Dutchman in a hospital tent here in Danzig, but the man had had witnesses who swore that he had served in the German Army faithfully, and had already been wounded at the time the SS guards were killed. There had also been a Norwegian who had been arrested in Oslo and deported to work as a slave-laborer on a Prussian farm for having Communist sympathies. But he too had turned out to be a dead end.

Meyer took in a last few drags on his cigarette then threw the butt into the waters splashing against the dockside. The trail of the mysterious foreign-born sergeant had grown cold. Was the case even worth wasting any more time on, now that he was leaving the city? Probably forever.

He could always inquire in Kolberg. The place where his ship was headed. Another Festung. Another city the Russians would soon swarm over. But he would only be there a week or two. At the most. Some shoring up of the local department. A few executions of traitors and spies. The brass had promised him a rise in command and a higher salary if he took the job before eventually embarking for Denmark. And if the situation in Denmark worsened, he would then fly to Norway. And if that didn't pan out, then a U-boat would make sure he got safely to Spain. A

Fascist nation that could use his services. But first: Kolberg. Meyer hoped he could find another whore there, to make the brief stay more pleasurable.

Foss awoke in the middle of the night to a pleasure he had not experienced since before the war. When Jutta finished with him, he lay on his back deliciously exhausted. He could not understand why some people equated such acts as being beastly. She snuggled up to him afterwards. No words were spoken—nor were they needed. Then sighing happily, Foss said, "I didn't think country girls knew about that."

Her eyes closed, Jutta cracked a smile. "We're more sophisticated than you can imagine."

Foss believed it. Shaking his head, he said, "All of this seems so unreal."

Jutta cocked one eye open, partly alarmed at the tone in Foss's voice. "Why unreal?" she asked.

Suppressing a cough, Foss shrugged. "I never expected someone like you to come into my life. Not here. Not now."

Jutta looked at him with both eyes. "I've been wondering the same thing. You're not regretting anything, are you?"

Clearing his throat, Foss ran a hand down Jutta's spine, only halting when he reached her rear end. He let the hand stay there. "No regrets at all," he said candidly. "Not concerning you. There are many other things I regret. Yet what's the worth in speaking about anything you can't undo . . ."

The drone of the war continued in the background. To both of them it was like the buzzing of a fly at a window. Noticeable, but not worrisome. Taking Foss's other hand in her own, Jutta squeezed it affectionately, then squeezed again. "Have you written me any poems?" she asked.

"I've written you dozens of poems in my head."

"And you haven't put them on paper yet?" She playfully cuffed him on the shoulder.

"Paper's a scarce commodity at the front. You'll get them someday."

Jutta's face turned serious. "Do you remember what you said on the road, Aksel? Just before we parted?"

Foss gave a nod. "I remember."

Jutta was quiet a moment. "Do you still feel that way?"

She was putting him on the spot. From their brief time in the hut, he recalled Jutta being a person who needed to get to the bottom of things—but there was not always a straightforward answer why people fell in love. Considering all that had passed since then, the loss of his remaining friends, the near-loss of his sanity, Foss wondered whether he had changed too much in Jutta's eyes. Or maybe new experiences in her own life in the past month had changed her. Foss realized that war often heightened or degraded people's normal life-patterns. To the extent that they could turn into saints or monsters. Love in war followed the same highs and lows. He would not hold it against her if she no longer felt a deeper love for him.

"Yes, I still feel that way," Foss answered.

Her eyes sparkling, Jutta pressed her lips against his. "So you love me?"

"I love you, Jutta."

She kissed him again, more forcefully. "I guess I'm in the same boat. I love you!"

Foss felt like he couldn't breathe—he was that thrilled, that happy. And he felt a fire reigniting in his loins. Gently pushing Jutta on to her backside, he once more joined his body with hers.

For a long time afterward Jutta lay on Foss's chest, cradled by his arms. They both soon fell asleep. Only to be awakened by the growing intensity of the Russian batteries pounding the German positions. Becoming all of a sudden afraid, Jutta gripped Foss so hard that her nails dug into his flesh.

"We have to survive this war, Aksel," she said, arching up so that she looked at him in the eye. "We simply have to. I've lost too much already—I don't want to lose you. I want to be with you always."

"But I'm going back to Denmark."

"Then I'm going to Denmark with you."

Foss suddenly remembered Tulm's opinion that nothing remained for him in Germany. The same could be said for Jutta. "I was told while recuperating at the hospital here that I would be boarding a ship to take me home soon. We could go together."

"We could . . . " Jutta appeared pensive. "There's an order that all women in the nursing corps must leave once the Russians are on the outskirts of the city. Which could be any day now. Though at the moment, the trains are still running in and out of Kolberg. Access across the Oder is not completely cut off."

Foss had seen the train station and knew that it was true. But he had no desire to travel anywhere deeper into Germany. "I don't relish the idea of sailing on a ship again—not after what happened. But it's far easier to reach Copenhagen that way."

"Sailing gives me the jitters too. I got seasick coming here." Jutta brushed a strand of hair away that had fallen over one of her eyes. "If we went by train, we could connect to another one heading north."

Images of the smashed train in East Prussia ran through Foss's mind. He had not told Jutta of that incident. "I'm not wild about going by train either," he reproved. "The Russians might cut the lines at some point. Then there'd be hell to pay."

Jutta opened her mouth to speak, then shivered. "There's no happy medium in this case."

"No, there's not. Unfortunately."

They lay silent awhile. The first gray light of dawn showed through the window. Foss heard voices outside. He stood up to look. A throng of refugees were passing down the street, headed toward the railway station. Foss felt Jutta beside him. She had wrapped the blanket around her.

"Kolberg is too small for so many refugees," Jutta declared sadly. "I learned the other day that we have more civilians than soldiers. And most of the soldiers are wounded or inexperienced."

Well aware that green troops would be no match for the veterans of the Red Army hardened by four years of war, Foss wondered what had happened to Tulm and Ziemans. Turning away from the window, he sat on the edge of the bed. He watched as Jutta began to dress herself.

"I have to work in an hour," she said. "But I know a place where I can scrounge up some breakfast. The Black Market here has become the main way of staying alive."

Donning his own clothes, Foss started to cough violently. Concerned, Jutta said, "I'll see what I can do about getting you some proper medicine. Why don't you stay in the apartment today rather than wander around in the cold." Jutta gave him a motherly look. "You don't want to get pneumonia again."

"What time will you return?"

"In the evening."

Foss considered this. He wanted to find out the time of the next outgoing ship. He decided not to tell Jutta this. "Alright, I'll stay in the apartment."

Jutta went out and got them some breakfast. There would be enough leftovers to tide Foss over through the day. For nearly a week they lived according to this pattern: Jutta working during the day and Foss spending most of the time alone in the apartment. She even brought him a notebook and few pencils. He wrote down some of his thoughts; jotted down the drafts for several poems. At night they fulfilled their urges, and slept contently in one another's arms. Foss had found passage aboard a torpedo boat and waited only for Jutta to receive permission to travel alongside him. But the decision was shortly taken from them. The Russians were probing the outer defenses of Kolberg, and finding them almost non-existent, had begun sending infantry and tanks along the Persante River that flowed in a northwesterly direction toward the coast. Jutta returned at noon one day instead of her usual time in the evening. Her face was flushed. Marks left by tears lined her cheeks. Foss sensed immediately the change in her mood.

"What's the matter, Jutta?"

A biting of lips, more tears. "I've been ordered to leave Kolberg," she said in a tiny voice.

Foss was at first joyfully startled, thinking she had received the official pass they both wanted. But when she cried harder, his hopes were dashed.

"Don't you want to leave?" he asked, wiping the tears from her face with his hand.

"I do . . . but not this way. All females associated with the military have been ordered to take the next train. The last train heading west. I'm being sent to Berlin, Aksel."

Something clutched at Foss's heart. "Can't you request reassignment elsewhere?" But he knew as soon as he said it, the inanity of such a question.

"I tried," she said tearfully. Jutta appeared as forlorn as Foss had ever seen her. "I even lied," she continued. "Told my superior I had relatives near the Danish border. He said everyone had relatives somewhere, but that we all have a duty to fulfill. No more wounded are being brought to Kolberg. The army doesn't want women nurses in the fighting areas."

Foss scoffed at this. "Then why the hell are they sending you to Berlin? Does Hitler think Stalin is planning a picnic on the outskirts of the capital? The situation will be a hell of a lot worse there!"

Jutta shook with sobs, and her nurse's hat fell to the floor. Foss retrieved it, then pulled her into his arms. He was about to speak when she spoke first. "That's not the only bad news. All able-bodied men are to report by eight o'clock tomorrow morning at the railroad depot." She hesitated. "And it's not to catch a train . . . "

It took a few seconds for Foss to understand her meaning. He was being ordered back into the army. For a moment, panic set in. It was not possible. He had been declared mentally unstable by a military physician. He had nearly drowned in a ship-wreck that had taken the lives of thousands. And he had only just gotten over pneumonia. They could not legally coerce him. He had already served his time.

"I won't go," he concluded, his voice stern.

"You'll be shot, Aksel. You know that better than I do."

Foss thought back to the time he had tried to escape in Denmark. Before he had even gone to boot camp. He'd been caught just outside the fence to the barracks and later given a thorough thrashing. In the Danish Army he might have received a bureaucratic slap on the wrist and brief prison stay. But Denmark was a democratic nation. The Nazis held different rules. Foss cursed inwardly as he remembered the many corpses he had seen the last several months, swaying from trees and poles with placards hung from their stretched necks proclaiming their supposed treachery toward the Fatherland. It made no difference that he wasn't German. *Goddamn them!* he fumed. For an angry moment he hoped the allies and the Russians destroyed the lot of them and their sick political vision. But then he recalled the Germans who had meant something to him; he recalled his comrades; he recalled Dreybach falling away from him into the sea. Thinking back to his time spent in the Soviet Union, Foss missed the camaraderie of his friends. A hand on his arm brought him back from his reverie.

"You were somewhere else for a moment," Jutta said, her voice anxious.

Foss nodded, slowly. "This war never seems to end. If I'm to serve again, I only wish it could be with those whom I trust. You get to know how men react in a battle—who will cover for you, and who won't. You don't build such cohesiveness in a week's time. And here . . . we might not even have a week."

"You make it sound so hopeless . . . "Jutta was too exasperated with fear and sorrow to speak. Then clinging to Foss as though he would leave her any second, she said, "We must survive this war, Aksel. We must find each other again! Somewhere in Germany, or in Denmark. We can't lose each

other! I've lost everything else . . . " She kissed him fiercely. "Promise
you'll come back to me."

Promises. Foss had promised Dreybach that they would reach land safely.
He now wondered whether promises should even be given in wartime. Foss
met Jutta's gaze and reflected on the fact that two months ago he didn't
know such a woman existed. Did he really love her . . . so much that he
was willing to spend the rest of his years with her? And why the doubt? He
had nothing else. Nothing, except a desire to return home. Jutta had begun
to shed more tears, and Foss realized he must give her an answer. *But what
answer?* Jutta was a beautiful person, a good person—but am I good enough
for *her?* And how would their feelings be in peacetime? They might share
endearments at this moment, but life could change in the blink of an eye.
Steenhagen had died in less time than that.

"If it's within my power," Foss said honestly, "then I'll come back to
you. Wherever you are."

Noises from the street broke in on them. Parting the curtains, they
looked down to see hundreds of refugees racing along the street toward the
train station. People were shoving and bumping into one another. A few
stumbled and fell, and were trampled under the stampede. Foss saw a young
woman fall with her baby. Somehow she managed to stand again, but the
infant was not in her hands. Frantically she searched the ground. Foss
closed the curtains again.

"I experienced worse in Russia," he said flatly. "People strangled each
other over a crust of bread."

"What is happening to us? We've become so beastly!"

After losing Dreybach, Foss was almost too weary and numb to care
about the plight of civilians.

"The train may already be here, Jutta. We better leave."

They left. And fought through the crowd to get to the station. Jutta had
her ticket ready. She carried only a small suitcase. All her other belongings
remained behind in the apartment.

"We're not allowed to take anymore than this," she said, trying her best
to keep control of her emotions. She was right. The luggage and valuables
of scores of refugees were strewn across the platform like the treasures from
a vanished civilization. But not everyone was going. Those not able to
obtain a viable transport pass would have to wait to travel by ship. People

wept, growled, prayed. Yet it made no difference. The Russians were coming—and the world was hurtling to an end.

Foss gripped Jutta in a bear-hug, feeling a new batch of her tears lather his face and neck. The blast of a whistle startled him, and he tried stifling the memories of the shot-up train.

"I'll write to you once I reach my destination." Despite the sincerity of her words, a stark uncertainty tinged Jutta's voice.

"Madam, you must board now." A sullen-faced conductor stood near them. He was peering at his watch.

"Goodbye . . . Aksel." Hesitating, Jutta only stepped toward the train when the conductor glared at her.

The second goodbye. The final one? Foss ran to Jutta, catching up to her just as she reached the coach doors. Not caring about proper etiquette, he kissed her one last time on the lips.

"Farewell, Jutta." He wanted to say more—much more—but an excess of words at such a moment seemed trite. The train was packed. He lost track of Jutta as she walked down the aisle. Because of the cold weather, the windows were kept closed. Foss kept pace with the train as it started and picked up speed. But no one waved. And no one waved from the platform. Those left in Kolberg were bitter, jealous, forlorn. Too soon the train was lost to view. The refugees unhappily trudged away from the station to wait at the harbor. Foss was one of the last persons standing near the railroad tracks. The smoke from the engine was the final thing he saw. Then it too disappeared. But he knew there would be more smoke in the coming days. And it wouldn't be from a train.

MARCH 1945

CHAPTER 14

The morning was gray. A sea wind with the tang of salt blew inland across the city. Given a brief respite from shoveling with the rest of the troops manning the front line, Foss took time to write a letter to Jutta. In the past day he had already written her two, but not yet knowing her address, he kept them folded up in his jacket to send later. *If he could send them.* He might not be in Kolberg that long. With less than a division in strength, the Germans planned to hold up the Red Army's advance long enough so that all the remaining civilians could escape by sea. With the soldiers to follow afterward.

Foss winced as he felt a tweak in his back. Seemingly every muscle in his body ached from digging anti-tank ditches. But some of the other men were in worse shape. Most of the soldiers defending Kolberg were too old or too young, or wounded men barely healed who had been thrust back into action simply because there were no other reserves. Given a brand new uniform and boots—*that was a surprise*—five grenades and an MP 40, the German-made Tommy gun, Foss had settled back in the role of assuming command over a squad of soldiers. The old skills of being a sergeant had returned quickly, and the men responded to him with respect. At least he thought so. He had not yet encountered any smart alecks like Ziemans. And unlike Ruder, not one man had broadcast a deep and abiding sympathy for Nazism.

Picking up his shovel, Foss started to dig again. Thankfully the ground had begun to thaw. Weeks earlier such toil would have netted little gain, with the ground being iron-hard, but now the semblance of a long trench took shape on the coastal side of the river. Actually, being so close to the water, the soil was not ideal for trenches. Too muddy. Too loose. And too likely to erode away at the first spring rain. Though the weather was still cold, a hint of the warmer season loomed in the air.

"Do you really think this trench will stop the tanks, Sergeant?" Expressing doubt, a young fair-haired soldier gazed at Foss as though anything he voiced would be accepted as truth.

Foss noticed the soldier had the smooth cheeks of one who had not yet begun to shave. *Should I lie to soothe his fears?* Foss decided to be candid. "It might stop them a short while."

"A short while . . . ?"

Foss knew only too well that no barriers, natural or man-made, had halted the Russians for any significant length of time. This one wouldn't either. "We'll have to beat them back with our weapons."

Taking a pause from shoveling, an older man nearby wiped a line a sweat from his brow. Shaking his head, he said, "Then why are we breaking our backs like this—if it's to no avail?"

Foss kept digging. "Because we're soldiers. And when soldiers are given orders, the orders have to be followed."

Foss had spoken a plain fact, but the older man took it as sarcasm. "So what are we supposed to do, fight them with our bare hands? We have only a dozen or so tanks to defend the whole of Kolberg, and these can hardly move for lack of fuel. We're just wasting our time here. The brass don't care if we die as long as they have their embarkation passes. Fuck them!" The man looked around at the other men, as though he wanted them to support his views. When no one else said anything, he cursed, then muttered one word: "*Sheep!*"

Foss narrowed his eyes at the man. "What did you say?"

"Sheep. That's what we are. Sheep. Taking this crap and for what end!"

Foss didn't know how to answer. When he remained silent, the man said, "I fought in the Great War—and though I was as patriotic as any other, I came to realize quickly that common soldiers are nothing but cannon fodder. The bigwigs were drinking their schnapps and bedding the ladies while we were drowning in mud and getting slaughtered by the thousands. And not a damn thing has changed. It's only gotten worse. They're sending single soldiers to tussle with T-34s—yet they still expect us to win. What do you think about that, Sergeant Foss? Do you agree with it?"

Enervated mentally and physically, Foss was in no mood to argue. "If you don't wish to dig, I won't make you. But if an officer walks by and asks why you are loafing, I'll tell him what you just told me. Then when you are lined up before a firing-squad, I might feel a little pity for you."

For a moment the older man stood gaping at Foss, then grumbling to himself, he lifted up the shovel and thrust it into the soil. Foss noted that all the other men who had paused to listen to the conversation, were once again digging earnestly.

Later in the day the first Russian shells began to fall. Men took cover in dugouts and in the cellars of abandoned buildings. Many of these men had never been in the thick of things, and their eyes were wide with terror each time an explosion went off close by. Especially when the Stalin organs slammed into the city, causing fire and devastation. Drowsy from fatigue, Foss shut his eyes and tried to nap. He knew some of the others would deem him mad for sleeping amidst a bombardment, but Foss knew as well that there was little to be done out in the open where shards of hot flying metal would shred flesh like giant cleavers. Someone began to whimper. Another, a mere boy of twelve, shouted for his mother. Foss was tempted to put a stop to such morale-destroying behavior—yet, what was the use. Outnumbered, outgunned, outmaneuvered, underfed, and without hope for adequate reinforcements, the defenders of Kolberg were no match for the Red Army. They would fight and die, and buy time for the remaining refugees who hugged the coastline as though it were the only sanctuary on earth. Any surviving soldiers would with luck, follow in their tracks. But Foss didn't count on this. The odds of returning to Denmark were becoming slimmer by the day. By the hour. And besides, he wasn't sure he ever wanted to take another boat-ride. Even with Ivan breathing down his neck.

An explosion smashed just outside the cellar. Dust scattered in the stuffy air. A man coughed.

"How much longer!" a shrill voice entreated.

The boy who shouted for his mother began to bawl. Then one of the few veterans of the group slapped him hard across the cheek. When the boy bawled louder, the veteran slapped him again. And again, until there was no more utterance. Inside Foss realized that he should assume the role of command over the squad—but the urgency to lead was gone. If discipline broke down . . . hell, then let the officers deal with it. He was too damned tired to care about anything. Except Jutta.

"Did you hear we're up against Polacks?"

Foss turned to notice next to him the man who had complained about the digging. "Yes, we're fighting a bunch of goddamned Poles," the man repeated, as though Foss had not heard him the first time.

Foss merely shrugged a response. He'd learned that along with the Russians attacking, an entire army of Poles sympathetic to the Communist cause were poised to lead assaults on the city. He had not a thing in the world against Poland. He along with most other Danes had empathized with Poland when the Nazis invaded. No, he didn't hold anything against the Poles—unless they were trying to shoot him.

The oldster, sensing that Foss was in no mood for small talk, went elsewhere. The shells continued to rain down. When it gradually grew quiet, Foss ascended from the cellar and stepped outdoors. He had not beckoned to the others to follow, yet he heard their boot-steps behind him on the stairs leading out to a street now smashed and littered with craters. Smoke penetrated Foss's nostrils and he gagged momentarily, as the odor of burnt flesh became prevalent in the air. Small arms fire became evident in the distance. A huge boom forced him to crouch behind the chipped wall of a ruined supermarket. He just as quickly stood up. Another boom. Foss guessed it was the guns from the armored train he had earlier seen at the main station. One of the few valuable chess pieces the Germans owned. It could not answer the Russians' firepower, but Foss was glad to know someone was firing back. Other cannons even larger than those of the train, now started to add to the crescendo. A few naval ships in the open sea beyond the range of the enemy, unloaded salvo after salvo on the Soviet lines. A direct hit from one of these guns could flatten a tank and obliterate an entire platoon of men.

But the firing was short-lived. Not enough ammo. The Germans had to be sparing.

Rising from his hiding place, Foss carefully tread a path toward the outer limits of the city. He was forced to constantly step over rubble, and even a few corpses. Refugees caught in the open. Feeling a bullet whip through the sleeve of his coat near his elbow, Foss sought cover behind a burned-out truck in the road. He heard a scream from one of his men, but he didn't turn to look. All of a sudden bullets began to whisk by from every direction. Foss thought at first his own men were shooting blindly due to nerves and inexperience—the same had happened throughout the war with soldiers accidentally slain by "Friendly fire"—but then he saw Russians, or Poles, darting in and out of the city's ruins from all angles. Not hesitating, Foss let out a burst from his gun at several of the enemy who appeared to his left.

He heard their screams, saw them fall. Then a grenade rolled at his feet. Kicking it out of the way, he leaped in front of the hood of the truck just as it went off. He lay a full minute without moving. He felt no pain. No blood on his uniform. A clanking noise alerted his senses. A T-34 rambled straight towards him. Just a few meters away a wounded Landser in the street was trying to crawl out of its path. But his legs were too mangled and he screamed hideously as the tank treads rolled over him, crushing his body to a pulp.

Mesmerized with horror, for a split second Foss was too stunned to move. Then forgetting his combat fatigue, his desire to go home, his love for Jutta . . . he became a stricken animal racing for its life.

Encountering machine gun fire, Foss ran, dodged, crawled, leaped and finally landed in a shell-crater where two hands stoppered his fall.

"You're a lucky man," a voice complimented him in a thickly-accented German.

Breathing raggedly, Foss noted the SS insignia on the man's right arm. Three other men with the same insignia sat beside him, all intently gazing at Foss. The Dane had seen members of a French division of SS troops some weeks earlier, but he did not recognize these men in front of him. As though to forestall any query, the man who had spoken earlier said, "We are part of the 1st Latvian."

Foss looked at him. He had heard of this unit fighting in Russia. They had the reputation of being tough soldiers.

"I'm not German either," Foss said offhandedly. "Danish. Forced into this war like the rest of us."

The Latvians smiled, and nodded. But their smiles just as quickly left them. The T-34 could be heard again, and was headed their way.

But instead of scrambling for better cover as Foss expected them to, the men calmly took stock of the situation. One of them held a Panzerschreck. The weapon's nickname, "Tank terror," was well qualified, especially with the man now wielding it. His face protected by a blast shield, the Latvian locked in on the Russian tank at less than a hundred meters, and with the pull of his finger, unleashed the small but deadly rocket at the tank. In the blink of an eye the T-34 went up in flames, its turret jarred loose and only one man staggering from the wreck. He didn't last long though. One of the other Latvians gunned him down with a single rifle shot.

Foss stared at the Panzerschreck with almost disbelief. He had seen them often enough, but such weapons continued to surprise him. That such a small rocket could knock out a gigantic tank seemed beyond amazing. Suddenly Foss thought of Ruder. The Reich might not have created the

"Wonder Weapons" he had hinted at so highly—but the Panzerschreck was certainly a formidable tool with the right person handling it.

"So you're a Dane?"

Foss turned to the man who had asked the question. "For better or worse, yes."

The man laughed. "Not fond of the Germans, eh?"

"Fond of some of them. Most I could care less about."

"I'd rather have the Germans than the Russians," another Latvian broke in, his brown eyes serious.

"The lesser of two evils," added the man who had addressed Foss initially. The man reloaded his rifle, then took out a pack of cigarettes and offered one to Foss.

The street had become quiet, except for the groans and shrieks of the wounded. Foss smoked with the Latvians and thought of the SS men he had mowed down in the East Prussian forest. Would these men kill him if they knew he had murdered their compatriots. For some reason he doubted it. The Latvians most likely had joined up as a way of retaliating against the Soviets for the 1940 invasion and conquest of their tiny nation. Pawns in the big stakes between Germany and Russia, they had little choice but to follow their hearts. Now the communists had overrun their country again, yet here they were fighting a losing battle for an ally that could no longer help them. Either extreme bravery, or extreme madness. And here I'm in the same damned predicament, Foss reflected with anger.

Foss had a desire to ask them about their feelings toward the war, but just then Soviet artillery started a barrage. The ruins of the city were to be leveled further. Wishing the Latvians well, Foss peered over the crater, then seeing the street clear, crawled over the edge and made a break for more secure shelter. Bullets again whizzed all around him. He sprinted toward the doorway of a bombed-out tailor's and reached it just an explosion went off overhead.

Foss could hear shrapnel pelting the door as he dove to the floor. He landed on something pointed. A brand-new pair of woman's high heels, and next to these, a long evening dress. A thought crossed his mind whether Jutta had ever worn such lady-like apparel. A farm-woman from East Prussia probably had little time for such finery. Foss's nose twitched. A rotten odor saturated the shop. Clothes were scattered everywhere amidst broken mirrors, fallen display racks, coat hangers. Kicking the debris out of his way, Foss nearly kicked a corpse in the leg.

An older man. Gunshot wound to the head. Dead for several days by the look and smell of him. Possibly the proprietor. Foss surmised that the man didn't want to leave a good life in Kolberg to start all over again.

The shells outside kept falling. Foss found a chair and sat down. He'd endured hiding in small places with foul smells before. He'd find other shelter soon enough. Pulling out his canteen, he wet his dry mouth with cold water. His stomach rumbled from sudden hunger. Once the bursting bombs ceased, he'd return to the streets and find his unit. Scrounge up some grub.

*

How the hell have I gotten myself into this mess? Meyer held his hands over his ears but to no avail. The hospital was crammed with screaming men, some having had a leg or arm amputated without anesthetics of any sort. He needed to get away from this nightmare. Espying an orderly tending to a wounded soldier with blood running from his neck, Meyer shouted indignantly, "Why am I still here?"

The orderly turned. His expression was one of utter fatigue and gloom. "You're here by orders of Doctor Klaffke," he said without preamble. "You've already been told that a dozen times."

Meyer resented being spoken to like a child. And especially by a social inferior. "I am a Criminal Inspector for the SS," he said bluntly. "I hope that wakes something up in your brain!"

The orderly had heard it all before. "An order is an order, Inspector. You know that as well as I do."

"But I am not to stay in Kolberg! I was meant to only be here a little while before continuing on to Kiel."

Shrugging, the orderly said, "I can't help it that your ship was attacked by planes. And that you got a nasty bump on your head while seeking cover. You were lucky the ship was close enough to shore to make it here without sinking."

"Yes, yes, I know all that." Meyer shook his head with impatience. "But that was a week or so ago. I should not still be lying in a hospital bed surrounded by a bunch of raving madmen."

His own patience dwindling, the orderly glanced around at the swarms of wounded, many of whom lay close to death. Not enough doctors and not enough orderlies to treat them all sufficiently. And this pompous SS bastard acting like a martinet. The man had been in out of consciousness for days upon arrival. And could very easily have kicked the bucket if not for the special care provided by Doctor Klaffke. The orderly wanted to tell him to stick his pompousness up his ass, but instead said with a tone of authority, "You will be released shortly, Inspector. Boats are leaving the jetty around the clock. I'm certain at some point you'll be put on one of them. So count your blessings."

The insolence of the orderly did not escape Meyer's attention. "I could easily have you arrested for using such a tone with me."

The orderly gave Meyer a hard look. "Alright, arrest me. It'll save the Ivans from wasting a bullet. Who knows—they might even overrun the hospital today. A man of your importance would be quite a find for them. Quite a find indeed." With that the orderly turned around abruptly and walked off.

Meyer swallowed. He had heard the roar of artillery for the past day or so, but he didn't know the Russians were that close. Sudden fright caused him to shiver. The back of his head where he had supposedly bumped it on a ship rail—he didn't remember a single detail—began to throb mercilessly.

In a hoarse voice he called out to the orderly to return, but the man either didn't hear him, or didn't care. Meyer was stunned that order was breaking down so rapidly—the same had been true in Danzig, but at least there he had not been incapacitated and reliant on others to look after him. The roof of the building vibrated as an artillery round landed outside. Shaking as with a fever, Meyer realized he had to get the hell out of Kolberg—and with no more delay. The worst scenario for any member of the SS was to be captured by the Reds. Death was to be yearned for when they got hold of you . . .

Meyer shut his eyes—trying to blank out the world, the pain—and by doing so, began to doze. When he woke again the throbbing had subsided. He could tell it was night. The little light in the room shined dimmer. He noticed movement. Two orderlies were removing a man from a nearby bed to a stretcher. The man's head and arms hung limply; his face bore the gray look of death. The rattle of gunfire outside was clearly audible. Another orderly appeared by Meyer's bed, holding a tray of food. The orderly started to speak when suddenly he disappeared from Meyer's view.

A great explosion. Meyer was thrown from his bed. All the lights went out. Lying on the floor in a daze, Meyer heard next to him someone groaning. This soon became a horrid choking noise. A hand gripped Meyer's leg like a claw, and in sheer panic he lashed out at whomever it was. A few feet away a voice shrieked in agony. Meyer crawled across a body, then shrieking himself, made hurriedly toward a glow in the distance. Narrowing his eyes to get a better view, he thought it a lamp at first that had not been extinguished. Yet why did he smell smoke? *Fire*. The hospital was on fire. A second explosion, then a third right after it. Rafters fell. Meyer felt something thud into his back and he yelled out in pain. Reaching a hand behind his back, he felt no blood. A minor injury. But he had to get away from the fire that was now snaking across the floor. Grabbing on to the frame of an undamaged bed, Meyer strained with every muscle in his body to stand. Surprisingly there was a crutch leaning against the bed. Meyer held on to it with dear life and limped in the opposite direction of the advancing firelight.

Other wounded were doing the same. A few medical staff unhurt by the bombs frantically scoured the premises for anyone still alive. One of them put an arm around Meyer's waist and led him to safety. Meyer noticed with surprise that it was the same orderly who hours earlier had been impudent. Escorted to an adjacent part of the hospital that was undamaged, Meyer was put in a chair and draped with a greatcoat over his shoulders. Unbelievably he was then given a cup of hot coffee—a rare treat in these times of absolute scarcity. Cradling the cup in his hands, Meyer sipped at the liquid. Despite the awful circumstances, he felt himself renewed. If he could survive a shell-burst, then he was ready to resume his trek to the west. He had not accomplished his mission in Kolberg—a few renegade Poles were to be executed for firing on German soldiers, but no doubt somebody would have performed the task already by now—yet there was still the matter of the murdered SS men. The logical thing would be to drop the case. Write it up as unsolvable. But in his mind he had given this case a priority. He still held a sense of honor toward his fellow SS. And since he was certain it would be his last case, he was determined to crack it. Time and events would not allow for any others.

*

The city of Kolberg was just a city in name. To the outside world it might still be recognized as a German coastal settlement along the Baltic

Sea, but to the current inhabitants—or rather the defenders and attackers—it had assumed the appearance of a burning wasteland. Shell-craters overflowing with the slush formed from blood and snow; mounds of smashed bricks and the twisted blackened steel of torched vehicles; the wreckage of gutted-out apartment buildings, laced with smelly corpses and the bomb-dismembered parts of what had once been human beings.

To Aksel Foss, such gruesome scenes had become part of the normalcy of war. Resting after battle with five other men in the dilapidated remains of what had once been a kiosk, Foss reflected without emotion on his current state. He couldn't recall ever feeling so dismal. So disengaged from any future goal or happiness. So beyond even apathy. The intimate time spent with Jutta now seemed like a mirage. Over the course of three straight days of fighting the Soviets and Poles in the streets, he had lost the notebook she had given him, along with the letters he'd written her. Ironically the pencil had not fallen out of his coat pocket—but what good was a pencil without paper . . .

A man next to Foss pulled out a cigarette and matches from his jacket. Foss thought of reprimanding him, but instead, looked away. He had once ordered Ziemans not to smoke—*a hundred years ago?*—yet what difference did it make now. The end was near. No help was coming. Just the day before two companies of reinforcements had been landed to bolster the defense, but the troops had been of such a low standard that most of them were ill-prepared to deal with the horrors of urban warfare. Overall only a few thousand Landsers remained in Kolberg to keep the enemy at bay long enough so that the last refugees and wounded could depart. Then and only then, if time and luck were with them, and the Ivans had not overtaken the quayside, Foss and the others might be fortunate to hop a boat to safety.

He didn't count on it.

He didn't count on anything except an unknown grave in this godforsaken place.

Cursing himself suddenly for his morbidity, Foss slammed the butt of his gun to the floor, causing the rest of the men to stir in alarm.

"Is something wrong, Sergeant?" One of the younger men, in reality a boy. He bore a look of apprehension.

Foss didn't want to talk. There was no Tulm or Dreybach here to confide in. But the men were gazing at him, wondering. He said finally, "We better find the rest of the unit before it gets too dark." He stood up.

"But we don't know where they are," another of the men stated, his voice hinting that he had no desire to venture outside where Soviet snipers lay hidden amid the vast rubble. "We don't even know where we are . . . "

Foss shrugged. He was going out into the inferno, even if he had to do so alone. The boy who had spoken earlier stood up beside him. Foss said, "This much we know: the Ivans are advancing along the river. The only option we have is to make certain we are not cut off from the port. If that happens, well . . . "

He didn't need to finish the sentence. Every man knew the consequences. They gathered around Foss. Taking the lead himself he slowly led them outside through a huge hole in the wall. The younger man stayed close to him. The air was filled with smoke from endless fires spreading throughout the city; what was left of the sidewalk was black from soot. Somewhere a machine gun rattled away. Then a bloodcurdling scream made them stop in their tracks.

Surveying the street ahead of them, Foss felt a finger tapping his arm. It was the boy.

"Sergeant . . . is it true the Communists kill prisoners?"

Foss was for a moment taken aback. Stark terror emanated from the boy's eyes. Deciding that truth gave one a better incentive to fight, and to fight bravely, Foss said, "It depends on the mood they're in. But don't bet your luck that you'll be taken alive. Even if you are—it's Siberia in the end."

The boy swallowed. "I heard a rumor yesterday. Someone told me the SS captured a lot of Polish prisoners. Then shot them."

Foss had heard the rumor too. He didn't doubt it's validity. "Both sides have killed prisoners throughout the war," he said at length. "One of the things you accept. And one of the reasons why you fight till your last bullet."

The boy gazed at the rifle in his hands as though it were the most precious thing he had ever owned. An explosion not far down street the caused the boy to jump inadvertently. Foss made certain all of them were well shielded behind a heap of rubble before deciding to sprint to the other side of the street where a road led toward the docks. "Cover me!" he commanded, then at a crouch ran like the devil was at his heels.

Whoever had been firing earlier, was briefly caught off guard. Then the bullets started pinging off the pavement again and Foss barely had time to dive into a crater. He stayed low, keeping his face close to the ground. A pause in the firing. He rolled over. Noticed a streak of blood on his hand. Apprehensive a moment, he realized quickly that he had scraped it on a broken brick. Looking back at the others, he saw that they were pinned down. Suddenly a Red was running down what remained of the sidewalk. In one swift motion he lobbed a grenade at the wall of the kiosk. Without a second's hesitation, Foss fired a burst at him, then screamed at his men to take cover.

A flower of red sprouted on the Ivan's chest as he fell back, crumpling to the ground—just as the grenade went off with a short but loud bang. Foss moved away from the crater—too conspicuous now. And it was dangerous to call to his comrades without giving away his location. Keeping low to the ground, he found momentary sanctuary in the ruins of a barber shop, trying all the while to see if any of the others had followed him. For some minutes he stared intently at the area around the kiosk, hoping they had survived. No movement. They were either dead, hurt, or too terrified to leave their spot. Foss was about fifty meters away now. He mulled on the situation. Too dangerous to go back. The enemy had their sights on him.

He heard the noise of tank treads crunching on stone. He surmised less than a hundred meters. A sense of desperation swept over him. He couldn't help feeling guilty about the boy—the others left no imprint on his mind—but the situation was out of his hands now. One had to continually wipe the slate clean in war. Not brood on the past. The lost. Calming himself by taking deep breaths, Foss focused on finding a German strong-point. A way to the pier. He knew from a report delivered to him a few hours earlier by a runner that the railway station had not yet been taken. The big train guns still fired at the enemy. But to go there would be to write his epitaph. The west bank of the Persante River was still under German control. *Yet for how long?* It was a wide river, but that wouldn't stop the Soviets from eventually encircling the defenders with their massed armor and men. Foss estimated it might only be days before the garrison at Kolberg was totally surrounded, then annihilated.

The massive booms from German naval vessels rang out suddenly. They continued to fire from their northern positions beyond the city for some minutes. Foss felt a sense of slight hope. If the navy was going out of its way to pound at the Poles and Russians, then that meant there were still refugees needing to flee. Nor would the Kriegsmarine abandon its fellow soldiers if there were a chance to get them out.

Remaining where he was, Foss came to a decision: find the quay when darkness fell. He might run into an enemy outpost, but the risk of running into one during daylight was greater. He quietly backed further into the destroyed shop, keeping himself hidden from view. According to his watch, it was just after 1500 hours. Another four hours or more before dusk. Resting, but staying alert, Foss kept his gun pointed at the entrance.

He waited. For night.

CHAPTER 15

Though darkness came to Kolberg, flames everywhere lit up the skeletal ruins of what had once been a flourishing town. Detonations burst with thunderous regularity. Small-arms fire chattered without stop. A smoke tinged with bright orange made seeing and breathing unbearable. For Major Meyer, he could not have imagined a nightmare more psychotic.

Dammit . . . I'm not even supposed to be here!

Losing his way in an alley, he began to cough as the burning smoke penetrated his lungs. A sudden blaze rippled through a door, nearly torching his face. Meyer stumbled on, holding to a rifle he'd been given several days before. He had been waiting at dawn to take a small ferry out of this awful place, when Russian aircraft flew overhead, scattering the long lines at the quayside with machine gun fire and damaging the boat beyond repair. When Meyer later sought to use his credentials as an officer of the SS to force a berth on the next boat, he'd been handed a rifle instead by a Wehrmacht colonel, and told that every man was needed to stabilize the front.

"I'm no soldier! I'm an Inspector of criminal activities," Meyer had complained with fury. "A Detective!" But the Colonel merely shrugged, saying, "I don't care what you are. The Fuhrer demands that every healthy male citizen stand and fight at this dire hour. If you refuse my order, I will haul you before an Military tribunal for insubordination." From the colonel's unyielding demeanor, Meyer knew instantly that the man held no liking for the SS. Rather than argue and risk arrest, he had taken the rifle and marched with a group of other men pulled out of the queue. Looking at the officer with unabashed loathing, Meyer promised himself that he would report this incident to his superiors once he was out of this mess.

Though now he doubted he would ever get out. Shaking from a chilling fear, Meyer eventually stepped out of the alley to a square of death. Bodies of Germans and Russians lay sprawled across what once must have been a market area. A few assault guns stood alone with shell casings scattered in all different directions. Their crews had either been killed or fled. Meyer recognized several of the dead Germans—some of the men who'd also been ordered to return from the pier and fight. Their sightless eyes reflected the growing glow of firelight. Meyer couldn't believe his destiny had led him to this. The steady resourcefulness he'd gained from years of police work was proving useless to surviving street battles. No longer sure what to do, Meyer began to whimper like a lost child.

Pull yourself together, Otto. Goddammit, you're a major in the SS.

Then instinct churned in his gut. Meyer turned to see a squad of the enemy dash out of a shell hole. A bullet clanged off his rifle barrel. Needing no other sign, he raced back down the alley, losing his helmet in the process.

Foss lay on the ground hiding at the edge of an alley. A blaze of fire swept the other side of the street, engulfing the barbershop where he had been hiding a short time before. An explosion behind the building had forced him to leave earlier than he had wished. Looking left to right and back again, Foss searched for a way through the chaos. If he wanted to reach the port he would have do to so in a hurry. Staying low to the street, he ran toward what he perceived was north when a man flew out of the alley, nearly colliding with him. The man screamed out in terror at the sight of Foss, then tripping over a loose piece of concrete, went sprawling head over heels. Stunned, the man lay immobile.

By his uniform, Foss saw that the man was German. SS. Bending down to check whether he was injured, Foss noticed blood seeping out from a gash on his cheek. With a groan the man slowly opened his eyes. Suddenly glimpsing Foss, he was ready to scream again, then refrained.

"You're German," the SS man said, relaxing.

Foss almost answered that he was Danish, but instead, simply nodded. He helped the man to his feet. "I'm heading for the docks." Foss had to raise his voice to be heard above the barking of automatic gunfire some blocks in the distance. "I don't advise staying here if I were you," he added over his shoulder as he once more set out.

Meyer felt the blood dripping down his face and was shocked to know that he had cut himself. Probably when he tripped. Not wanting to be left behind, he called out to the soldier. "I've lost my unit. May I join you?"

Foss didn't relish the idea of having an SS man tag along, but in a fight, two guns would offer more firepower than one. He waved to the man to follow him. Their senses on edge, they cautiously slipped through the dying city, watching for any movement that might betray armed men. Flames billowing out of a window briefly ignited Meyer's clothing. In a frenzy, he quickly extinguished them with his hands.

"Why aren't you wearing a helmet?"

The question startled Meyer. The two men had not spoken for some time. He was about to answer when it occurred to him that the soldier spoke with an accent.

"I was never issued one," Meyer lied. Walking to Foss's right, he scrutinized the soldier with a sidelong glance.

Foss shrugged. The dock area could not be far, but the city was not the same one he had arrived in more than a month before. In the street ahead, a German gun emplacement situated behind a makeshift barricade lay shattered in a tangled heap of melted metal. Surrounding it: the remains of four dead Landsers. A shell whistled overhead and Foss threw himself to the ground. The shell burst far in front of him, and the momentary light from its explosion for a second lit up the silhouette of a freighter milling about near the quay.

The port!

As more shells whistled by, Foss scrambled toward a bomb-hole in the pavement and flung himself towards it. The SS man tumbled in two seconds later.

All around them explosions. Somewhere screaming shrilled louder than the bomb-bursts. Then abruptly ceased. His heart pounding, his breaths coming in short gasps, Foss nevertheless was surprised at himself. His sanity was holding up. With the enemy now attacking this close to the pier—must mean the rest of Kolberg had been sealed off. Foss only hoped there were ships still coming to retrieve the last survivors. *But maybe they have stopped coming . . .*

He tried not to think about that. The SS man was squirming around with each shell blast. The pitiful sight brought back the memory of the SS men cowering in the forest as Russian planes appeared in the sky. It also brought back the memory of the emaciated women prisoners. Foss wondered what had become of them.

"How long will this last?" Meyer's voice was nearing hysteria as he looked at Foss as though the Landser could suddenly click his fingers and end the bombardment.

"We have to wait it out," Foss answered firmly. After a few minutes there was a pause. Then Foss said, "Likely they're short of ammo. This is our chance!" With that he peered out of the hole. Not seeing any imminent danger, he leaped up and ran toward the pier.

Then the shelling started up again. Foss found the roofless remains of a gutted building and entered it without a second thought. The Russians might already have occupied it, but he preferred the odds of facing a man with a rifle rather than an exploding shell. But luckily the place was empty. *Or is it!* Fingering the trigger of his Tommy-gun, Foss whirled around at the sudden sound of loud panting.

"It's me! Don't shoot!" With one hand, Meyer held his right side. He continued to pant. When his breathing was less erratic, he said, "Haven't run like that . . . in years . . . "

Foss lowered his weapon and was about to respond when the ungodly noise of Stalin Organs erupted over Kolberg. Foss had not heard the high-pitched Soviet rockets for some time, but now, as they roared into the city, he threw himself to the floor. The SS man yelled out in terror as explosions shook the street. The building swayed. A wall fell and crashed. Foss was hit by shards of wood and plaster. Shutting his eyes tight, he expected to die. But the rocket attack soon abated, the jarring detonations fading westward toward the opposite bank of the river. Rising slowly, Foss brushed the debris from his uniform. He noticed the SS man curled up in a corner.

"Is it over?" The man was shaking like a wet dog.

"For the moment it is." Foss glanced outside. Fires everywhere raged. In fact, the entire city looked to be engulfed in one gigantic flame. More reason to get the hell out. Kolberg was no longer defensible.

"What do we do now?" The SS man had stood up. He too stared at the fires.

"Depends on the navy," Foss said with a shrug. "Depends on if they think there's anyone left worth saving."

"You mean . . . they'd abandon us?"

"If the Russkis own the port then the Kriegsmarine won't risk losing any ships."

The distinct accent again. Meyer cast a shrewd glance at the soldier. Noting the shoulder-strap of a sergeant, he spoke on impulse. "You're not German-born, are you?"

Foss sighed. *The same as always.* "No, I am not."

"But you are a citizen of the Reich now?"

Foss shook his head.

"Pardon my curiosity, but what *is* your nationality?"

"Does it matter at this point."

"It might."

Three years at the front had taught Foss to rely on intuition. Countless times it had been a lifesaver. The SS man's demeanor had altered; his blood and soot spattered face made him appear almost like a gargoyle. The tone of his voice was altered too—a voice of command, a voice of not bowing down to others. Foss thought of telling a lie, then said, "Your nation invaded mine. And through circumstances I was unaware of, your military forced me to don a German uniform." Foss paused. "I didn't want to fight in your damned war, but as you can see . . . I have served with distinction."

Meyer was at a loss for words. Perhaps the nightmare of running through the streets of Kolberg to save his skin had caused him to miss the Iron Cross pinned beneath the foreign soldier's collar. Meyer stared at the medal as though hypnotized, then feeling an anger rise in him, he gripped his rifle tightly and pointed it at the soldier's midsection.

"You're the scoundrel who murdered half a dozen members of the SS!"

Foss said nothing. He noticed the gun aimed at him. His own gun was pointed at the ground.

"I knew . . . I would catch up to you sooner or later." Meyer moved closer. His finger was on the trigger. "My guess is—you're a Norwegian bastard."

When Foss continued to remain silent, Meyer lashed out at his head with the gun. Blocking the blow with his arm, Foss felt a sharp ripple of pain run from his hand to his elbow. Then a boot slammed into his ankle and he toppled. But instead of lying prone, Foss rolled and sticking out his own foot, tripped the SS man.

Meyer's rifle went off by accident. Not losing a second, Foss aimed a punch at the other man's chin but only grazed it as Meyer turned his face just in time. Both men leaped to their feet but Meyer had his gun raised first.

"Your luck's run out, you swine." A fresh spurt of blood trickled down Meyer's cheek where the cut had reopened. "If I could only do things by the book . . . I'd not only arrest you, but make you plead for death. We reserve special tortures for criminals such as you. Now drop your gun."

Foss was reluctant to let go of his weapon. "I said drop it!" Meyer ordered a second time.

Foss dropped it.

"Hands up in the air! Then turn around slowly. Very slowly."

Obeying, Foss turned his back toward the SS man. He was tempted to proclaim his innocence, but suddenly he felt a sense of apathy. The war had led him to this. Trapped in a burning city, confronted by a madman who at any moment would put a slug into the back of his skull, Foss oddly thought of the freezing waters flooding into Dreybach's lungs. *I didn't want to shoot you, Ernst. But you were right—the sensible thing to do. The humane thing.* His mind wandering even further back, Foss realized he could have easily chosen not to obey the initial order to join the Wehrmacht. A similar bullet would have pierced his brain in the same way as it would in a second or two. Yet he would never have suffered the misery of the war. *Never met Jutta.* The last thought annoyed him. Annoyed him because an SS thug was about to steal his future. Every muscle in his body tensed. He clenched his fists.

"What are you waiting for, you bastard?" Foss muttered grimly.

"I like to make men sweat a bit before they meet their doom." Meyer laughed, but it sounded more like a growl. He bent down and picked up Foss's Tommy gun. "A nice piece of work," he said, running his hand over the length of the weapon. "It'll do more damage than the rifle. Is that what you used to kill my comrades?"

Foss cried out as something slammed into his head. Falling to the floor, he lay there, stunned. It felt like he'd been hit by a hammer. *Am I dead?* But he was not dead.

"Just testing the gun-stock." Meyer placed a boot on the middle of Foss's spine. "Good German craftsmanship, wouldn't you say?"

When the soldier didn't answer, Meyer cursed him. "I might show mercy if you grovel. A quick shot to the heart. But you're too proud for that, aren't you? You foreign scum! You're no different than a subhuman Russian or a Pole. It's the ones like you . . . who force men in my position to dirty our hands." He ground his hobnails into Foss's back. When this produced a groan, Meyer ground harder. "That's it. Stop playing the tough guy, and I'll make it easier on you."

Foss thought his back was about to break. He tried sliding sideways but the SS man pushed down harder.

"I want your name and the names of the other soldiers involved in the murder." Meyer thrust the end of the gun barrel viciously against the soldier's exposed cheek.

Foss was surprised at the change in the man from a whimpering innocent in battle to a sadistic beast. But such was the characteristic of bullies. Bruised and humiliated, Foss could barely breathe let alone speak, yet no torture in the world would force him to betray his friends. "They're all dead."

Meyer kicked Foss in the ribs. "I don't care whether they're dead or not. I want names! This deed will go into the record. And their families will bear the brunt of their complicity in this crime. As will yours!"

A sudden bomb exploding outside caused Meyer to yell out with fright. A second explosion and he jumped, losing his balance. The boot came off Foss's back and the Dane moved as though a grenade had landed near him. He felt pain, but pain was bearable—death was the end. Further explosions; one knocked over a few remaining strands of roofing, these toppling down with a crash between Foss and the SS man. Dust particles rose into the air, temporarily blinding both of them. Still clinging to the Tommy gun, Meyer let out a burst, but anticipating this, Foss dived again to the floor, grabbing the other man's ankles and thrusting him backwards.

Meyer fell heavily and Foss was on him in a second, punching, gouging, and even biting one of the SS man's flailing hands. They wrestled and lashed out at one another like demented animals. Foss just avoided a knee aimed for his crotch, blocking it with the middle of his thigh. He felt fingers scratching his eyelid and screaming out in hate and fear, Foss backfisted the man across the nose, breaking it. Blood poured out of Meyer's nostrils as Foss hit him again and again. The man shrieked in terror before Foss crawled over his chest and took hold of both sides of his neck. Quickly finding the jugular with his thumbs, Foss thrust them downward as hard as he could. A raspy gurgling noise emitted from Meyer's open mouth. Foss pressed harder. The man heaved up his body, trying to throw the Dane off him. Long seconds passed. With the SS man's face turning blue, Foss thought he had nearly finished him when something sharp pierced the back of his thigh.

Foss cried out, releasing his grip. He felt the pain again, lower, in the calf. Grabbing his leg, Foss didn't see the fist that took him in the jaw. He fell over, stunned.

Breathing raggedly, Meyer with great effort pushed himself into a kneeling position. In his hand he held a knife. He looked at the soldier who lay half-senseless, and bleeding on the floor in front of him. His throat raw with pain, Meyer said in a scratchy voice, "Almost forgot about this little jewel." For a moment he ran his eyes over the knife. "A ceremonial dagger. Everyone inducted into the SS receives one. Never thought much of it until now." With a shaking hand he moved the knife towards Foss's throat. "I've killed men in worse ways than this." To give him a taste of what was to come, Meyer jabbed lightly twice at Foss's skin, drawing more blood.

Having heard stories that a man witnesses his whole life pass before him just as death is about to whisk him from the earth, Foss found himself thinking suddenly of his mother. Would she even receive notification of his death? He doubted it. He'd be written off as one of the thousands of unknown soldiers lost on the Eastern Front. Foss saw the SS man curling his lips in triumph, the dagger in his hand poised to plunge through Foss's veins, stealing his lifeblood. Accepting the inevitable, Foss closed his eyes . . .

He opened them immediately at the roar of a gunshot.

The SS man lay on his back. Half his face had been shot away. Foss thought he must be dreaming, but then a familiar voice:

"I couldn't let him kill you, Sergeant."

The boy from his unit. *The boy. My God, the boy!* Foss simply stared. "You're alive!"

But Foss could instantly see the boy was hanging on a thread. Dirty, bedraggled, and his face grimed with lines that denoted long streaks of tears, he leaned limply against a wall, looking wide-eyed at the SS man he had just slain.

"I thought this might be a good place to hide. I just wanted . . . " The boy broke off speaking. His face suddenly scrunched up as though he might begin crying again at any moment.

Still incredulous at the upshot at what seemed like the end, Foss noticed the dagger lying beside him. Picking it up, he began to slice the SS man's trousers into long strips. Not sure how bad his wounds were, Foss nevertheless tied several strips tightly around his legs as tourniquets. He looked at the boy. "Help me up."

Wobbly and lightheaded from the punch and from loss of blood, it took some moments before Foss felt he could stand on his own. The boy did not leave his side. "I'll be fine, " Foss said, trying to sound more certain than he felt. "Get my gun."

The boy retrieved the Tommy gun. Foss said, "I thought you were a goner. The grenade . . . I waited across the street, but, I saw no movement. No sign of life. Nothing."

"I had forgotten my canteen and went back in the building to find it." The boy let out an exhausted sigh. "Then I heard the explosion. When I went back outside, everyone was . . . "

There was no need to ask anything further. The boy had somehow escaped his predicament of being alone in the midst of a horde of Russians. Biting his lips so as not to show any pain, Foss patted the younger soldier on the back. "When we reach headquarters," Foss said, "the first thing I'm going to do is commend you to an officer about your bravery under fire."

Briefly, the boy perked up, then frowning, said, "I hope you don't mean to tell them that I killed the SS man?"

Startled that the boy had misinterpreted him, Foss shook his head. "You didn't kill an SS man. You killed a first-class bastard that should have been done away with years ago. But let's speak no more of it. I would have killed him first if he hadn't fished that dagger out of his pocket. You saved me." He patted the boy again. "And I thank you for it. No one but you and I will ever know."

Visibly relieved, the boy smiled. A *pitiful smile,* Foss thought sadly. A smile of lost youth. Just like his own youth was lost. Foss considered asking him about his family, parents, but decided it might only worsen his mood. Then he said, "I was making for the sea. Before this happened. The only route left." He noticed the young soldier listening intently to his every word. "If we're to get out of here, we have to go at once."

Outside the shelling had nearly died off, even the small-arms fire was sporadic. Yet Kolberg continued to burn. The searing molten glow from thousands of individual blazes had set the city alight and swept through the air with a searing furnace-like heat. Foss looked carefully in all directions before stepping again into the streets. The boy followed him blindly. Gritting his teeth against the pain coursing through his legs with each step, Foss headed toward the docks. Once more toward the Baltic. Remembering his last sight of Dreybach, Foss held to the notion that lightning didn't strike the same place twice.

But, there was only one way to find out.

CHAPTER 16

Crouched behind the barricade of an army truck lying on its side after being knocked over by the reverberations set off by an exploding shell, Foss tried to keep his eyes open and stay alert. He had not slept more than a wink in over twenty-four hours, and with another day drawing to its close, he had no choice but to remain awake. Remain awake—or miss the boat that might come at any moment.

If there is a boat. With ten other Landsers, he waited alongside a mooring beside the wrecked pier of Kolberg. The last thousand or so civilians had been taken aboard a destroyer the day before, and were now headed to safety. Only a small garrison remained behind to guard a short stretch of shore along the sea. Several hundred men down to their final bullets left to fend off the attacks of two Soviet armies. Gazing around him, Foss was not surprised that he didn't know any of the other soldiers. The boy—he had finally learned his name: Winifred—had been killed in the morning. A shell fragment from a tank had decapitated him while he went behind a building to take a leak.

Though the sky was dark and moonless, a continuous array of sparks drifted overhead from the flames that consumed what was left of the city's ruins. To keep his eyelids from drooping, Foss counted each spark his eyes caught sight of, until he finally gave up. Too many. Foss turned as someone tapped his shoulder. A man was offering him a cigarette.

"You alright?" the man asked.

Foss took the cigarette and nodded. It was the medic who had treated him some hours after the fight with the SS man. "Thanks to you, I am."

The medic shrugged, giving a brief smile. "Your wounds weren't that bad. More superficial than anything else. You said a Russki bayoneted you—luckily he wasn't able to jab too deep."

Foss had lied about his injuries. And the boy had backed him up. But regardless of the opinion of the medic, his legs still hurt like he'd had lava poured on them. He sucked in the smoke from the cigarette, then began to cough. His lungs ached with each heave of his chest; his whole body ached. It was not that long ago since he'd had pneumonia. Probably not fully healed. But he continued to inhale the tobacco smoke.

An hour passed; hardly anyone spoke. Russian artillery was booming from afar. His nerves taut with strain, Foss, every few minutes, eyed the sea. No boats. Then one of the men began sniveling that it was all up with them, until there was the sound of a slap, and another man cursing his defeatism.

Shots rang out close by. Several Landsers were suddenly seen racing out of the burning remains of a former naval installation. They were running toward the quay when a tank crashed through the same building, and fired at them.

The explosion killed both men instantly. Then to make certain, the tank charged over the bodies, grinding them beyond recognition. Soviet infantry followed stealthily behind the tank, checking and peering into buildings along the waterfront that were all on fire.

"I told you it was all up with us . . . " The sniveling man spoke up again. This time no one contradicted him.

His nerves stretched to breaking, Foss watched the enemy creep toward them. The tank turned and slammed through the wall of a warehouse, scattering bricks across the road. Not even a hundred meters away. Foss had been in countless battles where the end seemed imminent—somehow he had always survived. But he knew there'd be no getting out of this one. He checked to see that his gun was loaded. The tank slowly turned its turret towards the wrecked truck. Foss hoped death came quickly. No lingering agony of lying with a leg blown off while the city's flames incinerated him. A few of the other Landsers began firing their rifles. One man threw a grenade. Useless. Lacking even a single Panzerfaust, there was nothing they could do. There were no other places to hide—the rest of the waterfront was either in enemy hands or burned to cinders. If they tried running they'd be cut down instantly.

The tank's machine gun began to spray bullets against the truck. Someone cried out in pain. Another man doubled-over from a gut-wound, then slumped to the ground, screaming. Foss didn't bother shooting back. He'd use his Tommy gun on the infantry. If it came to that. He heard the clank of the tank treads rolling closer. The smell of hot ash filled the air. The smell of urine, excrement.

Men had pissed and shit their pants from fear. Foss thought he heard the sound of a motor coming from behind him. Thinking the Russians were making an assault from the sea, he turned to shoot.

Three men stood aboard a small motorboat in full sight of his gun. But Foss lowered the barrel. They were Germans. One of them, an officer, had cupped his hands around his mouth and was shouting:

"Hurry! Get aboard! We're leaving!"

Foss stood frozen. The words didn't register. Then they did. The boat pulled up alongside the mooring. Foss grabbed at the other Landsers, gesturing frantically at them to turn and leap on the boat. Not hesitating, the soldiers rushed to the safety of the small craft. One man stumbled and fell in the water, but was rapidly brought out with a long pole. Foss waited till all the others had boarded before readying himself to jump. Then something tugged at his ankle in a visor-like grip. Gripped with fright, he whirled around.

"Don't leave me! Please, help me!"

It was the man who'd been shot in the stomach. Stomach wounds were usually fatal. Probably wouldn't last more than a few hours. Then Foss heard the tank again. He remembered the two soldiers who'd been squashed beneath its treads. Bending down, Foss with a grunt lifted the man beneath the arms and legs and hauled him up. Several men already aboard reached back to the pier to assist. The machine gun from the tank continued to bark at them. Foss felt a round bounce off his helmet, nearly knocking him over. But the wounded man was now safely aboard. The boat started leaving.

Going back a few steps and ignoring the pain in his legs, Foss took a deep breath then raced forward at a full sprint. Leaping like a long-jumper, he made the distance to the departing vessel by scant inches, but not without mishap. Catching one foot on the boat's edge he was sent sprawling over the foredeck, cutting his chin. Just then an explosion from hell flashed a wave of light seaward. Where the truck had been, an inferno of fire now raged across the mooring. The figures of Soviet soldiers appeared in the fire's glow, yelling curses and shooting their rifles at the fleeing motorboat. Slugs hit the boat's starboard, but didn't deter its passage out to sea.

Holding his chin, Foss stared back at the flames of Kolberg with disbelief. That he had actually escaped was beyond a miracle. He thought of the boy. *If not for Winifred, I'd not be on this boat.*

But the grisliness of the boy's death had meant no chance to retrieve the dog-tag. His family would never know what had happened to him. Foss considered the senselessness of it all—the birthing of a baby, nurturing and rearing him through childhood and adolescence, only for him to die horribly before knowing what it was to be an adult. *To touch and make love to a woman. To raise his own family. To live, simply to live* . . .

Foss continued to stare for a long time at the fiery blaze of the city. This eventually faded; only the explosions remained to remind him of what he'd left behind, before they too dulled in sound and the world grew quiet. A quiet so stark that it could almost be heard. Quiet, and the chop of the waters as they flowed off the boat's sides. Foss didn't know what direction the boat was headed in, and, he didn't care. Engulfed by the night's utter blackness, he was for the moment, out of the fire.

CHAPTER 17

The medic checked the pulse of the man with the stomach wound—there was none. Babbling and groaning for nearly an hour, the man had suddenly fallen unconscious without reawakening. The medic had done all he could, but with no morphine to dull the pain, the man had died in terrible agony.

"Wouldn't have mattered that much if you'd left him at the dock," the medic said to Foss.

"Yes it would have. The Ivans would have yanked out his intestines, then wound them around his neck till he strangled. This way, he died among comrades."

The medic didn't answer. Just then Major Strobl appeared, the man who had rescued Foss and the other soldiers. He glanced briefly at the dead man, then looked at Foss, and raised his eyebrows as he noted the Iron Cross.

"I see you've already been decorated for bravery," the Major said, impressed. "When we reach a secure destination, I plan to put the paperwork in order to see that you are decorated again."

Not caring about any more medals, Foss shrugged. "Thank you, sir, but there's no need. Didn't want the Russkis to get hold of him. Sir . . . if there's anyone deserving a medal, it's you."

Most of the other dozen or so men aboard the motorboat spoke up all at once to lavish the Major with the same praise. As far as they knew, theirs was the last boat to safely sail from Kolberg. The Major, a quiet older man, nodded in acknowledgment, then said, "We're not out of it yet. We still have a ways to travel. Let's pray no submarines are prowling the Baltic tonight."

The mention of submarines caused Foss to look with sudden fear at the black water. Other men gazed with equal fear. The Major, knowing he had mistakenly created another worry, cleared his throat to regain their attention. "Subs are out for bigger game, boys. We're not even a morsel. And, we don't have far to go if I've guessed right."

The men were all ears. "Maybe three or four hours," the Major continued, "and we'll make landfall."

"Where . . . sir?" A breathless voice, eager.

"The Island of Bornholm lies 100 kilometers almost directly north of Kolberg. We have a naval base there—there will be plenty of provisions.

We'd run out of fuel if we aimed for Sweden, and I decided not to try for Stettin or any other ports west." His tone became grim. "The Russians might already be there."

Someone else spoke up. "We'll be able to reach Germany again from Bornholm."

"Precisely. We'll be able to fight again."

None of the men commented on the last statement. Most, if not all of them, had had enough fighting. They wanted to go home. They began to stir, almost in glee. Foss too, felt his spirits lifted. A shiver of excitement ran across his torso. *Bornholm. A Danish island.* The Germans had conquered it along with the rest of Denmark, but Germany now was losing the war. It might end any day. And I'll be on home ground, Foss thought with a growing sense of assurance that he would no longer have to face bullets and shells on a daily basis. *Never face them again!* For the first time since perhaps he'd been sent to the front, Foss felt an overwhelming joy. *Bornholm!* Growing up in the capital of Denmark, he had not paid much attention to Bornholm. Foss knew it was an island with a rugged beautiful coastline situated in the middle of the Baltic, was geographically closer to Sweden than to his own country, and the inhabitants spoke an odd Danish dialect—but beyond that, he knew very little. He was so elated he almost didn't hear the Major speaking directly to him.

"You will get another medal, Sergeant. That's a promise."

A soft, "Yes, sir," was all Foss managed to say. The Major turned from him to the medic, who in the meantime had clipped off the dog-tag from the man with the stomach wound.

"Wrap a canvas over him," the Major said.

The medic appeared puzzled. "You mean, keep the body, sir?"

"That's exactly what I mean."

"Sir, a sailor's grave would be easier."

"You mean dump him in the sea? No, we're close enough to Bornholm that we can give him a proper burial. The cold air will keep the flesh from deteriorating until then."

Close enough to Bornholm. The Major's words struck a bell in Foss' mind. Gave him an idea. A plan. A new course. A powerful feeling rose within Foss—suddenly he realized it was imperative that he get away from the Germans at the first opportunity he could, get away from the army. Get away from the war. As Foss watched the Medic cover the corpse with a tarpaulin, the idea sprouted, grew, reached fruition. There was undeniable risk—but the risk had to be taken. Otherwise, like the Major had voiced earlier, he'd wind up being sent to fight elsewhere.

The hours seemed to pass at a slug's pace. Not wanting to cross paths with any other vessels, Major Strobl ordered the few sailors aboard not to rev the engines until they were in sight of Bornholm. Knowing that full darkness was needed for his plan to have any chance of success, Foss sat on the deck keeping his arms crossed. His hands shook from nerves, and despite the pitch-black night, he was afraid someone would notice him. But the men were all occupied with their own thoughts and worries. Foss kept his eyes locked on the sea and tried to calm himself. He dared not sleep for fear of waking when it was too late to act. No one in the boat knew anything about the island they approached, except for one of the sailors. According to him, most of the German forces were concentrated on the southern part of Bornholm, serving as sentinels against enemy shipping. Besides that, the place was relatively peaceful compared with the rest of war-torn Europe. No large-scale battles or killings, while the resistance movement was hardly noticeable, if it even existed at all except in the unspoken thoughts of the people.

His chin drooping to his chest, Foss had unknowingly begun to doze when something tapping his boot startled him. "My God, wake up man! We're saved!" A male voice, exuberant. "Land ahead!"

Still too dark to see the face of the man who spoke to him, Foss realized after a few seconds that it was the medic. Rubbing the sleepiness from his eyes, Foss gazed beyond the boat's bow and felt his heart leap. A scant scratch in the darkness, but enough to show that they had nearly reached their destination. Foss stood up, drew a deep breath. The resolution he had made earlier had not left him, but fear of the unknown tugged at his gut. Fear of the consequences. *Am I getting cold feet?* Trying to bolster any flagging notion of making the effort to cheat fate, Foss quietly turned and stepped toward the stern. All the others had eagerly piled in the front of the boat to await landfall. He was sure they hadn't noticed him. *I am sure.* Even the medic had gone.

The sailors gunned the engine. Foss hoped the increased noise would shield what he was about to do. He waited, a minute, two minutes—he counted the seconds slowly to himself. Still alone, Foss looked eagerly and with more than a little fear toward the barely visible shoreline that the boat was rapidly approaching. The timing had to be perfect to avoid detection. Barely able to breathe due to tension, Foss waited another thirty seconds. No one came back to check on him. When he calculated that the distance to the shore was less than a kilometer, Foss silently removed his boots and threw them overboard. Then threw himself overboard.

A splash. A long pause—then gradually an uproar from the boat. Shouting. "Someone fell in the water!" "Who! Who was it?"

But the voices soon faded. There was no slack to the motorboat's speed as Foss swam underwater sideways from where he had jumped in. His lungs ready to burst from lack of air, Foss pushed himself further away. The ice-like intensity of the late-winter water bore relentlessly into his pores, causing him to shiver all over and stinging the wounds on his legs where he'd been stabbed, and also the cut on his chin.

Resurfacing, and seeing no sign of the boat, he put the cold out his mind and began to swim in a direct line toward the shore. He had always been a strong swimmer. At one point he thought he heard the boat circling back. He dove underwater again, continuing to push landward. But there was no sign of the boat. Treading water for a minute, Foss hurriedly ripped off his tunic and trousers, then let them sink. He wanted no trace of a military identity once he reached Bornholm. For a moment he regretted throwing away his Iron Cross, but keeping such a trinket was a dead giveaway. The water began to shallow. He touched bottom. Clad only in his undergarments, he began to plod shoreward. Despite the bitter cold, he didn't run. Any splashing might be investigated by guards patrolling the beach. The thought struck Foss that it would be the height of absurdity—shot in his underwear while running out of the sea.

Tiny wavelets lapped his bare ankles as he cautiously stepped from the water to dry sand. The swim had energized him, but now a stark gust of wind blew against his body, chilling him even more than the sea had. A sharp noise made him stand still. *The faraway barking of a dog.* Foss reflected that the boat must have landed, and troops ashore alerted to a man missing. Looking every which way, Foss saw not a single light. Beginning to panic, he was not certain where to go; but certain that if he didn't keep moving, he'd freeze to death long before the Germans began searching the coast.

He ran. The beach was long, but soon he reached a small incline leading to a woodland. The forest, though bare of leaves, was dark enough to keep him hidden. Several times he tripped on roots, stumbling and barely able to maintain his balance. His feet felt like blocks of ice. Slowing down due to exhaustion, he eventually came to a path that meandered toward a large grassy area devoid of trees. Doubling over, Foss fought against a sudden wave of dizziness. He held on to a tree branch. When he felt the dizziness pass, he stared at the sky where a smudge of light to the east presaged the coming dawn. If he didn't find shelter soon . . .

He began to move again. After a few minutes he noticed a hayrick. Then many hayricks, scattered across the entire area. *A farm.* From having relatives that were farmers, Foss knew that hayricks generated lots of heat. Frozen to the bone, and nearing the end of his stamina, he considered crawling inside the stacked hay to lie low, warm up, rest. Then something blinking caught his attention. Hiding behind a hayrick, Foss caught sight of a man in the distance bearing a flashlight. Slowly, the man crossed from one building to another. Then soon entered the second building and was lost to view.

Foss wondered if he had stumbled upon a German outpost. He looked carefully at both of the building structures. Even in the darkness he noted the thatched roofs. Unless his eyesight had gone bad—they bore the unmistakeable architecture of a Danish farmhouse and barn. His senses tingling, Foss crept up toward the buildings.

It occurred to him that for the first time in years he carried no gun. Not even a knife, no equipment at all. When Foss reached what he took to be the barn, a grunting noise from inside stopped him from going further. An open door. He hesitated, then peered inside.

The man he had presumed to see earlier was bending over a patch of straw-covered ground, feeding a group of hogs that grunted and milled about inside a large pen. The man had his back to him. But whirled around once Foss took a step.

The two men faced each other—Foss standing rigid, holding out his hands in a gesture of friendliness, the farmer gaping in astonishment. Not wanting to mince words, Foss said, "I escaped from a German boat. I'm Danish. I need help."

The man no longer gaped, but stared at Foss with animal wariness. Foss had not considered that the man might be a German sympathizer, even a collaborator, and there were certainly Danes who were. Might even be German, sent to farm on Bornholm. But half-naked and numb with cold and hunger and fear, Foss had no time to deliberate on whom to trust and whom to avoid. Suddenly woozy, Foss sank to his knees. Trembling from an unyielding weakness, he closed his eyes, trying to fight off the faintness that threatened to overtake him.

"Help me . . . " he said again.

And the man helped him. "Come with me," he said, giving Foss the support of his arm. The man was short in stature but bore the muscles of someone who had spent his life performing hard labor. He helped Foss outside, then to the other building. Foss could hardly drag his feet. "Hurry!" The man's face twitched with strain. "Into the house."

Foss collapsed as soon as he got in the door. The world was spinning. Lying on his back he noticed the face of a woman gazing down at him with shock. She had streaks of gray in her brown hair. She was speaking in a rapid tone to a red-faced man standing beside her. Foss watched them for a few moments, gesticulating at him. They were speaking Danish. He tried to answer them, but his mouth wouldn't move. All that came out was a croak.

Then losing focus, he closed his eyes. Their worried words trailed away and he thought of all the times his mother would sit on his bed at night worrying about his asthma. She would stroke his face and coo words of endearment until he slept. Ah, sleep. Foss wanted to sleep and never wake up again. He opened his eyes briefly, but everything was blurred. Once more, he shut them. *I must sleep.* Tomorrow he would have to find Dreybach, Tulm, and the others. They were waiting for him. To lead them into battle. *The Russians!* They had to stop the Russians. They had to. They simply had to . . .

APRIL - MAY 1945

CHAPTER 18

For a long time after he woke Foss focused his eyes on a ray of sunlight beaming through a window. Then he took note of the bed he lay on, the pillow under his head, the sheet and blanket covering the rest of his body. Comforts he had not known in ages. Not exactly certain where he was, he little by little observed the rest of his surroundings. Plain white walls, cracked and seamed in several places. A wide picture frame with the photograph of a young boy hanging from one of the walls. An antique chair in a corner with a dark blue sweater draped over it. A large cabinet. A small dresser. A closet. Several pairs of men's shoes on the floor. Beside the bed, a nightstand with a lamp and a few newspapers and magazines. Pushing himself to a seated position, Foss pulled his arm from underneath the blanket and grabbed the newspapers. He scanned the front page. *Fædrelandet*. Foss was shocked to see that it was a Danish Nazi paper. And dated from three years earlier. He put the paper down and looked at another one. The same thing. Also from about the same month and year. Hearing a knock on the door to the room, Foss hurriedly threw the papers back on the nightstand.

The knob to the door slowly turned. A man entered. Appearing embarrassed, he cleared his throat several times. "Hope I didn't wake you."

"You didn't wake me."

The man noticed the ruffled papers beside the lamp. He seemed more embarrassed. "Those papers were my son's."

"The one in the picture?"

The man nodded.

"He looks rather young to be reading such stuff."

"He was only ten when that photograph was taken." The man became silent a moment. "He'd be twenty now . . . "

The man's cheerless tone did not escape Foss. "I'm sorry for your loss."

The man shrugged. "I raised him to have a mind of his own—I just never thought he'd go in that direction. It was the Germans' fault." The man's voice was edged with bitterness. "They fed him with all that nonsense about saving the world from the Bolsheviks. That's what made him go to Russia."

"Russia . . . ?"

The man opened his mouth to speak further when another person entered the room. A woman. The lines in her face and the gray in her hair brought sudden memory to Foss's mind. He'd seen her somewhere.

"Glad to see you are feeling better," the woman said.

"He is better," the man echoed. He looked at Foss. "You've been in out of consciousness most of the past few weeks . . . so you might not remember us."

"I remember some things." Foss rubbed his head. He still felt like he was in a fog. "But I don't remember lying in this bed."

"We brought you here. For awhile we didn't think you'd make it. Did we, Karen?"

The woman gave a slight tilt of her head in agreement, then glanced at the man beside her. "We are being bad hosts. We haven't even given him our names. I'm Karen Holt. And this is my husband, Einar."

Foss smiled at each one in turn. He wasn't sure whether he should give his real name, or make one up. The Nazi literature beside the lamp was enough to give him caution. But the man's earlier tone was not complimentary toward the Germans. Aksel told them his full name, then began to cough.

The woman's face wrinkled with concern. "You're still not well. I just made a pot of pea soup. Give me a minute and I'll fetch you a bowl."

"No . . . I mean, yes. I would like a bowl of soup, thank you. But not in bed."

Foss got out of the bed and tried to stand—but his legs wobbled like a newborn colt's. He leaned awkwardly on the small dresser, nearly knocking over the lamp. The couple rushed over to assist him.

"You need time to fully recover," Einar said. "Give it a few more days."

A few days turned into another week before Foss became well enough to walk on his own. In the meantime he had been visited by a local doctor every afternoon. The couple had shared the secret of their "guest" with Doctor Lunding shortly after the nearly-naked man had collapsed one early morning in the living room of their farmhouse. The doctor had initially urged them to have the man secretly transported to the local hospital, but the Holts worried over the possibility that the Germans might find out. A person without proper paperwork, proper identity, would immediately rouse suspicion. Einar wanted no trouble with the occupiers. He had already made no bones in the community about disliking Germans since the loss of his only child.

Foss was in the kitchen sitting at a small table finishing a breakfast of rye bread swabbed with butter and a slice of cheese when Einar brought in Doctor Lunding, a tall well-dressed bespectacled man with gray hair and a slight stoop. The doctor always tried to visit the Holts in the hour after dawn before heading to his office.

"You seem to be much better, young man." Lunding gave Foss a quick look over before smiling.

"I feel better . . . and I appreciate your help." Foss returned the smile. "All three of you." He began to drink a glass of milk that Karen placed before him. "One day, I hope I'll be able to repay you."

The doctor waved his hand in a casual manner as though dismissing Foss's words. "No payment necessary. We don't turn away fellow countrymen in need of aid. But I'm afraid we're not out of the fire yet."

"What do you mean? Am I still ill?"

"No, you are well enough, though there were moments I didn't think you'd be with us much longer. As frail a condition as you were in, taking a long swim in the Baltic in wintertime was not exactly conducive toward strengthening your heart and lungs. You were like an ice cube when we found you. You also lost a good deal of blood from cuts on your legs. May I ask if you were bitten by a shark when you swam ashore?"

Cuts. The leg wounds caused by the SS man's knife. The trauma of surviving the aftermath of Kolberg must have given him a temporary amnesia. Foss had given that savage memory no thought.

Until now.

"No, I met no sharks," Foss said. "Unless you include the human kind."

Lunding exchanged glances with Einar and Karen. "Well, whatever you encountered, you hardly have an ounce of fat on your frame."

Rolling up his shirtsleeve, Foss took note of the thinness of his forearm. Then did the same with the pants covering his left calf. It too appeared extremely thin. He had not realized he had lost so much weight.

"Food was not always plentiful where I was . . . " Foss stated absently.

"I'm sure it wasn't," Lunding said, after a pause.

Stroking his forearm, Foss noticed the clothes he wore did not fit him properly. As though reading his mind, Karen brought forth a sweater and placed it on the table beside Foss.

"I was given this by a woman whose husband died," she pointed out. "He was tall like you."

Foss picked up the sweater, measured it against his body. "I'm sure it will fit. Thanks again for your kindness." Before the war, the idea of wearing a dead man's clothing would have given him the creeps. But in Russia he had snitched clothing from corpses without a second thought.

"The clothes you have on belonged to our son." Einar's eyes were downcast as he spoke.

"He was shorter than you," Karen added.

Foss didn't know how to respond. But the doctor let him off the hook. "Now that you are getting better, we'll have to make certain the . . . *authorities*, don't start sniffing about."

Foss looked at the doctor. "You mean the Germans?

"Yes, the Germans. There was a report issued across the island that a soldier had fallen—or dived—overboard. A few of his belongings were found washed up on one of the beaches—but *he* was not found. Patrols combed much of the coastline, yet not a trace. He has been listed as missing at sea." The doctor and the couple gazed at Foss. Then Lunding asked, "Were you that soldier?"

Foss sighed, suddenly desiring to be alone. He knew over the preceding days that it would come to this—he'd have to explain his appearance. He had considered telling Einar and Karen that he had been a slave-laborer forced by the Nazis to work in the East. But even if they believed such a story, he doubted Lunding would. The doctor had a sharpness about him; he was no simple farmer.

"And what if I am that soldier?" Foss said with reserve.

The three other people in the kitchen stared at Foss but remained silent. Then Lunding shook his head. "I don't know the reasons why you fled that boat, but your presence here endangers lives. The lives of the Holts, myself, and possibly others. There are enough people on Bornholm that listen illegally to the BBC to know the Germans are losing the war. But that doesn't mean they're lightening up on their tactics towards the populace. Precisely the opposite. We have heard that reprisals have been carried out against our countrymen in the other parts of Denmark for even the slightest infringements against German authority. We have mostly avoided that here on the island—mainly because our population is so small, and there is nowhere to hide if one of us commits sabotage. The majority of the German troops here pose no trouble to our daily lives, but there are certainly some who would relish the chance to execute anyone openly resisting their rule. Their nerves are on edge, and men on the edge often have trigger-happy fingers."

"You speak as if you are experienced in such matters."

"I am." The doctor frowned. "Unfortunately I happened to be in Germany studying medicine during the Great War. It didn't matter that I was a Danish citizen from a neutral country at the time. When the war began to drain Germany's manpower, I was forcefully drafted into the military and served in the eastern theater fighting the Russians."

Foss gaped, aghast. "I must be staring at a mirror! That's what happened to me . . . " He then told them of the night in Copenhagen, and the morning after, being sworn in to the Wehrmacht despite his protests.

"Our dear Lars did the same thing," Einar broke in miserably. "But he never came back."

Covering her eyes and letting out a sob, Karen left the kitchen. An awkward silence ensued. Then Lunding squeezed Einar's shoulder. "Einar's boy was manipulated by SS propaganda. And by our own Danish government telling young men that it was fitting to join the Germans in their crusade to the east. And he's not the only one that didn't come back. A whole division was sent there."

Over the next few minutes Foss told them briefly his own tale. They listened without interrupting, nodding occasionally in sympathy for all Foss had gone through. Foss said nothing about his deadly encounters with the SS. His diagnosis of combat fatigue he shrugged off as something nearly all soldiers got.

Lunding agreed. "I witnessed it in the trenches quite frequently. Had a touch of it myself. As well as trench foot. I was lucky the Armistice came. Otherwise I might have gone stark raving mad."

Listening to Lunding, Foss was reminded of the kindhearted doctor who'd given him the medical pass to leave the fire zone. He hoped that noble man too had escaped the hell in the east. He looked at Lunding. "You said earlier that Germany is losing the war. The soldiers at the front have known that since last summer. Even before. I just want to get back to Copenhagen. What's the possibility I could do so without detection?"

It was Einar who spoke. "Fishermen sail from Bornholm's harbors all the time. That's their livelihood—and the Germans have allowed them to fish freely. Our island's closer to Sweden. You might consider going there first. Lots of other Danes have taken that route of escape."

"I have no desire to go to Sweden. I've been trekking across foreign nations the past three years. Home's the only place I want to be now."

"We could probably drop you off somewhere on the eastern seaboard of Zealand," Lunding expressed while removing his glasses and cleaning them with a handkerchief. "Once there, you could walk inland. Find a town. Catch a train."

"What would I do for money?"

"I'll give you the money. Enough to tide you over until you reach the capital."

Foss shook his head. "You've already done plenty. I won't need money once I reach Copenhagen. Why can't I just sail directly to the harbor there?"

"The German guards at the harbor are used to seeing the same fishermen sail in and out. A new face would more than likely be noticed immediately."

"What if I enter at night?"

"There's a curfew in effect. With the Allies so near, the Germans are suspicious of everything. You don't want to be caught and executed in the last days of the war."

Tapping his fingers on the table, Foss considered what the doctor said. No, he didn't want to be caught. But being caught on Bornholm was just as much a possibility. "How far is it from here to Copenhagen?"

"About one hundred fifty kilometers to be precise, depending on what part of Bornholm you sail from."

"That means if I left now, I could reach Zealand by late afternoon."

"Depends on the type of vessel you sail. With decent weather, a warship could take you there in three, maybe four hours. A small fishing craft, you probably have to double the time."

Foss's heart stirred with excitement. "Perhaps I could sneak aboard one of your fishing boats. Cover me in a box and put me in the cargo hold. That might—"

"No!" The doctor interrupted, exasperated. "Young man, I sympathize with your plight, more than you can think—but carrying out such a plan jeopardizes the lives of at least two, maybe three other men. And not only the fishermen will suffer the consequences. Undoubtedly many more. The

Germans will question their families, neighbors, friends. Word might even reach back here, and impact Einar and Karen. You wouldn't want that on your conscience."

No, I wouldn't. Foss already had too much on his conscience. They spoke no more on the matter. Not then, and not in the days and weeks afterward. Foss grudgingly accepted the idea that he would have to wait in the small farm village of Pedersker till the day of liberation. In the meantime he put on weight and grew stronger, enough to help Einar with farm work. It gave him a strong appreciation of how grueling such toil was. Mainly he looked after the pigs—once he got used to the stench—while Einar cultivated the fields, planting rye and vegetables. Karen did her share too. Baking bread and planting a small herb garden that she tended to with great diligence, as well as cooking all the meals.

Taking a break one morning after feeding the pigs, Foss smiled at the irony of his predicament. After three long years of near-daily combat: *This.* Things could be worse. *A lot worse!* Watching the pigs gorge themselves day after day on scraps, leftovers, garbage, anything, he was reminded of Ziemans scrounging up food from seemingly anywhere. He could see Ziemans laughing his head off if he knew his former sergeant was shoveling pig manure each morning at the crack of dawn. Foss became wistful. Then melancholy. But the mood left abruptly when he heard a voice calling out to him. It was German.

"I see that you've fattened them up quite a bit," the voice said jubilantly.

Foss whirled around to see a German lieutenant and three enlisted men standing just inside the door. He almost answered in German, then barely catching himself, shrugged. "Yes, the hogs are getting fat," he said in Danish.

The officer knitted his eyebrows. "You must be new here. Never seen you before."

Foss held out his hands, palms up, as though he didn't understand. The officer narrowed his eyes at him. It was at that moment Karen entered the door behind them.

"Ah, Herr Kremelmayer, you have met our new worker," she said smiling. "He's helping us out temporarily. So that Einar has sufficient time to plant the crops."

The officer appeared skeptical. "Is he from Pedersker?"

"No. From one of the farms north of here, outside of Stenby."

"I'm not so well acquainted with Stenby. But why doesn't he speak any German? Most Danes know at least a little. Or perhaps he's just rude."

Karen was at a loss to answer when Foss said, "I'm not rude. I'm just shy." Foss spoke with a much thicker German accent than he normally used, one that was barely understandable. He hoped he sounded peasant-like to the officer.

"What's your name?" the officer's voice was grim.

Foss acted like he didn't understand the question. Then said, "Jonas."

"Well, Jonas, the next time I happen to come by, I hope you remember your manners." With that the officer turned, and with a slight nod to Karen, left the barn. The three soldiers followed after him.

Looking shaken, Karen crossed a finger over her lips. "Please, don't say anything. We'll speak more of this later."

Foss had to wait until supper was finished before the subject of the Germans was brought up. Word had been sent to Doctor Lunding. He joined them. The four people sat taciturn in the living room. With a long sigh, Einar ended the silence.

"I guess we should have mentioned to you, Aksel, that the damned Krauts periodically come by to purchase a hog or two. Every farmer in Denmark has to fork over a certain amount of surplus to the German State, but in this case, the local soldiers occasionally buy produce and meat out of their own pockets. Kremelmayer was just making a round to see what the pickings were. He and others do the same at many farms."

Foss was petting the family's tabby cat, which had jumped into his lap and was now purring. He looked at Einar. "Karen was quick-thinking enough to distract the officer. Nevertheless, he might return soon and ask more questions that I won't be able to answer."

"They don't stop here every single week," Karen put in, though her tone betrayed doubt.

"But they might if they're suspicious." Lunding stepped over to the window and glanced out as though someone had an ear to the glass. "There's little the Germans let slide by without finding out what it is."

A look of loss overcame Einar. "I was hoping Aksel would stay awhile." Einar's gruff voice dropped a notch, became almost a whisper. "We've gotten used to him being here. Isn't that so, Karen?"

The woman gestured with a sad nod, and Foss recognized that he must have assumed a place in their lives that their son once held. Touched, but embarrassed by the couple's sentiments, Foss kept his eyes averted. *What would it be like to lose an only child?* He remembered the little girl at the jetty in Pillau who lost both her parents. *Her name?* He recalled the face but not the name. It had slipped his mind, like so many other events attached to the war. Events he wanted to forget.

"If I didn't have a family to go back to . . . I *would* stay." Foss's statement was an honest one.

Another awkward pause. Then Lunding said, "Without identity papers, Aksel, it's best you leave as soon as we can find a suitable means."

Aksel was surprised. "A few weeks ago you said such a plan would put people's lives at risk."

"And it still might. But there's another matter at hand now. A rumor is going around—and it might be more than a rumor—that the Soviets are planning to invade and attack the German garrison on Bornholm. Or at least force them to surrender. And it doesn't shock me that the German commander refuses to consider the idea. His yearning is to surrender only to the British, or the Americans. Even if it is to only one allied soldier. He'd rather do that than give in to the Russians."

A chill ran across Foss's body. "Who can blame him. I'd rather surrender to a single Britisher any day than to a horde of Reds. It's a long way from here to Siberia—if a prisoner even makes it that far."

His mouth agape, Einar glanced at Karen, before turning to Lunding. "We knew nothing about this . . . "

"Not even as gossip," Karen added. "Who else on Bornholm knows?"

Lunding continued to stand near the window. "Only a few of us . . . privy to certain *information*.

Lunding's change of tone implied something illicit, and the couple knew it was best to curb their curiosity. With Bornholm being a small, isolated island, it was dangerous for the inhabitants to engage in open acts of defiance against the German occupation. A spirit of resistance existed, but it was a quiet resistance, made up of individual patriotic citizens who took note of all that the Germans did, and who kept their ears alert for any news of a clandestine nature.

Stepping to the center of the room, Lunding spoke in an apologetic manner. "Einar, Karen . . . I mean no rudeness by this, but I must talk to Aksel alone." He gestured to Foss. "If you don't mind, let's go outside."

Once outside Lunding led Foss around the barn. Though it was nighttime, he didn't want any eyewitnesses to observe what he was about to do. Putting a hand in his pocket, the doctor pulled out a revolver and held it toward Foss.

"I doubt I'll ever use this," Lunding said, keeping the barrel pointed to the ground. "Some Danes in exile smuggled it aboard a Swedish fishing trawler, along with a few Sten guns and grenades. Just in case *those* in a precarious position, needed to defend themselves. By the grace of God, it's never come to that."

Taking hold of the revolver and scrutinizing it from all angles, Foss noted that it was an Enfield, a common British model. He'd known several Landsers who captured such guns as war-booty in France and in North Africa. A decent weapon at short range.

"Be careful!" Lunding suggested. "The gun's fully loaded. Unfortunately, I was given no spare cartridges. Hopefully you'll never have to use a single round."

"I hope I never have to either." Though Foss was secretly glad that he owned a weapon again. He no longer felt naked. "So you want me to leave without delay?"

Lunding cleared his voice before speaking. "A number of us have come to a decision that it would be best for everyone involved. *You,* first of all . . . and the well-being of the Holts is also of major concern. We are well aware of what the Germans will do if they catch Danes harboring a deserter from the Wehrmacht. But there is the matter of the Soviets as well. I daresay, they will not look kindly on you if they were to find out the truth."

"No, they would not treat me kindly. Especially if they knew I had been shooting at them the last three years." His voice becoming surly, Foss turned away for a moment and took a deep breath. It irked him that Lunding had used the word "deserter." In his mind, he did not desert—but had merely escaped for self-preservation. It was on the tip of his tongue to tell the doctor that he had won a Knight's Cross for bravery, but to a Dane such openness would be misconstrued as boasting. Foss took another deep breath and for a second wondered where Jutta had ended up. "So, Doctor, what plan have you concocted to get me home?"

And Lunding told him. At the small harbor of Snogebæk on the eastern coast, Foss would stow away aboard a fishing boat manned by two local fishermen whom the Germans paid little attention to. Wanting to protect their identities, Lunding did not name them. "We'll hide you in a large crate reserved for fish," Lunding said. "It might not be to your nose's liking, but you won't be in it forever. You'll be wheeled aboard the boat on a dolly. Once at sea and far from the island, you can come out again."

"Where am I to enter the crate?" Foss asked.

"Here. There's a man who delivers milk at dawn. You've probably heard Einar and Karen mention him. He's taken his horse and cart around these parts for God knows how many years. He's more than trustworthy. Wants to do his bit to help Denmark. So we'll load the crate on the cart, then you'll get in it."

Though he had lost a lot of weight, Foss thought lifting a crate with him inside would be too much for two men. "And you expect a couple of men to lift me off the cart once we reach the dock?"

"Don't worry. There will be plenty of other fishermen getting ready for the day's work. They might not know the details, but their lips will be sealed."

"What about the Germans?"

"A few guards patrolling the perimeter of the pier. They've seen the same scene every morning hundreds of times. They won't snoop."

Foss ran his fingers slowly across the metal of the gun. It was cold. "You realize, if they do investigate, that I might have to put this to use."

Lunding opened his mouth to answer, but no words came out. With a frown, he eyed the revolver as though he now regretted giving it to Foss. "The vast majority of German forces are concentrated in our two largest towns, Rønne and Nexø," he then said. "Snogebæk is just south of Nexø—the guards there are practically old men. No more than a handful of them. They won't snoop. I'd bet my life on it."

Foss shrugged, remembering the many old timers in the Volkssturm, most of whom had been thrust into the war unwillingly. "All right—when do I go?"

"Sometime before the week ends. That is our goal. Preferably on a day with rain. The Germans won't be as active then. Or diligent. But the fishermen still have to fish for their livelihood."

The days passed and there fell no rain. Spring had come to Bornholm. Aconite and crocuses sprouted up from the earth. Trees began to reveal buds and blossoms. The warming sun showed signs of an early summer. Foss knew from years of experience that in the north, the sun rose earlier, set later. Nervous with excitement, each night he could hardly sleep, expecting the morrow to be the day. He lay on his back staring at the dark ceiling, wondering whether the Holt's boy had done the same before being shipped off to fight against the Soviets. *Lars, you were a fool.* To give up this life on the farm. To turn your back on your upbringing. I never wanted to go. You, on the other hand joined up out of zeal . . .

The image of the dead SS man with half his head blown off lying in the ruins of Kolberg made Foss flinch. Had Lars Holt died in such a way? Perhaps he had been a bastard as well; anyone who joined the SS couldn't be right in the head. Though maybe he had had regrets. Maybe he yearned only to return to his simple life on Bornholm. *Maybe.* But in this war, second chances were rare. Dreybach had lost his entire family to the horrible firebombing. Then, had lost his own life, drowning in a frigid sea. Fire. Water. Death was no less cruel, either way. You were just as dead. *Dead dead dead.*

Is Jutta dead too? Tulm. Ziemans. Keller. He couldn't get them out of his mind. He often woke shrieking from nightmares, bathed in sweat, trembling. Several times the Holts had burst into the room afterward, fearful that something terrible had occurred. Luckily, they didn't live in an apartment, or Foss might have woken the whole building. Recalling the conversation he'd had with Dreybach about what they would do after the war, Foss reflected that he might never be able to return to a normal life. What would his mother think if he woke her every night, screaming? She'd plead with him to tell her what was wrong . . . but he would never be able to tell her. How could she ever relate to the terror of leaping into a foxhole two seconds before the treads of a T-34 mashed you to mush? How could she understand the wrenching in the gut . . . at seeing a caravan of refugees being bombed on the Frisches Haff and falling under the breaking ice, never to come up again? How would she relate to the agony at witnessing young Winifred having his head torn from his body by a shell-burst?

Stop. Goddamn it, stop! This is pointless. Foss had always been known for his coolness under fire—he would not have extricated himself and his men from countless instances of danger if he had not kept his cool. *So why am I losing it now?* He rolled the thought over in his brain. A knock on the door caused him to jump.

"Aksel, you need to rise." It was Einar. "Doctor Lunding is here. Hurry!"

Foss rose and dressed quickly. He met Lunding in the kitchen. Einar and Karen stood on either side of the doctor, deep concern etched on their faces.

"What's wrong?" Foss asked.

"The Russians are demanding that the German garrison surrender." The words came out of Lunding's mouth slowly, but with an edge of fear that Foss detected instantly.

"You mean they've already landed?" Foss said, striving to stay calm.

"No, but they demand immediate surrender, otherwise they'll bomb the island."

"Shit!" Foss had not meant to swear in front of the Holts, though neither appeared offended. "How soon?"

"No word on that," Lunding responded. "There's been a request put forth that the Germans send negotiators to Kolberg, but nothing's come of it. The Commandant refuses to acknowledge any Russian communiques. He still wants to capitulate to the British."

Foss sighed with exasperation. "Dammit. We've gone over this. I can't be here when they come. I'd rather be shot by the Germans than captured by the Russians."

Astonished, Lunding stared at Foss, but understood his meaning. "Yes, we'll get you out."

"They killed my boy," Einar said suddenly.

The room became silent. Then Lunding said, "The cart is outside. We must hurry. The Germans may restrict all sailing. They don't want us making contact with the Soviets."

Despite the mildness of the day, Karen insisted that Foss take a coat and heavy sweater. "The weather may change at any moment," she said, handing Foss the extra garments which she had bought for him without his knowing. She also had packed bread, cheese, and several thick pieces of sliced ham.

"You won't have to worry about beer," Einar added, patting Foss on the shoulder. "The fishermen always have plenty of that."

Feeling awkward, Foss graciously accepted the gifts. He embraced Karen, taking the older woman by surprise. She smiled. Then he gripped Einar by the hand. "I'll be back one day to visit, if you don't mind putting up with me."

"You are welcome here always," Karen said, her smile fading as though she realized this would be the last time she'd ever see the young man who had so recently come into their lives.

"Goodbye," Einar waved.

Then Lunding and Foss were out the door. Without explaining himself, Lunding handed Foss an envelope that was taped shut. "We spoke about you needing assistance once you reach Zealand. This will tide you over. And I'll be insulted if you try to give it back." Smiling, the doctor punched Foss playfully on the shoulder.

Not knowing how to respond, Foss nodded his thanks and pocketed the envelope. The man waiting for them on the cart, burly and red-faced with a large purple-veined nose, winked at Foss but didn't utter a word. With Lunding directing him, Foss heaved himself up on the back of the cart between two rows of milk bottles. Stooping over, he carefully maneuvered himself slowly into a oversized wooden crate. Lunding gave him the clothes and the sack of food that Karen had prepared for him, then covered over the crate completely with several sheets of canvas, making certain the canvas was tucked securely underneath to keep it from flapping up in case of wind. A small hole in the canvas toward the driver's side gave Foss enough air to breathe, though as the cart began to move, he started to sweat from the growing heat of the morning. *Or was it from nerves?*

Walking for a short distance beside the cart as it headed for the main thoroughfare, Lunding reminded Foss to stay silent at all times. "The lives of others depend on you doing so. Best of luck, Aksel! You can send me a postcard. Once . . . you make it home."

"I will," Foss said evenly. Then there was only the sound of wheels turning, the horse's shoes clopping on the road, the creak of the cart. Several times the cart stopped as motor vehicles rushed past in a hurry. On the second occasion Foss heard the driver utter an oath: "German swine."

Foss's heart beat faster. He surmised that something was up for the Germans to be racing like that. Maybe the Russians had already landed. *God forbid.* Foss felt trapped, helpless, inside the crate. *A sitting duck,* as the old saying went. Then he remembered that he carried the revolver in his pocket.

Though he would have much preferred his old Tommy-gun.

The heat grew worse. Just as he was about to try and widen the hole in the canvas, the cart halted for good. Foss heard what sounded like a number of men speaking in low voices. Footsteps pattered on the pavement. Someone jumped up into the cart. Then someone else. Foss felt a jolt as the crate was shoved suddenly, then tipped slightly. Men were grunting as Foss guessed that he was being hauled into the air as the crate was lowered from the cart. He felt a thud as he hit the ground, then was tipped over again, this time at a greater angle. Foss panicked briefly, then remembered: *The dolly.*

The crate was being rolled. After what seemed like mere seconds, the dolly ceased moving. Foss heard more grunting as the crate was again lifted then abruptly dropped with a hard thud. Slamming his head against one of the wooden sides, Foss was for a moment stunned. He was even more stunned when he heard a loud German voice calling out.

"What do you have in that crate? A body?" The voice was not close, but nor was it far. Foss could not tell whether the questions had been asked in seriousness, or with amusement.

"Actually, we do have a body." A man sounding as though he stood just outside the crate, was speaking German with a thick Danish accent. "A lot of them. Would you like to see?"

"Bodies! Are you kidding?" The German's voice was closer. Very close. Foss froze. After three years of war he would meet his end on Bornholm. Trying to stay as still as possible, Foss began to slide the gun from his pocket.

"No, I'm not kidding, Corporal," the Dane continued. "We had a lot of leftover fish from the last haul. Usually we would sell them as fertilizer to the farmers, but the smell was so awful they declined." The Dane chuckled. "So we're bringing them back to the sea to use as bait."

As though his sense of smell had remained for some reason dormant, Foss only now began to smell the one-of-a-kind stench of rotting fish. Holding a hand over his mouth to keep from retching, Foss listened as the German cursed loudly.

"My God! How do you stand it! Smells worse than shit."

Laughter. "I've been fishing for forty years. You get used to the smell of fish."

"Well, you can keep that smell to yourself." The German's voice became more distant.

"Are you sure, you don't want to have a peek?"

What the German said next was inaudible. Then Foss heard another Dane speak in Danish.

"Best we shove off before the ass changes his mind."

And they shoved off. Briefly the boat clanged against the pier where it was docked, then as the noise of the motor revved into a higher gear, the vessel pulled away out toward the sea. Foss didn't see it happen, but the splash of water against the sides of the boat told him that he was leaving the land. Sighing, he still held on to the gun. The boat picked up pace. The wind that blew against the crate was cooler. There was a light flapping of the canvas, despite Lunding's efforts. Then sudden sunlight caused Foss to shield his eyes as the canvas was lifted off the crate. Two men stood looking in. They were grinning.

"You can come out now," the older of the two said. "If you want."

Foss crawled out. After all the build up of tension, the wind and spray of water coming off the sea were like elixirs to his mind and body. Arching his back, he stretched out his arms, then stretched his legs. "It was a bit cramped in there," he said, smiling back at the fishermen.

The younger fishermen handed Foss a bottle of beer. "I know it's still morning, but we start early."

Foss took the beer and chugged it. He doubted etiquette was of much importance with these two and he was right. The older man slapped him on the back after he had finished half the bottle. "A man after my own heart." He praised Foss by pointing at a case of beer nudged up alongside a large bucket filled with rotting fish heads. "Help yourself to as many as you want."

For a moment Foss thought he was pointing at the fish heads, then realized he meant the beer. "So that's where the odor came from?"

"You got it! I figured that Kraut was too stupid to check thoroughly once he got a whiff of these. Probably thought the whole boat was infested." The man barked out a laugh.

"I want to thank you for your bravery. Both of you." Opening the sack that Karen had packed with food, Foss offered some bread and cheese to the fishermen.

The older man waved his hand. "Keep it. We're not starving. Isn't that so, Kjeld?"

The younger man nodded, then began to darn a broken fishing net he had pulled out of a metal container. Foss remembered that he was not supposed to converse too openly with the men, and especially not ask their names. Now he knew one of their names. He decided it was best to keep himself aloof.

"If you don't mind," Foss said mildly, "I'd like to rest a bit."

"Whatever you wish," the older man shrugged. "Just lie back and enjoy the ride. I'll let you know if we need you to help us with anything."

For several minutes no one spoke a word. Foss watched a lone seagull drifting lazily over the boat. Probably eyeing the dead fish. The older man had noticed the gull too. Hauling up the bucket with the fish heads, he leaned over the side of the boat and dumped the entire contents into the sea.

"Some creatures will have a feast today," he said, setting the bucket again beside the crate.

Foss was surprised. "I overheard you say you would use them for bait."

"We already did. We baited the Germans."

The mention of Germans brought a thought to Foss's mind. "Any chance we'll bump into them out here?"

"You mean the Krauts? And so what if we do—they'll leave us alone. War's almost over anyway."

Another thought, a scarier one. "What about Russians?"

"Russians?" Confused, the older man narrowed his eyes. "Why would we run into any Russians?"

So Lunding was one of the few to know. Then again, maybe no one really knew. Maybe the British were on their way to accept the surrender of the Bornholm garrison at this very moment. Foss looked up at the sky, but the seagull had flown away. He turned back to the older man. "Oh, a silly thought I had."

"You're not a Commie are you?" His voice sharp with derision, the younger man stopped darning the net to glare at Foss.

"No, I'm not a Commie. Never have been and never will be. I hate them almost as much I hate the Nazis." Not wanting to speak anymore, Foss ate a little of Karen's food, drank another beer, and stared out over the calm flow of the Baltic. So different than the night the *Steuben* had gone down. So utterly placid, still, sunlit . . . beautiful. Yet Foss knew that Dreybach lay somewhere underneath the gray waves. Along with thousands of others.

The trip to Zealand, the main island of Denmark, took most of the day. Foss occasionally chatted with the fishermen about the weather, the changes in the sea, their trade, inconsequential things, but he steered clear of the topic of war. Though, it was hard not to think about. The war and the German occupation were the dominant theme these days. They affected everyone. Several times German merchant vessels were spotted speeding toward the east, even one warship. Foss was alarmed, but they paid no heed to the small fishing boat.

"I told you they'd leave us alone." Smirking, the older man cast a quick glance at Foss. "They're picking up all those refugees. Copenhagen is full of them now. God knows what will happen to them once the war's finished. Hope they don't plan on staying."

Foss wondered what *would* happen to them. Perhaps Jutta was one of the many who had disembarked in Denmark. He might even be able to locate her. Just then a pair of aircraft flew overhead, swooping down briefly to better observe the fishing craft. Foss clearly saw that the markings were British. The two fishermen waved at the pilots. Taking cue, Foss followed suit. The planes then swerved off and headed south.

"Won't be long now till we hit land." The older man opened a beer. "Why don't you grab another one and celebrate."

Foss declined. He wanted to be level-headed when he reached the harbor. "I didn't realize we were so close to Copenhagen."

"We are not going to Copenhagen."

For a second, Foss wasn't sure he had heard right. "What do you mean—we're not going to Copenhagen?"

"The capital is where most of the Germans are. I was instructed to take you to Køge."

Køge. A coastal town southeast of Copenhagen. That much, Foss knew, though he had never been to the place. Suppressing his disappointment, Foss surmised that Lunding was being cautious about exposing the fishermen to excess danger. And who could blame him? *He did all he could to help me.* Foss looked at the older man, then asked, "How far is Køge from Copenhagen?"

"I doubt it's more the fifty kilometers, as the crow flies. Not far."

In Russia Foss had nearly walked that distance on a number of occasions. Sometimes ran, when tanks were chasing him. And the weather wouldn't be as bad as Russia.

Another hour slid by before they caught sight of the coast of Zealand. It was late afternoon. Local fishermen were heading in the same direction, their day's work done as they sailed into port. A sense of exhilaration swept over Foss at the thought that he was almost home. Slowing the motor, the younger man maneuvered the boat into the harbor slowly, pulling up to a spot where it could be moored beside the jetty. Then tossing a rope landward, he leaped out and wrapped it around a steel pole, securing it with a series of knots.

Gathering his few belongings, Foss was ready to leap out after him when the older man took hold of his elbow.

"Let Kjeld scout around a bit first," he said in an even tone. "I advise you to stay close to us. At least till we're in the clear. It'd be a pity if everything fell apart at the last moment. Whenever we frequent Køge, which is not often, we have a beer or two in a local bodega. Kjeld plans to pop in there now and ask about the current situation."

Ten minutes later Kjeld returned. "More activity than usual," he said. "The Krauts are getting antsy. Rounding up anyone who looks suspicious."

Foss gazed across the entire pier. Nothing out of the ordinary. A couple of German guards some distance away. Keeping his voice low, he said, "I'll have to take my chances."

"You'll be fine," the older man said. "Act normal, like everyone else. Remember though, you must get off the street before dark. The Germans are strict about the curfew."

Foss wondered where the sailors would go for the night. As though detecting his thought, the older man picked up a handbag from the deck. "We'll be staying at a nearby hotel for sailors. You're welcome to come too."

Foss held out his hand. "I'll find my way. Thanks for all you've done."

"Let's not part with a handshake. Just act like you're a fellow sailor. Once we reach the center of town then we'll go our separate paths."

Letting them walk on ahead, Foss slowed his pace until the fishermen turned a corner and were no longer visible. During the boat ride he had opened Lunding's envelope and found two hundred kroner inside. A small fortune! The doctor had been more than generous. Continuing his slow pace, Foss contemplated finding the train station and buying a ticket to Copenhagen. It was then he ran straight into a German soldier standing guard outside a police station. Startled, Foss apologized, and noted the German was equally startled.

The soldier gave him a scathing glance. "Watch where you're going, you idiot!"

Trying to appear nondescript, Foss walked on casually for several minutes, then remembering the weapon, put his hand in his pocket.

The pistol was gone!

Goddammit. In a panic, he turned around and scoured the way he had come. Other pedestrians blocked his view. He retraced his steps. But found no gun on the sidewalk. Bicyclists raced by on the street. None stopped because a revolver blocked their route. Foss leaned against the wall of a building and felt his heart pounding. *Had it fallen out when he collided with the German?* His hand shaking, he hastily checked the pocket again. Nothing. Then checked the other pocket . . .

He grasped the envelope containing the cash, and beside it . . . the touch of metal. Metal that was warm from being exposed to the rays of the sun shining on him all day during the boat ride. Shifting the envelope to his other pocket, Foss wandered on. Several times he considered asking someone the direction of the station. But doing so would immediately mark him as a non-resident. Wary as a cat in the backyard of a Doberman Pinscher, Foss wondered whether there was anyone he could trust. There were certainly informers in Denmark, people in cahoots with the Germans, even with ties to the dreaded Gestapo, and just one wrong word could spell a man's doom. An arrest would be the end. They'd find the gun—*a British gun!*—and there'd be no talking his way out of that. Foss at last found the station—but groups of Germans stood near the entrance. Not all of them wearing uniforms, though Foss could see instantly from the long leather jackets that hung down past their waists what they represented. The Gestapo were in Køge as much as in any Danish city.

Foss strolled past the station, acting like he had all the time in the world. Once past, he realized it was too risky to take a train. He had no papers, no identification. Security personnel might board a train at any time and demand that he produce them. A truck rumbled down the road and it crossed his mind that he could hitchhike a ride. Then he just as quickly gave up on the idea. A lone truck driver might stop to give him a lift, but so might a German vehicle. He could find a phone booth somewhere and ask the operator to dial up his mother, his brother, maybe even Ingrid—yet who else might be listening? *What the hell's wrong with me?* I'm becoming paranoid about everything. Foss had led men through some of the fiercest battles of the war in territory he knew nothing about—and now he was back in his own country and frightened to take any chances. He'd have to walk the entire length to Copenhagen after all.

Then something caught his eye. A bicycle resting against a kiosk. Walk . . . *or ride a bike.*

Like most Danes, Foss had ridden a bike since his earliest youth. The main means of transportation. Making sure no one was around, Foss went over to the bike, walked it to the street, sat down on it, and began to peddle.

The first bike he had ever stolen. He had only gone a short ways when he heard a man behind him yelling "Hey, stop, you thief! That's my bike! Someone stop him!"

But Foss didn't stop. And no else tried to stop him. He increased the speed, and coming to an intersection, saw a sign pointing the way to Copenhagen. Thinking he heard a siren, Foss turned down the main road heading north. The sun, still bright in the sky, was now behind him. Other cyclists rode in the same direction, and Foss decided it was best to stay close to them. *Safety in numbers.* That's what he'd learned in Russia. It could only be the same in Denmark.

Trying to use the last light of dusk to knit a sweater for the new-born baby of a friend's daughter, Ketty Foss glanced out the window at the darkening sky. The Germans had enforced a strict policy that all electric lights inside houses and apartments, even candles, be turned off at the start of each night. Ketty grimaced as she felt a twinge in the back of her neck. She felt them often. Cleaning stairwells in nearby apartment buildings during the daytime, often for up to ten hours with hardly a break, Ketty usually came home to her own fourth floor apartment exhausted. Arne, her eldest son, also worked during the day, loading crates of beer on wagons and trucks at the Carlsberg Brewery just down the road from where they lived on Enghavevej.

Putting the sweater and needles down, Ketty stood up from her chair and took a long look out the window at the street below. Arne had not arrived home yet. She worried with all the recent tension stirring up against the Germans, that he might be involved in the resistance. Biting her nails, Ketty tried to stem the growing fear that gnawed away inside of her.

Oh God, not Arne. Please, leave me one son. Her other son, Aksel, she had
not heard from in almost six months. Had not seen—in three years! He had
been forced to fight for the Germans, and with no letters in such a long
time, Ketty feared the worst. Killed, captured . . . or missing in action. It
physically hurt to think such thoughts, but after the suicide of her husband,
Ketty had become a realist with everything. That way, the pain did not
linger. At least, she told herself that. Wondering at the fate of Aksel, she
often broke out in tears. And Arne had recently become engaged to the
daughter of one of his co-workers. The wedding was planned for August,
and he was trying to save enough money to get an apartment. It was in
another part of Vesterbro, the section where they lived, but in Ketty's
mind, not close enough. The thought of being alone had brought with it
an almost nightly insomnia. Tossing and turning for hours at a time, she
felt depressed. Old. *Useless.*

She had earlier in the evening cooked dinner, believing Arne would
come home at his usual time. Now the food had grown cold. *He'll be
entering the door any moment,* she told herself. She looked at her watch.
Already half past eight, the light outside had dwindled to almost nothing.
Irked by Arne's thoughtlessness, she planned to tell him she'd no longer
tolerate—

A knock on the door.

Ketty's heart nearly leaped from her chest as she stood. *Visitors at night?*
With the curfew in effect, people were not allowed on the streets. Only the
Germans were allowed. *Only the Germans . . .*

Had Arne been caught? *Or shot?*

Then the door opened. Slowly. The hinges, not oiled for some time,
creaked. Ketty remained immobile, her hand pressed against the wall. A
tall figure entered. In the shadows she believed it was Arne—yet something
was wrong; he was too silent.

"Arne?" Ketty's voice was barely a wisp of air.

"No, not Arne." The figure emerged, became visible, had blond hair, not
brown.

"Oh my God! My God! My God! Aksel . . . "

Running through the small living room to the door, Ketty embraced him
fully. Her younger son. She looked at him, noting each detail in a face that
was the same, but not the same. She noted his thinness. He had gone away
practically still a boy. "Aksel, we thought you were . . . "

The word was left unsaid. In many ways Foss *felt* dead. "Mother, if you don't mind, I need to sit down. My legs are like water. I biked here from Køge."

Ketty blinked several times, astonished beyond belief. "You biked all the way from there?"

"Took me almost three hours." Leaving out certain details—*the dangerous details, the gruesome details*—Foss then told her the rest of the story. The years he had been away. At one point he asked for a glass of water and she got it for him. Then she said, "Come in to the kitchen. I cooked some pork chops and potatoes. They're cold now, but I'll reheat them."

Foss ate. And while he ate, the door to the apartment opened again. A voice.

"Sorry I'm late, Mom. We had some extra orders to deliver and . . . " The voice drifted away. It was Arne. He stood at the entrance to the kitchen. His eyes wide, he gazed at his brother. For some moments he remained speechless. Finally he said, "Are you home for good?"

"I'm home for good. That is, if the Germans don't catch me."

"We won't let them catch you!" There was ire in Arne's words. "The bastards are done for anyway." He looked at Ketty. "Excuse my language, Mom."

Ketty shrugged and smiled. "I've heard coarser language. Your father was not the most delicate speaker in the world."

Foss was astounded at his mother's words. He could barely remember a time when she had ever mentioned his father in a single sentence. But she didn't elaborate, as Arne, eager to hear the entire tale of his brother's wanderings, pumped him with question after question. In the utter darkness of the living room, the three of them talked for some hours after the meal. Then suddenly Arne jumped up from his chair and turned on the radio.

"The BBC comes on now." he said, adjusting the knob for a few seconds to find the right station.

A distant-sounding Danish voice, crackly with static, suddenly boomed out of the box.

"Turn the volume down, Arne," said Ketty in a loud whisper. "If the Germans catch us listening to the BBC—"

"Screw them!" Still, Arne turned down the volume. Foss heard the voice speak of Allied victories all over Europe. Then the static gradually drowned out the voice, and despite Arne's best efforts, he was not able to find the station again.

"Won't be long before we can listen to the BBC legally," Arne said, after giving up and turning the radio off.

Overcome with weariness, Foss yawned.

"Shame on me, Aksel, I didn't think that you might want to sleep after all your traveling." Getting up, Ketty quickly went to her bedroom. She soon returned with a pillow and blanket, and placed them on the sofa. "You take my bed," she said. "I can sleep on the sofa. Unfortunately your old room is filled with clutter. Tomorrow I'll clean it up."

Foss protested, but she wouldn't take no for an answer. "I often sleep on the sofa anyway," she added, emphasizing her point by sitting on the sofa. "Now go. And sleep as long as you want. Arne and I have to get up and work tomorrow, but we'll be quiet, won't we, Arne?"

"Yes, we'll be quiet," Arne agreed, and Foss, knowing there was nothing more to be said, rose and went to his mother's bedroom. It occurred to him when he lay down on the mattress and closed his eyes, that he had last slept here as a boy. On a night after he had fallen from his bike and scraped his shin. His mother had cradled him in her arms. Foss reflected on the fact that he had fallen several times today on his way up from Køge. And the irony that he had again scraped his shin. Perhaps lightning does strike twice . . .

CHAPTER 19

Several days went by with Foss barely leaving the apartment except to go to the bakery twice, and drink a beer in a bodega a few blocks away. He desired to walk to the center of Copenhagen but his mother had pleaded with him not to until it was finally safe. Shootings were beginning to occur at all hours of the day between the resistance and the Gestapo, and she was afraid he might wander into a street battle unawares. Neglecting on purpose to tell her that he had been in some of the most ferocious battles of the war, he agreed to let things calm down first.

And so he waited. Wanting to do what he could to help out, he had given most of Lunding's money to his mother, who despite her job, and Arne's job, was never far from poverty. It had been that way since his father's death.

Foss had planned to visit Ingrid at some point, but his brother told him that she had attached herself to another man. The news stunned him at first, though what could he expect? He had not seen her in so long, and with the way the mail system in the Reich had broken down after the Russian onslaught, she probably had assumed like his family, that he was lost forever.

Much of the time Foss spent staring out the window at people walking on the street. The trams and the few cars and trucks that passed by, a woman pushing a baby pram, a horse-drawn wagon bearing crates of vegetables for the farmer's market in the city. The hustle and bustle of shops opening in the morning and closing in the evening. The routine of it all amazed him. Saddened him. Ordinary events he had once taken for granted, now seemed extraordinary. These same people going about their lives in the same manner every day all the time he was away fighting in the fields and swamps of foreign lands. They had not known he was away, and even if they had known, they wouldn't have cared. It didn't affect their lives. He could have died on the steppes of Russia, or drowned in the Baltic, and it wouldn't have altered their lives in the slightest way. He thought of writing a poem about this—this maddening indifference of the world toward individual suffering. But the words just didn't flow. The music was not there. And Foss started to wonder if he would ever be able to write again.

Arne had always teased him about his poetry, and no one else in the family, from grandparents to uncles and aunts and cousins understood his yearning to write. Everyone in the family had always been blue-collar; about the only thing they read were newspapers, gossip magazines. "Books are what you use to keep a fire going, when you run out of coal," his Uncle Henrik had told him with annoyance once when he found Foss sprawled on the sofa immersed in a translation of Shakespeare. But Foss had paid him no heed. If the rest of them wanted to remain ignorant, then so be it. And because there was no one in the family he could share his likes with, he had branched out, made friends with other youths who held similar literary leanings, formed writers' groups that read the works of the great poets aloud, and their own works.

His family's background was all the more reason why he had dreamed of eventually getting away from them. He had just not anticipated the Nazi War Machine being the fuel that got the piston moving. Now, he had come back to his family and . . . was already feeling the itch to leave again.

Why?

He cared for his mother, his brother—cared deeply for them. And had thought of little else the last number of months but to get home. Yet being home felt odd. Not what he imagined. After the first day or so, the homecoming had worn off. His mother and Arne had their own lives, Ingrid was out of the picture, and he himself was no longer the same person that had gone out on that long-ago eve to guzzle down brews in Nyhavn. He could not turn back the clock, any more than Dreybach could suddenly rise up from the bottom of the sea.

An attractive blonde stepping in high heels and a short dress on the sidewalk below, bearing her legs and swinging her hips like a woman who knew the strength of her appeal and was not afraid to show it, reminded Foss of Jutta. Though he doubted Jutta would have been so brazen. At least not in public. A physical ache overcame him as thoughts of her flooded his mind. It was fruitless to guess where she had ended up. Perhaps still waiting for his letter. To tell her where *he* was.

Maybe when the war was officially over, he'd return to Germany to look for her.

Foss heard the door to the apartment open. Arne, breathless, and sweating from apparent exertion, trudged in and lowered a case of beer to the floor. He then smiled at his brother.

"Have you heard the news, Aksel?"

Aksel shook his head. "I haven't heard anything."

"Hitler's dead! Goddamn it, this calls for a celebration." Grabbing two beers, he handed one to Foss. With a pocketknife, Arne pried off each bottle cap in turn, then he lifted his beer in the air. "Skoal, Aksel."

"Skoal."

For a few moments they remained silent. Then Arne said, "Happened a day or two ago. In Berlin."

"Assassinated?"

"No one knows. But the bastard's dead, and that's all that counts."

"So the war's finished."

Arne narrowed his eyes. "I wish. But the Krauts in Denmark are still holding on to their guns. Still patrolling the streets. Looks like we'll have to kick them out on our own."

"Meaning?"

"That the boys from the Underground will be shooting Germans soon."

Foss studied his brother. Ketty had intimated at Arne's possible involvement in the Resistance Movement. Deciding to pull no punches, Foss said tersely, "How close are you to the Underground?"

Arne seemed surprised by the question. "What does that matter to you?"

"It matters a lot to me, and to mother. Getting yourself killed in the last days of the war won't benefit her, your future wife, and certainly not you."

"Listen to yourself. You, who paraded in the enemy's army trying to tell me that I shouldn't help the Motherland in her hour of need. Don't be a damn hypocrite, Aksel. Or maybe you want to protect a few of your German buddies."

Foss's face turned crimson. If such words had come from anyone but his brother, he would have smashed the bottle of beer over the other man's head. "You don't know what you're talking about—"

"Neither do you!" Arne interrupted. "You haven't been here the past few years, Aksel. Haven't seen what the Krauts and their Danish cronies have done. Ever heard of the Schalburg Corps—those traitors have tortured and executed their own people without batting an eye. It's time for payback. And believe me, it's only a matter of time before they get what's overdue!"

"But you are not trained in warfare. It's not fun-and-games, Arne. People die in war, and they die horribly."

"Didn't you hear what I just said?" Arne glared at his brother with disgust. "Our people are dying. I know what's it's like. Do you remember Bent Frederiksen? I used to go to school with him. He joined the fight against the Germans early on, but they eventually caught him. The Gestapo yanked his fingernails out, slowly, trying to get him to reveal the names of fellow resistance men. Then they smashed his teeth out with a crowbar. When he still wouldn't give in, they fractured his legs and arms. At last they took to him to a field, tied his broken body to a wooden post, and shot him. So don't play high and mighty and tell me what war is like. I know, Aksel. I know!"

Perhaps Arne knew more than he gave him credit for. Yet he couldn't imagine his brother being able to fathom the full horrors of the Eastern Front. Trying to keep his temper in check, Foss kept mum. Suddenly he whirled toward the window when he thought he heard gunshots.

"It's happening more and more," Arne said weightedly, stepping over to the window to peer outside. "We're finally fighting back. In the open. We're not hiding any longer. By this time tomorrow we'll confront them anywhere and everywhere across all of Denmark."

Foss shrugged, realizing it was futile to argue any further. Arne had always been headstrong, and that had not changed. "Well, at least let me help you," Foss said straightly. "Despite what you think, I *am* Danish."

Arne shook his head. "They . . . don't want your help."

"Who is they?"

"Members of the Resistance. The top dogs. They don't trust you."

"What the hell are you saying?"

"You served with the Germans."

"I was forced to serve. They must know that!"

"I told them those very words, but they still don't trust you. They think you were in the SS."

Foss stiffened as though he'd been slapped. "Then you can tell them they're full of shit. I would have died before joining the SS."

Shooing away a fly that was buzzing around him, Arne plopped into a chair and sighed. "No one in the family doubts you, Aksel. It's just that few Danes these days acknowledge the fact that a fellow countryman might have been coerced at gunpoint into a German uniform. You may have the most rational story in the world as to why you did what you did—but they won't buy it. Others who willingly served the Germans are saying the same: that they were forced under pressure." Arne took a swill of his beer. "And it's all because of fear. They're afraid of the consequences, now that the Allies are winning. They're frightened of being incarcerated. Frightened of execution. Maybe they think we'll even torture them like they tortured us. Fear will make a man do anything."

Fear will make a man do anything. Foss rolled that thought around in his head. Dreybach was ready to blow his brains out rather than sink beneath the waves. Because of fear. I might have been able to save him if he had only let me. Then Foss realized realistically that he had hardly been able to save himself. He looked at Arne. The conversation had left him drained. But inside he knew Arne was correct. Why should they trust me? If the roles were reversed, would I trust someone who fought three years in the Wehrmacht? They would trust me even less if they found out I won a Knight's Cross. Foss was now glad he had dropped it in the sea.

But in a way, the loss of the medal also pained him. Not the loss of the actual metal pin, but rather what it implied—that those years of his life were given toward a lost cause, a despicable cause, a cause alien to everything he believed in, and what had he gained from it? Memories of brief friendships with friends lying mostly in unknown graves; a love affair that had amounted to no more than a few weeks. Other than that, it had all been anguish, tediousness, constant fretting, and horrors piled on horrors. Back at the Holts when Foss had gazed into a mirror for the first time in months, he had noticed strands of gray streaking his blond hair. It had stunned him. *I'm only twenty-four,* he had thought then. His forehead was also heavily wrinkled whenever he furrowed his brow. Too young. I'm too young to look like this. But the war didn't take into account how young a person was. The meat grinder chopped up young and old alike, innocent, guilty. The roads of Prussia were witness to that. The roads to Moscow and Paris, perhaps all the roads of Europe.

Reflecting on all this, Foss thought it probably best to allow Arne his little foray into the world of violence. As long as it wasn't too violent. Foss spoke no more on the subject as Ketty came home then and told them that she too had heard the news of Hitler's demise.

"We won't have to close the blackout curtains much longer," she beamed happily.

But for two more nights they did. Then hell unleashed its terrible fire on Denmark. And as Arne had predicted, old scores were to be settled. The

Freedom Fighters came out in droves. "Most of these people are just joining the bandwagon," Arne told Foss, the irritation thick in his voice as he returned from work early to grab a Sten gun he had hidden away in a locker in his closet. Foss was caught off guard seeing Arne dressed in a loose sweater, a black beret on his head, a gun in his hands, a cigarette dangling from his lips. He held the appearance of an irregular soldier from the Spanish Civil War, something almost out of a Hemingway novel. Foss told him this.

"I guess I have to play the part," Arne said, grinning. "Since I don't have a regular uniform."

You can't play the part of a soldier, Foss thought to himself, unless you are a soldier. He noticed Arne's nervousness, his quicker than usual movements as he checked the Sten gun over and over to see if it was in working order. Remembering the death of Winifred, Foss put a hand on Arne's shoulder. "You don't have to do this, you know. There'll be plenty of others to weed out the Fascists. Sit it out, brother. I heard on the radio this morning that the Germans are on the verge of surrendering. The British will be here soon. Let them mop up any fanatics still holding out."

"Your news is hours old, Aksel. The Krauts already *have* surrendered." Taking a stiletto-like knife from a coat hanging in the closet, Arne knelt down and rolled up his pants leg. A leather knife holder was strapped around his bare calf. Positioning the stiletto carefully in the strap, he rolled his pants down again and stood up. "I'll be all right," he said, assuming an air of confidence by patting his gun as though it were a faithful friend. "Like I said . . . the surrender is official now. All German forces except the Gestapo and the SS. Those bastards have chosen to shoot it out. They and all the Danish Nazis. So if that's what they want, we'll oblige them." He stepped out of his room. Walked to the front door.

Sensing that Arne was beyond listening to reason, Foss tried another tactic. "Have you considered what Mother wants? Have you?" When he saw Arne hesitate, he said, "If you die, she'll never be the same. For her sake, stay home today. I saw death in the east on a daily basis, and I have come to realize that there is little worth dying for. I knew many heroic men—but what good is being a hero when you're dead? You have a long life ahead of you. An upcoming marriage. Staying alive is more important than seeking revenge on a few embittered Nazis. The courts can deal with them."

Arne turned and locked eyes with his brother. For a moment he didn't answer. Then turning aside, he opened the door and left the apartment. "I have to do this," he called back over his shoulder. His boots tapping on the stairs echoed for a scant time before dissipating altogether. Foss heard him leave the entrance to the building . . . then silence.

Exasperated at Arne's willfulness Foss hurriedly put on the coat the Holts had given him. He then found the Enfield which he had wrapped in a dish towel and hidden in one of his old shoes that his mother had kept for him. Concealing the revolver in his coat, Foss sped down the stairs and outside.

The day was waning toward dusk. Foss heard gunshots in the distance, nearer to downtown. He wondered where his mother was. She usually came home to cook dinner. Foss kept to the sidewalk, cutting over at one point to the main thoroughfare that led to the inner city. He noticed that no trams were running. Several men wearing the distinctive Danish military helmet and bearing rifles were sprinting in the same direction. Plenty of people were in the streets, nearly all of them civilians, curious to see what was happening.

Foss stopped and crouched down when he heard a bullet ricochet off the brick wall of a building not ten paces from where he had been walking. Ahead of him in the road he saw a man kneeling behind a parked automobile, one of its tires flat. Not far from the car, a motorcycle was lying on its side. Next to it was sprawled a man on his stomach. Blood marked the spot where his head lay.

"The bastards shot him just as he rode up." A man with a German helmet was shaking his head and pointed at a building across the street. He appeared to be a civilian, and Foss wondered if he had stolen the helmet from a dead German. "Those scum are holed up over there," the man said angrily, continuing to point.

More shots ripped through the air. Foss ducked down behind the car. Then lowering himself like a lizard to the pavement, he crawled back the way he had come till he was out of view. A few random shots might hit the car's gas tank and turn it into a blazing torch. He looked back to see the man with the helmet crawling away in the same manner he had done.

Amateurs, Foss thought sadly. The dead motorcyclist had probably ridden in like a cowboy chasing a group of Indians. Not sure where Arne had headed, Foss made his way toward the brewery where he worked. But Arne was not there either. Foss spent the next several hours wandering across much of the city. In some places hundreds of people were milling around the streets, laughing and quaffing beer to celebrate the end of German occupation. Ongoing firefights kept other sections deserted. Foss noticed that most of the main roads were barricaded. Armed resistance fighters patrolled the middle of the roads at certain intersections, thoroughly checking the papers and physical identity of the occupants in each car that passed through. Since most motor vehicles at this time were used by the Germans and their Danish lackeys, Foss was not surprised to see men roughly dragged from their cars then punched and kicked into submission. Some lay on the streets, beaten into unconsciousness. A few had even been shot, trying to escape.

Foss didn't know what to feel. Brutality and revenge. The same savage emotions he had seen scores of times in the East; the same emotions he himself had acted out. An incredible despair swept over him, and he thought of the doctor who had diagnosed him with combat fatigue. Gripping the gun in his pocket, he decided to walk to the harbor and throw it into the sound. Be done with violence forever.

With war.

But as he made his way toward the water, he found himself in the midst of a throng of jeering people. Many swore unabashedly. They were hurling insults at two women dressed in nothing but their undergarments. A number of men restrained the women while another man shaved completely the head of one woman, then the other. When the last of their hair fell away, the crowd clapped and hooted. Ashamed and terrified, the women stared forlornly at the ground.

Knowing full well why the women were being humiliated, Foss nevertheless pitied them. A part of him wanted to step forth and protect them from further insults. Just then the women were led away by a group of men bearing rifles. One of the women started to cry, while trying to keep her bra-strap from slipping off her shoulder.

A man next to Foss turned to him and snarled. "Those bitches were mattresses for the Germans. They deserve worse! They're lucky we don't strip all their clothes off."

The man, expecting Foss to agree with him, was shocked when the tall surly-looking stranger shoved him away. For a moment he was speechless. Then he said, "Why the hell did you do that? You're not a German-lover are you?"

"I have reason to dislike the Germans more than you do," Foss said coldly, giving the man a menacing stare. "But I don't condone this."

Foss didn't wait around to hear the man's response. The crowd was moving elsewhere, and Foss moved in the opposite direction. He heard guns firing in the distance, individual shots, sometimes the staccato bursts of a Tommy or Sten-gun. He no longer thought it wise to dispose of the revolver.

The day crawled into night and Foss continued to roam the streets of Copenhagen. All across the city, candles were lit in nearly every window to denote the end of the hated blackout. As he made his way past the Danish Parliament building and crossed a small bridge over the Slotsholmen canal, Foss ran into an old schoolmate who was flabbergasted to see him.

"Aksel Foss! My goodness! I thought you were no longer among the living!"

"No, Nis, I'm alive and well, as you can see."

Still stunned, Nis Gundersen ran a hand through his bright red hair and swore. "Someone told me you were killed in Russia."

Foss shrugged his shoulders. "I nearly stopped a bullet a few times."

Changing his expression, Gundersen looked at Foss with skepticism. "What were you doing in Russia?"

Foss told him a brief version of the story.

"You mean you only just got back home?" Gundersen asked.

Not sure whether Gundersen believed him, Foss said, "Just a few days ago. Now I'm searching for my brother. You remember Arne? I'm afraid he might have joined the resistance."

"Well, good for him. I thought about joining too at one time. But with a wife and two little ones, I'm strapped paying bills."

Foss sensed that Gundersen was becoming uneasy, distant. "I've got some more ground to cover, Nis. Maybe I'll see you around."

"Yes, maybe."

As Foss cut through some of the older districts, he wondered if serving with the Germans would forever be a stain on his record. To other Danes, it didn't seem to matter that he had been coerced at gunpoint to donning the gray-green uniform of the enemy. Foss thought of Ingrid; wanted to see her. But perhaps, she too, would feel distant toward him.

With crowds of people all over town rejoicing, Foss was able to gather snippets of information about the last Nazi holdouts. Some had been wounded and killed; most were in the process of surrendering once they were promised there would be no retribution. The top German leaders were under house arrest. A few fanatics had escaped by plane or boat to Norway. Though the German forces in Norway had also capitulated.

Feeling he had done all he could to find Arne, Foss walked to his mother's apartment. He had not eaten dinner, and his feet hurt from treading pavement. He reflected that the fields of Russia and Prussia had been softer.

His mother was waiting at the door as he entered. Her face, a mask of worry.

"Thank God, you're home . . . " Then she saw he was alone. "Where's Arne?"

"I thought he might have come back by now." Foss kept his voice calm, not wanting to alarm her any more than she was. "He'll be home soon," he assured her. "The fighting's died down. I could go back out and look for him if that will make you feel better."

"No. Don't go back out. Stay here. I don't want to be alone."

Foss had not noticed before, but now he saw that his mother seemed older, frailer. Her once luscious hair hung slack to stooped shoulders; dark circles had developed beneath her eyes. His being away and Arne's commitment to the Resistance had aged her.

"Do you know why he joined the Freedom Fighters?" Ketty asked suddenly.

When Foss didn't answer right away, she said, "Because of you. When you went to Russia he felt you were more of a man than he was. I think he always felt that way, even though you were younger. Your height for one thing, which came from your father. Arne has my family's small genes. School came easy to you too, Aksel. And you were good in sports. And you always attracted the prettiest girls. The only downside you had was your asthma. But you eventually got over that. Arne hated school, and until recently, the girls were hardly aware of him. About the only thing in his favor is that he is a diligent worker. He won't hesitate to put in extra hours if they ask him. And he never complains." She paused as she heard someone climbing the stairs. Then a door clicked open and was shut abruptly. "I thought it was him," she said, sighing. "I was glad that he got the job with Carlsberg. Glad that he finally could participate with something that he liked. But it came to me through others that certain employees there were involved . . . with the resistance. It really never occurred to me that they would want to include Arne in their activities, but they did. I can't tell you how many times I've waited up for him, biting my fingernails and fretting. I've always been a nail-biter, but now I don't have any nails left."

For perhaps the first time in his life, Foss took his mother in his arms and kissed her lightly on the forehead. He led her to the sofa where they sat down and waited. Foss took note that she too had put candles in the window. Hoping to take his mother's mind off of Arne, Foss spoke of the times before the German invasion. Even back then the family had struggled financially, but at least they had not had to contend with curfews or arrest by the Gestapo. Ketty smiled thinking about the occasion when her youngest son found a tiny hedgehog in Frederiksberg Park, close to the zoo. He had placed the hedgehog in his school satchel and carried it home. Believing his mother would be as overjoyed as he was to find such a pet, he cried when she told him that he had to take it back. "It's a wild animal, Aksel," she had lectured him. "He wouldn't like being cooped up in a cage."

They also spoke of Ingrid. "I truly thought you two were on the road to marriage," Ketty said. "She's a lovely girl."

"She is. I wrote to her a lot from Russia."

"Did you meet any girls at the front?"

Foss hesitated, remembering Jutta. "No," he lied. "I was too busy trying to be a soldier."

"Your father was a soldier . . . for a while."

"He was?"

"A Danish soldier."

Foss thought he detected sarcasm in her tone. *Aimed at me, or my father?* "I ran into an old friend tonight. When I told him where I served, I got the feeling he considered me a traitor for being a German soldier. It seems like everyone here feels that way. They don't believe me when I tell them that I had no choice." He paused as a siren wailed outside. Then the noise trailed away. "Do you think I'm a traitor, mother?"

Eyes wide, Ketty looked at her son, incredulous. "Not in a thousand years! You might have had to wear an enemy uniform, but you were still a

Dane. Yes, you were a soldier. But you were a Danish soldier. I never sensed otherwise. Not when you were gone, and not since you have returned. And that's all that matters. Who cares what the neighbors or what anyone else thinks."

It was on the tip of Foss's tongue to say that Danes, of all people, worried constantly over what the neighbors thought of them. But he let the matter rest. When he didn't say anything, Ketty asked, "Do you still write poetry?"

"Not for awhile. Haven't been inspired." Foss knew his mother had never understood his desire to write.

"Well, maybe since you're home again, you'll get more inspiration.

"I hope so."

They continued to chat, until a commotion in the stairwell caused them to freeze. Foss went to investigate. The lamp had gone out in the stairwell, or else had been shut off when the Germans imposed the blackout. But Foss could see the figures of three people moving quickly up the stairs. One of them wore a beret. Foss stepped down to meet them.

"Arne, is that you?"

The figures halted. Then one of them said, "No, but who asks?"

As Foss got closer he saw the one with the beret was not Arne. "I'm his brother," Foss declared.

Even in the darkness Foss could see the men were hesitant, nervous. The one who had spoken earlier said, "We have . . . bad news. You better come with us."

A dagger pierced Foss's heart. "Did . . . something happen to my brother?"

No one answered. Finally, the man wearing the beret said, "He got shot. We attacked a house in Hellerup. Arne wanted to be the first in. He took a bullet in the chest."

"Is he there now?"

"We were able to drive him to the hospital. He was still conscious when they wheeled him in."

"How long ago was that?"

"Maybe an hour ago. We came here by car. Arne asked us to let his mother know."

His mind racing, Foss told the men to wait. Then he sprinted upstairs to tell Ketty he was going with some men to look for Arne.

They drove at a high speed, narrowly avoiding people partying in the streets. Several times they were stopped and questioned at road blocks, but continued once it was ascertained they were not Nazis fleeing justice. At the hospital they learned that Arne had hemorrhaged—his condition was grave. He was in surgery. Foss demanded to see his brother, but was restrained by other Freedom Fighters waiting outside Arne's room.

"The doctors are operating now," one of them said, trying to placate Foss. "Arne's tough. He'll pull through."

But Arne didn't pull through. Foss sat and waited several anxious hours before one of the doctors approached him to say that they had done all they could. Arne had been shot several times, one of the bullets perforating his lung and causing internal bleeding; the other, had gone in the side of his neck, eventually lodging near his upper spine. Foss stared blankly, hardly hearing all that was being said to him.

"He would have been paralyzed if he had lived," the doctor commented further, as though this news might comfort Foss in his bleakness. When Foss remained silent, the doctor said, "His body will be placed in the morgue temporarily. You and your family can discuss how you want to make arrangements for burial." The doctor put a hand on Foss's shoulder. "It's been a rough day. We've unfortunately treated a number of gunshot victims. I know this might sound pointless to you now, but your brother saved others by putting his life on the line. I wouldn't have had the guts to do what he did; most wouldn't. Sadly . . . war has a price. And he paid it. If there's any consolation, Denmark will not forget his sacrifice."

War has a price. Foss reflected on this as the doctor walked away. A small phrase, but one Foss couldn't help thinking epitomized everything in his life. Not knowing how long he sat, not knowing whether the night had ended and dawn brought with it a new day, Foss noticed an older man standing in a corner of the waiting room. The man held the demeanor of one who was utterly demoralized.

"I'm sorry," the man said, his voice barely carrying through the room that contained only himself and Foss. "I was Arne's foreman at the brewery. He was engaged to my daughter."

Unused to violence and extreme sorrow, the man needed to talk. He talked the whole time as he drove Foss home in a beer truck. "I felt we had to do something for the Motherland. I'd done nothing the entire war. Arne felt the same. A lot of us did. Almost a duty. You can only take being trampled on so long. So we joined. Only been about four or five months. It's all gone so fast. Now it's over—we won. But it doesn't feel that way. Not with what happened to Arne . . . "

He left Foss beside the curb of the apartment, with the invitation to come and visit him at the brewery some time. Now he had to return home and break the awful news to his daughter.

While Foss had to break the news to his mother.

He lingered for some minutes. Daylight was several hours away. Revelers continued to parade through the streets. Hundreds of people were singing happily. Perhaps the whole country was singing. For the war was over, the enemy beaten. The British would arrive tomorrow to issue in the official peace.

A smiling drunk stumbled by, raising a beer bottle in the air as a toast. But Foss had already turned to the entrance. Was already maneuvering up the stairs. The lights still had not been fixed in the stairwell. To Foss, it seemed darker than before. Almost too dark to see.

JULY 1961

CHAPTER 20

A single piece of mail fell from the slot in the door. Slid a little ways on the floor before stopping beside an old shoe. Aksel Foss, who was sitting holding a beer, looked at his watch. Twenty minutes before noon. The postman had come early today—usually he didn't come before one or even later. Sometimes he didn't come at all, since there was little mail to be delivered. The usual bills and not much else. Foss guessed it was just another bill. He finished the beer before pushing himself up from the chair with a grunt.

But it was not a bill. Putting a hand to his back as he stooped down, he noticed the address on the back of the envelope was from Germany. *A letter! From Germany.* A tingling sensation ran across his body. Sitting down again, he hurriedly pealed open the envelope.

For the next half an hour he did nothing but read the letter, re-read it, stare at it, read it yet again. Finally putting it down, he rose, went to the window, looked out.

It was raining. Had been raining most of the week. Despite the rain, some boys were kicking a soccer ball in the courtyard below. Life went on regardless of the rain.

Though he couldn't say the same for himself. He turned back to the table and noticed five empty beer bottles, an ashtray overflowing with cigarette butts, a partly eaten bun. Next to all this, the plain white paper of the letter seemed out of place. Foss again looked outside. The boys were gone. In the span of a few seconds they had disappeared.

But wasn't life too often like that. *Mostly like that.* Wincing at a sudden sharp piercing pain in his low back, Foss gingerly made his way back to the chair. Reaching for a packet of cigarettes near the ashtray, he pulled one out, then not finding matches anywhere on the table, put the cigarette back. He hurt too much to go looking through cabinets merely to find matches. He'd been hurting the last six years. Working for a moving company, he had lost his footing on a stairwell while helping to carry a piano down to a waiting truck. Toppling down the stairs he had sprained his ankle and wrenched his back—then the piano fell on him. He didn't recall much after that, until he woke in a hospital and was told he was lucky to be alive. He thought a lot about that statement—*Lucky to be alive.* Sure, he was alive, but no longer able to work, or do anything ordinary

without pain. The only compensation: a small monthly pension from the
government for the rest of his life. Enough for one person to live on . . .

One person. Once upon a time there had been two. Foss married several
years after the war—to a girl who had never known him prior to that
era—but the marriage had been brief. Had been a disaster. They had
quarreled frequently, mainly about his recurring nightmares—she, urging
him to get professional medical care, he, arguing that there was no medical
care in the world that could help him. The nightmares that often caused
him to scream uncontrollably during the night, had in the end, almost
made him a murderer. After one particular awful dream he had luckily
come to his senses the moment he squeezed his hands around his wife's
neck, trying to strangle her. Not even packing her things, she left him as
soon as he let go of her, as soon as she could draw breath again. Sad, but
realizing it would make no difference to seek her forgiveness, Foss accepted
the terms of the divorce. Though he had wanted children, there had been
none. It was just as well. Having a crippled insane man as a father was not
a legacy Foss wanted to leave to any offspring.

So he would never become a father. And he had failed as a brother, and
as a son. Ketty had never blamed him for Arne's death, but he blamed
himself. That was all there was to it. He had not done enough to save his
brother's life. And the result: Ketty physically declined afterward. It was
foolish to believe the cancer that took her life four years after liberation
had anything to do with Arne's killing. Yet she was not the same person
after her eldest son was gone. Her appetite dwindled to nothing, her stick-
like body reminded Foss of the women inmates he had seen in the forest
with the SS. Foss was willing to support her on his own meager salary, but
Ketty insisted on still slaving away at her ten-hour a day job. When Foss
moved out of the apartment she was too stoic to ask him to stay, but he
guessed later that it was the final stake through her existence, her meaning
as a human being. When she collapsed cleaning a stairwell one morning,
and was rushed to the hospital, the diagnosis did not take long. A cancer
had metastasized from her lungs to other organs, had spread through
practically her whole body. Given one month to live, she lasted two. But
the pain was so unbearable that constant morphine was the only way to
sedate her. In Foss's eyes, it was merely a another form of death. For his
mother was no longer the person he had known. During the infrequent
moments she didn't shut her eyes in a drugged sleep, she would wake and

hallucinate, calling for Arne to come to her, even calling for his father. When he explained it was Aksel that was tending to her, she would stroke his face, and ask about his asthma. To her he had become a four year old child again. Foss later thought that it was perhaps the best way for her mind to go; rearing two boys on her own had undoubtedly been the hardest years of her life, yet they were also her happiest. The last week she lay in a coma in the hospital. Foss went to visit every day, until one day, there was no need.

A coughing fit overtook him. His eyes watered, and it was some minutes before he felt that he could inhale normally. The asthma had returned. It was most terrible in the winter, though the pollen in spring also played havoc with his breathing. The cigarettes did too. He smoked a pack a day, sometimes two. And he knew he was an idiot for doing so. But what did it matter? Since the injury he had also begun to drink at least a dozen beers a day. Occasionally liquor. The vodka he'd had in Russia had whetted his taste for it.

He tried not to think about Russia, or about the war at all. The bad of those times far outweighed the good. None of his comrades had ever contacted him; he thought at least Tulm might have. But from what Foss heard later about the last tumultuous months of the Third Reich, the Germans had been trounced everywhere. And suffered—like they had caused others to suffer. Tulm most likely had not survived. Even if he had made it to Denmark, he would not have been welcomed.

Foss himself had not been welcomed; Danes in general were not a nation bent on revenge, but certain elements were. Certain politicians, often the very same ones who had first appeased the Nazi conquerors, after the war did an about-face. Fingers were pointed, mainly at the young men who had joined the Waffen SS supposedly to combat Communism. Trials were arranged, prison terms handed out. Few were sentenced for more than a decade in length, most two to three years. Foss was not especially surprised at such actions; what took him by surprise was a day in the autumn of 1945 when four policemen came by his mother's apartment bearing a summons to arrest him. Though Ketty had clawed tooth and nail with words decrying the outrageousness of locking up an innocent man, it was to no avail. Hauled before a magistrate, interrogated about his service under the Germans, Foss made no attempt to evade the facts of all that had taken place during the war. Despite being given a lawyer who halfheartedly defended his position, Foss had been handed a sentence of two years in prison, to be served immediately.

But Danes had begun to forget the war. It was a new era. Most people wanted to put the hostilities behind them. Foss's sentence in the end was commuted to six months. Physically he was no worse for the wear. He had eaten better than he had in the Wehrmacht. Had exercised daily. Mentally, however, a stinging bitterness lingered. He was certain one of the residents in the apartment building had leaked specific information about his time in the German military. Foss could not pinpoint who the culprit was, but it made him more eager to move out, despite his mother's protests.

He found his own apartment in the section of Østerbro, on the other side of town. A short distance from the sound, Foss initially took almost daily treks to the water. On clear days he could see the shoreline of Sweden, and it reminded him of his time spent on Bornholm. But though he often contemplated paying a visit to Einar and Karen, he always found an excuse not to do so. Similar to the excuses he made not to journey again to Germany. He had inquired about Jutta Scherbenske in the German refugee camps in Denmark, but no one bearing that name was ever listed. *Had she even made it as far as Berlin?* Foss could only speculate as to what happened to her in those last chaotic weeks. Foss learned that the Americans and British had flown daily bombing sorties over most of the Reich's cities. Berlin had taken a heavy toll. Perhaps Jutta had been caught in the open during one of the raids. He knew it was futile to compare types of death, but for a woman—*a good-looking woman*—being blasted to nothingness by a bomb might be preferable to being raped and murdered by a platoon of Ivans.

Foss gave up speculating after a while. He wished to be done with the war. Just like he was done with poetry. He had not written a single poem since the war-years. It was all past. Until . . . the letter. Picking it up once more, he scrutinized every line, every word. He couldn't believe after all this time, that she still remembered him. And had taken the effort to locate him. She stated so in the letter. Had searched around various libraries near and far to secure an up-to-date Danish phone book, where she had finally found the street address and phone number of an Aksel Foss. A pin pulled out of a haystack. Though Foss wasn't a common name in

Denmark, like Jensen, or Hansen, he nevertheless was impressed with her resolve to seek his whereabouts.

She hadn't stated much else, except to say where she lived, and to give him an address to write back to, he if chose. And if he chose to . . . she wondered whether he'd mind her paying him a visit—at the end of July. In exactly three weeks.

Three weeks! Foss scratched his head; a nervous shutter ran through him. He had not written a letter to anyone in . . . *God knows how long.* Did he even want her to come? Getting up, Foss shuffled to the bathroom, turned on the light, stared in the mirror. What stared back was a forty-year old face etched with permanent lines, sallow, the eyes bleary, the hair thinning and prematurely gray. He had a double-chin, and his stomach protruded over his belt from too much alcohol. He suddenly grew scared that his appearance would disgust her. She might even regret the trip. Her recollection of him would be that of a young soldier, a man in his prime. Yet . . . she would not be the same either. She too would have changed.

But this only made him eager to see her again. To learn all that had happened. It took him some minutes, but Foss found a pen and a notebook. Taking his time, he began to write.

Her response came to him within days. Having a short period of time off from her work, she could come by train to Copenhagen and stay a day or two. *Can you meet me at the station?* He had written back promptly to say that that was fine and he would. There was so much she wanted to see in the Danish capital. *Him*, first of all, Tivoli Gardens, of course—and if there was time, the statue of the Little Mermaid. She had always loved the stories of H.C. Andersen.

Over the next few weeks Foss went about remaking himself. He curtailed his drinking and smoking, took long walks and bike rides daily despite the lingering pain in his back, cleaned up his apartment, and even managed to begin work on a poem. A sense of thrill had come back into his life, he was clearing away the cobwebs. He saw a new face taking shape in the mirror. One day while throwing away clothes and shoes he had not used in ages, he was startled to find the Enfield hidden under a stack of old newspapers. When had he put it there? Whether on purpose or by accident, the gun reminded him of the months after his divorce. There had been sleepless nights when tossing and turning he had risen from bed, took the revolver from a drawer where it had then been, placed it against his temple and . . .

Almost pulled the trigger.

But he hadn't. Death, he did not fear—it was the life he had neglected to live that stayed his finger. And it was that life he was still trying to find.

Foss threw the newspapers away and put the gun in a shoebox. He didn't need such a weapon any longer, yet he was reluctant to discard it.

The day had come. Traveling first from Bremen to Hamburg, she was scheduled to arrive in Copenhagen in the early afternoon. Foss was sure she would dine on the train, but he was prepared to offer to take her out to one of the old seafood restaurants that stood along a stretch of one of the canals. Then they could walk beside the small harbor at Nyhavn. The irony of it was all too clear. *Nyhavn*. Where he had literally drunk himself into the German Army; now, he would go there without worry with a German woman who also had been affected by the war.

The weather was fairly warm. Foss strolled up and down the platform, checking his watch every few minutes while trying to say phrases to himself in German. He was afraid he would be rusty after so many years of not speaking the language. When he heard the sound of the wheels rushing closer, his heart beat furiously. The same thump thump thump that had occurred on the occasion when as a newly outfitted soldier in the Wehrmacht, he had waited nervously to board the train that would land him in the Soviet Union. He and all those other young men. The train entered the station. Foss stood at the midway point at the platform to get a good view of everyone leaving the coaches. They had arranged that she would hold a suitcase in one hand, a book in the other. Minutes passed as the passengers exited. Foss had bought a bouquet of flowers. The crowds thinned. He began to worry that maybe she had had to postpone the trip—a personal matter, job, or . . . she had decided not to come after all.

Then he saw her. Wearing a blue skirt and a white short-sleeved blouse, she was standing on the far end of the platform looking right and left, searching for him. If not for the suitcase and book, Foss would never have recognized her. Only when he waved to her did she spot him.

As they moved toward each other, Foss noticed first relief on her face, then her expression became one of surprise. *She's startled to see how I have aged.* But as they came together she smiled.

"Mr. Foss, forgive my forwardness, but I've been wanting to give you this for a long time." Putting the suitcase down, she hugged him warmly.

Foss was embarrassed by the open display of affection, then realizing this was a once in a lifetime moment, returned the embrace with equal fervor. When they pulled apart, he handed her the flowers.

"So nice to see you again, Traudl," Foss said, nodding his head at the little girl who had become an attractive young woman. A tall brunette whose blue eyes sparkled at him, she nodded back at him.

"Thank you," she said. "You really didn't have to do that, Mr. Foss."

"It's just a small gift. And please, don't call me Mr. Foss. That makes me sound older than I am."

"We're all a bit older," she seconded, still keeping her smile. "It occurred to me riding up here, that life repeats itself sometimes. The last time I saw you, I also carried only one suitcase."

"You obviously have a great memory." Foss recalled the tiny child with tears in her eyes tugging at his sleeve on the wharf at Pillau sixteen years before, searching frantically for her parents. He frowned. "I just hope life doesn't always repeat itself. Pray those terrible times never come again."

"Amen to that."

They took a taxi to a restaurant that offered typical Danish fare. Traudl had been too excited on the train to eat, so they decided to combine a late lunch with an early dinner. They conversed little while they ate, mostly Foss acted as a tourist guide, making plans to show Traudl the many sights of the city. When they finished, Foss proposed that they walk to the Little Mermaid. "I live on that part of town," he said, "but if it's too far—"

"It won't be too far," she assured him, smiling. "I love walking."

So they walked. First along the famous walking-street of Strøget, lined on each side by shops, bars, restaurants. Traudl window-shopped while Foss insisted on carrying her suitcase.

"I really don't mind carrying it," she said. "It's not heavy."

But Foss wouldn't let her. They left Strøget and crossed the street to the large square of Kongens Nytorv that led to Nyhavn and the harbor. If Foss had been alone he would have entered one of the seedy bars, but they were not places for a respectable girl. He and Traudl continued on, passing along the wharf where large cruise and industrial ships stood at anchor. From here they walked across the cobblestone courtyard of Amalienborg, the King's palace. When they eventually reached the statue of the Little Mermaid perched on a large rock in the water, Traudl gazed at it for some time in silence.

Foss sat on a nearby bench, observing her. The trek had left him winded. He envied her youth, and wished he were young again. She had roused in him a stirring he had not felt in years. But he quickly suppressed it. He was old enough to be her father. Besides, she had told him she was engaged to a young man in Bremen, the town where she lived. When she came to the bench and sat down beside him, Foss asked, "How long have you been engaged?"

"Almost a year," Traudl answered. "He's a teacher at the same school where I teach."

"And he let you come up here alone?"

Traudl laughed. "Not willingly. But this is something I wanted to do forever. He knows that."

"Do you like teaching?"

"I do. I like the younger grades. I feel like I missed out on so much when I was a child. In a way I can relive my own childhood by ensuring that my students are encouraged to remember that they are still just children—and should not be expected to act as adults. Like I was."

"You mean when you lost your parents?"

"Yes."

Foss detected in Traud's voice a hurt that had never been expunged. "So I take it you never heard any more about their fate?"

"No. No news whatsoever. There were thousands of missing people in those days. Thousands of refugees. Official records disappeared in those last months of the war. Or else the Nazis purposely destroyed them. And it won't help to go back there today. Prussia no longer exists, it's all part of Poland and Russia now. And you can certainly bet the communists aren't going to assist former German residents in finding their loved ones. Missing or alive."

Foss nodded in agreement. He'd heard the Soviets had often arrested returning refugees and at gunpoint forced them to toil in labor camps for years, or had killed them outright. They didn't want Germans to ever resettle the east.

"Whatever happened to that woman you got on the boat with?" Foss asked. "I remember she wore a fur coat, but I don't recollect her name."

A look of anger shone from Traudl's eyes. "Aunt Margot. At least that's what she called herself. She ditched me—as soon as we landed in Kiel.

Told me she was going to find food for the both of us. After that, I never saw her again."

Foss was not surprised. He remembered the haughtiness of the woman, her reluctance to take Traudl with her on the ship, though it had meant her own free passage to the west. "So you were all alone in the port of Kiel?"

"I was all alone. I must have wept non-stop. All the orphans and children with missing parents were gathered in the ruins of an abandoned school. I remember it like it happened yesterday. It was freezing, dirty, noisy. Food was scarce, and there was one latrine for everyone. Just the smells often caused me to vomit. An awful place." Traudl stopped to point to a heron that had landed next to the statue of the Little Mermaid. It flew away when it eyed the two humans sitting on the bench. "They moved us from the ruins after a few days," she continued. "The allies were bombing the docks. I didn't think about it then, but later it hit me how horribly tragic it was for the refugees. Coming all that way to escape the Russians, grateful for being saved, only to be killed by American bombs. I and most of the rest of the children by then had been moved to the outskirts of the city. We were lucky. In time, we were bunched together with other refugees. I was with a group that left Kiel and headed south. I won't bore you with the whole story—"

"But it doesn't bore me."

Traudl shrugged. "There's not too much more to tell. A kind woman in Bremen took me in to help her tend the house. Dora was an angel. She was frail from having battled with tuberculosis much of her life. Her husband and son were soldiers. Both had fallen in the war. She was alone, like me. Everyone in Germany back then had lost at least someone. So I lived with her and she raised me as her daughter. To the neighbors and townspeople I was a 'niece' whose family had perished in a bombing raid. Despite Dora's illness, she was a strong person. She taught *me* to be strong. She really hounded me to get an education, to become independent. 'The world is changing,' she would tell me. 'Girls today must learn to fend for themselves.' Not that I hadn't already been doing that, but her words reinforced the idea."

"You still live with her?"

Traudl seemed not to have heard him at first. Then she said, "Poor Dora died a few years back. Unbelievably, she left everything in her will to me.

It wasn't a lot, but I did get the house. Though I never thought of it as my real home. So after several months I sold it. Now I live in an apartment. That's all I need. I suppose Ulrich and I will buy a house once we have our own children."

Foss was about to ask a question when the sudden blast of a horn nearby meant that an ocean liner was readying to leave the port. When the sound ceased, he had lost his train of thought.

"I hope I'm not inconveniencing you by coming here to visit."

"No Traudl, not at all. The opposite. This is the nicest thing to happen to me in a long time. It's reawakened me."

"How?"

"I was becoming complacent. I was living in a cocoon of bad habits." Foss then shared his own story from the time he put her on the boat till now, minus the gory details. Danes didn't usually uncork the bottle of their lives to strangers, but he didn't feel completely Danish anymore, and she wasn't a stranger. When he finished, she placed a hand on his forearm.

"I appreciate you telling me that," she said sincerely. "It seemed like I was blabbing away without letting you get a word in. Goodness, you had to survive even more than I did."

"It was just different. I don't think anyone can compare woes."

"I think you're right."

Shaking his head, Foss grinned. "Your letter shocked me. I couldn't believe that you still remembered me—considering how you had so much else to deal with."

"How could I ever forget you?" For a moment Traudl appeared hurt that Foss could even broach such a question. "I wouldn't be here without you," she said decisively. You were the soldier that protected me. Saved me . . . "

Foss turned red. "There were plenty of others that would have done the same."

"I asked other soldiers, and civilians. No one helped me. You were the only one."

Foss was taken aback. How to respond? No one had complimented like this in decades. He had to swallow several times to keep himself from shedding tears.

Sensing his awkwardness, Traudl stood up. Grabbing Foss's hand, she gently beckoned him to stand too. Like this, they walked along the water's edge, silently. Other pedestrians passed them without even a glance. After awhile Traudl stopped, faced Foss, then kissed him on the cheek.

"Being a schoolteacher," she said softly, "I have the chance to mold a lot of lives. This might sound ridiculous, but I want to give to these children what you once gave to me—hope for the future. Germany is not the same as it was when I was a child. The rubble in the cities has all been cleared away. People are not afraid of a knock on the door at night. But that doesn't mean it couldn't all happen again. Bombs may fall on our homes tomorrow. The Russians and Americans may clash at any moment . . . "

"That's nothing but saber-rattling." But Foss wasn't so sure.

"I hope it is just saber-rattling. I hope there's never another war . . . but one never knows."

One never knows. Such a line could be the epitome of everything, Foss thought. Clouds were drifting over the sound from Sweden, dark clouds, bringing with them an omen of rain. Wishing he could stay here by the water and talk with Traudl forever, Foss knew that it was best they soon get indoors. He mentioned this to Traudl.

"You know the weather of your country better than I do," she said, taking hold of his hand again.

Traudl ended up staying three nights. Foss gave her his bed to sleep in while he took the couch. Wanting to prepare her, he told her not to be alarmed if she heard him screaming during the night.

"Dear Aksel, I was going to warn you of the same thing." Traudl let out a sigh of relief as though she had finally found another human with the same quirks. "I haven't even told Ulrich about my nightmares. It might scare him off."

"Not if he loves you."

But for those three nights neither Traudl nor Foss woke once panting and shrieking with terror. They slept peacefully. During the daytime Foss showed her Copenhagen. The many gardens, castles, towers, alleyways strewn with history. They ate pastries for breakfast and dined in cafes for lunch. Each evening Traudl insisted on cooking dinner. Foss protested that he was the host, but she would not back down.

She was a good cook. A good person. Intelligent, serious, but could just as easily laugh her head off at a joke. And she was not adverse to drinking a beer and smoking a cigarette. Foss was smitten with her. He wondered if he had ever been so happy in such a short span of time. Yet the happiness was mixed with confusion. Were the feelings he held for her that of a father to a daughter, or of a man wishing a closer bond? He decided not to push it. Though there were moments he desired to take her in his arms and make love to her.

Sunday came and Traudl had to leave early to catch the train to Hamburg. From there she would transfer to a line going to Bremen. They remained inside the station until the last minute. Outside, the day was gray and miserable with constant drizzle and an unseasonably cold temperature. Foss felt miserable too. He didn't want her to go. Sensing his downcast mood, Traudl sidled up to him, leaning her head on his shoulder.

"What's wrong, Mr. Foss?" she asked, using his surname lightheartedly, hoping it might cheer him.

Foss was on the verge of telling her his secret yearnings when he noticed her train was ready for boarding. Instead, he said, "I really enjoyed having you here. I'm going to miss you, Traudl. If you're not too busy with life . . . I hope we can meet again at some point."

"I'm going to miss you, too." Traudl hugged him. "Ulrich and I are getting married in the middle of August. It's to be a civil wedding, small, only his parents and a few others, otherwise I would invite you. But once we are settled, I would love for you to come down and visit. I want him to meet you. You're an amazing man, Aksel Foss."

"If only I was ten years younger," Foss partly mumbled, mostly to himself, though he knew she heard him clearly, and that she understood.

Traudl was still a moment. Putting a finger under her eye, she wiped away a tear. Then she looked at Foss squarely and kissed him on the lips—a slight peck, more like the caress of a feather. Pulling away from him, she said, "Not long after I began to live with Dora, I spent nearly an entire day crying. She didn't tell me to stop. She instinctively knew that I had to unleash all the agony that had built up since I fled my home in Lyck. After I calmed down, and lay in my bed exhausted, she consoled me with these words: 'Cry when you need to, but just remember: Regret poisons today.' I've never forgotten those words. I'm too weak not to regret certain people and events from my past. I think most of us are too weak to bury all our broken memories. Some things can never be. But we must not poison today with things that can't be changed. We must never poison today."

Foss watched her as she boarded the train, found a seat, opened the window next to it. Holding her hand outside it, she beckoned to him. He clasped her hand in his own until the train started to roll out of the station. She briefly waved, then pulled her arm in and he lost sight of her. Had not Jutta parted from him in the same way? Foss stayed at the station for a long time after the train was gone, his hair, face, shoes, clothes soaked by the drizzle. Traudl's presence was still with him. The brush of her lips he still felt, the touch of her hand. Yes, she was still with him.

She would always be with him.

*

In the fall of the next year Foss heard one morning the report on the radio that the Cuban Missile Crisis was over. The world had narrowly avoided an atomic war. A Third World War. It was a frigid windy day, but Foss rode his bike many kilometers up the coast to a stretch of deserted beach. During the summertime, the sands would be dotted with sunbathers, but now he was the only person. He wanted it that way. The world might be on the verge of another war, but Foss was breaking his final ties to the last one.

Glancing around to make certain he was indeed alone, Foss stepped to the very edge of the water. The waves were rough, the tide high. He didn't see a single boat.

Placing a hand in the pocket of his coat, he took the Enfield out and scrutinized it. Then slowly, he removed each bullet from the barrel and tossed them one by one far out into the sea. He scrutinized the revolver again. A gun was rather a useless thing without bullets, he thought. Without ammo, a gun, any gun, was just a toy, an object to place on a mantelpiece, a museum exhibit. If there were no bullets, there would be no guns. He wasn't sure if what he was about to do would bring the world any closer to peace. But at least he wouldn't bring it any closer to war.

Foss gave the gun one last look over, then grinning, it too, he heaved far out toward the darkness of the water.

HIST⊕RICAL N⊕TE

The exact number of German refugees that fled the eastern provinces of Germany, and from all parts of Eastern Europe, has never been officially calculated. The estimated total ranges from 12 to 14 million between the years of 1945 (the last year of the war) until the early 1950s. Though most fled on their own, a good many were forcibly expelled from their homes on the orders of the Soviet dictator, Joseph Stalin. Because of the unprecedented barbarity perpetrated by the SS and the German armies during their attack on the Soviet Union, Stalin wanted the Germans pushed as far away from Eastern Europe as possible. He wanted a buffer zone in case Germany became powerful again in the future. Areas that had been culturally and linguistically German as far back as the Middle Ages, such as the great city of Koenigsberg, were emptied of most of the German populace, and repopulated with Russians. Further west, portions of Prussia and Pomerania were given to the Poles, who also had suffered horribly under the Nazis. Danzig and Kolberg became Polish cities, and still are.

The sad fact about history is that often the idea of revenge from one tribe or nation against another becomes the motivating factor for initiating large-scale change in the world. Millions of Jews, Soviets, Poles, and other nationalities all across Europe were slaughtered in Hitler's quest to secure *Lebensraum* for the German Reich. When the tide turned, it seemed only fitting in the eyes of those who had been brutalized to give the Germans a taste of their own methods. At least half a million German refugees were believed to have been killed by the Soviets and their eastern allies, and the figure may have been greater than two million. The countless acts of murder, rape, mutilation and pillage by Soviet troops toward German civilians were savage and gruesome. As borne out in the novel, often Poles, Russian slave laborers, and even Allied prisoners of war chose willingly to flee with the retreating Germans rather than face the uncertainty of waiting for the Red Army. The passage of years always allows us to point fingers at actions that should or should not have been taken in an earlier era. But there were reasons for the way things happened. The Germans were the enemies at that time, the Soviets the good guys, and the western press either ignored, or downplayed Soviet atrocities as being part of the war.

What later became known as *Germany's Dunkirk*, Operation Hannibal was the largest sea-borne evacuation ever. Between the months of January and May 1945, upwards of two million German refugees and military personnel were safely withdrawn from the eastern provinces to western ports in Germany and Denmark. Despite the four worst maritime disasters ever recorded, including the sinking of the *Steuben*, overall, the operation was a stunning success. This was true even when considering how the German navy, low on fuel and adequate vessels, had to deal constantly with the threat of Soviet submarines, as well as air and ground attacks. Not to mention mines placed throughout the Baltic, and the occasional sorties carried out by the RAF.

It may seem that I spent too little time writing about the tragedy of the *Steuben*. But after being hit by the two torpedoes, the ship sank rapidly. By some estimates, it took only seven minutes to fall beneath the waves; and at most, no more than twenty minutes. By contrast, the *Titantic* stayed afloat for nearly three hours. The nearly 5,000 civilians and wounded soldiers aboard the German liner hardly had a chance to put on a life jacket, though many were not even issued with one. Around 650 people, including crew members, survived the disaster. The rest drowned, succumbed to hypothermia in the frigid Baltic, or took their own lives.

Marinesko, the Soviet commander responsible for the sinking, and for the earlier destruction of the *Wilhelm Gustloff*, ran afoul with the Soviet High Naval Command, mainly due to his alcoholism and to the lack of tact he used toward men outranking him. Too outspoken, and bitter that many refused to give him credit for his tallies, he was later arrested on trumped-up charges and sent to a concentration camp. It wasn't until nearly three decades after his death that he was finally honored as a *Hero of the Soviet Union* for his wartime accomplishments.

My wife is from Denmark, and this book is loosely based on the story of her grandfather's younger brother. Similar to Aksel Foss, he was forcibly conscripted into the German Army and sent to the Eastern Front. Unlike Foss, however, he never came back.

CPSIA information can be obtained at www.ICGtesting.com
Printed in the USA
BVOW08s1626191215

430641BV00004B/7/P

9 781515 403234